Also by Grace Burrowes

The Duke's Obsession Series
The Heir
The Soldier
The Virtuoso
Lady Sophie's Christmas Wish
Lady Maggie's Secret Scandal
Lady Louisa's Christmas Knight
Lady Eve's Indiscretion

Novellas
The Courtship
The Duke and His Duchess

The Lonely Lords Series
Darius
Nicholas
Ethan
Beckman

Scottish-Set Victorian Romance
The Bridegroom Wore Plaid

Once Upon a Tartan

GRACE BURROWES

sourcebooks
casablanca

Published by Sourcebooks Casablanca, an imprint of Sourcebooks,
Inc.
P.O. Box 4410, Naperville, Illinois 60567-4410
(630) 961-3900
FAX: (630) 961-2168
www.sourcebooks.com

Printed and bound in Canada
WC 10 9 8 7 6 5 4 3 2 1

To those struggling with grief. You grieve because you loved, and it's the love that will abide.

One

WHEN TIBERIUS LAMARTINE FLYNN HEARD THE TREE singing, his first thought was that he'd parted company with his reason. Then two dusty little boots dangled above his horse's abruptly nervous eyes, and the matter became a great deal simpler.

"Out of the tree, child, lest you spook some unsuspecting traveler's mount."

A pair of slim white calves flashed among the branches, the movement provoking the damned horse to dancing and propping.

"What's his name?"

The question was almost unintelligible, so thick was the burr.

"His name is Flying Rowan," Tye said, stroking a hand down the horse's crest. "And he'd better settle himself down this instant if he knows what's good for him. His efforts in this regard would be greatly facilitated if you'd vacate that damned tree."

"You shouldn't swear at her. She's a wonderful tree."

The horse settled, having had as much frolic as Tye was inclined to permit.

"In the first place, trees do not have gender, in the second, your heathen accent makes your discourse nigh incomprehensible, and in the third, please get the hell out of the tree."

"Introduce yourself. I'm not supposed to talk to strangers."

A heathen child with manners. What else did he expect from the wilds of Aberdeenshire?

"Tiberius Lamartine Flynn, Earl of Spathfoy, at your service. Had we any mutual acquaintances, I'd have them attend to the civilities."

Silence from the tree, while Tye felt the idiot horse tensing for another display of nonsense.

"You're wrong—we have a mutual acquaintance. This is a treaty oak. She's everybody's friend. I'm Fee."

Except in his Englishness, Tye first thought the little scamp had said, "I'm fey," which seemed appropriate.

"Pleased to make your acquaintance, Fee. Now show yourself like a gentleman, or I'll think it's your intent to drop onto hapless travelers and rob them blind."

"Do you think I could?"

Dear God, the child sounded fascinated.

"Down. *Now.*" That tone of voice had worked on Tye's younger brother until Gordie had been almost twelve. The same tone had ever been a source of amusement to his younger sisters. The branches moved, and Rowan tensed again, haunches bunching as if he'd bolt.

A lithe little shape plummeted at least eight feet to the ground and landed with a loud "Ouch!" provoking Rowan to rear in earnest.

From the ground, the horse looked enormous, and the man astride like a giant. Fee caught an impression of darkness—dark horse, dark riding clothes, and a dark scowl as the man tried to control his horse.

"That is quite enough out of you." The man's voice was so stern, Fee suspected the horse understood the words, for two large iron-shod hooves came to a standstill not a foot from her head.

"Child, you will get up slowly and move away from the horse. I cannot guarantee your safety otherwise."

Still stern—maybe this fellow was always stern, in which case he was to be pitied. Fee sat up and tried to creep back on her hands, backside, and feet, but pain shot through her left ankle and up her calf before she'd shifted half her weight.

"I hurt myself."

The horse backed a good ten feet away, though Fee couldn't see how the rider had asked it to do so.

"Where are you hurt?"

"My foot. I think I landed on it wrong. It's because I'm wearing shoes."

"Shoes do not cause injury." He swung off the horse and shook a gloved finger at the animal. "You stand, or you'll be stewed up for the poor of the parish."

"Are you always so mean, mister?"

He loomed above her, hands on his hips, and Fee's Aunt Hester would have said he looked like The Wrath of God. His nose was a Wrath-of-God sort of nose, nothing sweet or humble about it, and his eyes were Wrath-of-God eyes, all dark and glaring.

He was as tall as the Wrath of God, too, maybe even taller than Fee's uncles, who, if not exactly the Wrath of God, could sometimes be the Wrath of Deeside and greater Aberdeenshire.

As could her aunt Hester, which was a sobering thought.

"You think I'm mean, young lady?"

"Yes."

"Then I must answer in the affirmative."

She frowned up at him. From his accent, he was at least a bloody Lowlander, or possibly a damned Sassenach, but even making those very significant allowances, he still talked funny.

"What is a firmative?"

"Yes, I am mean. Can you walk?"

He extended a hand down to her, a very large hand in a black riding glove. Fee had seen some pictures in a book once, of a lot of cupids without nappies bouncing around with harps, and a hand very like that one, sticking out of the clouds, except the hand in the picture was not swathed in black leather.

"Child, I do not have all day to impersonate the Good Samaritan."

"The Good Samaritan was nice. *He* went to heaven."

"While it is *my* sorry fate to be ruralizing in Scotland." He hauled Fee to her feet by virtue of lifting her up under the arms. He did this without effort, as if he hoisted five stone of little girl from the roadside for regular amusement.

"Do you ever smile?"

"When in the presence of silent, well-behaved,

properly scrubbed children, I sometimes consider the notion. Can you put weight on that foot?"

"It hurts. I think it hurts because my shoe is getting too tight."

He muttered something under his breath, which might have had some bad words mixed in with more of his pernickety accent, then lifted Fee to his hip. "I am forced by the requirements of good breeding and honor to endure your company in the saddle for however long it takes to return you to the dubious care of your wardens, and may God pity them that responsibility."

"I get to ride your horse?"

"*We* get to ride my horse. If you were a boy, I'd leave you here to the mercy of passing strangers or allow you to crawl home."

He might have been teasing. The accent made it difficult to tell—as did the scowl. "You thought I was boy?"

"Don't sound so pleased. I thought you were a nuisance, and I still do. Can you balance?"

He deposited her next to the treaty oak, which meant she could stand on one foot and lean on the tree. "I want to take my shoes off." He wrinkled that big nose of his, looking like he smelled something rank. "My feet are clean. Aunt Hester makes me take a bath every night whether I need one or not."

This Abomination Against the Natural Order— another one of Aunt Hester's terms—did not appear to impress the man. Fee wondered if anything impressed him—and what a poverty that would be, as Aunt would say, to go through the whole day without once being impressed.

He hunkered before her, and he was even tall when he knelt. "Put your hand on my shoulder."

Fee complied, finding his shoulder every bit as sturdy as the oak. He unlaced her boot, but when he tried to ease it off her foot, she had to squeal with the pain of it.

"Wrenched it properly, then. Here." He pulled off his gloves and passed them to her. "Bite down on one of those, hard enough to cut right through the leather, and scream if you have to. I have every confidence you can ruin my hearing if you make half an effort."

She took the gloves, which were warm and supple. "Are you an uncle?"

"As it happens, this dolorous fate has befallen me."

"Is that a firmative?"

"It is. Why?"

"Because you're trying to distract me, which is something my uncles do a lot. I won't scream."

He regarded her for a moment, looking almost as if he might say something not quite so fussy, then bent to glare at her boot. "Suit yourself, as it appears you are in the habit of doing."

She braced herself; she even put one of the riding gloves between her teeth, because as badly as her ankle hurt, she expected taking off her boot would cause the kind of pain that made her ears roar and her vision dim around the edges.

She neither screamed nor bit through the glove—which tasted like reins and horse—because before she could even draw in a proper breath, her boot was gently eased off her foot.

"I suppose you want the other one off too?"

"Is my ankle all bruised and horrible?"

"Your ankle is slightly swollen. It will likely be bruised before the day is out, but perhaps not horribly if we can get ice on it."

"Are you a priest?"

"For pity's sake, child. First an uncle, then a priest? What can you be thinking?" He sat her in the grass and started unlacing her second boot.

"You talk like Vicar on Sunday, though on Saturday night, he sounds like everybody else when he's having his pint. If my ankle is awful, Aunt Hester will cry and feed me shortbread with my tea. She might even play cards with me. My uncles taught me how to cheat, but explained I must never cheat unless I'm playing with them."

"Honor among thieves being the invention of the Scots, this does not surprise me." He tied the laces of both boots into a knot and slung them around Fee's neck.

"I'm a Scot."

His lips quirked. Maybe this was what it looked like when the Wrath of God was afraid he might smile.

"My condolences. Except for your unfortunate red hair, execrable accent, and the layer of dirt about your person, I would never have suspected." He lifted her up again, but this time carried her to Flying Rowan, who had stood like a good boy all the while the man had been getting Fee's boots off.

"I have wonderful hair, just like my mama's. My papa says I'm going to be bee-yoo-ti-full. My uncles say I already am."

"What you are is impertinent and inconvenient,

though one can hardly blame your hair on you. Up you go." He deposited her in the saddle, bracing a hand around her middle until she had her balance.

"Oh, this is a wonderful adventure. May I have the reins?"

"Assuredly not. Lean forward."

He was up behind her in nothing flat, but that just made it all the better. Flying Rowan was even taller than Uncle Ian's gelding, and almost as broad as the plow horses. Having the solid bulk of an adult male in the saddle made the whole business safe, even as it was also exciting.

He nudged the horse forward. "Where I am taking you, child?"

Fee could feel the way he rode, feel the way he moved with the horse and communicated with the horse without really using the reins.

"Child?"

"That way." She lifted her hand to point in the direction of the manor, feeling the horse flinch beneath her as she did. "If you go by way of the pastures, it's shorter than the road."

"How many gates?"

"Lots. Papa has a lot of doddies."

"Has your upbringing acquainted you with the equestrian arts?"

He didn't even sound like a priest. He sounded like nothing and no one Fee had ever heard before. His voice was stern but somehow beautiful too, even when he wasn't making any sense at all. "I don't know what equestrian arts are."

"Do you ride horseback?" He spoke slowly, as if

Fee were daft, which made her want to drive her elbow back into his ribs—though that would likely hurt her elbow.

"I don't have a pony, but my uncles take me up when I pester them hard enough."

"That will serve. Grab some mane and don't squeal."

He wrapped that big hand around her middle again, and urged the horse into a rocking canter. The wind blew Fee's hair back, and it was hard not to squeal, so delightful was the sensation of flying over the ground.

"Hold tight." This was nearly growled as the man leaned forward, necessitating that Fee lean forward too. In a mighty surge, the horse leapt up and over a stone wall, then thundered off across the pasture in perfect rhythm.

The sensations were *magnificent*, to be borne aloft for a timeless moment, to soar above the earth, to be safe and snug in the midst of flight.

"Do another one!" Fee called over her shoulder, even as the horse bore down on a second wall.

They did three more, cutting directly across the fields, leaving the cows to watch as the horse cantered by, the placid expressions of the bovines at such variance with the utter glee Fee felt at each wall.

When the man brought his horse down to a walk at the foot of the drive, she leaned forward and patted the gelding soundly on the shoulder. "Good fellow, Flying Rowan! Oh, that was the best! I will write to everybody and tell them what a good boy you are." She lapsed into the Gaelic, too happy and excited not to praise the horse in a more civilized language than the stilted, stodgy English.

Behind her, she felt the man's hard chest shift slightly, and she fell silent.

"Mama says it's rude to speak the Gaelic when somebody else can't."

"I comprehend it. Is this your home?"

"I live here. Aunt Hester lives here too, but Mama and Papa are away right now."

"Shall I take you around to the back?"

He was scowling at the manor as he spoke, as if the house wasn't the most lovely place in the world, all full of flowers and pretty views.

"Here comes Aunt Hester. I expect she'll want to thank you."

Fee felt Rowan's owner tense behind her. It wasn't that his muscles bunched up, it was more that he went still. The horse beneath them went still too, as if both man and horse understood that the look on Aunt Hester's face did not at all fit with Fee's prediction of impending thanks.

❧

A female thundercloud was advancing on Tye where he sat his gelding, the little girl perched before him. Beneath his hand, he felt the child's spine stiffen and her bony little shoulders square.

This particular thundercloud had golden blond hair piled on top of her head, quite possibly in an attempt to give an illusion of height. She wore an old-fashioned blue walking dress, the dusty hems of which were swishing madly around her boots as she sailed across the drive.

He'd always liked the sound of a woman's petticoats

in brisk motion, they gave a man a little warning—and something to think about.

"I bid you good day." He nodded from the saddle, a hat being a hopeless inconvenience when a man rode cross-country. "Spathfoy, at your service."

Some perverse desire to see what she'd do next kept him on the horse, looking down at her from a considerable height.

"Hester Daniels." She sketched a hint of a curtsy then planted her fists on her hips. "Fiona Ursula MacGregor, *what* am I to do with you? *Where* have you gone off to this time, that a strange man must bring you home at a dead gallop, over field and fence, your hair a fright and—" The lady paused and drew in a tremendous breath. "*Why* are your boots hanging about your neck? *What* have I told you about running off barefoot, much less when you're in the company of horses, and *when* will you remember that we eat meals at regular hours, in a civilized fashion, and *what* do you expect me to tell your dear mother about this latest escapade?"

When she fell silent, Tye was somewhat taken aback to see the lady's eyes shining, quite possibly with tears.

"I am sorry," said the girl, hanging her head. "I went to visit the oak, that's all, and it was a fine afternoon for singing in a tree, and then I jumped down, but I landed wrong, and this fellow came along on Flying Rowan. I didn't mean to hurt my foot, but we had such fun galloping home, didn't we, sir?"

She turned around to spear him with big, pleading green eyes, leaving Tye feeling resentful, and perhaps… oh, something else too bothersome to parse at the moment.

"There now," he said, smoothing a gloved hand over the child's crown. "A very nice apology, and that should be an end to it. The child can't be blamed for my horse's loss of composure when finding himself beneath a singing tree. If anybody should be apologizing, it's Rowan here."

This was a ridiculous speech, attributing manners and morals to a mute and consistently self-interested beast, but it served to soften the lady's ire. Her hands dropped from her hips, her breath left her in a gentle sigh, and her expression became one of exasperated affection. "Did you come a cropper, then, Fee?"

"She wrenched her ankle," Tye said, swinging down. He was pleased to note that when standing, he was still a good deal taller than Miss Daniels, but then, he was a good deal taller than most everybody. "I'm happy to carry her inside, where some ice and a tisane might be in order."

Before Miss Daniels could summon a servant for the task, Tye lifted Fiona out of the saddle. The child obligingly perched on his hip, batting those guileless green eyes at her aunt while a groom came to take Rowan.

Gordie had had such eyes, though the lack of guile was far more genuine in the child than it had ever been in the man.

"If you don't mind carrying her," Miss Daniels said, "I would be obliged. Fee is getting quite grown-up."

"She means I'm too heavy."

"You are a mere bagatelle." He shifted her to a

piggyback position. "Lead on please, madam. The bagatelle has to be in some discomfort."

But the girl did not complain, which was interesting. She settled in on Tye's back, resting her cheek against his nape. "I like being a bagatelle. Do bagatelles sing?"

"This one does, and she chatters," Tye said. "Incessantly." Though she was also at the braids-and-pinafores stage of her development, so he limited his rebuke.

"I know what that means. I'm trying to make small talk. Why do we call it small talk? It's the same size as other talk, at least other talk inside the house. Is there such a thing as large talk?"

She huffed out a sigh while Tye followed Miss Daniels into the house. The dwelling was a tidy Tudor manor that looked to be laid out in the typical Tudor E, gardens overflowing with flowers all about the place and even in window boxes on the upper stories. The mullioned windows were sparkling, the gravel walks tidily raked, and the terraces neatly swept.

Which was . not disappointing, exactly, but not what Tye had been expecting.

"I hope this isn't too great an inconvenience," Miss Daniels said as Tye carried his burden into a cozy library. "I'll ring for refreshment as soon as we have Fee settled."

"May I have some refreshment?" the child asked.

Miss Daniels frowned at the girl clinging to Tye's back like a monkey. "You nipped out before breakfast, Fee, and missed luncheon. No doubt you pilfered some scones, but you'll make a pig of yourself at tea and ruin your supper entirely."

"I'll have one sandwich. Just one. Please, Aunt Hester?"

Tye had no doubt the winsome green eyes were working their wiles over his shoulder, but really, an active child couldn't go all day on a just a few scones.

"We might take our tea in here," Tye said, shifting the girl to seat her on the sofa. "It's a pleasant room with a nice view of the back gardens."

"Oh, very well." Miss Daniels looked unhappy with her capitulation, but moved off to speak with a footman at the doorway. Tye looked about, spotted a hassock, and moved to place it before Fiona. He tossed a throw pillow onto the hassock and pointed.

"Get your foot up, child. It will help contain the swelling."

"But then it won't look horrid enough."

"And it won't feel quite so horrid either. Besides, you've already winkled tea and crumpets out of your aunt, and that after playing truant the entire day. You ought to be ashamed of yourself."

God in heaven, he'd sounded just like his father.

"You should not have used foul language."

"I should not—" He closed his mouth. The impertinent little baggage was right, though foul language was a simple enough pleasure in a life where pleasure was otherwise in short supply. "I do beg your pardon. I was overset."

"You were not." She grabbed a green-and-black tartan blanket from the back of the sofa. "Grown-up men don't get overset, though they do get soused.

Aunt taught me that word, but I'm not to use it around company."

He stared at the child. Treated the little minx to a gimlet gaze that had settled overspending distant relations without a word.

She winked at him. "We're even now."

"The tea tray will be along shortly," Miss Daniels said, sweeping back into the room. "Won't you have a seat, Mr. Spathfoy?"

She betrayed her Englishness with the lapse—it was a Scottish title, after all, and a Scottish courtesy title at that. Her lack of familiarity with it confirmed suspicions originating in her proper southern speech and pretty company manners.

"I beg your pardon, Miss Daniels, I am the *Earl* of Spathfoy." He waited with some interest to see how she'd react to her faux pas.

"I do apologize, my lord. Shall we be seated?"

No blush, no stammering, no glancing all around or scolding him for not initially introducing himself properly.

Seeing no alternative, Tye sat, taking a wing chair flanking the sofa where the Duchess of Singing Trees reclined in grand estate. Miss Daniels took a second wing chair and turned a considering look on her niece. "I'm going to have to send a note to Uncle Ian at least, Fee. He might wire your mama and papa."

"Will they come home to see if I'm alive?"

"They will come home when they've completed their journey. They hardly had time for a wedding journey, so you must not begrudge them their travels this summer." She shot the child a speaking glance, as if visually reminding the girl not to argue before company.

Though Tye would enjoy seeing the two of them go at it. His money would be on the girl. "Where are they traveling?" he asked, mostly to break a growing silence.

"All over," Fiona said, slumping back on a dramatic sigh. "First Paris, then Berlin, Munich, Vienna, Venice, Florence and Rome. Madrid and Lisbon, then home again. I had a cat named Florence once. She ran off with a handsome marmalade fellow named Beowulf."

"This will be quite a journey." And quite a convenient development, given Tye's plans.

"Mary Fran and Matthew have been married a year," Miss Daniels said. "Their first priority was establishing a home here, near Mary Frances's family, but she has longed to see some of the Continent, and I was available to stay with Fiona while they traveled, so here we are."

She gave him a bright, false smile, and it occurred to him that he was in the presence of a Poor Relation. Miss Daniels was young, pretty, not sporting a ring on the fourth finger of her left hand, and by rights ought to be in London, trying to flirt herself up a decent match.

Instead she was here in Aberdeenshire, during the only months that location boasted pretensions to decent weather, idling away her youth with a child who sang to trees. A bleak prospect indeed, but a penniless female was at the mercy of the rest of her family.

"Have you written to your parents, Fiona?" He

put the question to the child, though making polite conversation with the infantry was not a skill he'd ever aspired to.

"I write to them every other day, but that's mostly so Aunt Hester can say I've practiced my penmanship." She regarded her propped foot. "I miss them."

Such a plaintive expression accompanied this declaration that Tye felt an unwelcome urge to comfort the child. Very unwelcome.

"We'll stay busy," Miss Daniels said. "The weeks will pass quickly, and then they'll be home."

"And then at Christmas, we'll have a new baby!" As melancholy as the girl had been an instant ago, she was that gleeful with news of her coming half sibling. "I hope it's a boy so I can teach him how to fish and make mud pies."

"Fiona." Miss Daniels put a wealth of repression in three syllables, and Tye was intrigued to see the lady was blushing hotly, right up her neck and both cheeks, which was almost as interesting as the news that Fiona's mother was again on the nest.

Within one year of marriage, no less. The woman was nothing if not an easy breeder. The food arrived before Tye could dwell on that unhappy subject, and Miss Daniels launched into a recitation of all the books Fiona might read while allowing her foot to heal. A chambermaid appeared with a bowl of ice and a set of towels, and Miss Daniels interrupted her litany of books to make a fuss doctoring the child's ailing foot. Tye used the time to fill the pit in his stomach with scrumptious ham-and-cheddar sandwiches and a delectable array of small tea cakes.

"You enjoy a hearty appetite, my lord."

He pause midreach toward the last chocolate tea cake, wondering if that was censure or amusement in Miss Daniels's voice. She was nibbling on a tea cake too, and while he watched, the pink tip of her tongue peeked out of the corner of her mouth to lick a dab of white frosting from her lip.

"The fresh country air and a tidy little gallop have left me peckish. Then too, I have been traveling for some time." Though the fresh country air was also addling his brain if he'd taken to staring at a decent woman's mouth.

"Were you in Florence?" That from the child, who was reaching for another sandwich. He met her gaze and realized she knew damned good and well she was exceeding her own stated limit of one sandwich.

"I have been in Florence, though not recently. A lovely city, if hot." And somewhat unfragrant, like many of the European capitals, including— emphatically—dear old London towne.

"My uncle Asher is in Canada." The girl took a bite of her second sandwich. "He went there when I wasn't even a baby, but I love him. My uncles are the best."

The child's words were a providential opening. Before Miss Daniels could nibble more frosting, before the child could cadge a third sandwich, Tye decided it was the only opening he was likely to have, and it was past time he presented himself honestly.

"Your uncles are the best?"

Fee nodded emphatically. "The very, very best. Especially Uncle Ian, because he looks after all of us—he's an earl—but all my uncles are capital fellows."

"It's fortunate you feel that way, because I myself am among their number."

❦

Hester had taken their guest for a Scot at first, in part because of his glorious size. He appeared to enjoy the breeding of many a Scot, a cross of dark Celtic good looks with Viking scale and muscle.

He inhabited his body like a Scot too, comfortable and rangy, at ease with both his proportions and his strength. Watching him ride across the pastures, she'd envied Fee, thinking at first that Ian had perhaps cantered over for a surprise visit and was treating his niece to a taste of adventure.

But then he'd spoken, and that voice… Spathfoy should be a mesmerist, with a voice like that. The English public school consonants were present, all crisply started, neatly executed, and cleanly finished off, but in the vowels there lurked something… more. Something suggestive of foreign antecedents and earthy inclinations. She could listen to that voice like a lullaby.

Except… he formed words, not just spoken music, and he'd said something extraordinary.

"I beg your pardon, my lord. Did you just pronounce yourself to be among Fiona's uncles?"

"I did. I am the older brother of Fiona's late father, and very pleased to make my niece's acquaintance."

The great beast of a man was lying—not about being Fee's uncle, but about being pleased. He even sounded beautiful when he lied—beautiful and believable. Oh, he'd done the proper thing and made sure Fee got safely home when she'd hurt her ankle, but the proper thing and the convenient thing were sometimes separated merely by the intention motivating the same act.

"Fiona would make her curtsy to you, I'm sure, but for her indisposition. I don't suppose you were merely in the area and calling upon a relation?"

Fiona shifted amid her pillows. "I don't know you. I know my uncles."

"I have been remiss in not calling before, but I reside primarily in London, which is some distance away." He looked directly at Fee while he spoke, and this, Hester realized, was part of his... not charm. He wasn't in any case charming, but part of his attraction. He had moss-green eyes, startlingly green, fringed with long, dark lashes. They imparted a sensual air to an otherwise austere countenance, and suggested the truth of the man was in that voice, in the caress and lilt of it, rather than in the stern features.

"You are here now," Hester said, though she was wishing it were otherwise, and that probably showed in her voice.

Fiona peered up at his lordship. "*Why* are you here now?"

For an instant, something flickered through lordly green eyes, impatience, maybe, or resentment. Or—a remote possibility—surprise, that a little girl would not remain silent and passive in the presence of this titled uncle.

"I am addressing a previous oversight. I'd written to Altsax of my intent, but he has apparently gone traveling with his lady. I will call upon Lord Balfour at the earliest opportunity in Altsax's absence."

"Papa doesn't use the title." Fee was frowning a particularly worried frown, and Hester could only imagine what was going through the child's mind.

She passed her niece the last tea cake and served up a reassuring smile with it. "After such a trying day, Fiona, you should probably rest for a bit. Would you like a book?"

"*Robinson Crusoe*, please." The please was an oddment, an indication of tension caused by Spathfoy's bald announcement, and the choice of story was the mental equivalent of reaching for a favorite doll.

Hester got down the book, noting that Spathfoy had gone quiet, probably the better to plan his next broadside.

"My lord, may I request a turn in the garden on your arm? The day is lovely, and Mary Frances takes great pride in her flowers." The request was as polite as Hester could manage, but her temper—her blasted, perishing temper, which had never been a problem until this self-imposed banishment to Scotland—was threatening to gallop off with her manners.

"But of course." He rose to his impressive height, looking handsome and proper. There wasn't a single crumb on his breeches, and his hair looked artfully windblown, not as if he was given to pelting over fences willy-nilly.

Hester led him to the gardens, lecturing herself all the while about decorum, Highland hospitality, and making good first impressions. When Spathfoy inquired as to whether "the child" had a governess, tutors, or music instructors, she did not wallop him across his arrogant cheek.

She limited her wrath to a mere ladylike tongue lashing, but she made as thorough a job of it as momentary inspiration and vicarious maternal instinct could muster—which was very thorough indeed.

∽

Where a prim little bit of poor relation had stood before, a raging tempest now boiled.

"What on earth can you be about, my lord, to come barging in here, misrepresenting yourself to all and sundry, insinuating yourself into the child's good graces when she's all alone and without her parents? You broke bread with that girl before you revealed yourself to her. And you've yet to explain why Fee's paternal family could turn their collective *English* backs on her for years, then show up here, without invitation, and trespass on the child's peace. Do you know how much upheaval and change she's gone through in the past year? Moving, acquiring a stepfather who loves her, losing the only home she's known, and parting from the family in whose care she has thrived? And then you, you *gallop* onto the scene, as if you have some right to make inquiries regarding Fee's care and well being..."

She ranted on quite impressively. Blue eyes were commonplace, and Tye had never been particularly partial to them—never noticed them, in fact, but these blue eyes were capable of sinking galleons, so effectively did they fire off indignation and protectiveness.

He was impressed, and he allowed the lady to rage on in part because he *was* impressed, but also because, as a member of Fiona's extended maternal family, Miss Daniels was entitled to her tantrum.

"Perhaps madam might permit me an edgewise word of explanation." He did not allow this to be a question.

She folded her arms over a bosom rendered impressive when heaving with ire, and turned her back on him—a telling shot. "Make it a good word, my lord. Fiona's father was a disgrace, and his family's behavior has only confirmed that his character ran true to his breeding."

A splendid insult, but enough was quite enough.

"And how is any of this your concern, Miss Daniels? As I understand it, you are the younger sister of Fiona's newly acquired stepfather. You are no relation to the child at all."

She turned to face him, somehow glaring down a rather determined nose, though she was a foot shorter than Tye. "I am her physical custodian at present, my lord, and *I love her*."

Clearly, this irrelevance was a decisive argument to the woman, and just as clearly, Tye was going to have to reassess the situation. A serving of contrition leavened with charm was called for—on his part.

"You are quite right to be indignant on Fiona's behalf, though I had expected to have this discussion with Altsax, or possibly with Altsax and Balfour. Shall we stroll a while, or would you prefer to sit?"

She blinked at the choice. "It matters naught to me."

He offered her his arm, a strategic bit of manners. She took it gingerly and let him lead her down a path among the roses. "Fiona's mother does take her gardens seriously, doesn't she?"

"Her name is Mary Frances."

He let a silence form, one intended to ease hostilities

and allow him to size up his immediate opponent—because they were opponents. He'd take on all the indignant aunts and doting—if absentee—stepfathers in Scotland, if necessary, to accomplish his ends.

"And is Mary Frances happy with your brother?"

Something shifted in the woman's demeanor. "They are besotted." Her admission was grudging and maybe wistful too.

"I concluded as much, owing to the brevity of their engagement. When a man has a title, though, these things become a priority."

She dropped his arm. "These things? These things, such as marrying the love of one's life, speaking vows with the person who can help one to face life's hurts and wrongs with courage, the person in whose love and trust one can repose one's entire heart?"

She spoke in flights and poems, and made no sense to him.

"I was referring to the need to secure the succession, to populate one's nursery. Procreation of legitimate offspring, that sort of thing."

She visually *walloped* him, smacked him hard, a good, cracking blow that no doubt would have left his cheek smarting mightily had she used her hand instead of those blue eyes, that nose, and a posture reminiscent of an outraged angel. "Fiona is *legitimate*, no thanks to your dashing scoundrel of a brother."

He did not touch his cheek, though it was tempting. "I did not mean to imply otherwise."

"Yes, you did. Dripping gentlemanlike condescension, using sly innuendo and subtle hints, you insulted my niece *and* her mother. If I were a man, I'd call you out."

He took two steps to stand right next to her, since the upper hand had to be reestablished, manners be damned. "Dueling went out of fashion thirty years ago."

And this entire conversation had blundered into something very like an argument with a lady, which Tye could not in his entire adult memory recall ever having engaged in before. It was almost… arousing.

"You're in the *Highlands*, my lord." She closed the remaining distance between them and stuck that arrogant nose in his face. "We settle our differences here in as expedient a fashion as necessary."

"And this is Highland hospitality? Railing in the garden at guests who come in good faith, guests who take tender care of injured children like, like a *Good Samaritan*?" Ah, that was gratifying, to flourish the biblical term and see her righteousness falter.

"Fiona would not right this minute be watching her ankle swell up with pain if your blasted horse hadn't necessitated that she jump down from a dangerous height. Good Samaritan, indeed."

Tye was formulating a riposte to that inanity when a quavery voice sang out over the roses.

"Why, Hester, we have a guest. Always so nice when friends come to call. Perhaps you'd introduce us?"

A Lilliputian in a purple turban advanced on them, if such a doddering progress could be called an advance. That turban bobbing along was all Tye could make out at first, until stooped shoulders and a frail personage came around the corner of a bed of roses. She leaned heavily on a thick, carved cane that looked to be more counterweight than support, and her face had the papery smooth transparency of great age. Her smile was sweet and slightly vague, but her green eyes bore more than a spark of intelligence.

"My dear girl," said the old woman, "you must introduce me to such a handsome fellow. Merely beholding him adds years to my life."

Old women could be great flirts. Tye had learned this startling fact while lurking on the edge of many a ballroom. They could also be powerful allies to their favorites, having connections that went back to Mad King George's day, and a knowledge of family history—family secrets—that went back even further.

He turned his best, most enchanted smile on the old dear. "Miss Daniels, I agree. you must introduce us this instant, that I might pluck for the lady a rose worthy of her attention lest she continue to bedazzle my feeble sight with her smile."

Miss Daniels heaved a great sigh conveying nothing so much as long-suffering.

"Lady Ariadne MacGregor, may I make known to you the Earl of Spathfoy, though I can't recall the man's name if he deigned to part with it. Your lordship, Fiona's great-aunt, possibly great-great, and a woman not to be underestimated. Fiona intends to grow up to be just like her. I warn you solely out of a sense of pity for helpless creatures."

"Oh, now, Hester. You'll have the man thinking you've no manners." But being a flirt, Lady Ariadne extended her hand to Tye for a gentlemanly bow, which he bestowed in lingering, adoring fashion.

"Spathfoy is the title for the Quinworth heir, am I right? And how is your dear mother, my boy? She was such a pretty girl. And you must call me Aunt Ree. Everybody does—I insist."

A slight trickle of unease percolated through Tye's vitals. He let the lady retrieve her hand and kept his smile in place. "My mother fares well." As far as he knew. He offered Lady Ariadne his arm, though it was about the equivalent of offering his arm to little Fiona, so tiny was his new, honorary aunt.

"I saw you galloping over the fields, Spathfoy. That black of yours looks like a handful."

And when she wasn't flirting or gossiping, an old woman might talk horses and hounds as well as many a squire. Tye relaxed his guard and prepared to move very slowly toward the house. "Flying Rowan is young, and he needs to work the fidgets out regularly, but his sense of distance to a jump is faultless, he has tremendous bottom, and he has a good heart."

"He has potential, then." She stopped and craned her neck to peer up at him. "My late husband—my second late husband—often remarked that a man will choose his dogs to complement his personality, but his horse must be a direct reflection of him."

He wasn't going to go near that sally—he rode a gelding, for pity's sake.

"And what of his cats, Lady Ariadne? On what basis does a man choose his cats?"

"Cats?" She twitched a little straighter as they meandered along. "Cats are like women, Spathfoy. They do the choosing. Come along, Hester. We must inform the staff we'll be providing hospitality to a guest." She stopped again, as if thinking, talking, and moving forward at the same time exceeded the energy she could muster in one moment. "How long can you stay, my lord? I'm sure Fiona will want to get to know her uncle, particularly when you will one day be the highest ranking among them all."

❧

Hester watched as Aunt Ree hobbled and swayed along on That Man's arm. While her body was frail, Aunt's hearing was remarkable, as was her eyesight. Without doubt, she'd overheard that unseemly disagreement Hester had undertaken with the earl.

Of Spathfoy, which Aunt had recognized as being an heir's courtesy title, and if the courtesy title was an earldom, then the man's father was a marquess at least, or—*Merciful Powers, deliver me*—possibly even a duke.

No wonder he had arrogance to spare and condescension oozing from every syllable. Hester considered lingering in the garden to cool her temper then discarded the notion.

Aunt Ree had joined the household to provide proper chaperonage for Hester, while Hester had joined the household to look after Fiona in her parents' absence. They formed a little parade of the cast-off and inconvenient females of the family, put in train to keep their eyes on one another.

And if anybody required supervision, it was Aunt Ree in the presence of a handsome and unsuspecting man. With a reluctant nod to duty and decency, Hester plucked herself a bud from a Bourbon rose, treated herself to a whiff of its fragrance, and made her way into the house.

She caught up with Aunt and her escort outside the library doors.

"His lordship tells me our Fiona has wrenched her ankle, Hester. I can sit with the child while you alert the housekeeper to our good fortune. Spathfoy says he's at leisure." Aunt beamed a guileless smile at the man. "He can stay with us for quite some time. Isn't that marvelous?"

Marvelous?

Marvelous! To have such a great, arrogant, interfering, argumentative excuse for a—

But Aunt was aiming her smile at Hester, communicating a more immediate message than how marvelous his lordship's company was going to be.

Hester smiled right back at Aunt Ariadne. "I'll confer with Mrs. Deal. I'm sure she'll be as happy as I am at the prospect of his lordship staying with us." She tossed a curtsy in the direction of His Marvelousness and ducked down the stairs to the kitchen before his two-inch inclination of a bow was even fully executed.

Aunt had known Spathfoy was Fiona's uncle, and there was some warning for Hester in that final observation—Spathfoy was the most powerful among Fee's uncles.

This was enough to give Hester pause at the foot of the steps. Fee had three, possibly four maternal uncles, each of them every bit as handsome and physically imposing as Spathfoy.

Connor MacGregor was married to a wealthy Northumbrian widow, one whom he was making wealthier still, if the family gossip could be believed.

A man who commanded wealth had significant power in these modern times.

Ian MacGregor was currently styled Earl of Balfour, though family gossip also suggested an older brother thought dead in the Canadian wilderness might yet be lurking among the provincial pines. Ian also knew how to make an estate profitable, and his wife, Augusta, was both titled in her own right and abundantly landed.

Gilgallon MacGregor was sporting about London as husband to Hester's own sister, and if he wasn't exactly wealthy, he was canny, ruthless, and quick with his fists.

And Spathfoy was going to be more powerful than any of these three?

Than all of them put together?

"Mrs. Deal?"

A woman built roughly along the proportions of a plow horse looked up from where she was pummeling a batch of dough at the wooden counter. "Miss Hester." A great, toothy smile creased Deal's ruddy face. "Are we to be serving up another round of tea? Damned English do love their tea."

And Deal loved her work. She was more cook than housekeeper, since Mary Fran's notions of how to run a household left little room for delegation. Deal personified the old-fashioned Scottish notion of "family retainer." She served MacGregors, and the specific capacity mattered less than the resulting loyalty and mutual obligation.

"We don't need another tea tray," Hester clarified, "but Aunt Ree is inviting Lord Spathfoy to stay with us for a bit. We'll need to serve more than bannocks or scones for breakfast, because he's one of Fiona's paternal uncles." By Highland standards he was family, as incongruous as that notion felt.

"Ach, aye. If the English couldn't get a proper breakfast, they'd starve but for their tea. That lot knows nothing of sauces and subtleties. Which bedroom shall we put his lordship in?"

She smacked the dough down with particularly fierce enthusiasm, as if showing his lordship the error of English culinary failures was going to be the satisfaction of a life's work.

"Let's use the corner bedroom in the east wing. It boasts nice views of the garden, and the chimney doesn't smoke."

Deal nodded as she started separating the dough into long, thick sections. "Putting him in the guest wing will keep him out of everybody's hair. I suppose you'll be sending a note over to Balfour House?"

"Of course." Belatedly, Hester realized this was the mission Aunt had tried to communicate between all those smiles. "At once."

"You, Dinlach." Deal barked at the potboy, who was doing a desultory job at the main sink. "Tell Festus we'll want a rider over to Balfour soonest. Miss Hester needs to warn the earl that Lady Mary Fran's worthless former in-laws have come skulking about at last."

"Mrs. Deal, you shouldn't say such things."

Deal deftly braided the dough into a fat loaf. "Flynns is border English, which is the worst kind. They recall enough of their Scottish heritage to hold their whisky and reave what they want, but they've got English titles, and English wealth to protect them from the consequences. Ask auld Ree. She'll explain it to you."

Deal used a pastry brush to dab melted butter over each loaf in curiously delicate movements, while foreboding settled cold and queasy in Hester's innards.

"He's a titled English lord, Deal. He won't be stealing cattle, trust me on this."

Deal set the butter and brush aside. "I'm just the help, Miss Hester. Far be it from me to speak ill of a guest. Hadn't you best be writing that note?"

Hester headed back up the stairs, but Deal, plain-faced, phlegmatic, and loyal to her bones, had suggested a potential threat to the household coming from the most likely quarter.

A perishing son of a titled family, as if Hester hadn't suffered enough already at the hands of the very same.

⁂

Being the Earl of Balfour was a damned pain in Ian MacGregor's muscular backside—his muscular and, according to his wife, adorable backside. The title involved responsibility for family members both cantankerous and unruly, stewardship of difficult and rugged land, and a bloody lot of ceremony and pomp for which no self-respecting Highlander had much patience.

In other regards, though, Ian was a very, very patient man.

His countess pinched the part of him she found so adorable.

"You're teasing me, Husband. I am not in a mood to lollygag."

"Hmm?" He kissed her ear, then bit down on the

lobe. "My hearing is a wee bit off today, most likely as a result of all that exercise our son gave his lungs before going down for his nap."

He plied her gently with his cock, listening for the telltale sighs, both audible and corporeal, that would signal that she was growing desperate. Augusta grew greedy and wonderfully passionate when she was desperate.

"You are teasing me, Ian. This is not well done of you. The baby will awaken, and then you'll wish you'd applied yourself with a little more—oh, my goodness."

He applied himself with a little *more*, not faster, just a trifle more. Too much more, and his self-discipline would go down in the flames of his wife's passion, but a little more, a few sparks on the dry tinder of her arousal, and she'd start up with those soft moans that inspired him to great feats of forbearance.

"My wife is given to chatter. I will kiss this tendency away."

He made her wait for even his kisses, running his nose along her jaw, then dragging his lips over each eyebrow. Beneath him, Augusta shifted her hips, catching him at a slightly deeper angle.

In their year of marriage she'd learned how to toss a few sparks of her own.

"So impatient, Wife. 'Tis a failing in you English. Always plundering when you could barter."

He eased a hand up and gently closed it over one full breast—very gently. Maddeningly gently. She sighed against his neck and bartered her luscious mouth right over his, an openmouthed, seeking kiss involving her tongue and his few remaining wits.

"Naughty girl. How I treasure you."

She sighed into his mouth, anchored a hand on his bottom, and then—oh, have mercy upon a poor married man—got her internal muscles into the negotiation.

"Lass, you mustn't—"

"Hush, laddie."

She offered him no quarter, just her luscious, loving body, her heart, and her very soul, and he gave her his in return.

And then… ah, then the cuddling, at which she also excelled, an attribute Ian privately thought was the influence of Scottish antecedents hanging a few branches back on his wife's family tree. Highland winters sorted out the priorities that effectively.

He tucked his sated wife against his side and hugged her close. "Could the little man be cutting teeth yet?"

"I certainly hope not. Mary Fran says that can presage months of intermittent misery for the child, and Fiona didn't start teething until she was six months old."

"So we have that to look forward to." He kissed her ear—it was a beautiful ear. "You are a wonderful mother, Augusta, never doubt it." She eased in his arms in some way, suggesting she'd needed the reassurance, but God in heaven, no baby was ever cosseted and cared for more conscientiously.

The entire family, the entire clan, seemed to dote on their son, and it warmed Ian's heart to see it.

"I want more children, Ian. I want a big family, and we've gotten a late start on it."

"And did you think I was exerting myself so

manfully in this bed purely out of selfish motives, Wife?" He dragged her over him, so she straddled his hips and cuddled down to his chest. "If my wife wants more babies, then I will do my utmost to see her pleased in this regard. My marital devotion allows for no less."

She ran her tongue over his nipple. "Such generosity. What was in the note, Ian? You got very quiet after you read it."

He rested his chin on her crown and let his hands wander over the long, elegant bones of her back. "We've trouble, Wife. Spathfoy has made a surprise raid on your cousin's household, and we don't know what his motives are."

"Spathfoy?" Augusta paused in her teasing to peer up at him. "I don't recognize the title."

"He's heir to the Marquess of Quinworth, and older brother to the worthless, conniving scoundrel who took advantage of my sister and got her with child." He tried not to let his anger show in his voice or in his body, because Augusta was that perceptive, but Mary Fran had given the faithless bounder her virginity, and Gordie Flynn had given her nothing but pain and humiliation in return.

"Spathfoy lost a brother, Ian. That cannot have been easy."

"And he has Quinworth for a father, but what if he's showing up all these years later to snatch our Fiona away, my love? Mary Fran will be heartbroken, and Matthew will stop at nothing to retrieve the child."

Augusta's fine dark brows knit, which made Ian want

to kiss them. He resisted this notion, because babies slept only so long, and he valued his wife's counsel.

"Maybe he's merely showing the colors, Ian. You can't assume because he's English his purpose is necessarily nefarious."

"Nefarious and English are synonyms in the Scottish lexicon, my love. The Flynns made it plain they considered the girl child of a handfast marriage little more than a bastard. They've never sent so much as a groat for Fiona's upkeep or a token for her birthday. I'm not inclined to trust Spathfoy's avuncular motives very far."

"Is his father perhaps ailing? That can shift a man's perspective on family matters."

Ian let out a sigh of his own. The topic was curdling any notions of further efforts to ensure the large family his wife sought, but Augusta was a good sounding board, and theirs was a marriage without secrets. "I'll ride over in the morning and get the lay of the land. Hester sounds like she's in quite a dither, though Aunt Ree will manage the man well enough I'm sure."

"You'll behave?" She rose off his chest to spear him with a look. "Charm at the ready, all Scottish good cheer to the fore? You can be very charming when you set your mind to it, Ian. I have your ring on my finger as a result of your charm."

"There was a bit more to it than that, my love."

"*More*, Ian?" She smiled a feline smile, feathered her thumbs over his nipples, and Ian barely had time to send up a prayer that the baby would sleep for at least another hour before Augusta was offering him *more*, indeed.

Hester had forgotten the pleasure of spending time with a man on his best behavior, particularly a handsome man with a gorgeous voice. If she'd known scolding a lordling would have this effect, she might have behaved very differently with her former fiancé.

Though it was irksome in the extreme to think she'd have to withstand Spathfoy's good behavior all on her own for the duration of an entire meal. Aunt had decided to take a tray with Fiona, which was probably as well, given the child's difficult day.

"I am sorry Lady Ariadne will not be joining us for dinner." Spathfoy offered his arm with all the courtly élan imbued by his breeding. "She gave me to understand she's something of a family historian, and I would love to hear the tales she has stored in her head."

"She's a treasure." *Also a terror.* "But her stories are not such as would flatter English ears."

He seated her at the table without replying, and he had the knack of even that.

A lady needed assistance taking her seat because she had to manage her skirts and petticoats, which involved two hands, generally, and that left the gentleman to manage the chair. Her brother Matthew was no good at it at all, usually catching hems under chair legs, or bumping the chair right into the backs of her knees.

Matthew was her brother. Spathfoy was... a pest. An elegant pest who'd bathed and changed for the evening meal, though even in informal attire, he exuded a kind of inborn grace that was not having a good effect on Hester's disposition.

"You might be interested to know I am *half* English, Miss Daniels."

He'd murmured that soft aside right near her ear as she'd fluffed out her skirts, and in addition to the impact of his silken voice twining through her awareness, she caught a whiff of his scent.

It was all she could do not to bat him away. He smelled of lavender and something lovely—attar of roses? Honeysuckle? She was still trying to dissect the incongruous sweetness in his fragrance when he took the chair to her right.

"Your mother is Scottish, my lord?"

"A Lowlander, but yes. I get my height from her side of the family. May I serve you?"

They were dining informally, with the food kept hot on the table in chafing dishes. This was how the household always dined, but Hester felt a pang not to have Fee chattering away on one side, and Aunt chirping along on the other. They were her family now, and she had quickly grown to love them.

His lordship was regarding her curiously, and Hester realized she'd let the conversation lapse.

"If you would do the honors, my lord. I am very partial to my vegetables. Have your things arrived from the inn at Ballater?"

"They did. I must say I was impressed with the quality of the accommodations. I take it Her Majesty's interest in the surrounds has done good things for the local economy."

He passed her a plate full of steaming food, but the

portions were such as a large man might consume after a busy day in the fields—an interesting miscalculation from somebody Hester took to be very calculating indeed.

"If I eat this much, my lord, I'll not be able to rise at the end of the meal." She set the plate down in front of him and started serving herself. "And as for the local economy, the royal family is here but a few months a year, and that only in recent years. Deeside owes more to the fish than we do to the Crown."

"Fish?" He watched her serve herself and frowned at the portions she put on her plate. "Miss Daniels, you cannot thrive on such meager fare."

"There's trifle for dessert, my lord. Will you say the blessing?" An inspiration, to stick him with something as mundane as blessing the meal.

Her cleverness backfired. He was sitting where Fee usually sat, and out of habit, Hester reached out her hand when it was time to say the blessing. When her fingers closed around Spathfoy's, she was too dumbstruck at her blunder to withdraw her hand.

Two

"I'D BE HAPPY TO SAY THE BLESSING."

While Spathfoy sat there holding Hester's bare hand in his, his gaze moved around the table, over the covered dishes, to the huge bouquet of roses starting to wilt on the sideboard, and to the window, where the long hours of gloaming were casting soft shadows. "For journeys safely concluded, for good food, for the company of family and friends, we are grateful. Amen."

He kept his hand around hers for an instant more, long enough for Hester to register several impressions: his grip was dry, warm, firm, and unhesitating. He wasn't cursed with bodily shyness, for all his other faults.

And it felt good—far, far too good—to join hands again with an adult male, to feel the latent strength in the clasp of his hand, to revel in simple human contact.

Hester reached for her water goblet at the same time Spathfoy reached for his wine, and their hands brushed again.

"I beg your pardon, Miss Daniels. You were saying something about fish?" He took a sip of his wine, not by word or gesture suggesting a little collision of hands might unnerve him the way it unnerved her.

"The River Dee is among the finest salmon streams in the world, my lord. Throughout Deeside, there are excellent inns and hostelries to accommodate the fishermen who come here for sport. His Highness is a great sportsman, and that doesn't hurt either."

"But the royal family is not now in residence at Balmoral, are they?" He ate almost daintily, and yet the food was disappearing from his plate at a great rate.

"Her Majesty usually removes here closer to August. We get quite the influx of English then, all mad for a walk in the Highlands in hopes they'll encounter the royal family on a ramble."

"You say this with some aspersion."

His lovely voice held not so much censure as curiosity. Hester collected her thoughts while she took a sip of her wine, though the truth came out anyway.

"I came to Scotland to be with family, my lord. To escape the social confines of London, and the expectations incumbent on the daughter of a titled man when she emerges from mourning that man's death. I do not relish the idea of coming across in the woods the very people I sought to avoid when I quit London."

He was regarding her closely, his expression hard to read, and then he did the most unexpected thing: he patted her hand. A gentle, glancing stroke of his fingers over her knuckles.

The gesture should have felt condescending, but instead it was… comforting.

"Society is the very devil." He topped off her wine. "As the heir to a marquess, I can only sympathize with your disparagement of it. And my condolences on the loss of your father. I'm hoping my own lives to a biblical age."

He sounded very sincere in this wish, very human. Hester tried not to be disconcerted by that.

She'd thought dinner would be a struggle, but by the time he was asking her to finish his serving of trifle, she realized more than an hour in Spathfoy's company had been... enjoyable.

"We've almost lost the light, Miss Daniels, but is there time for a short turn in the garden? A stroll before retiring settles the meal and is a personal habit of mine. If nothing else, I can look in on Flying Rowan."

She could not politely refuse, and it wasn't pitch dark yet. He assisted her to her feet, taking her hand then tucking it over his arm. He touched her with a certain competence, a male assurance that suggested handling women came instinctively to him.

She could not quite resent him for this—being handled competently was too rare a treat—but Hester vowed she would not be swayed by his abilities in this regard. He was an invading army of one, and his company manners did not make his mission any less suspect.

"The roses are particularly lovely," she said as they moved across the terrace. "Mary Fran spares no effort in their care."

"My grandmother was quite the gardener. My Scottish grandmother, that is."

"And you must have seen her gardens at some point?"

He walked along beside her, making a gentlemanly accommodation to her shorter stride, and yet she felt him hesitate at the question.

"I did. For a succession of boyhood summers, I was sent to my grandparents while my parents attended various house parties in the South."

He said nothing more, revealed no memories of those long-ago summers, so Hester was casting about for a polite topic they hadn't yet exhausted, when an odd, ugly sound split the evening gloom. Beside her, Spathfoy paused.

Hester shuddered, wanting to put her hands over her ears. "What *is* that? It sound like a child in distress, a very young child."

"It's a fox, and I've been told that sound is Reynard's attempt to attract a mate."

"Pity the poor vixen, then, if that's his best effort at courtship." Hester wanted to move, to get away from that unpleasant, raucous noise, though it didn't seem to bother her escort.

"The female's lot is often unenviable, or so my sisters would have me believe. Which is your favorite rose?"

They made a circuit of the entire garden, until Hester's head was beginning to ache with the unaccustomed amount of wine she'd consumed and the burden of being sociable to a man she did not like or trust. He left the impression that being cordially pleasant was no effort for him, so thoroughly ingrained were his gentlemanly inclinations.

"It is nearly dark," Hester said. "Shall you visit your horse?"

"Let's sit for a moment. It has been some time since I paused to appreciate the fragrance of roses on the evening air."

Mother of God, he sounded wistful, and there was

nothing for it but she must sit with him. Hester appropriated a wooden bench between the Bourbons and the Damasks, hearing the seat creak when Spathfoy came down beside her.

"I see a lamp burning in the opposite wing from my bedroom, though I doubt you have servants biding on the ground floor."

"Aunt Ree's rooms are on the ground floor to spare her the stairs and put her closer to the kitchens if she's in need of a posset at bedtime."

As they watched, Lady Ariadne herself bobbed past a window, her purple turban no longer in evidence.

"My grandmother had the same snow-white hair," Spathfoy said. "What do you suppose she's reading?"

Hester sensed that this too was part of his nature, a curiosity about anything and everything around him, because a man likely to inherit a marquessate would not comprehend that people with small lives treasured at least the privacy of those small lives.

"She reads old love letters before retiring and hopes her former swains will visit her in her dreams."

Ariadne's habit sounded daft, put into words like that. Daft and lonely.

And he had nothing to say to this, so a silence fell while Hester felt fatigue of both body and spirit seeping into her bones.

Spathfoy stretched out long, long legs and crossed them at the ankles. "At least she has love letters. Are you growing chilled, Miss Daniels? I can offer my coat, or return you to the house."

Hester rose. The idea of being enveloped in the warmth and fragrance of his clothing was more disturbing than any slight chill in the evening air. "No thank you, my lord. I'll see myself in, and my thanks, too, for your company at dinner. Breakfast is on the sideboard in the same dining parlor no later than first light."

He got to his feet. "My thanks as well, Miss Daniels. Pleasant dreams."

She might have tarried, might have reminded him to ring for anything he needed, and added admonitions that Highland hospitality meant their home was his for the duration of his stay, but she left him among the roses and shadows. Reminding Lady Ariadne to close her curtains was a far more urgent and worthy mission.

❧

Tye hadn't lied. A stroll after dinner was one of his personal habits. He'd acquired this habit in defense of his peace of mind when the alternative had been port and cigars with his father—a domestic ritual that invariably degenerated into vituperation of the Commons, the Prince Consort, his lordship's own marchioness, or the fairer sex at large.

And seeing Flying Rowan properly bedded down was also part of Tye's routine, though it served nicely to allow for discreet reconnaissance of Matthew Daniels's outbuildings and grounds as well.

If the stables and gardens were any indication, Daniels was no slacker.

"Unlike you."

Rowan flicked an elegant black ear as his owner approached. The horse stood in a loose box bedded in ample, fragrant oat straw. A full bucket of clean water hung on the wall, and the gelding's coat showed signs of a thorough grooming after his exertions earlier in the day.

"Don't get too comfortable here, horse. The poor of the parish—of which there are more than a few—could use a hearty stew."

Rowan wuffled and turned large, luminous eyes on Tye.

"Shameless beggar." Tye let himself into the stall and produced a lump of sugar from his coat pocket. "Does it trouble you, horse, that you have no love letters to read by your bedside of a night?"

Rowan dispatched the lump of sugar and used a big roman nose to gently nudge at Tye's pocket.

"You have no love letters, do you? Neither do I, thank The Almighty. Don't beg." He tapped the horse's nose. "It's ungentlemanly." Tye scratched the beast's withers, also part of his end-of-day ritual with the horse. "Quinworth reads old letters. One almost pities him when one finds him in such a state. Swilling whisky and chasing it with sentiment."

The horse groaned and shivered all over. When Tye dropped his hand, the gelding craned its neck to pin Tye with another pointed look.

"You have no dignity, horse." Tye moved around and started scratching from the horse's other side. "And Quinworth has too much. The old boy has me neatly boxed in, make no mistake. If I don't retrieve my darling niece, there will be hell to pay."

And for just a moment, Tye let himself wonder if the ends truly justified the means. A childhood served out on Quinworth's terms was not exactly a guarantee of happiness—far from it.

He slung an arm over the horse's withers and leaned in, resting his weight against the animal for a moment. Fiona would be better off being acknowledged by her paternal family, and she would want for nothing money could buy.

And that should be an end to it.

"We'll be heading back south before too much longer. Enjoy your Scottish holiday while you can."

Tye let himself out of the stall, made certain the door was securely latched, took a tour of the rest of the stalls to inspect for the same measure, and ambled out into the starry night.

A light was burning on the first floor in the wing opposite Miss Ariadne's, and the rest of the house, for the most part, was dark. The light wasn't in Tye's room—he'd been graced with a corner chamber of stately proportions—which meant it was possibly Miss Daniels burning late-night oil.

Did she, too, read love letters in hopes of inspiring amorous dreams?

He thought not. She didn't strike him as a woman who'd received many love letters, much less as a lady who'd treasure the ones she'd been sent.

~

"Serviette on your lap, Fee." Hester passed the child two sections of an orange. "And you'll not be haring off this morning. If you need to stretch your legs, we'll take a walk down to the burn."

"May we picnic?"

Aunt Ariadne turned the handle of the teapot so it faced Hester. "It's a lovely day for a ramble, my dears.

I'm sure his lordship would appreciate a chance to see some of our views, too."

Hester did not wrinkle her nose at this suggestion, because Fee was watching her too closely, even as the child also made short work of the orange sections.

"Perhaps his lordship would like to rest up from his journey," Hester suggested. "Write some letters assuring his loved ones of his safe arrival."

And perhaps his lordship didn't intend to stay long enough to make even that exercise worth his time. The inn had sent out one small trunk and a traveling bag, which Hester took as encouraging.

A man traveling that light usually did not intend to tarry.

Aunt Ariadne watched as Hester filled their teacups. "Did you sleep well, my dear?"

"Oh, of course."

Except she hadn't. Hester had heard his lordship in the chamber next to hers, heard the sound of his wardrobe closing, heard him stirring on the balcony next to hers, heard him opening and closing the drawers to the escritoire in his room.

He wasn't particularly loud, but he was *there*, where nobody ought to be, and this offended Hester's equilibrium to the point where she suspected the dratted man had made an appearance in her dreams.

"Good morning, Lady Ariadne." As if conjured from Hester's thoughts, Spathfoy paused in the doorway to the dining parlor. "Miss Daniels, Miss Fiona. A lovely morning made lovelier still by present company."

He advanced into the room, and Hester gave him

a look informing him that she wasn't charmed by his expansive good will. Last night, over a few too many glasses of wine, she'd exerted herself to tolerate his company out of simple good manners, but in the broad light of day, he needed to know she was not about to let down her guard again.

"Good morning, Uncle." Fee beamed up at him over sticky fingers and a sticky chin. "Do you want to share my orange?"

"I'll pass, thank you." He moved along the sideboard, piling eggs, bacon, ham, and toast on his plate. "But a spot of tea wouldn't go amiss. I must say, it has been quite some time since I've enjoyed my matutinal repast in such jejune company."

He took a seat at Ariadne's elbow while Hester wiped off Fee's chin.

Fee spoke around Hester's dampened serviette. "Your tootinal what?"

"His morning meal," Hester translated. "In the company of one so young."

"Is that English?"

Hester almost replied that such a lofty expression was very definitely *English*, but Aunt intervened.

"Maybe his lordship was offering me a compliment on my youthful good looks, for which I would have to thank him. You must accompany the ladies on their rambles this morning, Spathfoy. They're planning a picnic by the burn, which is a lovely spot. After traveling all day yesterday, you might want to work out a few of the kinks. Sitting on a train can be such an ordeal."

"I didn't, actually." He paused before he took up his knife and fork, which left Hester a moment to stare at his hands. She'd held one of those hands, if only briefly. "I do not enjoy train travel, though it serves well for long distances. I rode out from Aberdeen over the course of the past two days."

Fee sat up. "You rode Flying Rowan clear out from Aberdeen? That is miles and miles. Surely, your fundament—"

Hester put her hand over the girl's mouth. "Fiona MacGregor, you know better than to mention such a thing before a gentleman." Though sixty-some miles was quite a long way to ride when the train was readily available.

Aunt placidly sipped her tea. "One can wonder about such things, Fiona, my dear, but one doesn't ask at table, and not of a gentleman guest. Some jam, my lord?"

He was not afraid of good, hearty fare. In fact, he ate with the casual gusto of a man who had never known hunger or want, a man whose family hadn't weathered potato famines, clearances, or decades of outlaw status forbidding them use of their very name.

"You're quiet this morning, Miss Daniels. Did you sleep well?" He paused long enough to put down his utensils and take a sip of his tea while he considered Hester from across the table.

"I'm a sound sleeper, my lord. Thank you."

Fee seized on the minute silence following Hester's comment. "Will you picnic with us, Uncle? We could bring Flying Rowan if he needs to work out the kinks too."

"Rowan will work out his kinks ambling around a grassy paddock, but I will tell him you extended a cordial invitation. Perhaps tomorrow we might take him for a short hack."

"Does that mean I can go with you?" Fee fairly bounced in her seat with anticipation. "Can we leap the walls again and go really, really fast?"

Spathfoy set down his teacup. "I am guessing permission for such an outing will depend on your excellent deportment in the intervening hours, Fiona, and of course upon the Scottish weather."

He tossed a glance at Hester, as if making some clever implication about the weather, or Hester herself.

"He means you have to behave, Fee," Hester said.

"I'll behave. Aunt Ree, may I please be excused? I want to tell Rowan we might go on another adventure."

"You may be excused, but Fiona?" Aunt's countenance remained serene. "You are not to go into that horse's stall, my girl. You can visit with him perfectly well from outside his door."

"Yes, Aunt."

Fiona scrambled off her chair, remembered to bob something resembling a curtsy at the door, and departed in a patter of small feet.

"She is a wonderfully lively child," Spathfoy remarked. "And it appears her injury is healed overnight. More tea, Miss Daniels?"

He managed to imply that *lively* was a distasteful quality in a child—in anybody. "No thank you, my lord. I was wondering if you'd like us to post some letters for you. Surely your family will want to know you're safely arrived?"

"And here I thought I was among family, at least in the general sense."

Well, good. Sniping was far preferable to charm.

Aunt beamed him an angelic smile. "Of course you're among family, dear boy. You must prevail upon Balfour to take you shooting while you're with us, and fishing, though Hester is quite the sport fisher herself."

Hester put aside her irritation with this disclosure long enough to wonder what Aunt was up to.

"Ian knows the woods well, and a haunch of venison never goes to waste," Hester said. "I doubt his lordship wants to idle along the Dee with a fishing pole and a book."

"On the contrary, Miss Daniels. While I've been on many a shoot, I can't say I've had much opportunity to fish."

Bother and damnation. "It would be my pleasure to take you, then."

As soon as the words were out of her mouth, she realized he'd hooked her with only a few words. Plucked her from the current of her intentions and left her flopping on the verge of his own plans.

The last thing she wanted to do was spend time idling about with this spoiled, overgrown exponent of English aristocracy.

"I shall look forward to it, then," his lordship said. "Maybe tomorrow, after we take out the horses?"

Aunt clapped her hands together gently. "Oh, excellent! Hester so enjoys a good gallop, and she hasn't had a riding companion since she got here. What a pity Fiona has no mount of her own."

Hester tried not to let her consternation show: by some legerdemain of manners, she was now accompanying Spathfoy both riding and fishing.

"Perhaps I shall get the child a pony." Spathfoy looked intrigued with the notion. "My sisters all had ponies before they had tutors."

"Fiona's *parents* might have something to say about such an extravagant gift, my lord. I believe Matthew wanted to be the one to teach *his daughter* how to ride, though the thought is most generous of you."

Hester fired off a smile to go with her scold. Spathfoy smiled back, all even white teeth and genial condescension. "An *uncle*, particularly one newly introduced to the child, must be allowed to *dote*, Miss Daniels."

"I'm off to the kitchen," Aunt said, laying her folded serviette on the table. "I will alert Deal to the need for a picnic today, and likely one tomorrow as well, though you won't catch any fish if Fiona comes along."

Before she could put both hands on the table, Spathfoy was on his feet and poised to shift her chair. He waited with every appearance of solicitude while Aunt scooted to the edge of her seat, bounced a little on her backside, then heaved up to a standing position.

"Shall I escort you to the kitchen, my lady?"

"Lord, no. Deal would have kittens to think of such a great man among the scullery maids and potboys. If you'd hand me my cane, my lord, I'll toddle along under my own steam."

Deal might also be tempted to take a carving knife to the great man's self-importance, though Hester kept that thought to herself when Spathfoy resumed his seat.

"Our elders present us with a puzzle." He poured himself more tea and gestured with the pot at Hester's cup.

"Please." When tea was one's only source of fortitude, it would be silly to refuse another cup.

"I never know with my father whether he's being irascible out of habit, or whether he's provoking me into some display of dominance over him so he might retire from the duties of the marquessate, satisfied that I have sufficient pugnacity to step into his shoes."

That sentence was long, even for him. Hester searched through it for plain meaning while she drank half her tea. "Your father is too proud to ask for your help."

Spathfoy peered at his teacup, and it was a satisfying moment, both because she'd flummoxed him and because his father apparently flummoxed him. Spathfoy had mentioned sisters, too—in the plural—which boded well for Hester's spirits.

"It is perhaps more the case my father and I don't know how to ask for help from each other." He sounded unhappy to draw this conclusion, the honesty of the sentiment ruining Hester's gloat entirely.

"What help would you request of him, my lord?"

Spathfoy dabbed a bite of eggs onto a corner of toast the way an artist might add paint to a canvas. "Interesting question, though I don't seek the help he proffers enthusiastically. The man is forever tossing prospective brides at me. He has a good eye for horses, though."

"And the two don't correlate? An eye for a bride and an eye for a horse?"

Too late, Hester realized she'd left him worlds of room for sly innuendo about mounts, rides, and other vulgar jokes. Jasper would have been smirking lasciviously at the very least. She took refuge in draining her teacup.

Spathfoy wasn't smirking, though humor lurked in his green eyes. "My mother and my sisters would skin me alive did I intimate a connection between brides and horses, but if there is one, it likely has to do with tossing a man aside when his attention lapses and giving his pride a hard landing."

A polite, even friendly rejoinder, damn him, and yet Hester wished she could leave him to his own company at breakfast, even though he was a guest newly arrived.

"What of your own father, Miss Daniels? Was he inclined to provide helpful advice?"

"He was not." Even the thought of the late Baron Altsax had Hester's tea and toast threatening to rebel. "He provided his opinions to all and sundry nonetheless." She lifted her teacup to her mouth, only to find it empty, and when she set it down on the table, she realized Spathfoy could see quite well what she'd done.

"I never did offer my condolences on your loss."

If he patted her hand again she'd be smashing her teacup against the wall. "My thanks, Lord Spathfoy. You also never told Aunt how long you can stay with us."

The inquiry wasn't rude, exactly, put like that, but he clearly wasn't fooled.

"I am at leisure, Miss Daniels, and it has been far too long since I've enjoyed a Scottish holiday. When do we depart for this ramble Fiona seems so delighted to contemplate?"

❧

Scotland was good for the body. Tye had forgotten this in the years since his boyhood visits.

The old house bore the slight tang of peat smoke rather than the pungent stench of coal. Out of doors, the air was crisp, the light clear, and under all the other scents—garden, stable, breakfast parlor, or freshly turned earth—heather wafted gently through the senses.

The hills ringing the shire bore purplish hems of heather; the inn where he'd stayed in Ballater had offered heather ale. He'd enjoyed a tankard and enjoyed the freedom to sit in the common and simply watch the passing scene. He was also enjoying this morning respite on a tartan blanket by a gurgling little stream, though the company left a great deal to be desired.

"Is my niece always so prone to climbing?"

"Your height spares you the indignities and inconveniences of shorter stature, my lord." Miss Daniels did not even glance up from her book to deliver this insight. If she sat any farther away, she'd be on the grass. "Those of us built on a less grandiose scale enjoy what height we can appropriate from trees, horses, and the terrain itself."

Grandiose, not grand. Miss Daniels bore the scent of lemon verbena. Tye was not intimately acquainted with the lexicon of flowers, but he suspected lemon verbena might stand for, "May the ruddy bastard get himself back to England, the sooner the better."

If only he could.

"Miss Daniels?"

"Hmm?" She tucked an errant lock of blond hair over one ear and kept her gaze on her book.

"Have I somehow given offense? I realize you were not forewarned of my visit, but I did write to your brother twice."

She put her book down with particular patience and glanced at him as if he smelled a good deal less appealing than heather, but she was too much a lady to show it.

"My lord, it is curious to me that you would travel such a distance without any guarantee of your welcome. What if Matthew and Mary Fran had closed up the house during their summer travels? It was one plan under consideration."

"Then I should have paid my respects to Balfour, enjoyed the Highland scenery currently so much in vogue, and taken myself back south. Lady Ariadne seemed cheered at the thought of a house guest. If I am mistaken in this regard, I will be happy to remove to the inn in Ballater while I further my acquaintance with my only niece."

She closed her book, and Tye had the satisfaction of seeing her neatly cornered by manners and good breeding. When she did not speak but bit her full, rosy lip and regarded her closed book, he gave her a little more to think about.

"I am enjoying my stay, short though it has been. I am not much in the company of my female family, and yet your household at present is exclusively female."

"And you *like* staying with a child, a dowager, and a spinster?"

"A spinster, Miss Daniels?" She was damned pretty for a spinster. Also quite young.

She lifted her chin so his gaze collided with a pair

of solemn blue eyes. "There are worse terms for me, your lordship. Spinster is accurate. I'm not ashamed of it."

And abruptly, they were beyond the bounds of manners. Her gaze was steady, neither challenging nor defensive, though any fool could see her dignity was supported by some deep hurt.

"You have me at a loss, Miss Daniels."

She regarded her book of verse the same way Fiona had regarded her injured ankle the day before. "I am a jilt, at least, and others called me a tease—"

"Aunt Hester! I see a fish!" Fiona stood on her tree limb and pointed to the shallows of the burn, making the entire limb as well as its shadows shake. "He's a great big fellow and taking a nap in the reeds not two feet from the bank."

Wanting nothing so much as to escape from the faint accusation in Miss Daniels's somber gaze, Tye yanked off first one boot, then the other. "You mustn't wake him up. Stay where you are, Fiona. My grandfather showed me how this is done." He stripped off his socks and rolled up his breeches.

"Will you guddle him, Uncle? Can I watch?"

"You can watch quietly." Tye rose off the blanket. "Point to him again, then climb down slowly and without making a sound."

"There." Fiona stage-whispered and gestured to the dappled shallows. "You can see his tail sticking out from the reeds."

Tye set his boots and socks aside and stepped one foot at a time into the shallow water downstream from the fish.

"God in heaven." He stood for a moment, enjoying the shock of the near-freezing water. "This is invigorating. Do not think of dipping a single toe into this water, Fiona. Your word on it."

"But I want to guddle him too!" She clambered out of the tree and stomped up to the bank. "I saw him first, and I've never tickled a fish before."

"Then this is your chance to learn from your elders. Hush, child. This requires concentration."

It required no such thing. It merely wanted patience, common sense, and an inhuman tolerance for cold water. By degrees, Tye inched up along the streambed, keeping the delicately waving fishtail in his sight at all times. When he was near enough to the fish, he dipped down on one knee and slipped both hands into the water.

"You start at the tail," he said softly. If Fiona leaned one inch farther out, she'd fall into the water. "My grandda said to begin with one finger and stroke slowly, slowly along the belly."

He made contact with a cool, smooth fish belly, using the tip of one index finger.

"And you mustn't rush it. Mustn't disturb his dreams, but rather, steal into them." He added a second finger in a slow, back-and-forth stroking motion. "If you get greedy, you'll wake him rather than lull him deeper to sleep."

"Is it like a lullaby when you tickle him?" Fiona's voice was soft and wondering, just as Tye's had been when his grandfather had first shown him how to tickle a fish.

"Like a lullaby, or rubbing a baby's back to coax her

to sleep." He shifted his fingers up the fish's belly, half inch by half inch. "He's quite good size."

"I want to see!" Fee hissed out her frustration, slapping her fists against her thighs.

"Fiona." Miss Daniels's voice was soft with reproach from her place at Fiona's side. "Lord Spathfoy is not freezing his toes off so you can scare the fish away with your chatter."

Fiona fell silent as Tye stroked his fingers back and forth, back and forth. "I'm close." He was whispering, and when he glanced up, he saw both Fiona and Miss Daniels's expressions were rapt with expectation.

"Another moment." Another moment and his calf submerged in the burn would cramp or lose sensation altogether. Tye slid his hands around the fish and closed gently.

"That's it. There we go."

He lifted the fish up out of the water, feeling inordinately pleased with himself.

"He's enormous!" Fiona reached out a hand then dropped it. "May I touch him?"

"Of course, though he'll start to thrash here directly." The fish was panting, dazed, and soon to realize its mortal peril.

"He's very pretty, and cold." Fiona ran a finger over the fish's side. "He looks like the light from the water is caught in his skin."

"His scales," Tye said. "If we don't toss him back soon, he'll die."

"Toss him back?" Fiona glanced over at her aunt. "Won't Deal want him for the kitchen?"

Miss Daniels looked horrified at the very notion.

"We won't tell Deal quite how big he is." While Tye watched, Miss Daniels ran her fingers down the cold, scaly length of the fish's body. "Best toss him back quickly, my lord."

Tye hadn't expected her to touch the fish then command its rescue. He gently lobbed the creature to the far side of the stream, and they all three watched as it swam away down the current.

Fiona slapped her hands together. "That was capital! If we see another, may I try?"

"You may," Tye said, slogging up onto the bank. "With your aunt's permission."

"Not by yourself, Fiona MacGregor. The burn is a pretty little stream now, but one storm higher up in the hills, and it can rage over its banks."

"Why can't I ever do anything by myself?" The fish forgotten, the child repaired to her tree—a reading tree, rather than a treaty oak—and began to climb.

Tye waited while Miss Daniels resumed a place on the blanket, then took a spot immediately beside her just to see what she'd do. "You allow her to address her elders in such a manner?"

She picked up her book. "Why don't you give her a stern talking to, *Uncle*? Let her see that with merely a cross word, she can pique your interest and rivet your attention. As fascinated as she is with you—or perhaps with your horse—she'll be bickering the livelong day in no time. And she's right: she is left little to her own devices."

Miss Daniels turned a page, as if she were reading in truth.

"You've piqued my interest, Miss Daniels."

She looked up, her expression gratifyingly wary. "My lord?"

"You mentioned the words jilt and tease. These are pejoratives, and I would have you explain them." He kept his voice down out of deference to the child's proximity, though Fiona was warbling among the boughs in Gaelic about her love gone over the sea.

The lady closed her eyes and expelled an audible breath. When she opened them, as close as Tye sat to her, he could see flecks of gold in her blue irises and flecks of deeper blue.

"If you frequent London society, my lord, then you are as aware as the next titled lordling that I've recently broken an engagement to Jasper Merriman—Lord Jasper. The situation was particularly nasty, because the gentleman had been counting heavily on my dowry. He threatened to bring suit."

"God in heaven. Suit? Against you? I've never heard of such a thing—a lady is permitted to change her mind. Even the courts know that."

"Breach of promise, though he was convinced to take the more gentlemanly route."

"Convinced by a goodly sum of coin, no doubt." He couldn't keep the anger from his voice. A woman brought suit for breach of a man's promise, because a man's word was the embodiment of his honor. A young woman's word was hardly hers to give, because she was in the care of her parents if the match involved a lady of any standing.

"You censure him for this?" Her tone was careful, merely inquisitive.

"Of course I censure the bas—the beggar. Living

on one's expectations is foolishness, and threatening to drag a woman's good name through the courts, when that woman was previously considered adequate to mother one's children... Of course I censure him. What was his name? Merridew?"

"Merriman. Third son of the Marquess of Spielgood."

"For God's sake... A third son, no less. He should be horsewhipped. I hope your brother dealt with him."

"My brother paid him off."

And from the way she took to studying the burn, Tye divined that this was the real hurt. Not the gossip, not the labeling, not Merriman's legal posturing and dishonorable conduct. The real shame, for Hester Daniels, was that her brother had been put to embarrassment and expense on her behalf.

"He doesn't blame you."

She glanced over at him fleetingly, then resumed her perusal of the burn, the banks, the fields and hills beyond. "I beg your pardon?"

"Your brother does not blame you. He blames himself. If he'd been more attentive, you would not have taken up with a bounder like this Merrifield idiot." Her lips quirked at his purposeful misnomer, the smallest, fleeting breach in her dignity. He wanted to widen that breach.

"Matthew did not approve of the match. Because my older sister was not yet betrothed, my father kept his agreement with Jasper private. Then too, Mama wanted me to have my own Season once Genie was engaged."

"But your father died, and there were no more Seasons for you." She nodded, and Tye might have seen her blinking at the book in her hands.

"I had only Jasper's word for the fact that Altsax had agreed to the match. The solicitors could only tell us my father had instructed them to draw up the settlements. He never signed them or sent them to Jasper's solicitors."

Now this purely stank. "How would breach of promise have been proved if there were no signed agreements?"

She set the poetry aside and smoothed a hand over her skirts, putting Tye in mind of his younger sister's habit of twisting a lock of hair when unnerved. "Jasper proposed to me in the park one afternoon, directly after I'd concluded my mourning for Altsax. Before one and all, his lordship put a ring on my finger and kissed my cheek."

"That is utter *rot*." He wanted to throw her bloody, bedamned book into the water. "The bastard ambushed you, caught you unawares, and set you up so you could not refuse. He must have been very deep in debt indeed, and my guess is old Spielgood cut him off."

She abruptly found Tye worthy of study. "Do you think so?"

"For God's sake, Miss Daniels, I know so. Younger sons face a choice—I know, my brother was one. They can either try to be more noble than their titled fathers and brothers, or they can spend their lives pouting because they were born two years or two minutes behind their older sibling. This Merriberg fellow was entirely beneath you, you're well rid of him, and he's lucky your brother didn't arrange a bare-knuckle encounter with him in some dingy alley."

Her lips were threatening to turn up again. "You are carrying on like a brother now."

She sounded *approving*, damned if she didn't. Tye wrestled the urge to hunt down Jasper Merridamn and introduce him to some of Tye's favorite pugilistic theories.

"I *am* a brother. I have three younger sisters, not a one of them married, and if I understand anything, it's the perils of Polite Society."

"You truly think I'm well rid of him?"

She sounded plaintive, which left Tye wanting to have a word with the woman's brother. "Has no one told you as much?"

"Aunt has. My cousin Augusta. Fiona."

But she hadn't heard it from her menfolk, or apparently from her own mother. Tye schooled himself to sound older and wiser, and not bloody angry on her behalf.

"You think you are destined for a life of obscurity, and that your great shame will follow you all your days. I am loathe to inform you, Miss Daniels, that your great shame has already been forgotten by every tabby and tattletale in London. At least four scandals have crowded in on the heels of your little contretemps, each juicier than the last. You are tormenting yourself for nothing. The man took advantage of you when you were grieving, pressed an expectation never legally his, and embarrassed you unforgivably in the process. Take a few turns around a few ballrooms next Season, and the matter will be at an end. I will be happy to stand up with you for this express purpose."

He fell silent because there was no disguising the

anger in his tone. Was chivalry to die such an easy death at the hands of the men of England?

The lady at least looked interested in his version of events, which was an odd relief. He much preferred her spewing hail and lightning on all in her path.

Or possibly, he preferred to see what would happen if she permitted herself even one genuine smile aimed in his direction.

"Did you know, Miss Daniels, that Henrietta Mortenson was caught out in a punt on the Cam when a downpour started, and though her escort offered his coat, she was drenched through to the skin before he could row her ashore? This occurred not two weeks past, and I was told repeatedly, whether I wished to hear it or not, that every stitch of the embroidery on her underlinen was visible through the wet fabric of her dress, and very nice stitch work it was, too."

"Oh, do be quiet. Fiona will overhear you."

"Good. Then she'll know what to expect when she makes her bow. I also have it on good authority that to win a dare from her sister, Sally Higgambotham allowed Sir Neil Forthambly to kiss her, but her brothers overheard the dare and placed side bets on whether they could compromise the couple into marriage. The couple was caught, but I do not know if an announcement has yet been issued."

"But Sir Neil…"

"Is eighty if he's a day."

She tried to hide it. She made a good effort, a good stout firming of her mouth, but then her lips curved up, curved up higher, and parted to reveal two rows of white teeth. Her discipline crumbled apace as her cheeks lifted, her eyes lit, and merriment suffused her countenance.

She *smiled* at him, and the grace and beauty of it, the sheer loveliness, was such that Tiberius Lamartine Flynn, for the first time in his nearly thirty years of life, felt as if a woman's smile illuminated him from within.

❦

An hour by the stream, which should have been a simple, even tedious outing to humor Fiona's need for activity, had presented Hester with three problems, each disturbing in its own way.

First, there was the realization that Fiona was predisposed to love uncles—any uncles who came into her life. Because Fiona had been raised without a father, her three maternal uncles had showered her with the love and affection less easily shown to their sister, her mother. Any man sporting the title "uncle" would bear positive associations for Fiona.

Second, Spathfoy was good at this uncle-ing business. His manner of doting was brusque, even imperious, but he neither hovered nor ignored Fiona, and because he was an older brother and an astute man, the role of uncle was not that great a leap for him.

Well, so be it.

Perhaps a wealthy, titled English uncle would be an asset to Fiona as she grew older, provided he kept to his wealthy, titled English world except for the occasional summer visit.

But then there was Difficulty Number Three, which devolved to Hester personally: the man himself.

A woman inured to the injustices of the world was in a sorry case indeed when she envied a gasping trout. Or salmon—whatever that poor fish had been.

"This requires concentration... Stroke slowly, slowly along the belly... mustn't rush it... like a lullaby... I'm close... That's it. There we go."

Had the fish been as seduced by that voice as Hester had? Inside her body, things had lifted and shifted as Spathfoy had entranced the fish. His wet, dripping hands had secured that hapless fish with gentle implacability, and the thing had been willing to lie in his grasp and gasp itself to death while Hester looked on and tried to breathe normally.

Mother of God, had Jasper been right? Did all women seek a man's intimate attentions?

And that wasn't the worst of the problem. Spathfoy walked along beside her as they made their way back to the house, Fiona swinging his hand while she pestered him about sea monsters and tree sprites.

"But what if a sea monster fell in love with a tree sprite? How would they marry, Uncle?"

"Turtles walk on dry land and yet dwell in water, and I know many trees sink roots into a riverbank. I should think they'd marry fairly well."

This silenced the child for three entire strides. "What if a troll fell in love with a beautiful princess?"

"This is easy, Niece. The princess kisses the troll, he turns into a handsome prince, and they live happily ever after. Your education has been neglected if you don't know that one."

"I knew it, but my papa didn't, and neither did Uncle Ian. Uncle Con said trolls who fall in love with princesses are to be pitied, and Aunt Julie smacked him, and then he kissed her."

"Which was likely his aim. I'm for a visit to the stables. Will you ladies join me?"

"I will!" Fee started kiting around madly on the end of his arm. "I want to tell Flying Rowan all about the fishy, and I can guddle the next one."

"Not if you're making this much racket."

At her uncle's simple observation, Fee quieted.

"I will excuse myself," Hester said. "With company in the house, Mrs. Deal is understandably concerned regarding the menus. Fiona, I'm sure Aunt will want to know all about the fish when you read to her this afternoon."

"Yes! And I can tell her he was this big!" She stretched her hands about three feet apart, which for Fiona was only a slight exaggeration. She snatched her uncle's fingers in hers and dragged him off toward the stables, until, as Hester watched, Spathfoy hiked the child onto his back.

Leaving Hester to again enumerate the growing list of difficulties relating to the Earl of Spathfoy.

The worst problem revealed by the morning's outing was that Spathfoy—for all that his vocabulary and his conceit were in proportion to the rest of him—was a decent man.

Hester had expected he'd recoil upon realizing she was *that* Miss Daniels, the one who'd tossed aside the son of a marquess. She was the Miss Daniels who'd left a young man to the mercy of his creditors and to the mercy of a father for whom the term "old-fashioned" was a euphemism.

She was the Miss Daniels whose own mother had banished her to the far North, thrown her on the mercy of a brother newly wed to become, at not even twenty-five years old, an object of pity.

Spinster was beyond a euphemism. It was a fairy tale, a benign mischaracterization Hester had been all too willing to accept—though Spathfoy had not.

This endeared him to her, which was a very great disruption of Hester's plans for the man. He'd *teased* her. How long had it been since she'd been teased with relentless, gentle good humor?

And then, when she'd indicated he'd made his point, he'd smiled at her. Not one of his buccaneer grins, or a condescending quirk of the lips accompanied by a haughty arch of his brow.

His smile was a blessing. A radiant, soul-warming benevolence just for her.

And—assuming the man was going to head back south without a backward glance—therein lay the sum and substance of Difficulties Number Three through Three Hundred.

❧

Tye was by no means done reconnoitering enemy territory, but he could start maneuvering his artillery into place nonetheless. Lollygagging by the stream was defensible as an information-gathering expedition— also a pleasant respite after a demanding journey—but his time was limited, and each day had to count.

"This is Hannibal. He's Uncle Ian's horse, but he's getting on. If I'm tall enough, I can have him when Uncle says Hannibal needs a lighter rider."

Hannibal was every bit as substantial and elegant as Flying Rowan, but there was gray encroaching on the horse's muzzle, and above his eyes, the bone structure testified to advancing years.

"Wouldn't you rather start off with a pony, Fiona?" She stood beside him on a sturdy trunk, her hand extended through the bars into the horse's stall, and yet Tye could feel every fiber of her little being go still. "Mama says I can't have a pony until I'm nine."

"That seems a very long way off." To a child, even a few months could feel like forever, and a year or two an unfathomable eternity.

"It is *forever*, a terrible, awful, perishing long time." She turned around, and with a hearty huff, plopped her backside onto the trunk. "Mama never changes her mind. Aunt Hester says Mama is the Rock of Gibraltar on matters of importance. I think she's stubborn, and Uncle Ian once told me I wasn't wrong. I'm stubborn too—so is Uncle Ian."

Tye had to wonder about a belted earl sharing confidences with a girl child, but then, here he was himself, attempting the very same thing. He took a seat beside his niece on the trunk. "Does your mother have a reason for making you wait such a terribly, awfully, perishing long time?"

"Yes. Mama has a reason, and Papa says it's a sound reason, so I must not wheedle. Her reason is this: ponies are small, but I am going to be a great, strapping beauty, and so I will outgrow ponies very quickly. The longer I wait for my first one, the fewer ponies I will outgrow. Mama wanted me to wait until

I was twelve, but Papa said I was already quite tall, so Mama compromised. They had an argument."

"Arguments can be loud."

"They go in the bedroom and lock the door. It isn't loud. Sometimes I hear Mama laughing." She hopped off the trunk and crossed the aisle to lean over Rowan's half door. "He's very handsome."

Tye remained where he was, oddly reluctant to pry further information from the child. "Will you miss Rowan when he goes?"

She whirled, which caused the gelding to startle in his stall. "You *just* got here. You can't be going away so soon! Why doesn't anybody want to stay with me? Aunt Ree is too old to travel, and Aunt Hester is only here for the summer to look after Aunt Ree and me. It isn't fair."

She turned again to extend a hand to Rowan. The gelding overcame his nerves enough to sniff delicately at her fingers.

"He smells that fish," Tye said. "Would you enjoy traveling, Fiona? Seeing the sea and the north country, Edinburgh and London?"

She was quiet for a moment while Rowan went back to lipping his hay. "I've been to Aberdeen. There are lots of horses there, everything is made of stone, and it smells like fish by the sea. I don't like the ocean."

"Come here." He patted the place beside him. "There's a menagerie in London, and the royal mews too, which is where the great golden coronation coach is."

She scrambled onto the trunk and crammed right up against his side. "Is it *really* made of gold?"

"Sit with me for a moment, and I'll tell you about it." He tucked an arm around her small, bony shoulders and tried to recall what had first impressed him about the coach when he'd seen it as a small and easily enchanted boy.

❧

Augusta MacGregor, Countess of Balfour, worried about her cousin Hester, and thus Ian MacGregor, Earl of Balfour, was prone to the same anxiety. The girl looked far too tired and serious for her tender years.

"Is Fiona running you ragged, Hester?" Ian bent to kiss his pretty cousin-in-law's cheek, catching a pleasant whiff of lemon as he did.

"Fiona is a perfect angel, but the nights grow short, and I'm not quite settled in here yet."

A month had gone by since Ian and Augusta had collected her from the train station at Ballater, it being familial consensus that no less person than the earl himself should welcome her back to Aberdeenshire. She'd been pale, brave, and so dauntingly proper in her behavior Ian had wanted to get on the damned train, head to London, and pummel the daylights out of a certain marquess's youngest son. Matthew and Mary Fran had talked him out of it, lecturing him about sleeping dogs and an earl's consequence.

He tucked Hester's hand onto his arm and led her toward the family parlor. "Will Aunt Ree be joining us, or is she resting?"

"She rests a great deal, Ian. I try not to disturb her, but she'll want to see you."

"Interrogate me, you mean. Where's Fiona?"

Hester untangled her hand from his arm. "I left her in Spathfoy's care. They were visiting the horses, which seemed like a good way for them to get further acquainted."

"Brave man, to take on Fiona in her favorite surrounds. Do you trust him?"

She took a seat in a rocker by the empty hearth, the same chair Aunt Ree usually favored. "I do not trust him, Ian. Spathfoy came here without any acknowledgement that he'd be welcome or the house even occupied. His family has shown no interest in Fiona since her birth, and yet here he is, when Mary Fran and Matthew are far, far away."

Ian took the corner of the sofa. "Augusta has a theory about this, and it makes sense to me."

Hester said nothing and didn't even set the chair to rocking. Last summer, she'd been lively, good humored, and bristling with energy. This summer, she was a different and far sadder creature entirely.

"Augusta believes old Quinworth is getting on and the young lord is preparing to take over the reins. Showing an interest in Fiona is one way Spathfoy can do that. Then too, by sending his son to look in on the girl, Quinworth isn't quite admitting he's neglected his only granddaughter all these years."

"Men." She spat the word. "Titled men in particular." Ian allowed a diplomatic silence to stretch when what he wanted to do involved travel south, cursing, and fisticuffs. "I don't mean you, Ian. I mean titled Englishmen."

"Has Spathfoy been so insufferable as all that? I can have him over to Balfour, and if that screaming infant doesn't send him back to London hotfoot, then Augusta's discussions of nappies and infant digestion will."

At long last, humor came into Hester's blue eyes. "Ian MacGregor, are you complaining?"

"Bitterly. I finally find a woman I want to keep for my own, a woman courageous enough to marry me, and she's stolen away by a wee bandit no bigger than this." He held his hands about a bread-loaf's distance from each other. "Shall I subject Spathfoy to my son's hospitality?"

"I think not." She answered quickly and with some assurance, which was interesting. "He's very well mannered, and Aunt Ree enjoys flirting with him."

"Ariadne MacGregor has an affliction. She can't help herself." Aunt Ree was enough to give a man in contemplation of daughters pause.

Hester rose from her chair to go to the window. "He flirts back, and he's very good with Fee—patient, but he doesn't let her get away with much."

Ian moved to stand beside her, marveling anew at how petite she was. "Give it a few days. He'll be cowering under his bed to hide from his niece, or she'll be having him up the trees, into the burn, and down the hillside. I have to admit when Fee and Mary Fran left Balfour House, the place felt like a library, so quiet did it become."

"It's not quiet now, is it?"

When the baby slept it was quiet. "You're quiet, Hester Daniels. How are you getting on?"

She crossed her arms and glowered at the roses beyond the window, but did not retreat to her rocker, ring for tea, or indulge in any of the other genteel prevarications available to her. "I am indebted to my brother for his hospitality. We're having a lovely summer, or we were until unexpected company arrived."

"And you don't want to hand your company over to me and Augusta?"

She wrinkled her nose, which reminded Ian that his cousin-in-law was nigh ten years his junior, with all of one social Season under her dainty belt. That her father had been a conniving scoundrel did not mean Hester herself was worldly, and she'd said little about her reasons for breaking off what ought to have been a very promising match.

"Ian, I like Spathfoy. I don't want to like him, and he has no charm whatsoever, but he's..."

Ian watched as a tall, dark-haired man in well-tailored riding attire was led up the path from the stables by Fiona, who appeared to be chattering away all the while. "He's a good-looking rascal."

"He's arrogant," Hester said, dropping her arms. "He uses vocabulary unsuited to communicating with a child, but she likes him for it. He fascinates her, a shiny new uncle with a fancy accent appearing just as she's about to die of missing her parents."

"They'll be home in a few weeks, and then Spathfoy will be forgotten until he next recalls he has a Scottish niece. By then he'll have a countess of his own to keep him out of trouble."

She gave Ian an unreadable look. "I'll ring for tea."

Ian watched Fiona tow her shiny new uncle along, and felt a sense of frustration that Augusta had not accompanied him for this visit. Hester was pining for something, or someone, and Ian was at a loss about what to do for the girl.

Mary Fran had suggested peace and quiet would help, but exactly what they were supposed to help *with*, Ian had not asked.

"Uncle Ian!" Fiona pelted into the room, throwing herself into Ian's waiting arms. "I spied the biggest fish from up in my reading tree, and we guddled him right to sleep. Uncle said I can do it next time, but not if there's a storm to raise the burn. Did Aunt Augusta come along? Will you tell her we guddled a huge fishy?"

Ian wrapped his arms around his only niece. "I will tell her you are grown half a foot since I saw you on Saturday. You'll soon be dancing with your cousin, at this rate."

She wiggled away, her face a mask of disgust. "Not until he's out of nappies."

Ian let her go and saw Spathfoy hanging by the door, wearing the look of an uncle who'd just learned his niece could forget his existence in an instant.

"This must be the great guddler." Ian extended a hand. "Balfour, at your service." He bestowed his best, disarming smile on the man, and received a firm handshake in return—no smile.

"Spathfoy, pleased to make your acquaintance."

Augusta would know how to describe that voice— sophisticated, or portentous, or some damned big, pretty, stuffy word.

"Uncle Spathfoy caught the fish," Fiona supplied. "I wasn't allowed in the burn, but next time it will be my turn." She seized Ian's hand and turned to regard "Uncle Spathfoy" pointedly.

"Be glad you weren't allowed in the burn," Ian said. "Your wee teeth would still be chattering."

"And," Spathfoy said, eyeing the grip Fiona had of Ian's hand, "your clothing might still be damp. If you'll excuse me, Lord Balfour, I'll see to my attire before we observe further civilities."

He nodded—perhaps the gesture approached some form of bow by virtue of its proximity to his prissy little speech—and withdrew.

"Uncle Ian, what's a tire?"

Three

NOT TWO YEARS INTO PUBLIC SCHOOL, TYE HAD understood why Duty and Honor must be elevated so high in the esteem of the budding flowers of English manhood: Duty and Honor were required to fill a boy's vision so he might lose sight—if not entirely then at least substantially—of his Resentments.

The result of this insight was for Tye to focus intently on those resentments, until he could list them, recite them to himself like a litany of souls to be prayed for. He resented his younger brother, whose scrapes and pranks were forever earning Tye a birching or, worse, protracted lectures about setting a worthy example. He resented his younger sisters when they came along, for they appropriated attention from a formerly devoted mother and very indulgent staff.

He probably resented his mother too, though even in his lowest adolescent lows—and those were melodramatically low, indeed—he did not quite manage to add her to his list.

And he still had not, though in the privacy of his thoughts it was a near thing.

He resented his father. There were sublists and footnotes and nigh an entire bibliography appended to the resentment he bore his father. He suspected other fellows in expectation of a title carried similar lists in their heads, but by tacit understanding, each honorable, dutiful boy nurtured his resentments in private, if he acknowledged them at all.

And now, Tye could resurrect the list that had died a quiet death in his university years—resentment was an indulgence, after all—and add several more items to it.

He resented Scotland. This struck him as a solid, English sort of addition to the list, and if it meant he resented half his own heritage, well, he'd borne that burden for his entire life.

He resented nieces who charmed and provoked protective instincts at variance with the demands of Duty and Honor.

He resented, bitterly, fathers who made a son choose between duty and conscience, particularly when both options were rife with negative consequences to people not even involved in the choice.

He resented Scottish earls, Balfour in particular, who could exude such bonhomie and graciousness that Tye nearly believed Balfour shouldered the burdens of his title without suffering any resentments at all.

Tye mentally polished his list while changing into dry morning clothes, dragging a brush through his hair, and returning to the family parlor from whence he'd come. He figuratively left his resentments at the door, fixed a smile on his countenance, and prepared to match Balfour's pleasant good humor with every semblance of credibility.

"Uncle!" This time, Fiona bolted toward *him*, which was a fleeting triumph until Tye realized he was supposed to sweep her into his embrace, though they'd parted not ten minutes earlier.

"Niece." He set her on her feet. "I see you left a scone or two on the tray."

"I didn't, but Uncle Ian did. He said he's going to reave Deal back to Balfour, because she makes the best."

She escorted him across the parlor to the sofa and indicated he should take the seat to the left of Miss Daniels. Tye did, only to find his niece wiggling herself between him and the end of the sofa, which forwardness necessitated that *he* shift closer to Miss Daniels.

"Uncle told me about the coronation coach. He said the wheels are almost as tall as he is."

"That is your last scone, Fiona MacGregor. You'll spoil your luncheon." Miss Daniels spoke pleasantly while she passed Tye a cup of tea.

"And I'll not be stealing Deal until your aunt Augusta weans the little shoat, particularly not when Deal can be cooking for an English earl here." The dainty teacup in Balfour's hand looked like doll china, though the man's fingernails were clean and his turnout every bit as well made and spotless as Tye's own.

Balfour snitched a bite of his niece's scone and went on speaking. "I have petitioned the Sovereign to pass a law that the offspring of titled men should be weaned at birth. The succession of many a title will be more easily assured. The Prince Consort has told me privately he endorses my scheme, but I've yet to prevail."

This was humor. Tye understood it as such, but

there were females present, and it was humor relating to, of all things, *weaning*.

"I haven't an opinion on the matter."

"You will, laddie." Balfour winked at him, reminding Tye strongly of their mutual niece. "Give it time, a countess of your own, and a few assaults on your beleaguered paternal ears, and you will, particularly when the ruddy little blighter must invade your very bed. That's mine, Fee."

He used two fingers to slap his niece's wrist, but she crammed a piece of his scone into her maw and drew back against Tye, giggling all the while.

"Would you like a scone, Lord Spathfoy?" Miss Daniels wasn't oblivious to the misbehavior of her family members, but she didn't appear bothered by it either.

"None for me, thanks." Because though he was hungry, how on earth was he to react when some niece or earl or other pilfered the food from his very plate?

"We'll have none of that." Balfour passed him a plate with two scones on it. "You'll hurt Deal's feelings if you turn up your nose at her scones. The vindication of English diplomacy lies in your grasp, Spathfoy, and, Fee, I'll not take you up before me for a week if you try to raid a guest's plate."

Well. Tye bit into a scone.

And while he consumed both scones—he'd forgotten the pleasure of a fresh, warm, flaky scone full of raisins—Balfour proceeded to quiz his niece on her sums and her Latin, her French and her history. This was a version of an earl executing the duties of Head of the Family that Tye had not previously seen, and one he had to approve of.

Grudgingly, of course.

Still, Fiona was given a chance to show off a bit before her elders, and while she conversed in basic French with her uncle, some of her little-girl mannerisms fell away.

She sat more quietly beside Tye. She set her plate aside and folded her hands in her lap, her expression convincingly demure.

"But, Uncle Ian? What is the French word for guddle?"

Tye spoke without thinking. "*Voler.*"

"Nay." Balfour's expression lost a measure of its geniality. "You are mistaken, Spathfoy. To guddle is not to poach or steal, it is more in the nature of *chatouiller*, to tickle or tease."

"My mistake."

Balfour's smile changed in some way, becoming edged not with threat, exactly, but with... challenge. "You'll walk me to the stables, Spathfoy? Good manners and my continued good health require that you accept an invitation from my countess to dine with us while you're visiting. I will try to have his little bellowing lordship taken up by the watch between now and then."

While Tye looked on, Balfour hugged and kissed both his niece and her aunt. The girl went willingly into his embrace, as did Miss Daniels, to whom the man had only the remotest family connection.

"My regards to Aunt Ree," Balfour said, releasing Miss Daniels. "She's been naughty, I know it. She'd face me like a proper auntie if she weren't trying to hide some misdeed. Fiona, you behave for your aunts or I'll make you change your cousin's dirty nappy when next you visit."

The young lady disappeared into the little girl amid giggles and expressions of disgust as well as more hugs. Tye undertook the walk to the stables with more relief than foreboding.

"So, Spathfoy, to what do we owe the honor of a visit?"

Balfour's tone was not accusing, but it wasn't genial either. This interrogation, too, was a part of being the head of a family, and Tye respected it as such.

"My father sent me along to ascertain whether the child was thriving, and to investigate her circumstances generally."

Balfour ambled along beside him, when Tye wanted to stop, stand still, and admire the way sunlight had a sharper edge this far north, even in high summer.

"Why?"

"I beg your pardon?"

"Why," Balfour said, "after leaving Fiona in my care since birth, has Quinworth chosen now—when Mary Fran and her husband are off on an extended journey—to finally make inquiry regarding the child?"

"You had the care of her?"

"For God's sake, man." Balfour stopped walking, and in his voice Tye heard a trace more of the Gaelic, the mountains, and the laird of old. "I'm Fee's uncle, Mary Fran's older brother, and head of my branch of the clan, such as it exists in these enlightened, damned times. Of course I provided for my niece. I also wrote to your father regularly regarding the girl's progress and health, and I never once received a reply."

"You never once received money, you mean?"

To put it like that was rude, but goading Balfour would expose how much opposition Tye was likely to face.

"You're trying to convince me you're stupid," Balfour said mildly. "Brave, but stupid. I suppose it's the most one can hope for from an Englishman. That, and pretty manners." He resumed walking. Tye fell in beside him while trying to determine if he'd heard pity, humor, or resignation in Balfour's insult.

"If my father was asked for funds and refused your request, perhaps he intends to make amends. Fiona is arguably his responsibility."

"Morally, yes. Legally, I doubt it. But he has failed spectacularly in this responsibility, and now he sends you around to charm the ladies and whisper in Fee's little ear about gold coaches."

Tye remained silent, resenting Balfour's astuteness.

And the trickle of shame it dripped into Tye's conscience.

"I want what is best for Fiona," Tye said. It was the truth—despite the marquess's machinations, Tye could be honest about this much.

Balfour sighed mightily as they approached the stables. "That's what I'm afraid of. The English have ever wanted what is best for Scotland, and the Scottish have wanted only to be left the hell alone. Give Quinworth my respects when next you report to him, and warn him he'll have a fight on his hands if his intentions toward Fee are less than honorable. We'll expect you at Balfour House tomorrow night for dinner. Be prepared for an assault on your ears."

He walked off without a bow or a backward glance, and Tye was reminded that for now, Balfour outranked him and had the advantage of fighting on home turf.

For, apparently, a fight it would be.

❧

Sitting next to Spathfoy at morning tea, Hester had noted a resemblance between him and the Earl of Balfour. They were both tall, dark-haired, and green-eyed, true, but the resemblance went deeper, to a force of personality that had little to do with brawn or wit per se. Ian was relentless when committed to a goal; Hester had the sense Spathfoy would be no different.

When the opportunity to best him came along later in the morning, she could not resist.

"If I give you a few lengths head start, my lord, will you race me to that cow byre?" She pointed across the valley to a small stone building set half into the earth of the hillside.

Spathfoy drew his horse up. "A few lengths head start? Should I be insulted, Miss Daniels?"

"I know the terrain, my horse hasn't recently been ridden half the breadth of Scotland, and I'm the one challenging you."

He looked thoughtful, while his horse capered and curvetted beneath him. "No head start, and not to the cow byre, but to the wall just beyond it."

"To the last jump then."

"The lady gives the start."

She brought her mare alongside his gelding at the

walk, collected her horse with a few simple cues, snugged her knee to the horn, and gave the signal quietly. "Go."

The valley was a good mile across, and Dolly was fresh and eager to show the fidgety gelding her heels. Hester bent low and let the mare have her head.

They flew effortlessly across the ground; the wind sang in Hester's ears; and the rhythm of the horse thundering beneath her beat away every worry, woe, and anxiety she had ever claimed. She urged the horse faster, aware that Spathfoy's gelding was keeping pace half a length back.

Of course he was. The beast was a good hand taller than the mare, giving Spathfoy an advantage of height, even mounted. And the damned gelding jumped so smoothly in stride, Spathfoy barely had to get up in his stirrups, whereas Dolly chipped at the first wall and overjumped the second.

Hester ran a gloved hand down the mare's crest even as she whispered to the horse for a hair more speed.

They cleared a burn that Spathfoy and his gelding weren't prepared for, and it put Dolly a full length in the lead. As the last wall loomed closer, Hester could feel Spathfoy gaining, pushing his horse hard to close the distance. She knew better than to look over her shoulder.

"Don't let them catch us, girl." With a touch of her heel, she urged the mare into a flat, flowing gallop that sent them sailing neatly over the wall.

Like a perfect lady, Dolly came down to the walk on cue, her sides heaving, her neck wet with sweat.

"Well done, my lady." Spathfoy's horse was winded

as well and blowing hard, but still dancing with nervous energy beneath its rider.

Hester gave Dolly a solid pat on the shoulder. "Did you let us beat you?"

"I did not. Rowan has tremendous stamina, but your lighter mount has more native speed, particularly for a short distance. Then too, Rowan is young and wastes energy fretting. Shall we walk for a bit?"

They turned back through the meadow, the race having eased something inside Hester's body and mind. That Spathfoy would honestly pit his horse against hers was a compliment; that she'd beat him was a lovely boon.

"You ride quite well, Miss Daniels."

"You're being gentlemanly again. You needn't bother."

Some of her pleasure in the ride dimmed at the exchange, but Spathfoy remained quiet on his horse beside her until they came to the burn.

"Shall we let the horses rest? We're a good way from the manor."

"Rest and have a drink."

Too late she realized this would require that he assist her off her horse. When Ian or his brothers offered the same courtesy, it meant nothing. Gilgallon was inclined to flirt, Connor to handle her like a sack of grain, and Ian to turn it into such a gallantry as to be a jest. To a man, they had to comment on her diminutive size each and every time.

Spathfoy turned it into... something else entirely.

Hester unhooked her knee from the horn, shifted sideways in the saddle, and put a hand on each of

Spathfoy's shoulders—surpassingly broad shoulders when measured thus. His hands went to her waist, which was standard protocol for such a courtesy.

When she boosted herself from the saddle, she expected his hands to merely ride along her sides until her feet met the ground, but no. His strength was such that he could control her descent, so she did not jump to the ground but was borne there by his hold, until she stood quite close to him.

Dolly swished her tail and took one step to the side with a hind foot, nudging Hester such that she was pitched into the solid expanse of Spathfoy's chest.

"Steady there." Not quite at her waist, but lower, almost on her hips, his hands held her for a moment. He didn't presume, didn't take untoward liberties, and yet…

It was the closest thing to a true embrace Hester had enjoyed in too long to recall. Yes, her brother hugged her, fleeting, brusque, mostly one-armed gestures of affection entirely foreign to their interaction until he'd married Mary Frances.

And Ian, Connor, and Gil were affectionate men, but always with Hester, there was a carefulness to their affection. It drove her mad, that carefulness.

"I won't break, you know."

She didn't slide away, didn't elbow the horse to make room for a backward step.

"I do believe you are one of the shortest women it has ever been my pleasure to assist from a horse." He sounded curious, and before Hester could shake her riding crop at him for his rudeness, his hand settled on the top of her bare head and then measured her height against his breastbone.

She went still, staring at the shirt and cravat covering that breastbone while he did it again, only this time, his hand did not pass from her crown to his sternum. It slid down over the back of her head in what felt heartrendingly like a caress, and then settled at her nape.

"Your hair is an absolute fright. Come here."

He steered her by the shoulders to stand before him, but facing away. Behind her, he was taking off his gloves with his teeth, admonishing her through a clenched jaw.

"You've no doubt lost half your pins, for which, somehow, you will blame me. This is the recompense I'm to be served for allowing you to win."

"You did not let me win." She half turned to remonstrate with him, but his fingers loosening the braid at her nape prevented an adequate range of motion. "Your horse was still fatigued from riding the length of the River Dee, you did not know the terrain, and it is not your fault if I lost a few of my pins."

"Hold these." He passed a dozen pins over her shoulder, and Hester felt her braid hanging down her back.

"Is there a reason why your hair must be so long?"

If he was examining its length, then he was noting the tail of her braid swinging against her fundament. This notion was enough to provoke a blush, and *that* was enough to spark Hester's temper.

"A woman's hair is her crowning glory, my lord. Surely even you have been sufficiently exposed to Scripture to understand this?"

"Hold still, I tell you, and yes, I've had as much

Scripture drummed into me as any English schoolboy, though my grandfather explained to me that the reason for this is because the print in the damned Bible is so small, one can read it only with the eyes of youth. In old age, memorized passages are the only comfort Scripture affords. There. You will soon be marginally presentable. Give me the rest of those pins."

A few minutes later, she patted the bun he'd secured at her nape and turned to regard him.

"The damned Bible, my lord?"

"Yes, the damned Bible. I will explain once I've loosened the horses' girths."

He dealt with the horses and passed Hester the mare's reins so they could offer their mounts a drink from the stream. The gelding had to snort and dodge and caper around while Dolly slaked her thirst. When the mare raised a placid eye to the other horse, he condescended to take a few dainty sips beside her.

"He lacks confidence," Spathfoy said, "but this makes him work hard to please, and I have hopes for him."

"I noticed you did not pet him after his exertions."

Spathfoy peered over at her from the other side of the horses. "An oversight on my part. Horse, pay attention: my thanks for your efforts. Next time, I will not allow the ladies to win. Is that better?"

She could not help the smile that emerged from some dark corner of her soul. "You are diverting, my lord, and not just because we beat you and your flighty beast."

For a few minutes, they did not speak. Spathfoy unrolled a tartan blanket from behind his saddle and spread it on the ground. The stream gurgled along, the horses soon took to cropping what grass there was, and a kind of peace seeped into Hester's soul she would not have expected the moment to yield.

"Shall we sit, Miss Daniels? The day is pretty, and I'm enjoying the outing. I think you are too."

He gestured to the blanket and began shrugging out of his jacket. To be alone like this was arguably improper, except they had a niece in common and they were in plain sight, and what had being proper ever earned Hester, except a fiancé bent on the worst of improprieties? She unbuttoned the jacket of her habit and spread it on the blanket as well.

When she had settled beside their coats, Spathfoy came down beside her. "Care for a nip?" He waggled a silver flask, unscrewed the cap, and held the flask out to her.

"Please." She reached for it, expecting cider, lemonade, or water, and got... *fire*. Whisky scorched its way down her gullet into her entrails, leaving her lungs seizing, her eyes watering, and heat blooming through her limbs.

"Oh, Merciful Powers, Heaven and Earth, Mother of God." She tried to breathe evenly, but this provoked a coughing spell that inspired Spathfoy to sit directly at her hip while he thumped her soundly in the middle of her back.

"For God's sake, take shallow breaths. I should have warned you. I do beg your... what did you think I'd have in a flask if not spirits?"

"You drink that *on purpose*? Stop beating me."

"I'm not beating you, for God's sake." His hand went still, but he switched to rubbing her back, causing a warmth of a different sort where he touched her. "I drink it on purpose and in quantity on occasion." His hand fell away, but he did not move from her side. "I suspect Balfour does likewise."

"Of course, but a lady does not drink strong spirits. I can understand why now. Augusta said it's an acquired taste."

He took a pull from the flask before tucking it away, then hiked his knees and started shredding a sprig of heather plucked from a nearby bush. "Augusta would be Balfour's countess?"

"And my cousin. What were you going to explain to me about the damned Bible, my lord?"

He turned up his substantial nose. "My lord this, my lord that. I have a name, and since we're drinking companions, you might consider its use." He did not look comfortable to be making this offer. He snatched up another sprig of heather and set to destroying it as well.

"What is your name?" She did not add *my lord* for fear of agitating him further.

"Tiberius Lamartine Flynn. My sisters call me Tye."

His friends—if any he had—would call him Spathfoy, though. Hester wasn't sure being lumped in with his sisters was a good thing.

"You may call me Hester. We are practically family, and if I call you Tye, then Fiona will have an alternative to Uncle Spathfoy."

He tossed away the bits of heather. "Fiona, my one and only niece. Balfour asked me what I was doing, skulking about the child after my father had neglected her for years."

So Ian's visit hadn't been about tea, crumpets, and fish stories. "What did you tell him?"

Spathfoy—Tye—looked away, and Hester sensed he was choosing words, choosing the more attractive versions of the more attractive truths to share with her.

"I told him my father was likely seeking to redress his previous neglect of the child, and that I wanted what was best for my niece."

He snatched up a third little branch of heather, but Hester put her hand over his before he could wreak more destruction. His hands were warm and much larger than hers. "You were prevaricating, weren't you?"

He kept his gaze on their joined hands. "I do not know what my father's motives are, but you should not trust me, Hester Daniels. Not when it comes to that child."

She withdrew her hand and regarded him. Sitting this close, she could feel the heat of exertion coming off of him, catch a hint of the flowery shaving soap he used, along with the pungent scent of heather, and could almost count the long, dark lashes framing his eyes. She could also sense that Tiberius Lamartine Flynn, the Earl of Spathfoy, was troubled by these half confidences he reposed in her.

"You represent no threat to me, sir. It's the men crooning their trustworthiness behind closed doors who must be avoided at all costs. If you want what's best for Fiona, you are no threat to her either."

His lips thinned, but he remained silent.

"Tell me," Hester urged.

"She runs wild, barefoot even."

"I have seen no less personage than the Earl of Spathfoy himself unshod. This is no great crime."

"So you have." His lips turned down, when Hester

had wanted the opposite reaction. "She climbs trees, she sings to them, reads to them."

"You were denied these pleasures as a child, but I've no doubt you sneaked into a few trees anyway."

"A few."

"So solemn, and over a child's summer pastimes?"

He looked away, toward the horses, but this was more than prevarication. Predictably, he changed the topic. "I'm to dine at Balfour House tomorrow."

"Then you'll want to work up an appetite. Ian believes in feeding his countess, for she sustains his heir."

"I cannot believe he said as much in mixed company." He was back to plucking at heather.

"Are you fascinated at his forthrightness or appalled?"

"Impressed, I suppose, and intrigued to know what sort of woman would take on such a barbarian."

Hester leaned back on her hands. "Ian MacGregor is more a gentleman than ninety-nine percent of the men I stood up with in London. He loves his wife."

Spathfoy's fingertips were turning gray with all the heather he was shredding. "Was that Merriburg's shortcoming, he did not love you?"

This was no business of his, but it kept them off the topics of Fiona's behaviors and Augusta nursing her own child. "Jasper loved none but himself, but no, that was not the reason I tossed aside my reputation, my future, my hopes for a family of my own, and my welcome in my own mother's house. Shall we be going, my lord? I think the horses are quite rested enough."

She struggled to her feet when a dignified exit stage left was called for. A riding habit was an odd garment though, not symmetric, and shown to best advantage only when a lady was mounted. Hester managed to tramp on her hem twice while she tried to gain her balance, until only Spathfoy's grip on her forearms kept her from landing in a heap at his feet.

He glowered down at her with particular intensity. "Merriman was an idiot, and Hester Daniels, *you should not trust me.*"

She was so close to him she could see the verdigris gradations in his pupils—green, gold, agate, amber, black, brown, an entire palette of colors—and she could feel the warmth and strength of his grip through the thin cotton of her sleeves. The urge to comfort him—to soothe him—was strange, unwelcome, and irresistible. She smoothed the fingers of one hand down his chest, marveling at the heat he gave off.

This simple caress was a mistake, or possibly the smartest thing she'd ever done.

He bent over her, firmed his grip on her forearms, and pressed his mouth carefully but relentlessly to hers.

Hester had been kissed before and hadn't found it at all appealing. Men who'd had too much wine with dinner, chased by a few cigars and port, did not have much to recommend them when they were bent on mashing their teeth into Hester's lips or slobbering on her neck.

On Spathfoy, the wee dram of whisky tasted lovely—all dark, smoky apples, and spice. He didn't mash, he caressed with his mouth. His hands shifted to Hester's back and held her close; his strength and heat enveloped her. She moaned with the pleasure of his nearness, and then the damned man took his mouth away.

She grabbed a fistful of his cravat. "Don't you..."

"Hush." He ran his open mouth along her throat, leaving heat and wanting to trickle down through her vitals. When he brought his mouth back to hers, Hester sank a hand into his hair and opened her mouth beneath his.

He groaned, a soft, sighing breath into her mouth—so intimate, Hester felt as if she'd downed the whole flask of whisky. She burrowed closer, until he took his mouth away again, and she wanted to howl at the unfairness of the loss.

His hand cradled the back of her head while she stood in his embrace, her forehead resting on his chest. "This will not serve, Hester Daniels. I owe you a sincere apology for taking liberties no gentleman would think of appropriating. I offer you my most—"

She reached up without lifting her face from his chest and put her hand over his mouth, more to feel the shape of his words than to stop him from speaking. His apology didn't matter, but the sound of his voice was something she wanted to take into her senses through every possible means.

"Tell me about the damned Bible."

He expelled a bark of humorless laughter, which she felt against his chest. "The damned anything. I have a theory that a good bout of swearing helps settle the nerves. Foul language re-establishes a sense of equilibrium and diverts uncouth feelings into their natural expression."

She did pull back then, far enough to peer into the bleak depths of his eyes. "So this is a damned kiss?"

"A bloody awful, misguided, bedamned, miserable

excuse for a bleeding kiss. I told you not to trust me, Hester."

He looked as unhappy as Hester had seen him. This was a small comfort. She went up on her toes, kissed his cheek, and offered him a small comfort in return. "I do not now, nor do I have any intention in the future, of trusting you."

He caught her to him for one more brief, fierce hug, then let her go. When he helped her into the saddle, he managed it while barely touching her, and not looking at her at all.

He did not shake the blanket out, but simply rolled it up and stashed it behind his saddle, then vaulted onto Flying Rowan's back. They went directly home, trotting and cantering through the heather without a single word of conversation.

In her head, Hester was testing his theory, using every naughty, off-color, and outright bad word she knew to describe his advances. It didn't work. When they ambled into the stable yard to hand the horses off to a groom, Hester was still hoping Spathfoy would offer her another bloody awful, misguided, bedamned, miserable excuse for a bleeding kiss—rather damned sooner than later.

❧

"Is all in order with our visiting earl?"

Augusta kissed Ian before he could get out a reply, and then he had to kiss her back, and *then* he had to hold her and pet her while he tried to recall what her question had been—even as she was stroking her hand over his arse in the most proprietary fashion.

His adorable arse.

"Spathfoy is a great big lout, speaking the Queen's English with such precision it nigh left my ears bleeding. He's cozening Fiona with tales of the golden city to the south, and likely bedazzling Aunt Ree with his university-boy manners."

He patted her bottom then recalled they were standing in the rose gardens where any servant peering out of any window might see them. "I've invited his lordship to dinner tomorrow, but I think he's afraid you'll start nursing The Terror right at the table."

"You were naughty." She rested against him more heavily. "Ian MacGregor, must I remind you of the requirements of proper behavior?"

"Yes, Wife, I fear you must. At great length and in considerable detail. The privacy of our bedchamber would be an ideal location for this reminder." He growled this command into her ear, which caused her to cuddle against him, her shoulders shaking with suppressed mirth. She was such a dignified woman generally that he loved to make her laugh. "I would have reported earlier for my lesson in proper deportment, except I cut into Ballater to arrange for a few wires to be sent."

He turned her under his arm so they could start walking toward the house before Ian's interest in his wife's scolding reached embarrassing proportions. "Wires are expensive, Husband."

"But expedient. Matthew and Mary Fran need to know there's an English lordling slithering about in their garden."

"Is he slithering?"

"The poor bastard is here as the old man's emissary. I think Spathfoy has orders to reave little Fee right out from under our noses, and the guilt of it is nigh killing the man."

"Do you mean reave in the legal sense, or in the Scottish sense?"

"That's what one of the wires was about, to see if there are any custody suits recently brought regarding our niece, and to see where Quinworth is lurking while his son is on holiday in our backyard."

"You didn't send one to Mary Fran and Matthew?"

"I sent three. Now about that lecture you promised me, Countess? I have been exceedingly remiss, I am planning on being naughtier still, and my only hope of proper guidance rests with you."

He scooped his wife into his arms and carried her up two flights of stairs, only to hear a certain Terror waken from his nap in a predictable state of loud and hungry indignation just as Augusta was on the point of unfastening her husband's breeches.

A list of known aphrodisiacs had circulated among Tye's confreres at university, but lemon verbena had assuredly not been among the foods, fragrances, and substances named.

Nor had fresh air, or the scent of heather, or the sound of a burbling Scottish stream, or proximity to tartan wool, but something or *someone* had so unbalanced the relationship between Tye's self-restraint and his base urges as to violate every tenet of common sense.

One did not accost decent young women, no matter how much in need of kissing they might seem.

One did not kiss young ladies who had given no overt indication they were receptive to such advances.

One did not allow oneself into compromising situations where any wandering neighbor might come upon one.

But one was also having great difficulty forgetting the kiss, *and* the compromising situation, *and* the decent young lady from whom the kiss had been stolen.

Behind his closed door, Tye wrote a letter—*not* a report—to his father, who was rusticating at the family seat in Northumbria. To his sisters, he dashed off notes full of drivel about the fresh Scottish air and beautiful Scottish skies. He wrote to the steward of his estates in Kent and outside Alnwick, and in sheer desperation, he even wrote to his mother in Edinburgh.

And still, when he sanded the last epistle, he had not in the least changed the fact that he'd kissed Hester Daniels.

Thoroughly, but somehow, not thoroughly enough.

And worse yet—*far worse*—she had kissed him back.

He tossed his pen down and leaned back in his chair, his gaze going to the view of the gardens, stables, and grounds stretching between the manor and the surrounding hills.

Maybe the fresh Scottish air was to blame.

He enjoyed sex enthusiastically when it came his way, and it came his way frequently. Friendly widows were thick on the ground in the social Season, and if they were ever in short supply, Tye had been accosted by any number of wives intent on straying. Then too, there were women on the fringes of Polite Society with whom arrangements involving coin and exclusive sexual access could be discreetly made.

Those women were available once terms were struck. Hester Daniels—jilt, tease, spinster, or whatever inaccurate label she wanted to put on herself—was *unavailable* to him.

And always would be.

A quiet triple tap on his door interrupted another round of self-castigation.

"Come in."

"Uncle!" Fiona literally skipped into the room, leaving the door open behind her. "I read to Aunt Ree, and we spoke French, and she said I could write to Mama in French tomorrow if I look up five very big words tonight. Are you writing letters?"

"I was." He shifted the stack of missives to the side while the infernal child scrambled up onto his knees.

"May I see?"

"No, you may not. Shouldn't you be at your lessons?"

"I did my reading lesson. Tell me some big words in French. You have to spell them."

"Here." He passed her a pencil. "Spell this: p-e-s-t-i-l-e-n-t-i-e-l."

"What does it mean?"

"It's French for niece."

She squirmed around to scowl at him. "Niece is the same word with an accent like this over the *e*." She drew her finger down in imitation of an accent grave. "Are you in a bad mood?"

"Yes."

"Why?"

For God's sake… He set the child aside and rose. "Because I came up here for privacy, and you have intruded."

Her brows drew down in an expression that put Tye in mind of her step-aunt, though Miss Daniels was unrelated to the girl except insofar as both females bothered him. "Then, Uncle, you should not have let me come in."

"That would have been rude."

"You're being rude now."

He wanted to bellow at the little imp, wanted to transport her bodily to the corridor, but she was regarding him with such an air of mischief he felt his lips quirking up. "My apologies."

"You could tell me what's bothering you." She skipped to the bed, hopped up the three steps on one foot, then hiked herself onto the mattress. "Aunt Hester was in a bad mood when she came here a few weeks ago, but she explained to me that she'd had her heart broken. She came here for it to get better. Is your heart broken?"

"It is not. Please remove your person from that bed."

She hopped down, again on one foot. "Aunt said her beau took unseemly liberties, and she should have coshed him on the head." Fiona swung her fist in a fierce downward arc through the air while Tye smoothed the wrinkles from the counterpane of his bed. "I told Aunt Hester there are no beaus here in Scotland, we only have braw, bonny lads. Aunt Augusta said we had braw, bonny earls too, but she meant Uncle Ian. He winked at me when she said it."

"Is that where you acquired such a lamentable habit, from your uncle Ian?"

She winked at him. "It's a secret. I'll see you at tea." As quickly as she'd invaded his privacy, she skipped right back out to the corridor.

The ensuing silence had a peculiar, relieved quality. Tye had just sat back down at his desk when Fiona poked her head around the doorjamb. "May I call you Uncle Tye? Aunt Hester said your real name is Tiberius, which would be a grand name for a bear, I think."

"It's a perfectly adequate name for an earl, but yes, you may call me Uncle Tye."

She grinned at him, a huge, toothy expression of great good spirits, winked once more, and disappeared.

Tye stared at his stack of letters. He had not mentioned any kisses in those letters, just as Hester Daniels hadn't mentioned her worthless excuse for a fiancé taking unseemly liberties or needing his head coshed.

Which left Tye pondering why his own head had not been coshed by that fair lady when he'd taken unseemly liberties. Why she'd kissed him on the cheek without any provocation on his part at all.

He picked up the pencil and started making a list.

ॐ

"I have been foolish." Dear Hester made this pronouncement in tones indicative of an impending bout of martyrdom, so Ariadne set aside her third husband's journal and resigned herself to patience.

"I hope you at least had a grand time being foolish."

The girl dropped into the rocking chair by the hearth—a feat Ariadne hadn't attempted without assistance or planning for more than a decade. "I am not jesting, Aunt. I was very rag-mannered to Lord Spathfoy."

Ariadne gave the kind of snort an old woman was permitted even in public. "That one. He could do with some rudeness. He's handsome as sin, in expectation of a title, and wealthy to boot. I hope you took him down several pegs."

"I kissed him." A furious blush accompanied this confession.

"I'm envious. Did he kiss you back?"

"You're *envious?*" Hester shot to her feet and started pacing the small confines of Ariadne's sitting room—small rooms were easier to keep warm—leaving the rocking chair to bob gently, as if inhabited by a ghost. "I toss propriety to the wind when I know the fate of my good name is hanging by a thread, and you are envious? Spathfoy isn't some younger son trying to cadge a dowry so he can keep up with his gambling cronies. He's going to be Quinworth, and I've disgraced myself utterly, *again.*"

The girl was overdue for some dramatics. She'd been pale and composed for weeks, only rousing from her brown study when Fiona dragged her out-of-doors or Ian got her onto a horse.

"You are not to blame for Merriman's mischief, Hester Daniels. He was a bad apple, as my fourth husband would have said. Spoiled rotten and contaminating all in his ambit. Do you know how many men I've kissed?"

"I beg your pardon?"

"Such pretty manners. Do have a seat. You're making my neck ache with all your stomping about."

Hester popped back into the rocker. She was nothing if not considerate of her elders.

"I asked if you knew how many men I'd kissed."

She looked guardedly intrigued. "Of course, I can't know such a thing."

"I've lost count as well, but I'll tell you, Hester Daniels, from where I'm sitting now, waiting to shuffle off this mortal coil, it wasn't nearly enough."

"Aunt, perhaps in a former era, when society was less—"

Ariadne waved a hand. "Bah. Society has always delighted in catching the unwary in their missteps, and there have always been missteps. Old George ran a proper court, I can tell you. To bed at a reasonable hour, up early to ride for hours, and yet, look at his get. A crop of fifteen children. Even his princesses were not entirely chaste, and old King William had more Fitz-bastards than some people have fingers. Do you think you're the first woman ever to steal a kiss? Merciful sakes, child, men are so blockheaded one must sometimes draw them a map."

Hester's brows drew down, suggesting Ariadne's outlook wasn't one shared by whatever tutors and governesses had raised the girl.

"But, Aunt, I *enjoyed* kissing him."

"I kissed his grandfather once, the one he's named for. The man knew a thing or two about comforting a widow—all in good fun, of course."

"He's named for a grandfather?"

Bless the girl; she didn't hide her interest in even

such a crumb of information as this. "He's named for his maternal grandfather, a Lowland Scottish earl who knew how to turn a coin practically out of thin air. Quinworth's wealth today owes much to the dowry and financial abilities Spathfoy's mother brought to the match."

"He's never mentioned his parents."

"They are cordially distant, as happens in the later years of many a dynastic match. Was Spathfoy flirting with you when you kissed him?"

"Yes." An unequivocal answer, which suggested his strapping, handsome lordship had been engaged in more than pretty compliments.

"Then kiss him some more, for pity's sake. You're both at loose ends, he's handsome, and who knows, you might form an attachment."

"Aunt, one is supposed to form the attachment before one appropriates any kisses."

She was so certain of this progression, Ariadne felt sorry for her. "And were you attached to young Merriman?"

Hester stared at her hands, which rested in her lap. Her expression was wiped clean of all intentional emotion, but Ariadne had buried four husbands, and the misgivings and griefs of women were familiar to her.

"This is your real worry, isn't it? The man you gave your hand to, however temporarily, did not charm you with his kisses, and yet this arrogant intruder has you sighing and glancing on only a few days' acquaintance."

Hester sprang onto her feet again and went to the window. The girl spent a lot of time considering the views from various windows. "What if I am unnatural?

What if I can only have feelings for things and people forbidden to me?"

Ariadne considered Hester's poker-straight posture and the tension in her fists.

"What if you are completely natural, healthy, and attracted to one of the finest specimens of manhood I've seen in decades? What if he's attracted to you, and what if you're both sensible enough to explore the attraction—within reason?"

Hester turned to face Ariadne and crossed her arms over her chest. "Are you encouraging this foolishness?"

"Yes. Yes, I certainly am. I am encouraging you to put the unfortunate situation with Merriman behind you. The man was a cad and an idiot. I suspect he rushed his fences with you and showed you the low cards in his hand far too plainly. *Get back on the horse*, my girl. Toy with Spathfoy's affections all you like. He can manage for himself, and you might find you suit."

"But what if he toys with mine?"

The question was bewildered, anxious, and sincere. Ariadne did not permit herself to smile.

"Then you *enjoy* it. And when he trots back to England in a week or two, you thank him for a few kisses and remember him fondly. All need not be drama and high dudgeon, Hester, and if you didn't want to kiss a man like Spathfoy, I would be worried about you indeed. Now, we've missed our Gaelic since Spathfoy has joined us. Shall we practice?"

Hester rang for tea, and with the determined mispronunciation of the young and serious, started her daily session mangling the language of her own maternal ancestors—while being very clear about where her current interests lay.

"If you please, Aunt Ariadne, what else can you tell me about Lord Spathfoy's family?"

⁓⁓⁓

The shame had caught Hester quite by surprise, as if she'd risen from a chair to stride across the room, only to find her hem caught under some malefactor's boot.

She'd ridden over several miles of countryside with Spathfoy in silence, pondering his kiss—and her kiss—and feeling for the first time as if ending her engagement might have been among the better decisions she'd made.

Feeling a stirring of that most irksome of emotions: hope; but it was a hope so amorphous as to leave her wondering if Spathfoy himself had anything to do with it, or if a kiss from any handsome gentleman might have served.

No matter what she'd said to Ian, it wasn't as if she liked Spathfoy, after all.

But then they'd trotted into the stable yard, and Spathfoy had swung off his horse and turned to assist Hester to dismount. His expression had been so severe she'd nearly scrambled off the far side of her horse. He'd deposited her on the ground as if touching her had burned his hands, bowed shortly, and stalked off toward the house without a word.

Leaving Hester to doubt herself so badly, she was making confessions to Aunt Ree and butchering a language normally more pleasing to the ear than French.

"But are there rules, Aunt? If a gentleman kisses a lady, is it still forbidden for the lady to kiss the gentleman?"

"Oh, my heavens, child. If a gentleman kisses a lady, he is unquestionably opening the negotiations. He's *hoping* she'll kiss him back."

Spathfoy had not looked the least bit hopeful.

Hester was saved from explaining as much by Fiona's arrival. The child skipped into the parlor and plopped down beside Aunt Ree on the sofa.

"Uncle Tye is writing letters. He wouldn't give me any big words in French, though he was happy enough to give me some in English."

Aunt Ree smoothed a hand down the remains of one of Fiona's braids. "We're practicing our Gaelic, Fiona. We can look up the big English words in the French translation dictionary if that would help."

Inspiration struck, and Hester didn't pause to question it. "Maybe Uncle Tye will help you think up some big French words over dinner."

Fiona sat bolt upright. "I can come to table with Uncle and Aunt and you? I can stay up late and have dessert?"

"If you take a bath and change your pinny, yes, just this once."

Fiona bounced to her feet. "I must put this in my letter. I'm to dine with company. Mama and Papa will be very proud of me." She skipped off to the door, stopped, and frowned. "Will Uncle mind if I join you for dinner?"

Aunt Ariadne answered. "Of course, he won't. What gentleman wouldn't want to have three lovely ladies all to himself at dinner?"

❧

Tye had friends who'd served in the Crimea, men who'd gone off to war in great patriotic good spirits only to come home quiet, hollowed-eyed, and often missing body parts. The Russians had developed a type of weapon referred to as a *fougasse*, though various forms of *fougasse* had been around for centuries.

A man walking through deep grass would inadvertently step on one of these things and find himself blown to bits without warning.

Dinner loomed before Tye like a field salted with many hidden weapons, each intended to relieve him of some significant asset: his dignity, his composure, his manners, or—in Fiona's case—his patience.

"I've made you a list," he said. "Not less than ten of the largest words I know in French, and you shall have it after we dine. Now, might we converse about the weather?"

Lady Ariadne presided over the meal with benevolent vagueness. Miss Daniels—he could hardly call her Hester now—limited her contributions to gentle admonitions regarding the child's deportment, leaving Tye to converse with... his niece.

"Why do people talk about the weather?" Fiona queried. She aimed her question at a piece of braised lamb gracing the end of her fork.

"Eat your food, Fee dear, don't lecture it."

The girl popped the meat into her mouth and chewed vigorously.

"I'm just asking," she said a moment later. "The weather is always there, and we can't *do* anything about it, so why bring it up all the time as if it had manners to correct or ideas we could listen to?"

Tye topped off his wine and did the same for the ladies. "I will admit, Fiona, that weather would make a less interesting dinner companion than you, who have both manners to correct and all kinds of unorthodox ideas."

"What is the French word for un-ortho-ducks, and what does it mean?"

He took another sip of his wine. He was beginning to feel that slight distance between his mind, his emotions, and his bodily awareness, that suggested he'd had rather too many sips of wine.

Lady Ariadne murmured something in Gaelic that Tye did not catch—the child had addled his wits that greatly—and a servant brought Fiona a small glass of wine.

"For your digestion, my dear, but take small sips only, or it could have the opposite of its intended effect."

The girl took a dainty taste of her libation, showing no ill effects, which was the outside of too much.

Properly reared children did not dine at table with adults.

They did not run roughshod over the dinner conversation.

On this sceptered isle, they did not sip passably good table wine as if it were served to them nightly.

And a proper gentleman did not sit across from a decent young woman and mentally revisit the feel of her unbound hair sliding over his hands like blond silk. He did not watch her mouth when she drank her wine. He did not wonder if she would cosh him on his head if he attempted to kiss her again.

The longest meal of Tye's life ended when Lady Ariadne pushed to her feet. "If you young people will excuse me, I'll retire to my rooms and leave you to turn Fee loose for a gambol in the garden. Fiona, I am very proud of you, my dear. Your manners are impressive, and we will work on your conversation. Fetch me my cane and wish me sweet dreams."

Fiona scrambled out of her chair to retrieve her great-aunt's cane from where it was propped near the door. "Thank you, Aunt. Good night, sweet dreams, sleep well, I love you."

Tye rose, thinking this reply had the sound of an oft-repeated litany, one that put a damper on the irritation he'd been nursing through the meal. He frowned down at Lady Ariadne.

"Shall I escort you, my lady? I'm sure Miss Daniels can see the child to the gardens."

"No, thank you, my lord. Until breakfast, my dears."

She tottered off, leaving an odd silence in her wake.

"Aunt is very old," Fiona said. "It's easy to love old people, because they're so nice."

"It's easy to love you," Miss Daniels said, "because you're very kind as well, and you made such an effort to be agreeable at table tonight. My lord, please don't feel compelled to accompany us. Fiona and I are accustomed to rambling in our own gardens without escort."

Except they weren't *her* gardens. If she'd taken his arm quietly, without comment, he might have let her excuse him at the main staircase, but she had to intimate he was not welcome.

"I would be delighted to join you for a stroll among the roses, and I have to agree. Fiona acquitted herself admirably, considering her tender years."

He winged his arm at Miss Daniels, half expecting—half wishing for—an argument.

She placed her bare hand on his sleeve. "Come along, Fiona, the light won't last much longer, and you've stayed up quite late as it is."

They made a slow progress through the house and out onto the back terrace. With the scent of lemon verbena wafting through his nose, Tye came to two realizations, neither of which helped settle his meal.

First, when he kissed a woman, it was usually a pleasant moment, and possibly a prelude to some copulatory pleasant moments, but the kiss itself did not linger in his awareness. Kissing was a means to an end, a means he was happy enough to bypass if the lady perceived and shared a willingness to proceed to the end.

With Hester Daniels, the kiss itself had been his goal. He'd wanted to get his mouth on hers, and yes, he'd wanted more than that from her too. What had irritated him over dinner was not the child's chattering, or her forwardness. It was not the paucity of adult conversation or the unpretentious quality of the place settings or the simplicity of the food itself.

What irritated him was the memory of that kiss, lingering in his awareness like some upset or shining moment—he wasn't sure which. He'd enjoyed that kiss tremendously.

The second realization was no more comforting: he should not kiss Hester Daniels again, no matter how much he might want to.

And he did want to. Very much.

❧

"Aunt Ariadne insists I owe you no apology, but I'm proffering one nonetheless."

Hester watched as Fiona went from rose to rose, sniffing each one. The end of her nose would be dusted with pollen at the rate she was making her olfactory inventory.

"An apology?" Sitting beside Hester, Spathfoy stretched out long legs and crossed them at the ankles. He'd been his usual self at dinner, both mannerly and somehow unapproachable, patient with Fiona, solicitous of Aunt Ree, and toward Hester—unreadable.

"I kissed you, my lord. This is forward behavior, and regardless of Aunt's interpretation of the rules of Polite Society, I am offering you my apologies for having taken liberties with your lordship's person."

He was quiet for a moment in a considering, strategizing sort of way. This was rotten of him in the extreme, when he might have simply accepted Hester's apology and remarked on the stars winking into view on the eastern horizon.

"Correct me if I err, Miss Daniels, but I don't believe yours was the only kiss shared between us."

"That is of no moment."

Another silence, one Hester did not enjoy.

"*My* kiss was of *no* moment, but yours—a chaste peck on my right cheek, I do believe—requires that *you* apologize to *me*?"

Hester could not tell if he was amused or affronted, but *she* was mortified. The damned man could probably detect her blush even in the fading light.

"Young ladies are expected to uphold certain standards, my lord. Gentlemen are expected to have lapses."

Fiona sank down in the grass some yards off and started making catapults out of grass flowers. She shot little seed heads in all directions, then lay on her back and tried launching them right into the evening sky, though they fell to earth, usually landing on or near Fee's face.

"Miss Daniels, you would not allow me to apologize for my lapse, if my recollection serves, but if you insist on apologizing to me, then I insist on apologizing to you."

A little torpedo of grass seeds landed at Hester's feet. "You have nothing to apologize for." *Except this ridiculous conversation.* She wondered if the son of a marquess was somehow exempt from the manners every other gentleman—almost every other gentleman—had drilled into him before he was out of short coats.

"I have *nothing* to apologize for. I am fascinated to hear this." He sounded utterly bored, or perhaps appalled.

"I was getting back on the horse." She would explain this to him, lest he be mistaken about her motives. Aunt's version of events, upon reflection, had been helpful after all.

"You were mounting your horse? Before or after I kissed you, using my *tongue*, in your *mouth*, and my bare *hands* on various locations a gentleman does not presume to touch?"

Wretched man. "I wasn't getting back on the horse in the literal sense. By kissing you, I was demonstrating to myself that my failed engagement was not permanently wounding."

His arm settled along the back of their bench. To appearances, he was a man completely at ease after a simple, satisfying meal, while Hester was a lady who wished she'd not had so much wine. Again.

"What did Merriman do to make you wish you'd coshed him on his head?"

"I beg your pardon?"

"Your esteemed former fiancé. You were tempted to resort to violence with him, which makes me suspect he attempted more than a mere kiss."

Mere kiss? Mother of God. But how to answer?

He did not harry her for a reply, so Hester sat silently beside him, aware of him to a painful degree, staring at his hand where it rested on his thigh. His arm was at her back, his length along her side, his attention focused on her intently despite the lazy inflection of his voice and the apparent ease of his body.

It became difficult to breathe normally.

"Do I conclude from your silence, Miss Daniels, that your former fiancé attempted to anticipate the conjugal vows, and you were not impressed with his behavior?"

His voice held no more inflection than if he'd been complimenting Mary Fran's roses, though Hester's heart began to thump against her ribs.

"You may conclude something of that nature."

His silences were torturing her even as she dreaded the next question.

"In that case, I accept your apology, madam. I would regard it as a kindness if you would accept mine as well. The Bourbons are without equal when it comes to scent, whereas the Damasks lack subtlety, don't you agree?"

She managed a nod, becoming aware of the fragrance perfuming the evening around them only

when he'd pointed it out to her. She became aware
of something else too: Spathfoy's arm lightly encir-
cling her shoulders, a solid, warm weight, perhaps
intended as a comfort, more likely intended to mean
nothing at all.

Four

THE MACGREGORS HAD EARNED COIN UNTIL THE previous summer by opening Balfour House to paying guests while the royal family was in residence at nearby Balmoral Castle. From Quinworth's perspective, this was more contemptible than if they'd resorted to trade.

It was one thing to labor for one's bread or to make a profit off those laboring for their bread. The land alone could no longer sustain the lifestyle the upper classes maintained, and even Tye's father acknowledged that much. To make money out of nothing more than social and geographical convenience, though, was in Quinworth's estimation indefensible—a complete disregard of the standards and dictates of social propriety.

Tye suspected his very practical mother would have had a thing or two to say about such a conclusion, if she'd been on hand to hear it.

Tye found the MacGregors' choices resourceful, and doubted his own family could have been creative enough to seize such an opportunity in the wake of famine, massive emigration, and decades of political persecution.

"Welcome to Balfour House." A tall, black-haired woman with a gracious smile on her lovely face and an arm around Ian MacGregor's waist greeted Tye on a wide stone terrace. "Ian warned me you could be his cousin in coloring and height."

"Augusta, my heart, may I make known to you Tiberius, Earl of Spathfoy, and Fee's uncle. Spathfoy, my lady and I bid you welcome. I hope you're hungry, because the kitchen has been bankrupting the larders the livelong day in anticipation of feeding a genuine English lord."

Tye bowed over the countess's hand. "A courtesy lord only, and I hope a courteous lord. Your home is beautiful."

"My wife is beautiful," Balfour said, smiling shamelessly at his lady. "The house is just a place to raise our children. Come along. Augusta will want you to see some of the gardens before she lets us down a wee dram in anticipation of the meal."

"Ian will try to get you drunk," the lady interjected, slipping a hand through Tye's arm. "It's his duty as host to ply you with whisky, and mine to ply you with food. What brought you to the Highlands, my lord?"

It was another gauntlet, with husband and wife handing off the examination of the witness as neatly as two seasoned football players would pass the ball between them down the field.

How was his family? *And* his dear mother?

Was he missing the social whirl in Town?

Only as the meal wound down—and an excellent meal it was, too—did Tye understand they'd been toying with him, amusing themselves in a manner only a closely attuned married couple might consider entertaining.

"I must excuse myself," Lady Balfour said, getting to her feet. "My routine calls for a stop by the nursery at this hour, so I'll leave you gentlemen to your port. Lord Spathfoy, I bid you good night. Once I get to the nursery, it sometimes takes Ian prying me away from our son bodily before I'll leave that baby."

Balfour leaned in to kiss his wife's cheek, and Tye heard him whisper something in her ear in Gaelic about dreams and lectures. The lady smiled prettily and withdrew, her husband watching a part of her anatomy Tye dared not even notice.

The Scots were daft, and apparently marriage to a Scot resulted in daftness even in women raised among the English aristocracy. Tye wondered what his mother might have said about the effect on a Scottish woman of marrying an English noble.

"If you prefer port, Spathfoy, I'm bound as your host to provide it, but I've some whisky I typically bring out only for special occasions, if you're game."

"I'm a special occasion?"

"To your family you likely are, but it's plain to me I haven't gotten you drunk yet, so I'm resorting to my best stratagems." Balfour offered this comment with such candid good cheer, Tye almost believed he was teasing. Almost.

"And why must I become inebriated?"

"Let's take our drinks on the back terrace, shall we? I love the gloaming, and if the dew is falling just so, I'll hear my wife singing the bairn a lullaby. I can become *inebriated* on that alone."

Balfour was shameless about his family attachments, which was so different from what Tye had been raised with, Tye couldn't find it in himself to be appalled.

They stopped by a library, which wasn't exactly crammed with books, and Balfour opened a sideboard and passed Tye a decanter. "We'll use glasses in case her ladyship tries for a sneak inspection from the nursery window."

"Somehow, Balfour, if she's spying from the window, I doubt she'll be doing so for the sake of evaluating our etiquette."

Balfour smiled wolfishly. "Perhaps she won't be." Tye was surprised when the man did not wink but led him through French doors straight to the terrace.

"You are a guest under my roof and distant family, so I will appreciate some honesty," Balfour said as he took a bench at the edge of the terrace. He poured them each a drink and passed one to Tye, who remained standing. "To your health."

"And yours." Tye sipped his drink cautiously, but *God in heaven,* it was sublime libation. He took a place beside Balfour on the stone bench. "What *is* this?"

"We've taken to calling it the laird's cache. My master distiller and I came across about twenty barrels of this when we were doing an inventory last year. I suspect it's at least twenty years old, but McDowell claims it's twice that. We're decanting it one barrel at a time."

They sipped in respectful silence for some minutes. Tye tried to mentally describe the flavors gracing his palate, but it was pointless when faced with such variety and subtlety. The drink didn't burn its way into his vitals, it illuminated him from the inside out—like a certain young lady's smile.

"Do your royal neighbors know you've drink like this to offer your guests?"

"Oh, of course. We send over a few bottles in welcome every summer. Albert is a man of refinement, so at least we know it isn't going to waste."

More silence as Balfour topped off their drinks. "I'm plying you with my best whisky, Spathfoy. I expect a few honest answers in return."

Ah, so the real questioning was going to begin. "I am generally considered an honest man."

"Did you know Matthew Daniels has initiated a suit to assume legal guardianship of Fiona?"

Tye let the glow of his last sip of whisky fade before he answered. "I did not."

Balfour's disclosure made sense though. This might account for Quinworth's sudden interest in the child. A marquess might ignore his granddaughter, but only as long as nobody else—no other wealthy, titled Englishman, for example—was stepping into the breach. Still, Tye felt a spike of resentment that his father had sent him into battle less than well informed.

"Neither did I. I'm not sure Mary Fran knew. Matthew is devoted to the child."

As Quinworth had not been; as Tye had not been. "That is commendable."

"To see the girl leave Balfour House about tore the heart from my chest."

Scottish hyperbole, no doubt. "She's a delightful child." Which was English hyperbole.

"She's a damned force of nature, like her mother.

She's also the first good thing to happen to this family in nigh fifty years. I say this, though it means I must overcome my reluctance to admit anything good could come of yet another decent Scottish girl's rape at the hands of an English soldier. Excuse me. Perhaps I am the one becoming inebriated." He lifted his glass to peer at his drink. "I meant seduction, not rape."

Tye set his glass down between them on the stone bench. "You accuse my late brother of rape?"

"No... no, though I'd like to." Balfour's tone was thoughtful. "I accuse him of seducing an innocent, getting her with child, and having every intention of leaving the girl ruined if she refused his suit."

"Now this is interesting." Tye kept his tone speculative, though the insult intended was blatant. "My family regards Fiona's origins as an example of yet another loyal English soldier being led astray by a local woman intent on insinuating herself into the coffers of his wealthy and titled family."

"Interesting, indeed. I think I would have noticed my own sister doing this insinuating you mention, particularly when we haven't a Quinworth copper to show for it—nor a single letter or note from the wealthy, titled family since Fiona's birth years ago."

A valid argument. Tye remained silent while Balfour poured him another two fingers.

"Mary Fran was barely eighteen, her virtue something I, my three brothers, my grandfather, and assorted uncles and cousins would all have staked their lives on. She was headstrong, true, but not wicked. The woman knows not how to scheme when direct measures will serve. You have sisters, Spathfoy."

God yes, he had sisters. If he'd had no sisters, there was no power on earth that could have sent him on this fool's errand for Quinworth. "A woman at eighteen generally knows her own mind."

"And is this why English law forbids her to wed without parental consent until she's twenty-one?"

Now why would a Scottish earl bother himself with English law? Tye took another sip of his drink, and in his head began to count to one hundred in Gaelic.

Balfour gazed up at the darkening sky. "I read law, Spathfoy, lots and lots of it, with lots and lots of English barristers and solicitors. Here is what I want you to ask your dear papa: What Scotswoman in her right mind, much less the daughter of an earl, would cast herself into the arms of a penniless English soldier if she were intent on marriage? As I heard it, your own mother, who was no more wellborn than Mary Fran, was reluctant to take on a marquess and hasn't exactly remained at his side since the nuptials.

"Your brother was pretty," Balfour went on, "but prettier, wealthier officers were thick on the ground. Mary Fran was the highest-ranking eligible female in the shire. She had no need of Gordie Flynn's hand in marriage. She took her flirting too far perhaps, but Gordie was older, more worldly, and arguably raised as a gentleman. My sister married well beneath her justified expectations and very much against her preferences."

He sipped his whisky placidly, but his arguments settled into Tye's thinking brain and blended with several other trains of thought.

The marquess had not told Tye that a guardianship suit was pending. What else had the marquess failed to tell his firstborn son and minion? That Balfour was a lawyer certainly didn't help matters at all.

Mary Frances MacGregor, as described by her brother, was wellborn enough to have no need of association with the Flynns, something the marquess had also never acknowledged in Tye's hearing.

And there was more. In a casual tour of the house, Tye had seen a portrait of Mary Fran as a young mother. The lady was gorgeous, putting Tye in mind of his own mother's height, red hair, and feminine figure. This too, would have given her more marital options besides a marquess's younger son sporting around in regimental colors.

And eighteen in a proper household could be innocent—very likely *had been* innocent.

"More whisky?" Balfour was the soul of good manners now that he'd rattled swords and upset Tye's enjoyment of very fine spirits.

"No, thank you. This is drink to be savored."

"It is. Just as Fiona is a child to be loved."

Damn the man. "I cannot fault my father for attempting to redress what could be seen as previous neglect of his granddaughter."

"He can redress all the neglect he wants—set up a trust fund, send you along on annual inspections, have Fee down to visit her aunties when she's old enough to sit still on the train. An old man is entitled to deal with his regrets. He'll not be taking our Fee, though, not unless Mary Fran herself tells me to allow it."

"And that good woman is not here, is she?"

Balfour drank in silence, his gaze going to a window on the third floor. "Ask your father what he's truly about, Spathfoy. The child's happiness matters more to me and mine than your father's consequence or his queer starts. Meaning no disrespect to present company, your brother was a cad and a bounder, and your father had the raising of him. Taking possession of Fee as if she's some prize of war will not bring Gordie back, nor will it change what Gordie was."

And this was most damning of all, because Tye had known his brother—he better than his father had known him, though perhaps not better than his mother. Tye had seen his younger brother for the spoiled, self-indulgent boy he'd been.

He'd seen Gordie's venal streak, and borne the brunt of it more than once, and he'd desperately hoped some years in the military would mature the selfish streak into something more honorable.

So Tye compromised. Balfour had treated Tye honestly. Tye offered a truth in return: "If my brother dealt with Lady Mary Frances in a cavalier fashion, it would disappoint me. While it might surprise my father, it would not surprise me." He rose from the bench. "I thank you for a wonderful meal, and for sharing a memorable drink with me, though if I tarry much longer, I'll lose the light for my journey home."

"We'll call for your horse, but let me fetch you a bottle for your papa's cellars before we send you on your way."

That was Scottish of Balfour. They were a tight-fisted race of necessity, but Balfour was making a statement: even a marquess condemned to lose a legal battle was entitled to a last, decent drink.

The man was entirely too trusting of the marquess's

honor. Balfour's earlier point had been telling: Gordie's honor had been wanting, and Gordie was Quinworth's son. Tye was on his horse and headed down the lane before it occurred to him: he, too, was Quinworth's son.

⤬

"I will be more than relieved to see your son weaned, Husband." Augusta MacGregor shifted over to give her spouse the warm side of the bed, though in moments, his sheer size and brawn would have the whole thing toasty.

"I will be relieved as well, Wife, though likely for different reasons. It does send the lad to his slumbers, though." He moved about, rocking the bed until he was wrapped around Augusta from behind.

"Was Spathfoy very tiresome?"

"The man needs to indulge in good spirits more often, but no, he wasn't any worse than he was raised to be. Maybe a little better."

Augusta felt Ian's lips trailing over her neck, then his nose. He was particularly adept at the nose-kiss, or nuzzle, and especially… "That tickles, Ian."

"A sweet spot." He kissed the place right below her ear that made Augusta both sigh and shiver. "I think Spathfoy was honestly surprised to hear Matthew has brought suit to become Fee's guardian."

Augusta caught her husband's wandering hand before it lifted her nightgown any higher on her thigh. "You were surprised. I'm Matthew's cousin, and I was surprised. Do you think Hester knows?"

"That one." Ian squeezed Augusta's fingers, then

freed his hand from her grasp. "For the life of me, I can no longer read her, Augusta. Last year, she was full of mischief, carefree, and happy to enjoy the fresh air and sunshine. This year, she seems blighted."

"Blight kills."

"She's not a potato vine, my love." His hand started its stealthy stroking over her hip again. "I believe our Hester has caught Spathfoy's notice."

"Did he ask about her?"

"He stood before the daguerreotype we had taken of her at our wedding, and he'd have to be blind not to notice the changes in her. She was petite a year ago. She's a shadow now."

"And a cranky shadow." Augusta shifted ever so slightly, so her backside nestled more snugly against a certain part of her husband's anatomy. "Did you learn anything from Spathfoy over the manly tot of truth potion?"

"He's not his younger brother. I left enough insults in the air to be risking my good health, but Spathfoy is cannier than that. I couldn't bait him, and if I'm not mistaken, he was trying to pass along some information without being blatantly disloyal to the marquess." He shifted as well, so there was no mistaking his arousal. "My love, I never did get that lecture on proper deportment."

"I had hopes my good example might be inspiration enough."

But a thought was trying to edge its way through her growing arousal. "Do you think Gordie had despoiled other innocents?"

Ian went still. Bodily, this manifested as a simple

absence of movement, but Augusta was his devoted wife, and even lying on her side facing away from him, she could feel his mind focus on a single still point as well.

"Wife, you are brilliant. I would bet the rest of the laird's cache that's exactly what Spathfoy was intimating. He said he wouldn't be surprised to find Gordie had taken advantage of Mary Fran— disappointed, but not surprised. My wife is a genius." He rolled her to her back and caged her with his much larger body.

His kisses were tender, enthusiastic, and captivating. His kisses were part of what had endeared him to her when their chances of lasting happiness had seemed so dim.

"Ian?"

"Your Brilliance?"

"Have we heard from Mary Fran and Matthew?"

He lifted up and scowled down at her. "We have not. I will worry about that in the morning, Wife."

"Will you also worry about any will Gordie might have left?"

He smoothed a big hand over her hair and sighed gustily, some of the lust seeming to go out of him. "My heart, I thought you wanted a large family, though why you'd aspire to such a thing when one baby has already turned this household upside down is beyond the understanding of a simple man such as myself."

"You *are* worried." Augusta urged him down against her chest and wrapped her arms around him. "Did Gordie leave a will?"

"I've people looking into it. Gordie was an officer,

so making a will ought to have been something he saw to in the ordinary course. The question is, was it a will that provided for the guardianship of any minor children, and if so, what did it provide?"

"You think he'd leave his children in his father's care, don't you?"

Ian settled more closely on her, though even preoccupied, he was careful of her breasts. "Gordie was a heedless, selfish younger son. Such prudence and consideration would have been foreign to his nature."

"But you're worried." She stroked a hand through his thick, dark hair. "You're worried for Fee, for Mary Fran, and even for Matthew."

"No." He lifted his head to meet Augusta's gaze. "In the morning, I might be a wee bit concerned, but right now, I'm in bed with my wife, and the only thing *worrying* me is that I might once again be left with only the dubious comfort of my wife's example of proper deportment."

As it turned out, that example was not among the comforts to befall the Earl of Balfour, and by the time he fell asleep entangled with his loving wife, neither did his lordship feel the least bit worried.

❧

Hester watched from her vantage point as Spathfoy led his horse into the stables. He was talking to the animal, though she was too far away to hear exactly what was said. No doubt it was a lecture of some sort on proper equine deportment.

Her perch on a garden bench gave her a clear view into the barn. By the lantern hanging in the aisle, she could see Spathfoy didn't wake the lads but tended to the animal himself—and didn't skimp either. The saddle and bridle came off and were properly stowed, then a grooming ensued from one end of the gelding's glossy dark hide to the other.

Then—this surprised her—a scratching about the beast's withers and shoulders amid more talk.

Spathfoy left the horse in the cross ties while he scrubbed out, dumped, and refilled a water bucket. He picked out each hoof, which could be a messy proposition for a man in informal evening attire, then forked some hay into the stall.

Hester wasn't sure the grooms would have been quite that considerate, which was perhaps why Spathfoy was tending to his mount himself: an English lord in unfriendly territory needed a sound horse for his eventual retreat.

After making a circuit of the stables for which purpose Hester could not divine, Spathfoy started up the path, and still he didn't notice her sitting on her bench in the moonlight.

"Good evening, my lord." She hadn't intended to speak, but lurking any longer seemed rude.

"Miss Daniels, good evening." In the moonlight, his voice seemed different—richer, darker, less English and less of all the things that clouded its inherent beauty. "May I escort you to the house?"

He *would* offer to observe the proprieties.

"No thank you. You may join me if you like. I trust you found Ian and Augusta in good health?"

He settled beside her, a piece of the night taking a seat. "They did not terrorize me with the company of their offspring at table, if that's what you're asking, and the meal was above reproach."

"The meal was delicious. If Ian broke out the laird's cache, then the drink was among the finest you've ever been served."

He sighed, a big gust of male emotion that would never be accurately labeled. "I don't want to bicker with you, Miss Daniels. Are you sure I can't escort you to the house?"

"So you can lurk out here among the roses and brood in solitude?"

In the darkness, she saw his teeth gleam. A smile or a grimace? "Yes, if you must know. Solitude is my preferred state, in fact, and if I don't get regular doses of it, I become restive."

"You usually like bickering with me." And she liked bickering with him. The realization was not as lowering as it should have been.

"Your observation is no compliment to one who aspires to the status of gentleman."

"It wasn't an insult either." He was in some sort of mood. Hester recognized it, because she'd been in the same mood ever since Lord Jasper Merriman had left bruises on her person that had only recently faded. "And you don't deny it, either. You enjoy our spats."

"I'm tired, Miss Daniels, and yet I am not comfortable leaving you out here without companionship at such a late hour. What do you want of me?"

Even for him, that was brusque.

"Ian worked you over properly, didn't he? And Augusta abetted him, smiling and nodding all the while."

"Ian—*Lord Balfour*—reminded me I have a

conscience, and the realization is not at all convenient, even when softened by marvelously smooth whisky."

She didn't think he'd intended to be that honest, but she seized the opening before her courage deserted her. "Please call me Hester. We are practically family, and our paths are likely to cross on occasion if you remain interested in Fiona's well-being."

"Very well. May I escort you to the house, *Hester*?"

He was truly rattled. Whatever Ian had said or implied or otherwise insinuated, Spathfoy was wrestling with it.

"Will you kiss me, my lord?"

"For God's sake, no, I will not kiss you." He didn't get off the bench though. Didn't shift the slightest bit away from her.

"It's just that I don't particularly like you," Hester said, "so I think it's safe to try out your paces, so to speak. You've already had your tongue in my mouth, after all, and your bare hands on my person."

"We're back to your equestrian analogies?"

Still he didn't leave. Didn't get to his feet or cross his arms or otherwise reject her proposition.

"There is something amiss with me," Hester said, speaking slowly. "You say you are restive if too much in the company of others. I comprehend this, though I would not have even a few months ago. It's why I left London, why I so very thoroughly enjoyed a good gallop yesterday. Fiona says I'm out of sorts, and Ian and Augusta look at me like I'm a powder keg whose fuse they must not inadvertently light. Sometimes, I can't get my breath, and I feel like I *am* a powder keg."

She fell silent, because the more words she let spin

forth, the faster they wanted to come—and to *him*, of all people.

"You feel as if a fuse has been lit," Spathfoy said slowly—reluctantly? "You feel as if you're watching it burn down, and there's nothing you can do to stop the impending mayhem."

She nodded, because speech abruptly seemed a chancy thing. Her heart began to thump palpably, and she had to part her lips to draw breath.

"Any further kissing between us is ill-advised in the extreme." He stood and marched half a dozen steps in the direction of the house. Hester knew the urge to scream, to drag him back to her side by the hair, to rage and cry out and destroy the entire peace of the night around her.

Then he turned and stalked toward the bench. He kept coming, until to her shock, he knelt over her, one knee by each hip, so the great bulk of him was straddling her lap. "Very ill-advised."

He framed her face in his hands and paused, his mouth just a whisper from hers. "You will regret this, *Hester*. I will regret this."

His mouth descended onto hers firmly, nothing tentative or reluctant about it, and inside Hester, something eased. All the tension and frustrations she'd been corralling behind her manners and her benighted self-restraint found an outlet, a way to express themselves. She didn't think about Jasper Merriman or bruises, or her idiot mother, or her silently worried family.

With just his mouth on hers, Spathfoy obliterated all thought and all memory from Hester's awareness, leaving her to feast her senses on him alone.

He was warm all around her, and clean and yet male too, in the scents of horse and night and well-oiled leather clinging to his clothing. When Hester opened her mouth beneath his, his arms came around her, and hers lashed around him. She held him desperately tight, letting herself cling and *need* for just a few moments.

His tongue was a marvel, tasting first the corners of her mouth, then tracing her lips, then retreating to invite her into similar boldness. She accepted the invitation, went plundering into the hot, wet reaches of his mouth, sent her fingers into his hair, arched her body up into his.

"For God's sake, woman."

He hung over her, panting, while Hester pressed her face to his chest and resented his clothing. She could feel his erect male flesh, could feel curiosity in her vitals where distaste ought to be, and she rejoiced that it should be so.

"Do you want me to swive you right here on this bloody damned bench?" He climbed off her and turned his back, likely to arrange himself in his clothing. Then he faced her, scrubbing a hand back through his hair. "I assume you comprehend the term?"

"I comprehend the term better than you imagine, my lord. And what would you say if I replied in the affirmative?"

She'd shocked herself with her own question, but she'd shocked him as well. His posture shifted with it, as if she'd smacked him physically.

"I would say, madam, that you are overwrought for reasons I cannot fathom, and I would offer once again to escort you inside the damned house, where I would leave you in blasted peace and hope you might offer me the same ruddy courtesy while I try to forget this whole misguided encounter."

He resumed his seat on the bench when Hester had expected him to stomp off into the darkness. They sat there in silence until Hester realized she'd synchronized her breathing with his.

"Ian upset you."

He leaned back and ranged his arm along the bench behind her. "It might delight you to know, Miss Daniels, that *you* have upset me. You are family to the lord and lady of this home, family to the child who is my niece. You are young and innocent, despite what you think of a few wicked kisses, and it has never been an ambition of mine to despoil innocents."

"Now you're scolding me? I asked you to kiss me, I did not toss you bodily onto your lordly back and force my wiles upon you. I can't help that I like kissing you."

"You sound damned unhappy about it yourself. God knows a taste for you—for your kisses—doesn't make my life any easier."

Now he was disgruntled, or likely amused. The worst of his ill feeling was passing, perhaps as his arousal faded. He wasn't going to kiss her again, and to Hester, this seemed like a great, miserable unfairness on top of many other injustices.

"I know about that word you used."

"Swive—a lovely, old Anglo-Saxon monosyllable never to be uttered in the presence of women or children. My apologies for an egregious breach of propriety."

She closed her eyes, because she was going to

confide in this large, unhappy, often rude English lord. "I know about it."

"You've said as much. Congratulations on the depth of your naughty vocabulary, Miss Daniels. Please do not share this dubious accomplishment with my niece."

"My name is Hester, and I don't mean merely the word. I know about *it*."

A few beats of quiet went by, while off in the distance the fox started up lamenting his solitude. This time, Hester found the tortured sound appropriate to the discussion.

Spathfoy turned his head to regard her in the moonlight. "Are you telling me you have been relieved of your chastity?"

His voice was arctic, the verbal embodiment of barely contained affront. Hester hunched forward, gripping the edge of the bench with both hands.

She nodded.

He muttered something under his breath that sounded Gaelic. "Merriman?"

She nodded again, but inside her, something was coiling up more tightly than ever.

"Does your family know?"

Hester shook her head.

And then very gently, so gently she barely recognized it as the voice of the Earl of Spathfoy, "Hester, are you carrying the man's child?"

❧

The quiet wraith beside Tye shook her head again.

"I am not w… with child. It's not that I wanted to be, but still…"

He understood, probably better than Hester did herself, what she was trying to say. Children were the great consolation offered to women for every trial in life. Tye's mother had explained this to him, and further explained that the fact that children were among those trials was of no moment.

"Come here." He settled an arm around her shoulders and brought her close to his side. "You should tell your family, Hester."

"Can't."

Perhaps she meant she couldn't tell her brother because he was off gallivanting around the Continent with his new wife. Perhaps she meant something more complicated.

No matter. Tye traced the slender bones of her shoulder with his hand, hurting for her. Oh, he could catch a train south, hunt up Merriman, and mete out some rough justice, but this woman would still be hiding up here in rural Scotland, upset and unhappy when she should have been planning her wedding and picking out names for her firstborn.

"Did he hurt you?" The question was not prompted by conscience, but by something more problematic.

The daft woman tried to shift away. He gently prevented it.

"Not the way you mean." She sounded tired now, and for the first time in Tye's experience, defeated. To hear it made him furious, though he had wisdom enough to keep his anger to himself. "He confused me."

Tye waited. Hester Daniels was intelligent and articulate. She'd sort through what she wanted him to know, and he'd sit on this bench until his backside fell asleep while she did.

"Jasper could be so sure of himself, so convincing. He said I'd inflamed his passions, that I wanted what he was doing, and it was my duty, and everybody anticipated their vows. He was very confident of what he said."

Bastard. "You began to doubt yourself."

"I didn't *begin* to doubt myself. I lost track entirely of what I knew to be true. I've never inflamed a man's passions in my life, you see. I'm the girl none of the fellows needs to take seriously. I'm *cute*. Adorable, a whacking good sport, or I was."

At Balfour House, he'd seen a picture of the woman she described. She had the same gorgeous hair and the same wide, pretty eyes as Hester, but that woman had an innocent gaze and a laughing smile. Even sitting still for the interminable length of time necessary to form a photographic image, she'd projected high spirits and joie de vivre.

That woman had not known bitter self-doubt, and Tye doubted he would have found her half so intriguing as he did the bewildered, passionate creature sitting beside him in the moonlight.

And now was not the time to tell her she was still adorable. "I suppose a cute, adorable, adoring fiancée allows her prospective husband any liberties he demands. Was that Merriman's reasoning?"

She was silent so long worry started to flap around inside Tye's head, creating all manner of awful scenarios.

"Jasper isn't built on quite as grand a scale as you, my lord, but he's a good deal stronger than I suspected."

"The bastard *forced* you?" Though it made no difference whether the coercion was physical, or physical and emotional, or solely emotional. Hester's choices had been taken from her, and with them, any confidence she might have had in her right to decide.

"He says *I* forced *him*. I drove him to unbridled lust."

She ought to have snorted with disgust to relay such tripe; she ought to have laughed with incredulity that a grown man could posit such nonsense in the Queen's English.

But she still doubted. Tye heard it in her voice, felt it in her tense posture. Because of the violation of her person and her will by a man who ought to have died to keep her safe, Hester Daniels still doubted *herself*.

"I'll kill him for you, if that will help. I'll castrate him first, with a dull, rusty knife. I'm Quinworth's son. I won't be held accountable. You know what it means to castrate a man?"

Beneath his arm, her shoulders lifted and dropped, as if she'd found what was very nearly a sincere offer amusing. "A rusty knife, my lord?"

"A dull, rusty knife. A dull, *dirty* rusty knife left to lie about on the floor of a stable for a few days first."

Against him, she eased at his exaggeration. "I lie awake at night, dwelling on such thoughts. I want to maim him, socially if not physically. I want to see him humiliated."

"So you jilted him. Good for you."

She scuffed her foot across the grass beneath them. "Jilting him wasn't enough. I'm doomed to spinsterhood while he's free to charm his way under some other young lady's skirts and frog-march her up the church aisle as a result."

The lady lifted her face to the stars and sighed, not necessarily a sigh of defeat, but maybe of soul weariness. The conversation had been extraordinary in Tye's experience, not one they could have undertaken in daylight. In the morning, he would resent these confidences from her because they made what he must do to appease his father all the more difficult.

It wasn't morning yet. The moon was rising full over the eastern horizon, and Hester Daniels was becoming a warm, comfortable weight against his side. He didn't think before he acted, he merely indulged in a selfish impulse and scooped her onto his lap.

She fit there nicely, a soft, tired, inconveniently delectable, fragrant bundle of woman to whom life had not been very kind. He knew how that felt, knew what it was like to see options disappearing with nothing to take their places.

He desired her. More than he wanted to be her willing and enthusiastic sexual hobbyhorse, however, he wanted her laughter and confidence restored to her. "Go to sleep, Hester."

She made some little sound of contentment. This wasn't how she'd intended for the evening to go between them, he was sure of that, and it sure as hell didn't fit with his plans either.

Still, for her to fall asleep in his arms was good in a way Tye couldn't put into words. In the moment, holding her soothed and comforted him probably more even than it did her, regardless that this encounter would complicate their breakfast conversation considerably.

After a time, after even the lonely fox had gone silent, Tye carried Hester into the house and up to her bedroom, laid her on her bed, kissed her forehead, covered her with a soft tartan blanket, and withdrew to his room.

❧

"The mail, your ladyship."

Deirdre, Marchioness of Quinworth, eyed the pile of correspondence with misgiving but took the salver from the maid and set it well to the side on the breakfast table.

"Is Quinworth sending you more love letters?"

Sir Neville Pevensy had waited to ask until the maid had departed. He was a handsome fellow who did not care that he was ten years Deirdre's junior, any more than she cared that his affections would always be held first and foremost by his business partner, one Earnest Abingdon, Lord Rutherford.

If Deirdre found it curious that Rutherford had three half-grown children, none of whom resembled their father, well, these things happened in the best of families.

"Hale is a reliable correspondent." Deirdre poured them both more tea, being of the belief that at breakfast, at least, one shouldn't have to guard one's tongue against gossiping servants.

Or servants taking her husband's coin in addition to her own.

"You are very likely the only woman on earth who even knows the old boy's given name. Cream, my dear?"

"Please, and peel me an orange if you wouldn't mind."

He gave her a slow smile, a man who enjoyed a woman comfortable giving orders. "With pleasure. What do you call a reliable correspondent?"

"You are trying to pry confidences from me."

She poured a generous amount of cream into her tea, cream being the best part of the business, then drizzled a skein of honey into her cup as well. Neville watched her do this, and she liked that he watched her.

And had to wonder if that didn't make her just the smallest bit pathetic.

"You're restless," Neville said, starting on an orange. "Your salons are part of what makes Edinburgh a summer destination, your kitchens are the envy of the North, and you've just spent a fortune in Paris on new dresses. And yet, you aren't entirely enjoying yourself."

She wanted to ask him if he treated Rutherford to as careful a study as he made of her, but watched him make short work of the orange instead. A man with competent hands—her husband had competent hands—would always have a certain attractiveness.

"Quinworth's communications follow a pattern. He asks politely if I'd be interested in joining him at this or that house party, claiming that for appearances, we ought occasionally to be seen together."

The scent of oranges blossomed in the cheery breakfast parlor. "He has a point. Your daughters are not married, and cordially distant doesn't mean complete strangers." He passed her a section of orange and appropriated one for himself as well.

"He has a point? Quinworth always has points and sub-points and supporting arguments for his sub-sub-points. When the girls have serious prospects, then I'll swoop in and impersonate a mother hen. Do not hog that entire orange, Neville."

He passed over three more sections and gave her a sleepy, rascally look that did nothing to assuage the ache Deirdre felt for the company of her daughters—and her only surviving son.

"So you tell your husband-his-lordship you've made other plans and he must endure one house party after another all on his own. You're a cruel marchioness."

"I'm a marchioness whose Papa at least made sure she had her own money." She paused to butter a scone, wondering if Papa would be pleased to see his little marchioness now. She was estranged from her husband and son, missing her daughters, and growing old in the company of mostly male acquaintances whose friendship did not abate a loneliness that became more bitter with each year.

"Are you going to stare that butter into submission or put it on your scone, my dear?"

She slapped a pat of butter onto the scone. "When he's fed up with offering casual invitations, Hale resorts to seeking my business advice." She took a bite of scone then passed the rest of it to Neville.

"I ask for your business advice, and then Earnest becomes fascinated with my ingenuity when I quote you."

"Earnest is fascinated with your ingenuity under most circumstances." She took a sip of her tea, wondering if she'd sounded like she were whining—and over a man she'd never wanted to more than kiss, for God's sake.

"My favorite marchioness is out of sorts. Hale must have gone beyond soliciting business advice."

"I provide him business advice in great detail, in my

finest hand, on scented stationery. His next move is usually to demand that I take my place as a proper wife."

"Doesn't the man know you better than that?"

"No, Neville, he does not. I've borne him five children and been married to him for nearly thirty years, and he does not realize that I take a very dim view of men who comport themselves like domestic field marshals." A few months shy of thirty years, but who was counting?

"I will endeavor to keep this in mind." He popped the last section of orange into his mouth, holding her gaze while he chewed, the scamp. "Why did you marry such a blockhead?"

The question was fair, one she'd asked herself many, many times. "He was tall enough."

Neville's elegant, manicured hand stopped midreach toward his tea. "My dear, when prone or supine, a man's height hardly matters."

"I was seventeen years old, you dratted idiot. I wasn't thinking about anybody being supine or prone, I was thinking about waltzing with him. Do you know how desperately a girl who is almost six feet tall longs for a partner worthy of her height?"

"I've wondered why you tolerate my company. Height would never have occurred to me as the *sine qua non* of my many charms."

"Nor humility. Hale had height and a wonderful smile, and his papa was stupid enough to sign the marriage contracts my papa had drawn up. I was besotted with Hale's beautiful manners and his beautiful speeches." Also his beautiful body, but it would be disloyal to Hale to bruit that about. "We had some good years, and whatever else is true, my children are well provided for and welcome in every drawing room."

Neville took a slow, silent sip of tea.

"Just say it, Neville. I consider you a friend."

"What comes after the blustering? When dear Hale finally figures out that blustering and lecturing and cozening aren't going to work, what then?"

"I don't know." She buttered another scone and took a bite lest some uncomfortable truth try to find its way onto the breakfast menu. Neville was a friend, but he was a man, too.

In less than two years, Deirdre would turn fifty years old, an age unthinkable to that girl waltzing around all those ballrooms years—decades—ago. As a wife and marchioness, she'd learned that nobody could make her as angry as Hale; nobody could bring out her stubborn streak as effectively.

And when he stopped lecturing and cozening and blustering, there was nobody whose letters she'd miss more.

She rang for her confidential secretary, bid the man copy the missive, then told him to fold it back up and return it to the sender with a fresh seal of the same colored wax as it bore when delivered—just as she'd done with every other epistle from her stubborn, pigheaded, high-handed husband.

≈∂

"I was hoping Fiona might be free to join me for a short hack this morning." Tye sent the child what he intended as an avuncular smile, and she grinned back at him and started fidgeting in her chair.

"May I go with Uncle, *please*?" She swung a pleading gaze from her aunt to her great-aunt while Tye busied himself with whatever he'd put on his plate.

Anything was preferable to meeting Hester Daniels's eyes after that interlude in the garden last night. Sleep had eluded him for far longer than it should have, and for all the wrong reasons.

"My old bones tell me we're to have rain later today," Lady Ariadne said. "A ride this morning might be just the thing. Hester, you'll accompany them?"

Half a question, half a command, both in the gentle tones of a matriarch whom Tye would have pitted against the late Duke of Wellington—with whom the lady had probably flirted in her younger years.

"You'll want to change into old clothes, Fee." Miss Daniels aimed a tolerant smile at her niece, a much-softer smile than Tye had seen on her even a day ago.

"If you'd like to join us, Miss Daniels, we'd be pleased to have your company." Manners required him to say that. Manners did not require that he watch her mouth when she replied.

"I will let Dolly rest up today and maybe join you tomorrow. Fiona will be on her very best behavior if she has you all to herself."

Even her voice was different, more musical, less clipped and strained. She looked like she'd slept well, too. For which he tried to resent her—unsuccessfully.

Fiona kicked rhythmically at the rungs of her chair. "Then may I please be excused? I have to change my clothes and ask Deal for some carrots and find my boots."

"Look under your bed," Tye suggested, helping

himself to the bite of toast left on Fiona's plate. "When I was a boy, my boots migrated there every time I didn't want to make time to wash the mud off them."

Lady Ariadne smiled while Miss Daniels hid behind her teacup.

"You're excused," Lady Ariadne said. "You might want to wipe off your boots lest you track mud onto your mama's spotless carpets."

The child was off like a shot, leaving a domestic quiet in her wake.

"It's good of you to take her up," Miss Daniels said. "She was used to having three uncles to tag after before her mother married, and everybody at Balfour treated her as a sort of mascot. This isn't a MacGregor property, so her situation has changed some."

"Rowan enjoys frequent exercise, and so do I. She'll be no bother."

This went beyond gentlemanly manners to an outright falsehood, and Miss Daniels let him know it by smiling at him directly.

"Eat your eggs, Spathfoy." Lady Ariadne picked up a buttered toast point. "You'll need your sustenance."

Eggs. Tye glanced at his plate, where several bites of steaming omelet yet remained. He didn't recall serving himself eggs, but then, neither could he recall three consecutive monarchs of the English royal succession when Miss Daniels smiled at him like that.

Fortunately, Fiona came pounding back into the breakfast parlor before Lady Ariadne could abandon Tye in Miss Daniels's exclusive company. He let the child physically tug him from his seat and out to the stables.

"I want to hunt for the fox," she was saying. "I hear

him at night sometimes, and I think, what if he can't find his family? What if he's lonely or homesick?"

Or lust crazed.

"What if his mama signed him up for singing lessons?" Tye shot back. "What if he's practicing his serenades for all the young lady foxes, or what if he's had one pint too many at the local fox pub and he's yodeling his way home?"

"Foxes don't yodel."

"In Switzerland, everybody yodels. They're proud of their yodeling and their cheese. He might be a fox of Swiss ancestry." Tye picked the girl up when they reached the stables and sat her on a pile of clean straw. "You are to sit there and not move until I lead Rowan out to the mounting block, do you understand?"

"Yes, Uncle Tye."

And there she did sit, but ye gods, it seemed the less she moved physically, the more her mind hopped around and her mouth chattered on. What was his favorite bird? Did he know how to yodel? When was he in Switzerland? Her mama and papa might go to Switzerland, because it was near Italy.

By the time Tye had Fiona up on Rowan before him, he realized why the parents of young children wore a perpetually dazed expression. The adult mind was not meant to keep up with such gymnastics. He stopped trying just as Fiona's chatter slowed to an intelligible rate.

"I like Rowan, even though he's not very grown-up."

"Why do you say that?" The gelding was rising five and muscling up quite nicely.

"He's working on his manners. Like there, when he scooted at the puddle? He wasn't sure if he was supposed to say may-I-please or just walk right through it. You're a good boy, Rowan." She whacked him soundly on the neck, but the horse—perverse beast—didn't take umbrage. If Tye had attempted to pet his horse thus, they'd be dancing all the way into Ballater.

"Shall we take a fence, Niece? Rowan particularly enjoys showing off his jumping style."

"Oh, yes, let's!"

She had the natural seat of the very young, and Tye himself enjoyed hopping the stone walls with her up before him. When Rowan had taken enough fences to have worked off some of his energy, Tye brought the horse back to the walk.

"Your father was not very keen on jumping, but he was a great whip."

"My father?"

"Your first father." He didn't want to say her *real* father. Fiona had never met the fellow responsible for her conception—how real could such a man be to her?

"He didn't like jumping on horseback?"

"He learned, eventually, but give him the reins of any vehicle, and he was quite at home. He abhorred the trains, said they'd put the horse out of business."

"What else?"

He was learning to read her little body, to know an eager stillness from a tense one from a relaxed one. She was hungry—nigh starving—for knowledge of her father.

"He liked animals, like you do, and he hated asparagus."

"*I* hate asparagus too. Even with butter and leeks, it's still green and mushy."

They came to a divergence in the path, and Tye took the left fork, away from Ballater. He'd considered making inquiries at the local livery regarding a pony—making them right before his niece's dazzled eyes—but realized he had something even more fascinating than a pony to offer her.

"Shall I tell you a story about when your father was a young boy?"

"Oh, yes! Tell me every story you know, even if my papa came a cropper or got a birching. Children sometimes make mistakes, you know."

"I would never have guessed."

He gave Rowan a loose rein and cast back beyond the difficult years of adolescence to when he and Gordie had still been friends, confidantes, and conspirators. They'd run away together, tippled Papa's brandy together—and gotten sick together as a result—and even tried smoking the old man's cigars when they weren't much older than Fiona.

He could see her getting into the spirits and trying to light cigars without even a sibling to limit her mischief. And while the house went up in flames, her aunts would scold her gently and blame themselves.

"Your father and I once came across a barn cat whose leg had got stuck in a trap," he began. "We knew if your grandfather or the stable lads got wind of it, they'd shoot the thing. Gordie was young— probably about your age—and he thought we could take the animal to the local surgeon."

The surgeon had humored them, and the damned cat

had lived for years on three legs, too. Every time they'd come home from school, Gordie had gone looking for it, feeding it cheese and sneaking it up to their rooms.

"But what did you name the cat?" Fiona asked some minutes later. "He must have had a name?"

She asked for a detail, the kind of detail that would mean a great deal to a child. The kind of detail Tye had long since put from his adult mind.

"I didn't want Gordie to name the cat. I told him when you name things, they mean more."

"My papa named me."

"Your father was sent to Canada before you were born. He could not possibly have named you."

"Yes, he could." Her certainty held an ominous note of impending upset. "He knew my mama was going to have me, and he said if I was a girl, I should have the name Fiona, because it was the prettiest name for a girl. He said if I was a boy, I should be named Lamartine, because it was the name of one of the finest men he knew. My mama told me this, and my papa said it."

The horse had come to a halt while a strange sensation shivered over Tye's skin. "I believe you, Fiona." It seemed they had stories to tell each other. Tye nudged the horse forward.

"So what did my papa name the cat, Uncle Tye?"

He swallowed past the tightness in his throat. "He named her Fiona. Said it was the prettiest name he'd ever heard. She was his favorite, and came to him when he called her name."

Never for Tye though. Not even when he brought the little beast cheese and tried for hours to coax her to his hand.

Five

"YOU TWO WERE GONE MOST OF THE MORNING." Hester watched while Fiona pitched off the big dark horse and into her uncle's waiting arms. "I feared the rain might catch you."

"Aunt Hester!" Fiona charged up and lashed her arms around Hester's waist in the kind of spontaneous display of affection Hester still wasn't accustomed to. "We jumped every stone wall between here and old Clooty MacIntyre's, and Rowan was wonderful. We didn't yodel, though Uncle Tye says there are foxes who yodel in Sweden."

"Switzerland," her uncle corrected, loosening the horse's girth. He ran his stirrups up and brought the reins over the gelding's neck. "And one might consider adopting a more decorous tone of voice, Fiona, lest you scare the hens off their boxes."

Fiona let go of Hester's waist and instead grabbed her hand. "The hens aren't afraid of me. I pet them, and they let me take their eggs most mornings."

Spathfoy passed Rowan's reins off to a stable lad. "You've been petting Rowan, so why don't you hie yourself to the house and wash your hands?"

If Hester had made the suggestion, Fiona would have argued that Rowan was a clean horse and wiping one's hands on the grass would serve just fine and the house was too far away.

The girl pelted up the garden path, and Spathfoy watched her go.

"Fiona claims my horse enjoys hearing stories."

Any animal with ears would enjoy hearing the man talk. "She can be about as subtle as a thunderstorm. My thanks for allowing us a morning of peace and quiet in her absence."

His gaze shifted, taking a visual inventory of Hester. She wore an old high-waisted dress, a floppy straw hat, and gardening gloves.

"I was getting after some of the weeds. Mary Fran has high standards. Aunt Ariadne came out for a bit to supervise."

"She came out to breathe the scent of heather, which I suspect is the secret to her happy old age. Might I hope luncheon will soon be served? Making up stories can leave a man hungry."

He winged his arm at her as he spoke, and Hester took it.

"Now that our guest and the household princess have returned, luncheon will appear in not less than thirty minutes."

They strolled past the very bench where Spathfoy had kissed her the night before. Kissed her and held her in his arms and heard all manner of difficult things from her.

"You should garden more often, Miss Daniels. It puts roses in your cheeks."

She enjoyed the compliment. Didn't look for innuendo in it, didn't suspect it of having false motives. She let his words bring her a smile and then waft away on the gathering breeze.

"I like to dig in the dirt. I hadn't realized this until my father died and I was practically immured in the Kentish countryside for months. Gardening let me escape my mother's eye. Did you have to make up stories for Fiona?"

He gestured to a shady bench. "No, actually. Shall we sit?"

The ease of his invitation warmed Hester's insides agreeably. The morning was still trying to be pretty, though overhead, the clouds were forming into increasingly massive gray banks between shafts of sunshine.

"I told Fiona of her father."

She hadn't expected him to say that. He took a seat beside her, the feel of him on the bench comfortable and comforting. "I'm not sure she knows very much about him, my lord. Mary Fran and Gordie were not well acquainted when Fiona was conceived."

"Gordie wrote to me about Lady Mary Frances. Said he'd encountered a young Scottish goddess."

This was perhaps a confidence, but more likely a reminiscence. "And did your younger brother encounter goddesses often?"

"He encountered women frequently, not goddesses. Mary Frances hasn't tarnished his memory for the child. I'm grateful for that."

And that was neither reminiscence nor confidence, but rather a revelation, probably to him too. "She's very fair-minded, Mary Fran is. Fiona has some of the same quality."

"I told her as many flattering stories about her papa as the time allowed. I'd forgotten some of them myself."

"Was it difficult to speak of your brother?"

They weren't talking about her, they were talking about him, his family, and his role as an uncle. His willingness to do so was intriguing and suggested a trust in her Hester tried to ignore.

"Yes and no. My parents separated shortly after Gordie's death. My father's manner of coping was the proverbial stiff upper lip. His drinking certainly picked up, though."

She wanted to take his hand. "And how did you cope?"

"Not by writing letters to my only niece about her papa's brave boyhood exploits. It was some time before I even knew of Fiona's existence."

A dodge. Hester was surprised he hadn't dodged any sooner in this unusual conversation. "What did you do?"

"I managed my sisters. I dealt with the estates, since his lordship seemed disinclined to do aught but ride his hunters over the property at breakneck paces. The solicitors turned to me as well, and there is no putting those fellows off for long when the press of business is upon them. I suspect the year of mourning is very different for men than it is for women."

"Maybe not. I'm sure Fiona will treasure the stories you gave her. She'll tell them to her children and to her grandchildren."

He was silent for a moment, while a fat bee assayed

the roses one by one. "I have Gordie's old journals.
Someday, Fiona might want to read them."

This was a purely selfless thought, one that confirmed
Spathfoy was by no means as cool and indifferent to
others as his English diction and uncompromising
nose might suggest. Hester slipped off her glove, and
between them, linked her fingers with his.

"You were good to give Fee those stories. No one
else could have done that. They're the kind of stories
my sister will have to tell on me. My parents don't
know those stories, Matthew doesn't know them."

"I felt a little guilty for bringing them up." He did
not take his hand from hers, but his gaze was fixed on
the distant purple hills and the tall crags beyond them.

"Guilty because you'd forgotten them?"

He gave her an odd look. "That too." They
remained thus, hands linked in a peculiar sort of quiet,
until Hester felt a raindrop hit her cheek. Spathfoy
dropped his coat around her shoulders and very properly escorted her into the house.

*

Tye was limited to writing letters, because the staff at
the telegraph office in Ballater was unlikely to keep the
contents of any wires confidential.

And because he was so easily distracted by the
sound of Fiona's little feet thumping down the corridors, or the slow tattoo of Lady Ariadne's cane, he
was limited to writing his letters late at night when the
house had finally gone quiet—though even the quiet
was a maddening kind of distraction.

Riding with Fiona had been intended to foster the

child's trust, to tantalize her with the pleasures she craved most, and it had likely achieved those ends. It had achieved other ends as well, inconvenient, complicated ends, like making Tye aware of Fiona not as a pawn in the ongoing chess match with his father, but as a child who missed her mother.

Tye's sisters missed their mother.

Hell, *he* missed his mother.

Fiona's shameless craving to know more of her father reminded Tye that he was also a man who missed his brother, flawed though the adult fraternal relationship had been. He rose from his desk and went to the window, where a full moon was casting the gardens in silvery shadows. A drink was in order, a nightcap.

Several nightcaps.

He passed through the darkened house quietly, but had to pause at the head of the stairs. A sound disturbed the peace of the old house, a sound from within the walls. He followed that sound into the family wing, pausing outside a closed door.

Lady Ariadne slept downstairs, Miss Hester slept in the guest wing. He tapped on the door. "Child, open this door."

If anything, the weeping became more distinct. Tye pushed the door open and entered Fiona's room. She should have been housed on the higher floor, near if not adjoined to the nursery, though with Lady Ariadne downstairs and Miss Daniels on the opposite side of the house, the family wing was almost as isolated as the nursery.

"Fiona, are you hurt?"

"Yes." She hoo–hoo–hoo'd into her pillow, making Tye regret the impulse that brought him here.

"Is it your foot again?" Stupid question, but he'd ask her a hundred questions to stop her damned racket.

"It's not my f-foot. I want my mama."

She threw herself over on her side and sobbed afresh into her pillow. "I want my m-mama, and my papa, and they're gone, and I don't even know where Berlin or those other places are!"

"For God's sake…" He took a seat on the bed. "See here, child. This won't help."

God help him, he sounded like his father. More than ever.

"Go away. You're *mean*, and I don't have to listen to you."

Back to that. Tentatively, he reached out a hand and tugged one ratty red braid free from where it was creased along her neck. "Sending me away won't make your parents come home sooner."

She lifted her head off the pillow far enough glare at him in the moonlight. "I *know* that, but I *miss* them. They hardly ever write, and I'm stuck here. Uncle Ian and Aunt Augusta never come visit because of that stupid, stinky baby, and they're supposed to help look after me."

"Well, I've come to look after you. Move over."

Fiona moved about two inches left. The little bed creaked under his weight as Tye shifted to lean back against the headboard.

He got out his handkerchief. "I went to public school when I was about your age, you know."

"Is that where you learned to talk like the Wrath of God?"

She allowed him to wipe the tears from her face, then caught his hand and held the handkerchief to her nose while she honked.

"I do not speak like the Wrath of God." He folded the handkerchief and set it aside. "One doesn't dare cry in public school. All the fellows will make his life miserable if he does."

They made the first formers' lives miserable in any case.

She stirred around in her blankets until, after a sharp little elbow had dug into his ribs, she was budged against Tye's side. "But you got to go and *see* things, you got to do more than collect eggs and ramble to the burn, and wait for your uncles to come visit."

"I got to memorize more useless Latin than most children know English. I got my eyes blacked by the older boys. I was punished for things they did, and I missed my bro—"

"You missed my papa. I miss him too."

It was on the tip of his tongue to say that she couldn't possibly miss a man she'd never met, but Tye was beginning to get the knack of being not just an uncle, but *her* uncle.

"It's all right to miss him, Fiona. He would have loved to have known you."

"Mama says he was handsome."

This observation held a plea.

"He was damned good looking, and you are not to tattle on me for swearing. I'm stating a simple truth."

"Uncle Ian says it's not swearing to call them the damned English or the damned taxes. What did my father look like?"

The same queer feeling he'd experienced out riding with her washed over him again. He knew what his father looked like. He knew what Quinworth sounded like, knew the scent of his cigars, the way he studied his wineglass while the blessing was said over the evening meal.

Fiona knew none of these things regarding her progenitor, and that was arguably Tye's fault.

"I have a picture of him with me. I'll show it to you in the morning."

She bolted to a sitting position. "You have a painting of *my papa*? I want to see it now. I've never seen a picture of him. Does he look like me?"

She was scrambling across Tye as she spoke, digging knees into his shins and bringing to mind more swearing.

"It's the middle of the night, child. This can wait until morning."

"He's my papa. I want to see him now."

She stood there in her nightgown, a thick red braid coming undone over each shoulder, impending hysterics framing every line of her form. Her lips trembled with it, her shoulders quivered, and her tightly clenched little fists promised a great, noisy outburst in the very next instant.

"Come along then." He rose off the bed and took her by the hand. "And don't be complaining to me if you catch your very death, running about at all hours without your slippers."

"My slippers are under the bed." She wrenched free of his grasp, darted forth, and held them up.

"Give those to me." He snatched them from her and knelt to put them on her feet. "You will return to bed when I've shown you the portrait, do you understand?"

"Yes, Uncle Tye." She seized his hand and dragged him toward the door. "I'll go right to bed, and I won't bother you again tonight. I won't bother anybody. In the morning, may I see the picture again?"

She didn't require an answer. The entire length of the house, she blathered on about her good-looking, handsome papa, who was a brave soldier for Her Majesty and danced so very wonderfully at the regimental ball that Mama let him kiss her, and then they got married.

Kiss, indeed. But at least Fiona's mother hadn't burdened the child with less attractive truths—not yet.

Quinworth might not be so careful of the child's sensibilities regarding his view of her mother. Tye paused outside his door and looked down at Fiona where she smiled up at him. Trust shone out of her eyes, trust and hope and all manner of things that had Tye dropping her hand and pushing the door open.

"The portrait is in my traveling satchel. Are your hands clean?"

"I took my bath. Aunt Hester would skin me alive if I got my sheets dirty because I skipped my bath."

Aunt Hester would pat the girl on the head and murmur the mildest reproach. Tye rummaged in his bag and withdrew three small framed pictures. He passed the first one to her. "That's your papa."

She snatched it up and brought it to her face. "Why isn't he smiling?"

"His eyes are smiling, but to have a photograph made, one must sit still for a very long time, and facial expressions are discouraged as a result."

"You can't move at all?"

"If you do, it makes the image blurry. I think you can see a resemblance between you and your papa, around the chin and jaw."

She padded over to his dressing stand and peered at herself in the mirror, then back at the image of her father. "He *is* handsome. Mama wasn't saying that just to be nice."

Which suggested the girl suspected her mother had been diplomatic in some other regards. "I have two other pictures you might want to see." He hadn't planned to show these to her, but the moment seemed convenient.

"Is it a picture of you? I'd like a picture of you." She kept her father's portrait in her hand and came back to Tye's side.

"These are your paternal aunts. That's Dora, Mary Ellen, and Joan. Joan has red hair like you."

"I like Joan. She looks like you."

"She's quite tall, too, and loves to be out-of-doors. She likes painting and designing dresses, of all things."

She shot him a curious look. "Do you paint?"

"Not like she can. These are my parents, which makes them your grandparents." It was the most flattering image Tye had of his father, either photographic or hand drawn. His lordship was standing with one hand on his seated wife's shoulder. Their expressions showed a rare, congenial moment between them. Mama had insisted on being seated, lest her height be unnecessarily obvious, and his lordship had indulged her.

For once.

Fiona studied the image with the intensity she

did everything else. "My grandda looks like you too. Grandmama is very pretty, but not as old as Aunt Ariadne."

"Not nearly." The older Tye got, the more aware he became that his mother was only eighteen years his senior.

He didn't want to take the picture out of Fiona's hand, but neither did he want her up half the night staring at it. "You may borrow the portrait of your father for the night. Do not put it under your pillow, or you'll break the glass framing it."

"I can keep it?"

"You may borrow it."

She hunched up her shoulders and clutched the small picture to her skinny chest, her face suffused with joy. "I won't break it, Uncle Tye. Not ever."

He was about to point out to her that a loan until morning would afford no opportunities for "not ever," but he became aware of movement by his open door.

"Fiona, are you keeping your uncle up past his bedtime?"

Miss Daniels stood in his doorway, clad in an elegantly embroidered green silk nightgown and wrapper. On her feet, incongruously, were a sturdy pair of gray wool socks, and her hair hung over her right shoulder in a single shiny plait.

"Aunt, I have seen the very best thing *ever*. Uncle Tye has a picture of my papa." Fiona scampered over to her aunt and held out the miniature. She did not give it up to her aunt's possession even temporarily.

"My, what a good-looking fellow he was." Miss Daniels sank to her knees so she and the child could gaze at the good-looking fellow together. "I especially like the merriment in his eyes, as if he knew happy secrets he was just bursting to tell somebody."

Tye closed his eyes, trying not to picture his brother's expression of suppressed glee. Gordie had had charm, about that there was no dispute.

"I look like him," Fiona announced. "Uncle Tye said."

"Yes, I can see a resemblance. You must thank your uncle for showing you this. It was very considerate of him."

"Uncle said I may have it until tomorrow morning."

"I believe the term used was borrow, but as morning fast approaches, perhaps I'd better rethink my offer."

Fiona turned her body half away from him, the portrait held out of his sight. "It's hardly even nighttime, and the moon is still up. I'm going to bed now."

She shot between the two adults, leaving her aunt kneeling on the floor and a silence where a child had stood a moment before. Tye crossed the room and extended a hand down to Miss Daniels.

"My apologies if we woke you."

She came to her feet gracefully, her small, warm hand in his providing a curious blend of comfort and upset. To see her thus, ready for bed, her hair hanging in a gilded braid, those ugly socks on her feet... Tye's heart sped up, and the blood began pooling in inconvenient, ungentlemanly locations.

Which would never do. "May I see you back to your door, Miss Daniels?"

And still, he did not release her hand.

❧

Spathfoy looked tired and a little frazzled, probably from dealing with Fiona on a bad night. Unfortunately for Hester's composure, the Earl of Spathfoy tired and a little frazzled had a particular appeal.

As did the Earl of Spathfoy holding forth at breakfast.

And the Earl of Spathfoy in a contemplative mood under the stars.

And the Earl of Spathfoy demonstrating casual equestrian mastery over his unruly young horse.

She went up on her toes and kissed him. He was tall enough that he might have evaded her sally, but instead he stood slightly bent toward her, though very still, as if he wasn't sure if his brain had heard his mouth aright.

"I don't especially like you sometimes," she said. "Though other times, like when you're being so kind to Fee, I more than like you. I am coming to realize that liking and attraction do not necessarily go hand in hand."

Solemn green eyes blinked at her. "You are determined on more ill-advised behavior."

"Not determined, perhaps spontaneously tempted." She permitted herself to breathe in through her nose, to make an olfactory treat of his clean, floral fragrance. "I came over here to rescue you from Fiona, and now…"

"Who shall rescue me from you? Has it occurred to you, Miss Daniels, *you* might need rescuing from *me*?"

He was adorable when he tried to bluster. She added that to a growing list of things she had to admit she liked about him. "You would never force a woman."

He wouldn't have to.

"I might pick one up bodily and carry her back to her own room, then shut her door very firmly, return to my own chambers, and lock my door against her further invasions. My gentlemanly resolve goes only so far, Miss Daniels, and I've already told you that placing your trust in me is bound to end in disappointment."

He thought *disappointment* was going to dissuade her?

"Duly noted, your lordship." Was all this chatter on his part supposed to make her more determined? For that was the effect it had on her. She cupped his jaw, let the tension of it seep into her fingers. "I did not look for this attraction to you either, but ignoring it doesn't make it go away. Wasting it seems unthinkable."

"*Nothing* makes it go away." He muttered this last a quarter inch from her mouth, so she could feel the way the words shaped his breath and taste the frustration in his voice.

"Nothing you've tried so far, in any case." Hester put them both out of their respective miseries and pressed her mouth to his. She might have been content to explore him lazily, to let the kiss build as some of their previous kisses had built—slowly, wonderfully, terribly—but his arms came around her, mooring her tightly to his body. He widened his stance and growled as his mouth opened over hers.

And it was *heaven*, to be held and kissed by a man who knew exactly what he was about. A man sturdy enough in body and masculinity that Hester could let go of everything—propriety, thought, physical balance—and kiss him back.

"I love your hair." She spoke against his neck, which tasted of soap and lavender. "I love your height."

"Hush." He loved her mouth on his, apparently, seeking his kisses and his tongue and every oral detail of him she could lap up. She arched into his embrace, reveling in his height, because it meant she had nearly to climb him to get closer.

"Miss—Hester, for God's sake." He trapped her hands behind her back and rested his forehead against hers. "Do you seek your own ruin?"

He was breathing heavily. So was she.

"I *am* ruined. Merriman has seen to this, but if I'm going to be ruined, I want to *know*."

"One unfortunate encounter does not a lady ruin."

She did not point out that by his reasoning, she should be entitled to at least one lapse with him, then. "Jasper has put it about that he was sampling used goods, and eager used goods. I did not understand how any woman could be eager for that... poking business, but with you, I think I could."

"You could...?"

"Be eager. I can't seem to be anything but eager."

"For God's—" He brought her hands up, kissed each palm, and looped her arms around his neck. "My dear woman, if you were any more eager, I'd be lying on the floor, thoroughly ravished. The male mind boggles to consider such a thing."

The thread of amusement in his voice encouraged her.

"I apparently can't help myself around you, Spathfoy. I find your attractiveness unlikely and inconvenient, but undeniable."

This ought to have given him a little purchase on his lamentable resistance, ought to have put him a bit off. But no, Hester realized as he draped his arms around her shoulders and rested his chin on her crown. He was male, and that she was reluctant, even in theory, piqued his interest.

"How will you bear to look at me over breakfast, Hester? I've been to all the house parties. I know how to be cordial and flirtatious the next day without it meaning a thing. Despite what Merriman wants you to think of yourself, you are innocent."

He was a good man, to try so hard to dissuade her. Hester had suspected this; she only hoped he wasn't *too* good. "I managed breakfast this morning, didn't I?"

He was quiet as he held her, and Hester could feel two things. First, she could feel his mind doing some sort of emotional gymnastics, vaulting between the dictates of traditional honor—which would have him tossing her bodily into her own room, as threatened—and the whispered suggestions of opportunity, lust, and maybe even of a different kind of honor.

"Here is our dilemma," he said, his hands moving slowly over her back. Hester liked that it was *our* dilemma. "If I take you to bed and avail myself of your charms, I am a cad and a bounder, regardless that you endorse such behavior. Nonetheless, you are in the grip of misguided female notions about proving something to yourself, and one doesn't speak reason to a lady on such a course. If I send you on your eager, misguided way, you will be disappointed and emboldened to try again, if not with me, then with some other man who might not be at all considerate of you."

He fell silent while Hester focused her awareness on the second thing she could feel.

His erection, big, hard, and intriguing against her belly. Maybe he was allowing her to experience his arousal in an effort to bring her to her senses; maybe he was so wrapped up in his philosophical debate, he didn't realize how closely he was holding her.

She rocked her hips forward.

He did not shift away.

"If you get into my bed, Hester, there will be no undoing it, no taking it back in the morning. You'll know, and I'll know, and I promise you, there will come a time when we'll wish we hadn't. We will both wish we hadn't."

"Stop talking." She anchored her hand in his hair and went up on her toes again to kiss him. Men this size should come with a mounting block if they were going to be so shy about receiving kisses. "I live with regret well enough."

When he kissed her back this time, it was different. Slower and *hotter* somehow. He'd reasoned his way to some conclusion that allowed him at least to kiss her, to insinuate his tongue into her mouth and his hands around her derriere.

"Spathfoy, I want—"

"Tye."

"Tye." She tried it out against his throat. "Tiberius Flynn." He was going to be her lover, and he had a name, not just a title. It was a good, substantial name, imposing, like his kisses—and his erection.

She knew a moment of doubt, even as she subsided against him. "Blow out the candles, please."

Laughter rumbled in his chest. "Don't you want to see the prize you've captured, Hester?"

She did, but knowing him, that would mean he'd expect reciprocal privileges. She felt his chin on the top of her head again, a comforting weight that let her know exactly where he was in a way his arms around her did not.

"Now, she falls silent. Come." He stepped back and encircled her wrist with one hand. They went on a short progress about the room, with him blowing out all the candles but the one nearest the bedside.

"Do you know, Hester, if you asked me to blow out this last candle, I would?"

She found she did not want him to, though his offer was consideration itself. "You'd proceed in complete darkness?"

"For your modesty, or your courage. And listen to me when I tell you, every man you seek to intimately accost should be willing to do likewise for you. He should let you bind him, blindfold him, or keep your clothes on while you remove his."

His voice had gotten very stern, leaving Hester torn between pleasure that he was protective of her and irritation that he'd lecture her about future lovers when she hadn't properly availed herself of him first.

And *bindings*? "You'll let me undress you?"

He dropped her wrist and gave her a smile of such riveting sensuality Hester felt the heat of it on her skin. "I did imply that very thing, my dear, and I would love to undress you."

The game was on, the game Hester had campaigned and pleaded for. She'd lain in wait for him, ambushed him in the garden, accosted him in his own room—his word was appropriate, she didn't flinch from it—and now she had no idea what to do, didn't know the rules, didn't know what would constitute victory or defeat.

He took a step closer. "Or you can watch while I undress for your pleasure."

Oh, *God*. She would stare him directly in the eye over breakfast, lunch, and dinner, but she was going to have to cover her ears.

That *voice*. It was the same beautiful, masculine voice, but grown naughty and lazy with innuendo, and so intimate it ricocheted through Hester's body to land burning at the feet of her reason.

"Or," she said, resisting mightily the urge to unbutton his shirt, "you can stand about listing possibilities all night." And she could listen to him, too.

His smile shifted into a sweet, wicked curve of his lips that lit all manner of mischief in his eyes. And while he smiled, his elegant, nimble fingers went to the fastening of his trousers and stilled.

Hester's mouth went dry, and she was unable to look away from his hands, hovering over the bulge in his trousers—the sizable bulge.

He caressed himself once, then set about taking off his shirt. She tried to swallow and managed to blink. "You're teasing me."

"Turnabout, my dear. If you'd like to get into bed, I won't stop you."

He was daring her, or perhaps giving her dignity and self-possession a reprieve. The bed was only a few steps away, though on her unsteady knees, it seemed a long journey indeed.

Spath—*Tye*—lifted her into his arms, carried her up the steps to the bed, and laid her on the mattress.

Such gallantry restored a measure of her confidence. The earl—*Tye*—would be kind in bed and generous, even in his arrogance. He would know exactly what to do when she knew nothing, and he'd share his knowledge without her having to ask. This was part of what she needed from him, and that he'd understood it better than she had was reassuring.

So reassuring, she shamelessly watched him when he moved to lock the bedroom door, shed his shirt, and crossed to the washstand.

She lay on the bed and watched while he washed his face and hands and then under his arms. He was unself-conscious about his ablutions, as if demonstrating for Hester exactly how intimate they would be. He used his tooth powder while she watched too, and though his behavior would have been the same if she hadn't been sitting on the bed, she sensed he was every bit as aware of her as she was of him.

Which was very aware indeed.

"You might want to take off your wrapper and nightgown," he said, crossing the room to sit on the bed. "Sometimes, delicate apparel can get torn when it comes between me and a lady in my bed." His set his boots beside the bed, exposing big, stockinged feet.

Hester felt as if she were observing one revelation after another: the hair of his armpits, the way he leaned over the washbasin to rinse his mouth after brushing his teeth, the movement of skin over his rib cage as he prowled up to the bed.

All new, and all wonderful, if vaguely worrisome too.

He was allover defined muscle and sinew, a body sculpted by ceaseless activity, good nutrition, and masculine pursuits. As he bent forward to strip off his socks, Hester watched the play of muscle and bone along his spine.

She wanted to touch each knob and bump of his backbone, wanted to press her hand over his shoulder blades to feel what it meant bodily when all that power moved this way or that.

"Has the cat got your tongue, my girl, or are you planning my downfall?"

He stood, and without giving her a chance to reply, started unfastening his trousers. He shoved them off his hips, taking down trousers and underclothes in the same movement and stepping free of them as easily as Hester would have shoved a few pins into her hair.

He tossed his clothing onto a chair with unerring aim and then stood beside the bed, gazing down at her, his fists propped on his hips.

"Somebody has on more clothes than somebody else, far more clothes than the situation calls for. Are you having second thoughts, Hester?"

Naked, naked, naked. He spoke coherently even when naked. He managed a very credible taunt when naked. Hester wasn't sure she could speak at all when *he* was without clothing. How on earth was she to manage when he had *her* in the same condition?

She reached out a hand to touch his torso. "You are... undressed."

He was magnificent. The skin over his ribs was warm and smooth, with a trail of dark hair arrowing down from his chest to his groin. When she realized she was staring at *that* part of him, she jerked her gaze north, to the muscled expanse of his chest.

He leaned forward, over her. She thought—she hoped—he was going to kiss her.

"Shall I blow out the candle, Hester Daniels?"

He made it a dare, and though she was flat on her back, she tried for a taller posture. "You shall not. Get in this bed, Spath—Tiberius. I find your chatter boring."

This amused him. His lips split into that wicked smile to reveal teeth and a good deal of masculine tolerance. He was going to *humor* her, which meant at some point he might stop humoring her. *What on earth had she gotten herself into?*

He climbed across her and lay on his back on top of the covers. "Mind you take care with my sensitive parts, but touch me. Touch me all you like. Never say I allowed a lady to be bored when I might amuse her."

Resting there in her thick socks, nightgown, and wrapper, Hester felt sufficiently armored to take him at his word. She shifted to put the flat of her palms on the solid plane of his belly. His erection twitched, brushing the underside of her arm.

She closed *her* eyes, the better to focus on the warm, hair-dusted male skin beneath her hands. She leaned in and caught a whiff of him, paused and took a deliberate sniff, only to feel the palm of his hand come up to cradle the back of her head.

He didn't move, didn't direct her explorations in any manner, but for him to touch her like that closed a tactile circle between them. It put both of them in that bed, put both of them on this different and fascinating ground.

"There's no rush, Hester. We have all night."

A new note in his voice, not taunting, not pronouncing immutable truths, but offering something. More reassurance? *Himself?*

She rested her face against the hard shelf of his chest, took a swipe of him with her tongue. He tasted clean with a hint of lavender soap. She did it again and felt a tension leave his body. His hand was still palming her nape, so she rolled her head on her shoulders to feel his touch more intensely.

He captured her hand and moved it down to settle her fingers over the base of his erection. "Touch me, Hester. I certainly intend to touch you."

Another warning, one that told her she was keeping her clothes on only at his sufferance, at his whim. She could be tied naked to this bed and blindfolded if he chose, but he was allowing her to do the choosing.

The enormity of the trust involved began to seep through her arousal. This wasn't going to be some hurried, fumbling interlude with clothes pushed aside, the library door locked, and the curtains hastily closed on an otherwise lovely day.

This wasn't going to be quickly over once she realized what a mistake she'd made.

And for that reason, it *wasn't* a mistake. She feathered her thumb over a flat male nipple—what an odd texture.

He arched into her hand. The movement was slight but telling.

"You, sir, like this." She watched his face as his eyes opened, his gaze so alert it felt as if he'd been staring at her even with them closed. In addition to damnable quantities of English self-possession, a prodigious vocabulary, and an excellent seat when mounted, Tiberius Flynn had an ample store of hedonistic tendencies.

And—of all things—a well-hidden streak of generosity.

"More to the point, Hester Daniels, *you* like this."

Not an accusation, but a restatement of his priority when she was in his bed. She smiled at him, knelt up at his hip, and used both thumbs on both nipples. "They change when I touch them."

"As yours will when I touch you."

Her puzzlement must have shown on her face. Her nipples puckered when cold; she'd casually observed this and decided it wasn't unusual, though one could hardly ask anybody about such a thing.

He rested his hand on her thigh, giving her a moment to prepare, and then she watched while that big, knowing hand slid inside her wrapper and came to rest over her breast.

Through the cotton of her nightgown, she felt warmth from his touch and a coursing sort of lightness through her body. Jasper had been so rough, grabbing at her as if he were testing the ripeness of fruit at a shop of questionable quality. He'd hurt her dignity as well as her body, and for the first time, Hester could feel directly the residual anger his mistreatment of her had left behind.

Thoughts of Jasper evaporated as Spathfoy's hand closed gently on her breast. "Breathe, love. If you faint, I want it to be from pleasure."

His arrogance again, but what a lovely way to be arrogant. She wasn't angry at that moment; she was instead grateful to share a bed with Spathfoy, grateful for his confidence and even his arrogance.

Hester put her hand over his, the better to experience the sensations he gave her. As she drew in an unsteady breath, their hands rode the lift and fall of her chest.

How... marvelous. She breathed again and let her head fall back, surrendering the timing of this education to him. He closed his free hand around the hand she'd let drift to her side and brought her palm to rest over his genitals.

Another circle, a circle of pleasure, trust, and desire. She did not open her eyes, but traced her fingers along the warm, smooth length of his member. Jasper hadn't allowed her this either, not the luxury of time to explore, not the gracious sharing of bodily knowledge.

Another increment of Hester's ire dissipated as Spathfoy drew her fingers over the crown of his erection, the skin so oddly smooth. "I'm most sensitive here," he said, "but I can't imagine a way you could touch me that wouldn't bring pleasure."

She was to pleasure him, which opened up universes of possibilities, wonderful, daring, bold... *The trust went both ways*. This was a revelation of such magnitude, Hester had to scoot down and hide her face against his chest. He let go of her breast and encircled her shoulders with his arms.

Hester straddled him, and between their bodies, closed her fingers around the hard shaft of his *membrum virile*. She knew the proper name for that part of him. Tye could probably tell her a dozen terms for it, each naughtier than the last.

"Hester?"

"I'm all right." She was so much better than that. Edges inside her mind grown jagged with self-doubt and recrimination were being smoothed over; places in her body left aching with regret were easing.

And she still hadn't even taken off her nightgown. She lifted off his chest and shrugged out of the wrapper, feeling the fabric fall down her bare arms in a sensuous caress.

He lay on his back, resplendently naked by candlelight, resplendently erect, simply watching her. His gaze on her body was another caress, but she lacked the courage to be as exposed as he was.

Spathfoy apparently understood this. "Come here." He held up one arm, implying that she was to cuddle against his side. She went willingly, though when he hiked her knee across his thighs, she was taken a little aback. "For such a bold woman, you are surprisingly shy, Hester."

He sounded puzzled rather than disapproving. Just when she thought they might get into a contest of vocabulary—comparing "shy" and "reserved" for example—he shifted so her leg was hiked up over his hip, and he was on his side, looming over her while she lay mostly on her back.

How had he done that?

He peered down at her. "But not too shy."

She didn't bother forming a reply. Instead she drew her fingers along the architecture of his jaw, caressed the strong bones and lean muscle that created a sense of resolution and strength in his countenance. He caught her hand, kissed her palm, and set her fingers on his chest.

And his mouth on hers.

Kissing him was a relief of tremendous magnitude. When he settled his lips over hers, Hester felt as if a current ran between them, everywhere they touched. A current that had been damming up inside her body since she'd first laid eyes on him.

And perhaps in his body as well.

He was good at this. He could kiss and go plundering with his hand at the same time. Into her hair, to anchor her head on the pillow, down her arm, to squeeze her fingers gently, and then up her rib cage to... there.

Through the fabric of her nightgown, he teased her nipple to an aching peak, then covered the fullness of her breast with his hand. She moved into the caress, used her leg around his hips to pull herself closer to him, confident in the knowledge that her desire was a precious, wonderful thing to him. On that liberating thought, she hitched closer still.

And felt his erection against her belly.

"Kiss me, Hester."

She needed the reminder, because his intimate flesh was that distracting, that fascinating. She opened her mouth for him, welcoming his questing tongue, savoring him, and letting him tease her into exploring his mouth as well. When he pulled back and grazed his nose over her eyebrows, she fisted a hand in his hair and manually ordered him to resume his attentions to her mouth.

He smiled against her lips, a lovely sensation, but one that suggested he wasn't as absorbed in what they were doing as she was. Hester ran her hand down his torso and closed her grip around his shaft.

Only to feel his hand on her bare torso.

"My nightgown—" Somehow, he'd untied the bows down the front.

"Hush. Kiss me."

He plied her breast with exquisite focus, even as his mouth tried to distract her from those breathtaking sensations of pressure and want—and pleasure. She shifted her hold of him while he peeled her fingers loose from his member and set them on her own breast. Was the skin on the underside of her breast as soft as the crown of his male part? What that what he was showing her?

"Tiber—"

His touch delved lower, until he was teasing his fingers through the curls shielding her sex. She gave up on speech altogether, gave up on trying to figure out how she ought to touch him, gave up on thinking.

"Part your legs a little for me."

She did not give up on listening, but had to push back a wave of self-consciousness to comply.

"Yes." He set his palm over her sex, which should have been an act of dominion, except it wasn't. His hand brought warmth and a vague sort of relief, but frustration too.

Even when she said not a word, he heard her body's needs. This time when he kissed her, there was nothing coy or teasing about it. He consumed her with his mouth, using his tongue to set up a slow, sinuous rhythm Hester felt beneath the pit of her stomach.

"Move for me, Hester."

He glossed his fingers over her sex, his touch delicate and yet assured. The touch came again, slightly different, higher. Jasper hadn't touched her like this, hadn't done more than pummel her body with his own while he told her to hold still and be quiet.

She could not hold still; she had to move against that knowing male hand. Her hips flexed, and Spathfoy growled into her mouth. "Yes, like that. Again."

As he fell silent, Hester felt music start up in her body. With his hand and his mouth and even the pressure of his chest along her side, Spathfoy started a drumbeat of wanting in Hester's veins that ran hotter and hotter while his fingers kept up the same steady, teasing caress.

She should be touching him; she should be asking him what all this was in aid of; she should be… breathing.

The last was all Hester could manage. Though she knew the bed was solid beneath her, she felt behind her closed eyes as if she were suspended over some great chasm, her balance no longer her own but entirely dependent on the man touching her so intimately.

"Let go, Hester. I've got you."

Let…?

Her body understood. When pleasure coalesced into convulsions of soul-scorching ecstasy, she clung to him, flailed herself hard against his hand, and felt him slip two long, male fingers deep into her heat.

Bliss and bliss and more bliss deluged her, and he moved those fingers to ensure the flood did not recede until Hester was panting, her fingers manacled around his wrist, her body a foreign and thoroughly pleasured feminine territory she'd never inhabited before.

He understood about this part too, for which

Hester nearly loved him. He did not slip his hand free of her body, wipe it on a handkerchief, and climb on top of her. She could not have protested if he had.

"Hush, now," he murmured in her ear. He gathered her close, rested his chin on her temple, and trapped her leg between his two. When she pressed her cheek against his chest, she could hear his heart and feel it too. They lay like that, entwined, breathing in synchrony, as feelings rioted through Hester in silence.

Tiberius Flynn was arrogant, but also generous, kind, affectionate, considerate, attentive, and... two more words came to Hester's mind as she panted against his throat. First, Tye was *decent* in a gentlemanly sense that one had to be naked with him to understand, and second, he was *lovable* in the sense that a woman could find many reasons to esteem and desire him greatly.

And the man who'd just given her such indescribable pleasure, and who was holding her so tenderly, was also himself yet unsated. According to Jasper, men needed to spend regularly if dire bad health wasn't to result, but then, Jasper had apparently known next to nothing.

Oh, how that realization pleased her. She kissed Spathfoy's breastbone, wishing she could tell him, but lacking the courage. Then, too, there was his male member, hard, warm, and lying between their bodies as a rampant reminder that she had not provided him the pleasure he'd showered on her.

"Spath—Tiberius?"

"Tye."

"Are you all right?"

❧

"I'm fine."

Tye silently chided himself for having graduated from dissembling to outright lying. "Just catch your breath, hmm?" He buried his nose in her silky hair and wondered when a plan to scare her back into possession of her common sense had transformed into a burning need to cover her naked body with his own.

And when had that plan—perhaps understandable, if not excusable under the circumstances—shifted to a craving to bring her pleasure and comfort?

"But this?" She brushed her fingers over the head of his erection. "It can't be very comfortable." She let go of his cock but smoothed her hand down his chest and lapped at his nipple—for God's perishing sake.

He caught her hand in his own and brought her knuckles to his mouth for a lingering kiss. Where the resolve to leave the bed, pour himself a drink, and make light of the situation ought to be, he found a stubborn unwillingness to hurt her feelings to quite that degree.

She hadn't been a virgin, and yet she was still an innocent.

A passionate innocent, and Tye was only a human man.

He wrapped her hand about his cock, and then set his hand around hers. "This way, nobody risks conception. Every schoolboy becomes proficient at it if he isn't to lose his reason."

He fell silent, the pleasure of her hand on him eclipsing his ability to explain. She wasn't shy either, accepting the firmness of the grip he preferred and giving him the exact rhythm he demonstrated.

And she had the knack of slipping her hand over the head of his cock just loosely enough to make his breath catch in his throat. His hand fell away, and she didn't falter. "Don't stop."

She didn't. Of all times for her to turn up biddable, now Hester Daniels did exactly as he'd directed her. For long moments, he withstood the siren call of pleasure, hanging suspended over a cauldron of erotic sensations: Hester's hand on his swollen cock, the warm weight of her body plastered to his side, her leg flung over his hips, and the way the scent of her winding into Tye's brain became the scent of every pleasure he'd ever forbidden himself.

"Hester—" He'd meant to tug her hand away, to finish himself, but she gripped him tighter, wonderfully tighter, and it pushed him beyond the call of volition. Between their bodies his seed spurted, his body seizing with the force of his satisfaction. His ears roared, his mind went blank, and when he could next claim to have awareness of anything save pleasure, he was breathing like a bellows, his arm lashed around Hester, and his cock trapped between their naked bodies.

When he could recall how to form words, he tried to speak. "I've made quite a m—"

She didn't lift her head from his shoulder, but she put her hand—bearing his intimate scent—over his mouth. "You hush. Catch your breath."

How in the hell did a woman become so quickly attuned to the man who was supposed to be much more experienced than she was?

Who *was* much more experienced?

He shut up and subsided into her embrace. Yes,

he'd made the predictable, inconvenient, indelicate mess on their bellies. Yes, he'd completely failed in his plan to shock Hester back to her own room, permanently cured of boldness where he was concerned. And yes again, he'd failed utterly to control his own attraction to her.

But she was right. He needed to catch his breath, to locate his reason, recollect his duty—honor being a sketchy concept under the circumstances—and to forget for all time the sensation of her soft wool sock brushing provocatively across his arse as he gave himself up to soul-deep pleasure in her arms.

❦

"Where are you going?" Hester tightened her arms around Spathfoy. He was strong enough to break her hold, of course—he was strong enough to break her neck—but he paused in his flight from the bed.

"We are untidy, my dear." He kissed her temple, and this time she let him go. They were untidy—sticky, at least, and there was musk hanging in the air Hester found more fascinating than unpleasant. Her body was still humming with the revelations she'd experienced in Spathfoy's arms, leaving her both languorous and energized.

Pleased with herself—also pleased with *him*—and curious about what other aspects of the dealings between men and women she'd been kept in ignorance of.

"Lie back." Spathfoy approached the bed, a damp cloth in his hand. "The only water to be had is cold. I do apologize."

His torso glistened with dampness, and his skin was red where he'd scrubbed himself clean. He was gentle but brisk with her, swabbing her belly with no more sexual innuendo than if he'd been grooming his horse. And then he sat on the bed, regarding her where she lay in her opened nightgown and wool socks.

"What a picture I must make." She tried to bring the side of the nightgown closed over her naked body, but his hands stopped her. He leaned down, pressing his face to her midriff.

"You are beautiful, Hester Daniels. Never doubt it. Never." He kissed her sternum and laid his cheek over her heart, an oddly submissive posture from a man Hester wouldn't think capable of such a gesture. She settled her hands in his hair, reflecting that she'd learned a great deal from him in the past hour, not the least of which related to the man himself.

"Is there a name for that messy business?"

He stayed where he was, though he might have smiled against her skin. She liked the weight of him on her chest, liked the feel of his hair in her fingers, his breath on her skin.

"Onanism, casting one seed's upon the ground, to use the scriptural reference."

"I've wondered what the passage meant. It made sense to me as a girl that seed should be cast upon the ground."

"There are other names for it, some of them vulgar."

He seemed in no hurry to leave her embrace, which was perfectly acceptable to her. Maybe he even sensed she needed this time to steady her nerves and appease her curiosity. "Is it the same term when you do it to me?"

He raised his head. "You can do it to, or for, yourself, madam. The more genteel term is masturbate, from the Latin *masturbari*, of the same meaning."

"We've sinned in Latin. I'm impressed. Maybe that's why it felt so marvelous." Though she suspected it had felt so marvelous because he'd been the one responsible for her pleasure. "And what, if I may ask, is the proper term for—" She frowned and kissed his hair. "That lovely business, inside my body."

"The French call it *la petite mort*, which will serve."

"But there are less genteel terms?" She wanted to know them. Wanted to hear the less genteel terms from a man who could spout Latin when naked and make it sound beautiful and imposing.

"Coming. When pleasure overwhelms you, you come, or I bring you off. Move over." He extricated himself from her arms and climbed onto the bed. She moved over, finally casting the nightgown to the bottom of the bed. This earned her a smile as Spathfoy lay back beside her.

She treated herself to the sensation of his lean, warm, naked length all along her body, then tucked her leg across his torso, which put her sex in close proximity to his hip.

"Comfy, Miss Daniels?"

"Not quite. I like it when you hold my foot."

"You will not avail yourself of my nipples, if you please. They are overly appreciative of your touch."

"Yes, your lordship." She rubbed her cheek over one of these overly appreciative parts and sighed with the wonder of him. "How can you sound so unassailably proper when you're not wearing a stitch and I'm not either?"

"You are proud of yourself for this accomplishment." He took her foot in a lovely, firm grasp about the arch. "Well you should be."

"Good. If you'd scolded me, I might have started laughing."

"I need to scold myself. I have no business allowing you into my bed, Hester."

She wanted to bite him, to grab him by his now-curiously-unassuming male member and make him shut up. "And yet, here I am. You can't undo this, Tiberius Flynn, you can't take it back. I have that on the very best, most certain authority."

He fell silent, which was better than if he'd started spouting off about propriety, and gentlemanly deportment, and God knew what else. As his hand kneading her foot conjured a lovely bouquet of sensations, Hester realized that for all they'd been intimate, for all they'd been naked and trusting with each other, they hadn't joined their bodies in the sexual act itself.

And yet, he was preparing to flagellate himself.

"Tiberius Flynn, I forbid you to fret over this. I accosted you in your room, demanded attention from you, and left you no alternative but to accommodate me. The male of the species is weak and easily led astray. There is *biblical* authority for this."

He let her foot go and brought up his hand to stroke over her hair. "Even the devil can cite scripture for her own purpose."

Maybe his lordship intended that they have a nap, and then they'd become lovers in truth. Hester was beginning to doubt it. She had allowed him to catch not just his breath, but his damned gentlemanly scruples.

"Go to sleep, Tiberius." She kissed his jaw, which was now scratchy with an inchoate beard. "Whatever moral hammers you are using to beat yourself, set them aside. You can pick them up in the morning and resume your punishment."

She hoped he'd be reassured by the implication that she wouldn't demand further attentions from him, and she hoped he wouldn't toss her out of his bed just yet.

"Hester?"

"Hmm?" She resisted the urge to wrap her hand around his flaccid member.

"This has been a mistake. I know you don't agree with me, but you aren't in possession of a proper perspective on the situation. When you do have that perspective, I hope you will recall that I am apologizing for taking liberties, and that I did *not* take every liberty you would have granted me, including those that ought to be reserved solely for your husband or a man committed to becoming your husband."

"Go to sleep." She brushed her hand over his eyes, bringing his lids down before the damned man said anything further to ruin what had been breathtakingly lovely, sweet, and precious.

Six

"I WISH YOU HAD LET ME GO WITH YOU."

Fiona was frowning at Tye as if considering scolding him further. He hoped she would—he hoped the hand of God Himself would reach out of the clouds and scold the hell out of him for last night's mischief with Hester Daniels, if not for the whole misguided undertaking that was this journey to Scotland.

"It's pouring rain, child, and riding is a tricky proposition when the ground is wet. I went straight to the posting inn at Ballater and came straight back, risking my saddle and my horse in the process."

"Are you going to catch your death?" She sounded ghoulishly pleased with the possibility.

"I could not possibly be that lucky. What are you reading?"

After he'd changed out of his sodden riding clothes, Tye had come into the library to hide, of course, and to read the letter he'd retrieved from the inn at Ballater. One letter, in his father's inimitable black scrawl. Tye supposed that at least meant his sisters were staying out of trouble.

Which was more than he could say for himself.

"Do you want to read with me? I'm reading old Aesop." Fiona's voice was heartrendingly hopeful. She patted the place beside her on the couch. "It's nice and cozy here in the library, and there's nobody to make you do lessons or tell you not to get in the way."

He knew this trap. He'd laid it for his own mother at bedtime as a boy. He'd been ensnared in it by his younger sisters on many a stormy night.

"One story only, and I get to read."

She bounced over a few inches on the couch and passed him the book when he sat beside her. "You get to read, but I get to pick."

"We'll negotiate, because you'll just pick the longest one in the book." He leafed through the pages and looked for one with a picture, because his sisters had always preferred the ones with the pictures. He paused at an illustration of a Greek boy holding the paw of a huge, fanged lion. The beast's face was contorted into a grimace, and a horrific splinter, roughly half the size of a railroad tie, protruded from the animal's paw.

"This was your father's favorite."

"Read that one." She budged up so tightly to his side, she was all but sitting in his lap. "I don't read it often because it's toward the back and I can't say the name."

"Androcles." Tye launched into the tale of a boy who'd come upon a fierce lion in the woods, the lion's stated agenda being to make a snack of the boy. Androcles offered instead to remove the awful splinter from the animal's paw in hopes of improving the lion's disposition. The lion granted the boy a favor as a result, to be called in at the time and place of the boy's choosing.

Tye turned a page slowly, while Fiona fidgeted beside him. "How did they make friends if the lion couldn't talk?"

"This is a fable, child. Make believe. It has no bearing on reality but serves for entertainment only or perhaps to make some moral point. Now…" Predictably, the lion and the human met years later, when the mature Androcles was to be fed to the lions. The favor was called in—though the lion was hardly going to devour his old friend—and the emperor was so impressed that both man and lion were returned to their forest to live happily ever after.

"I wonder if he ever got another splinter." Fiona seized the book from Tye's hands. "You said there are lions in London."

"There are, at the Royal Menagerie, and all manner of strange beasts."

"I want to go there. I want to make friends with the lions."

Tye gently pried the book from her grasp and set it aside, thinking about tangled webs and old men too stubborn to consider the happiness of their daughters over political gain and financial machinations. "They aren't very happy lions, Fiona. They're far from home, and they miss their families."

Fiona retrieved her book. "I miss my mama and my papa."

Oh, not this bloody nonsense…

He slipped an arm around her shoulders. "I know, Fiona. They miss you too." *How could they not?*

She turned her face into his arm for one moment then sprang off the couch. "I'm going to draw them a picture for Uncle Ian to send them. I'll put the lion in it, but it will be a girl who saves him. A brave girl from Scotland."

She whirled off to the desk, leaving Tye without any other way to put off reading his father's damned letter.

❧

"Our guest certainly has a penchant for riding about the countryside in the rain."

Hester glanced up from her needlepoint to regard Aunt Ariadne. "He's English. They hardly notice the rain."

"Now that's odd." Aunt put down her letters and sent Hester a puzzled look. "I could have sworn you yourself hail from England."

Hester had the sense Lady Ariadne saw a great deal more than she let on, some of which was going to come inconveniently into evidence. "I was born in England, true, but the only family members I can rely upon are married to Scots. I have Scottish grandparents, and it appears I'm now dwelling in Scotland."

"While Spathfoy would have us believe he's English to the bone."

Hester gave up. "I took liberties with his person, Aunt. Substantial liberties."

"I suppose we must have you arrested then. Men can't abide it when we take liberties with their delicate, frail persons. And Spathfoy is such a pale, sensitive creature too."

"He's not delicate or frail in the least." Hester was

being baited shamelessly, but she couldn't resist. "He is the loveliest, most considerate man." And perceptive, possibly even sensitive too.

"We *are* discussing our guest, the Earl of Spathfoy?"

Hester put down her embroidery hoop. "Tiberius Flynn. His sisters call him Tye."

"I call him a damned clever fellow if he's put that look in your eye on such short acquaintance."

"You were the one who told me to get back on the horse."

"So I did." Aunt shuffled her letters in her lap. "And so I do. Merriman took a worse toll on you than he should have."

She *would* bring up that name. "I am not pleased with myself, Aunt."

"A few twinges of conscience are all well and good, my dear. The point of the exercise is for you to be pleased with Spathfoy. I trust you are?" Such an innocent question, but Aunt speared Hester with a look that brooked no prevarication.

"He has been everything that is gentlemanly, and I am not in the least disappointed." Though she was puzzled. He'd denied himself pleasures with her she'd freely offered, and she was at a loss to understand his reasons.

"Then that is an end to it. He'll go on his way, you'll wish him well, and everybody's spirits will be the better for his holiday here. Shall I ring for tea?"

Hester assented, not at all deceived. Aunt Ariadne was matchmaking, pretending any entanglement with Spathfoy was a casual frolic, easily put aside, when for Hester it might not be any such thing—as Lady Ariadne likely knew.

As she sipped her tea and listened to Aunt's parlor Gaelic, Hester realized what was bothering her. Not propriety, not her reputation—Spathfoy would die before he'd gossip about a woman of his acquaintance—but rather an alarming mixture of doubt and hope.

Hope, because the man who'd shown her such consideration last night, not only in his attentions but also his reticence, was a man she could respect as greatly as she desired him. She might even—only in the privacy of her mind could she admit this—*like* him.

Like him a very great deal.

But the serpent in her garden, the doubt, was that initially, she'd thought she could like Jasper a very great deal as well.

～

"The Earl of Spathfoy to see you, Laird."

Ian looked up from his ledgers in surprise. "In this bloody downpour?"

The footman's lips quirked. "His lordship is dripping in the foyer, my lord. We've taken his greatcoat to the kitchen to hang before the fire."

"Show him in, then. Her ladyship is not to be disturbed."

Ian rose from his desk and peered out at the rain pelting the library's mullioned windows. A peat fire burned in the hearth, which served only to reinforce a sense of premature autumnal gloom.

"His lordship, the Earl of Spathfoy, my lord." The footman withdrew, closing the library door quietly.

"Spathfoy, welcome." Ian extended a hand, finding

Spathfoy's grip cold but firm. "You'll need a wee dram to ward off the chill."

"My thanks, though you might want to save your whisky when you hear why I'm calling upon you."

"Anybody going about in such a deluge needs at least a tot." A tot of common sense, perhaps, though Spathfoy's features were so utterly composed, Ian poured the man a drink with a sense of foreboding.

"To your health." They drank in silence, Ian sizing up his guest and assuming Spathfoy was sizing up his host. "You've the look of a man with something serious on his mind. My royal neighbor frowns on dueling, and while I've the sense you could hold your own in a bare-knuckle round, my countess frowns on violence in the house. This leaves a man few options outside of unrelenting civility."

While Ian watched a bead of moisture trickle from Spathfoy's hair onto his collar, Spathfoy grimaced and stared at his drink. "Civility."

"Shall we sit? The fire's throwing out a little heat, thank God. And do I assume her ladyship's presence will not be needed for this tête-à-tête?"

Ian moved to the sofa, while Spathfoy lowered himself to a wing chair. The man's boots squeaked, which more than anything announced that Spathfoy's errand was not a social call. No English gentleman would jeopardize the welfare of his favorite riding boots had he any alternative.

"No, we will not need to bother her ladyship." Spathfoy fell silent then met Ian's gaze with a glacial green stare. "Fiona is my niece."

"She's my niece too, and a lovely little girl if I do say so myself."

"I'm to bring her back to England with me."

A shaft of pain lanced Ian's chest, pain for the child mostly, at being ripped from her home and family—if Spathfoy had his way. So many Scottish children had been uprooted at the behest of English convenience. The clearances had gone on since time out of mind, into Ian's infancy, but his own niece…

And pain for Hester and Ariadne, who had cobbled together a household around the child's routines and joie de vivre. Ian had done likewise almost since Fiona's birth.

And then there was Mary Frances's pain, should her own child be lost to her. This pain was too great to contemplate at any length.

"And why will you be taking Fiona from the only family to love her?"

Spathfoy rose and braced one arm on the mantel. "You're not going to argue?"

"Answer the question." Ian kept his seat, the better to watch his guest.

"Familial duty. The marquess has said it should be so, and I'm the logical one to retrieve the girl." Spathfoy contemplated the fire as if he'd prefer leaping into it to this familial duty.

"What aren't you telling me, Spathfoy? Quinworth forgets about the girl for years, all but denies her patrimony, and now he wants to reave her away from home the first time her mother isn't on hand to go with her. Even an English marquess wouldn't take that queer a start without some provocation."

"I wish to hell I knew what the old man's game was." Spathfoy threw himself back into the chair.

"When I came up here, I thought I'd simply collect the child, leave a bank draft with her mother, have a brandy with Altsax, and promise them they could visit her while she was with us. Altsax has a title, and nobody winters up here if they have a choice."

"I winter *up here*. Fiona has spent every winter of her life *up here*." Something wasn't making sense. Spathfoy looked not chagrined, but rather, miserable.

Torn.

"I know that, Balfour. I know now that Fiona is well cared for here, and I know her mother and stepfather aren't on hand to prevent me from taking the child. I did not know these things when I left England."

"So your own dear papa is not showing you all his cards, and you're his son and heir. How can you speak for his intentions toward Fiona?"

Spathfoy ran a hand through his damp hair, suggesting Ian's question had hit a tender spot. "My father has assured me it was Gordie's express wish, conveyed in his last will and testament, that any of Gordie's children be raised by Gordie's surviving family. My father would not lie about such a thing."

Ian had read law. There was lying, and then there were the English versions of the truth, which were many, varied, and often grossly inaccurate without being what English barristers would call lies. "Have you *seen* your brother's will?"

The knuckles on Spathfoy's hand, the hand holding his drink, were white. "I would not insult my father by demanding such a thing."

"Ah, but he'd insult you by sending you up here to steal a child without giving you the lay of the land. He'd insult me by sending you to do it without contacting me first as head of Fiona's family and the man who has been writing to the marquess regularly regarding the child, and he'd insult Lady Mary Frances by failing to extend an invitation to the child's mother to visit the almighty Flynn family seat with her daughter."

Ian did not raise his voice, though the urge to shout and break things—Spathfoy's handsome head included—was nigh overpowering.

"Let me be clear, Balfour." Spathfoy didn't shout either. "I am not borrowing Fiona for the rest of the summer. I am taking her to place her in the sole care and custody of the Marquess of Quinworth, her paternal grandfather. That is the purpose of my visit."

"You will be sure Quinworth's affairs are in order when you head south, won't you?" Ian took a sip of his drink, needing spirits to calm his heart as it pounded slowly against his ribs.

"Quinworth's affairs are always in order." Spathfoy replied with such assurance, Ian concluded it was Spathfoy's responsibility to ensure those affairs remained in order.

"That's just fine then, for Mary Fran will kill your father, Spathfoy. Altsax will load and reload her gun for her if necessary. Fiona's mother would consider it worth her life to keep Fee safe from Gordie's family, and particularly from her grandfather. More whisky?"

Spathfoy had the sense to cast a wary glance at Ian's offer of more drink. The threat to Quinworth's life if Fiona were kidnapped was far from a jest.

"The whisky would be appreciated, and I will

consider that your description of your sister's behavior is mere dramatics."

"Laddie, that was not dramatics. That was a promise." Ian went to the sideboard and brought the decanter to the coffee table. "Help yourself."

He wasn't trying to be rude, but he wanted to note whether Spathfoy's hands shook when he poured himself a drink. "I have to wonder, Spathfoy, why you didn't simply ride out with Fee, bundle her onto the train in Ballater, and send us a wire she's being held for ransom."

"Ransom?" Spathfoy set the decanter on the table—his hands were steady, damn the man. "That is a ridiculous notion. Quinworth's finances are quite sound. My mother and I have both seen to it."

Ian would bet his horse Spathfoy hadn't intended to make that disclosure. "Well, then your dear papa has gone daft, perhaps. I've yet to meet an English marquess who ignores his own granddaughter for years, only to demand possession of her with no warning or explanation. Does your father know how much trouble young females can be?"

Spathfoy studied the decanter. "Likely not. He's turned my sisters more or less over to me, and never had much to do with them when they were younger." He tossed back his drink and reached for the decanter.

"Then Fiona will at least have the company of some doting aunts, *if* you take her south?"

"I shall take her south, Balfour. I know my duty, but no, her aunts do not reside at the family seat."

"Married, are they?" Ian put the question casually while Spathfoy poured himself his third whisky. This was beyond chasing the damp away, past the medicinal tot, and fast approaching manly indulgence. Spathfoy was a big bastard, but he was drinking aged Scottish whisky like it was water.

Or like he was Scottish.

"Not a one of them is married. Not yet, which is the entire—" He fell silent, his drink halfway to his mouth. "They are lovely young women who enjoy the hospitality of various aunts and cousins for the summer. This is very good whisky, Balfour."

"It is. When are you supposed to take Fiona into the loving arms of that stranger known as her grandpapa?"

Spathfoy stopped staring at his drink to peer at Ian. "Oh, yesterday, of course. With his lordship, everything is yesterday if not the day before."

Which explained a few of Spathfoy's unfortunate tendencies. "I can't allow that. I need time to wire Fee's mama at least. They will very likely head directly home by way of London, and Hester and Ariadne will need time to pack up Fee's effects. I'll want some assurances in writing regarding Mary Fran's right to visit, as well as my own, Connor's, Gilgallon's, and Asher's."

"Who?"

"My brothers. With the exception of Asher, they've had as much of the raising of Fiona as I have."

Spathfoy nodded. Being in anticipation of a title, he would comprehend a need to document any understandings. "You'll draw something up?"

"Give me a week. This will require communicating with my men of business in Aberdeen, and they are not the most responsive bunch." It would require no such thing, but Spathfoy was hardly going to deny Ian a week's grace.

The English were stupid that way, though they called it being sporting.

"I'll write to my father that we've had this discussion." Spathfoy rose, and he did not weave on his feet in any manner.

Ian rose as well. "That's all we've had, Spathfoy. This is discussion on my part, not agreement. I have one demand, though."

"What would that be?"

"I'll be the one to explain to Fiona what's afoot, if and when the need arises. You're not to be enticing the girl with fairy tales about golden coaches and spun-sugar castles."

"Fair enough. You have a week, Balfour, and then I'll be taking my niece south."

"Our niece."

They shook hands, and then Ian watched while his guest departed to once again get soaked to his English skin in the bone-chilling Scottish downpour.

❧

A mean Scottish rain was sufficient to clear Tye's head in short order, that and the sloppy lanes, which would have Rowan bowing a tendon if Tye weren't careful. He brought the horse back to the walk and resigned himself to again getting thoroughly drenched.

Balfour had reacted with surprisingly good manners to Tye's announcement, which pointed to two conclusions.

First, the man was up to something. At the end of a

week, Tye would very likely have to snatch the child and make a dash for the south.

Second, Balfour had not, in the years of Fiona's life, done a thorough enough investigation of the legalities involved in Fiona's situation, or he would have known about Gordie's will and possibly even sent the girl to her paternal relations. As head of the MacGregor family, particularly as the head of the local branch of the clan, Balfour would have had that authority.

This suggested Quinworth was up to something as well, which made Tye positively grind his teeth with frustration.

Rowan shied hugely at a bush swaying and bowing against the increasingly stiff wind, bringing Tye's focus back to his horse.

"Settle, young man." He ran his hand down the horse's wet crest. "Nobody's going to eat you until I'm safely out of Scotland."

The horse walked on, though it managed to do so with a put-upon air. Tye was as relieved as the beast must have been to spot the stables when they trotted up the lane toward their temporary home.

And yet, guilt and resentment colored even such a simple emotion as pleasure at being warm and dry. Perhaps guilt and resentment were the dark twins of duty and honor. Tye put up his horse, discussing that very notion with the only being on earth who even appeared to care.

When Tye squished and slogged his way to the house, he went in by the kitchen entrance, finding Fiona sitting at the worktable doing sums.

"You should take your boots off, Uncle. The aunties will be wroth if you track mud on Mama's carpets."

"Oh, and what do the aunties look like when they're wroth?" He peered over the child's shoulder, but was careful not to drip on her.

"You're cold," Fiona said, shifting away from him. "Did you rub Rowan down before you put him up?"

"I rubbed him down, picked out his feet, sang him a lullaby, and listened to his prayers." As the horse had so often listened to Tye's. "Are you adding these?"

"I am. You can check them when I'm done."

"Lucky me." He moved away from the child, and finding the kitchen undefended by the indefatigable Deal, tossed some kindling under a burner, lit it, and took the kettle from the hob.

While the water heated, he went to the raised hearth and sat to remove his boots, which took some struggle. He didn't have his boots made so tightly they cut off his circulation, but they were snug and wet, and had Fiona not been sitting several feet away, the occasion would have served nicely for a bout of swearing.

Fiona picked up her paper and eyed it, as if admiring a piece of artwork. "I'm done. Will you read me another story?"

"I am soaked to the bone, about to catch my death, and I have no doubt you can read every story in the library on your own. I will decline the proffered honor." He put his boots in the back hallway, away from the damaging heat of the kitchen fire, then set about making a tea tray.

"I can't read the French ones. We have the fairy tales in French and German. I like the German."

"How is it you know the German?"

She shrugged. "The neighbors. When I go to Balmoral Castle to play, we sometimes speak German, though I don't know all the words."

The kettle started to whistle, and while Tye poured water into a teapot, he considered that perhaps his father knew of this too, and was having him kidnap—*retrieve*—Fiona because she counted princes and princesses among her playmates.

"Would you like some tea, Fiona?"

"If it's after lunch, I have to have nursery tea, but yes, please. Are you going to check my sums?"

"You can't possibly have gotten them all correct if you did them this quickly."

She pulled the end of a braid from her mouth. "I can possibly too. There are scones with raisins in the bread box."

"You may have no more than one, or the aunties will be wroth with me." He added a few scones and the tub of butter to the tray and took a seat across from the child. "Let me see your sums."

She passed over the paper and regarded him solemnly. "The subtraction is on the back. I like the subtraction better because it's not as obvious."

"Give me your pencil." She passed it over too, the brush of her little fingers making Tye realize how cold his hands were.

"Are you going to make my tea, first?"

"No, I am not. You can butter me a scone, since it's a lady's responsibility to preside over the tea tray."

Her eyes began to dance as she picked up the butter knife and a scone. Tye went back to checking her sums. When he looked up, Fiona was holding out a scone liberally slathered with butter.

"Fiona, you took a bite from it."

"Because we're family. Uncle Ian says food tastes better when you share it, and Aunt Augusta says Uncle is never wrong." She winked at him and waved the scone for him to take.

"Your sums are all correct, as is your subtraction." He traded her the paper for the scone, when he should have lectured her on the inappropriateness of Uncle Ian's poor manners when displayed before a guest.

A guest who was family, and who would soon be taking her from everything and everybody she knew and loved. He took a bite of the scone.

"That's why I don't like the math." She set about buttering a second scone. "I never get anything wrong, and so the aunties hardly spend any time with me on it. Aunt Hester has started teaching me the piano though, so I can play for Mama and Papa when they come home."

"I'll pour your tea." He moved away from the table, lest he have to look at her innocent, happy countenance, knowing she wouldn't be here when her parents came home. She wouldn't play for them; she wouldn't give them her sums to check.

He poured hot water into a mug, added a tablespoon of his own tea, a generous splash of cream, and a few lumps of sugar from the tea tray, and set it down before his niece.

"Did my papa drink nursery tea?"

"I think every English child drinks nursery tea, at least in the colder months. Your grandmother is quite competent with arithmetic."

"My grandmamma?"

"The Marchioness of Quinworth. Her given name is Deirdre. She has red hair just like you, and you might meet her one day." Except Quinworth and his lady were estranged, leaving Tye to wonder how the hell Quinworth expected to manage his granddaughter's upbringing. Seeing to a young lady's happiness involved a great deal more than hiring a governess and paying the dressmaker's bills. A great deal.

"Do you know any stories about my grandmother?"

The hope in her eyes slew him. This child subsisted on stories, on rambles to the burn, on the company of gentle women and doting uncles. She made friends with trees, and she was entirely, absolutely, and utterly too trusting for her own good.

Like another lady in the house.

"Fiona, dear, are you—Oh. You're back." Hester stood in the door to the kitchen, looking lovely and comfortable in a worn dress of light blue velvet. Inside Tye's chest, emotions collided and drew apart, then collided again.

"Miss Hester, good day. Fiona and I were sharing an early tea."

"Mine's plain," Fiona interjected from her place at the table. "I got all my sums right, and my subtractions too. Do you want to share a scone with me?"

"That would be delightful." Hester advanced toward the table, and it seemed to Tye as if she might have been blushing. "How do you know your maths were correct, Fee?"

"Uncle Tye checked them. He said my grandmamma likes to do math too."

And rather than meet his gaze, Hester took a place across from the child and started buttering a damned scone. The bossy cows of Scotland could be assured long and happy lives at the rate butter was consumed in this household.

"I might like another myself." Tye came down beside Hester and reached for the teapot, making sure his hand bumped hers, exactly as he had the first night when they'd shared a meal.

Yea, verily, a blush. For certain, seeing him and touching him provoked her to blushes. "Tea, Miss Hester?"

"Please."

He fixed her a cup with cream and sugar, while she troweled butter onto a scone. Thank God the child was there to chaperone, or he might have begun asking the lady personal questions about what caused her blushes.

Fiona kicked the rungs of her chair, the same way Joan still did when bored. "Uncle Tye said he sang Rowan a lullaby. Nobody sings *me* any lullabies."

Tye passed Hester her tea. "Shall you be going to bed before supper, Niece? I'll be happy to sing you a lullaby right now if you are."

"No." She smiled, generously conceding the point. "But I'll be going to bed after supper. You could sing to me then."

"No such luck." Tye peeled a raisin from the scone in Miss Hester's hand. "I'm engaged to serenade my horse after supper. It helps settle his equine nerves, to say nothing of my own." He popped the raisin in his mouth, but not before he caught a half smile from the woman trying to ignore his presence while they sat side by side on the same bench.

She smelled good—clean, flowery, lemony, and feminine, and it made his male brain recall that fragrance of hers combined with lavender-scented sheets and the earthy aroma of spent lust.

Spent lust being a degree short of *sated* lust.

"Did Rowan's nerves necessitate a hack in this rain, my lord?" Hester hid behind her teacup, reminding Tye he'd dodged the day's first two meals. No wonder the lady was hesitant.

"Rainy days are hard on the beast when he's confined to his stall, and a call on Balfour was in order. He sends his greetings." Tye resisted the urge to appropriate a bite of Hester's scone. She was eating slowly, tearing off a nibble or peeling off a single raisin and putting it into her mouth.

Innocent behavior. He could observe her doing the same thing any morning in the breakfast parlor—if he wanted to start the day losing his sanity.

"I'd best be changing into dry clothes. Fiona, if no one has explained multiplication to you, I will take on that challenge tomorrow."

"Like be fruitful and multiply?" Fiona's innocent question hung in the air, while Miss Hester's lips curved, and she abruptly appeared fascinated by her remaining bite of scone.

"That is an archaic biblical reference, child. What I have in mind is done on paper with a pencil and a good deal of careful thought. Miss Hester, I *will* see you at supper."

He managed a dignified exit in damp socks, which

was no small feat, even for the firstborn son and heir of
an English marquess. He was standing before the fire in
his bedroom, peeled down to his damp breeches and
bare feet with a tumbler of whisky in his hand, when the
first glimmer of a fascinating—if improbable—idea stole
into his tired, frustrated, and not a little resentful mind.

∽

"I hope Uncle Tye stays with us until Mama and
Papa come back." Fiona reached for a scone, but
must have seen the promise of retribution in Hester's
eyes. The child snitched a single orphaned raisin from
the tray instead.

"He's a busy man, Fee. I doubt he can bide with
us the entire summer." She doubted her nerves could
stand such a thing either: Tiberius Flynn, sleeping one
unlocked door down from her, night after night.

"Why is he busy? Does he have other nieces?"

"Not that I know of, but he has estates, younger
sisters, and parents. I'm sure there are many demands
on his time."

Fiona frowned, but it wasn't a frown of displeasure.
Hester was coming to know the child well enough to
see that this was an expression of thoughtfulness. "Why
doesn't Uncle want anybody to know he's nice?"

Why, indeed? Spathfoy wasn't a friendly man, and
he certainly made no effort to cultivate charm. She no
longer viewed this as a shortcoming, having met a few
too many friendly, charming scoundrels.

"Maybe he's shy." Shy enough that he'd fix her a
cup of tea, touch her hand, and steal a raisin from her
scone, but never once smile at her.

Fiona snitched another orphaned raisin. "Uncle is shy? I don't think so, but he's very careful. He guddles people the way he guddles a fish."

"What is that supposed to mean?" An image of Spathfoy's hand stroking slowly over Hester's stomach had her pulse fluttering.

"He is stealthy." Fiona hunched down closer to the table and dropped her voice. "He is polite and quiet, and uses a great lot of big words, but he has very good manners. My other uncles don't have such good manners."

"Your other uncles know you better, Fee. Spathfoy is more guest than uncle. When you know him better, he might be less formal."

"He made me a cup of tea, right here in this kitchen. Mrs. Deal will have kittens."

"He made me a cup of tea too"—exactly the way she preferred it—"so she'll have to have two litters. Would you like to help me practice my Gaelic over a game of matches?"

"You *promise* you won't let me win?"

Hester rose and carried the tray to the counter. "I shall pummel you flat, but we must practice my Gaelic while I defeat you."

"I bet Uncle could pummel you flat."

Hester took the child's hand and remained silent. She feared in some of the ways that mattered, Spathfoy had already pummeled her flat. She very much looked forward to her next pummeling, when she hoped she might return the favor to him. Aunt Ariadne had been quite correct to recommend that Hester avail herself of Spathfoy's subtle charms.

And if he stayed the entire summer, Hester would avail herself of those charms as often as the gentleman's *shyness* allowed her to.

❧

Tye tried writing to his father.

He needed to convey to the old man how dim-witted—and unsporting—this plan to uproot an innocent child was. He wanted to intimate to his father how urgent Tye's own exodus from Scotland had become—how close he found himself to committing irredeemable mischief with one Hester Daniels, who might not be best pleased to see Fiona taken south. He had to explain to his father how very decent Balfour had been to Fiona and to Tye both, and how deserving the Scottish earl was of decent treatment in return.

All of which would be so much wasted ink. Quinworth had spoken, and the universe was to promptly order itself accordingly.

Despite the impact on a little girl.

Despite the strain on Tye's self-discipline.

Despite the stain on Tye's honor.

Tye stared at the empty glass in his hand, and once again the sly, outlandish idea called to him. He dipped the pen and tried to start his epistle to the marquess, except the plan taking shape in Tye's brain was too fascinating, too strangely appealing, to permit the composition of a properly filial epistle. A list developed on the piece of paper before Tye, a list of reasons why this plan made perfect sense:

As his father's sole, direct male heir, Tye had to marry.

His father was pestilentially determined that Tye should marry sooner rather than later.

Tye's mother would have to attend the wedding ceremony, and it would please Tye inordinately to see his parents behaving as a couple in public.

The young lady was in need of a husband—all young ladies were in need of husbands, but this one needed a husband of sufficient social stature to scotch the remaining whiff of scandal clinging to her good name.

The lady was of childbearing age, for all her attempts to retire to the shelf.

The lady was impoverished and would be at pains to make a good match without a decent dowry.

The lady was quietly pretty and sensible, also quite passionate.

Tye scratched out the last line. A gentleman wouldn't remark on a woman's capacity for passion—a gentleman wouldn't allow himself the opportunity to notice such a thing.

He wrote the same line again and underlined the last word. Two minutes of staring at the list, and he added another line:

The lady was aunt by marriage to the niece Tye must kidnap.

Another lining through.

The lady was aunt by marriage to the niece whom Tye would escort to the family seat, and the lady's presence would aid the child in adjusting to her improved circumstances.

Improved was a stretch. He scowled at his list, scratched out "improved," and wrote "new."

Two minutes later he balled up his list and tossed it

into the fire. Hester Daniels was a nobody—a younger daughter of a mere baron, and her brother was all but disdaining to use the title. As much as Tye might find the lady suitable, Quinworth would make her life hell.

Whisky was putting odd notions in his head. He stared at where the fire was consuming the crumpled list, turning paper to ash.

Hester wasn't his mother, though. She wouldn't run off if Quinworth turned up difficult. Hester could give the old man what for and never even raise her voice.

And she was *quite* passionate.

He started making another list.

❧

Ian watched his wife climb into bed, something a year of marriage ought to have made into a prosaic, end-of-day sight.

Though it hadn't. Each and every night, he feasted his eyes on the way firelight brought out red highlights in her dark hair. Each and every night, he waited for the moment she settled on the mattress, drew her nightgown over her head, and ranged her warm, female curves along his tired body.

"Come to bed, Husband. You've been brooding at that fire since we came down from the nursery." She tossed off her nightgown, drew the covers up over herself, and lay back against the pillows.

Ian crossed the room, laid his dressing gown over her nightgown at the foot of the bed, and climbed in beside her. "The rain has made your son sleepy, I'm thinking. He hears it like a lullaby."

"Growing has made him sleepy. He'll likely be

every bit as tall as you." She cuddled up; he looped an arm around her shoulders and felt some of the day's tensions ease out of him.

"He'll be taller, because his mama is a fine, strappin' countess who brings her own height to the equation. Do you think the lad would be up to a social call later this week?"

"To see Lady Ariadne? Of course." She traced a single finger over Ian's breastbone. "What has you in such a taking, Husband? I know Spathfoy came to visit this afternoon, but he didn't stay long."

Ian trapped her fingers in his and brought her knuckles to his lips. "Damned man is intent on taking Fee south, Augusta. I'm not sure I can stop him."

She rose up on her side, peering at him by the dying firelight. "How can he just take Mary Fran's daughter, Ian? Do you mean for a visit?"

"No, my heart, I do not mean for a visit. Quinworth has taken some notion to retrieve his long-lost grand-daughter, and Spathfoy is charged with seeing it done."

Augusta was silent for long moments after she resumed her position at Ian's side. "This is not good, Ian. Quinworth is an old-fashioned aristocrat who probably thinks children should be seen and not heard."

Old-fashioned aristocrats were capable of worse notions where little girls were concerned—or not so little girls. "Spare the rod and all that rot. Fiona will not deal well with such treatment. Mary Fran grew more rebellious the more Grandfather tried to set limits for her. Fiona will be no different."

"Doesn't he need to file some sort of lawsuit?"

"Yes, he does, but I'm thinking he'd do so in

English courts." Ian stroked a hand over his wife's hair, the very feel of it soothing his worries. "Gordie was English, so his children would arguably be English."

"But Fee was born in Scotland to a Scottish mother."

"Who was married to an Englishman at the time of the child's birth."

Augusta cradled Ian's jaw, then drew a finger scented with lavender across his lips. "Do we know exactly when Gordie died? I thought Fee was a post-humous child."

"She…" He fell silent. They'd gotten word of Gordie's death after Fee's birth, but the ocean was wide, the Canadian wilderness almost as vast, and Ian had never gotten an exact date. "Wife, you give me hope, but at best, all I can do with this issue is slow Quinworth down. Spathfoy says the old man has Gordie's will, and Gordie's wishes are made very plain therein. Fee's to go to her father's family."

"If I didn't hate Gordie Flynn before…"

"He was trying to do what was best for his child, Augusta."

"And I will do what is best for my husband." She rose up and straddled him in all her naked glory. "When do Mary Fran and Matthew plan to get home?"

"That's just it." Ian wrapped a hand around her nape to urge her down within kissing range. "I haven't heard a damned thing from them. I've sent a dozen wires, and they haven't answered a one."

She brushed his hair back from his brow, flipped her braid over her shoulder, and set about distracting him from the substantial worry Fee's situation had become.

∽

For two days, a cold, miserable rain fell without pause, though in Hester's heart, she felt a slow sunrise. Spathfoy did not ride his horse out, but had a footman take correspondence into Ballater for him both days.

Hester had peeked at the addresses. They were letters to family, to the marquess, and to Spathfoy's sisters, at least one of whom was residing at the family seat in Northumbria.

Hester liked that he wrote to his sisters, didn't just append little postscripts for them to the marquess's missive. She liked that Spathfoy took tea with Aunt Ariadne in the afternoon and listened to the old woman prattle on about "dear Prinny" and "poor old George," as if they'd been neighbors of hers for years.

Which, given that Aunt had bided in London with two of her husbands, they very nearly had.

Hester also liked that last night's evening meal had been shared by her and the earl alone, Aunt Ariadne claiming the damp was making her bones ache fiercely.

Hester did *not* like that Spathfoy hadn't made one single overture of an intimate nature, though he was doing a creditable job of entertaining Fiona at cards as the afternoon wore on.

"You can't cheat at this game," Fiona admonished him. "I'll watch you every minute, you see, and the cards are all right before us. There are two ways to cheat. You can peek at the cards as you lay them down, or you can peek at them if I have to get up, say, to fetch a cup of tea."

She was shuffling the cards as she spoke, her hands appallingly competent for such a small child.

"And are we permitted to wager?" his lordship asked. They were on the rug in front of the hearth, the earl sprawled on his side, while Fee sat cross-legged on a pillow before him.

She paused in her handling of the cards. "Is wagering permitted, Aunt? I haven't much money, because I'm saving it up for a present for Mama when she comes home."

"I'm not going to be a banker for either of you." Hester put her novel aside. She hadn't absorbed a single word the entire time she'd been curled in her wing chair, though the pretense had allowed surreptitious enjoyment of the sight of Spathfoy at leisure. "You could wager favors, I suppose. Say, a ride on Rowan for some favor of the earl's choosing."

"Uncle already promised me a ride."

Spathfoy eased up to tailor-sit across from the child. "We could wager future favors." His gaze traveled from the cards Fee was shuffling to where the ruffled hem of Hester's petticoat peeked from beneath her skirt.

Fiona peered at the top card, then returned it to the deck. "You mean we could ask each other for *anything*? I could ask you to teach me to ride Rowan?"

"You might." He studied Hester's hands now, making her skin heat as she tucked her hem over the lace at her ankles. "Or we might agree on some limits, like something that can be done in the space of an hour."

His voice had taken on a particular depth, reaching into Hester's body and creating low and private stirrings—and she was certain he knew exactly what he was about.

"I could ride Rowan for an *hour*?" Fee started

laying cards face down in tidy rows. Then she paused. "What favors would you ask of me?"

"Now that is a challenge." Spathfoy considered Hester while he spoke. "What could a lovely young lady offer that I might seek to gain through a wager rather than simply by asking?"

Hester picked her book back up. "You can talk about wagering all afternoon, my lord, or you can go quietly to your fate. Fiona is wicked smart at the matching game. She has a gift for it."

"You've a passion for the game, Niece? Your grandmother enjoys cards as well, though there are few who will play against her when she's on her game."

He took part of the remaining deck and set about finishing the rows Fiona had started. Hester concluded the verbal skirmish was over, but it put the past two days in a different light. She recalled Spathfoy holding her chair at breakfast, leaning down just a little too far to wish her good morning while she adjusted her skirts.

Oh, the scent of him, first thing in the day…

And the utter wonder of awakening in her own bed, only to realize Spathfoy had carried her there as she'd slept, covered her up, then laid her nightgown and wrapper across the foot of her bed.

He'd handled her clothing.

He'd handled *her*.

And when they were at table, she could not reach for the salt without his hand brushing hers, though he never by word or expression gave it away as anything other than inadvertence.

He was *flirting with her*. His approach was so subtle, so utterly Tiberius Flynn, she hadn't recognized it.

She turned a page. "When you beat him, Fee, you mustn't ask anything too terribly difficult of him. Your uncle isn't used to being humbled by young ladies and their passions."

Hester was still congratulating herself on that salvo when Fiona went down to defeat, having a mere eight matches to the earl's eighteen.

~

Tye finished brushing his teeth and glowered at himself in the mirror. For two damned days, he'd acquitted himself like a perfect gentleman. Such behavior ought not to have been a burden, because he *was* a perfect gentleman—most of the time.

And yet... nothing. No overtures from the lady other than a little repartee, which had hardly encouraged Tye to bolder flirtation. And his plan—the plan his father would have to accommodate if the man's grandchildren were to know their grandpapa—required that Hester contribute more than some tart rejoinders.

Tye was going to have to storm her citadel. His time was running out, and while there were lines he would not cross, he was going to maneuver his heaviest artillery into the fray. If she expected him to bat his eyes at her or beg for a touch of her hand, Hester Daniels was sadly mistaken.

He jerked the belt of his robe closed, decided the moment did not call for any footwear—and particularly not any goddamned gray wool socks—and glanced at himself in the mirror.

For God's sake, he looked as if he were going to war.

He didn't stop to repair his appearance but stalked off to Hester's closed bedroom door.

To knock or not to knock? *To hell with it.* He knocked twice, then put his hand on the knob.

"Come in."

He swung the door wide as the lady bid him enter. She reclined on a chaise by the fire, her hair unbound, her nightclothes modestly covering her from her neck to her infernally sturdy gray wool socks.

"Good evening, my lord." She did not look surprised to see him, but he was surprised by all that hair. In the firelight, it gleamed like new pennies and old gold, made him want to get his hands on it and bury his nose in it.

"Good evening, Miss Hester." And *now* what? His brilliant plan was proving lamentably thin on details.

"Perhaps you'd close the door, my lord? You're letting in quite a draft."

He closed the door, though a part of him wanted to protest that propriety demanded it be kept open.

"I am no bloody good at this." He glanced around the room, hoping some other idiot fellow had made that announcement.

"At what?" She rose from her chaise, belting her robe with snug efficiency and crossing the room to stand before him. "Your hair is damp."

"Everything is damp in this damned rain."

"Come." She took him by the hand and tugged him closer to the fire. "We can enumerate all the things you're not good at, and perhaps a few of the endeavors at which you excel."

There was innuendo in her words—*she* excelled

at innuendo, turning innocent remarks over cards into smoldering flirtation. He let her tow him to the carpet, where she sat on the end of the chaise, behind and above him when he lowered himself to the floor.

"Tell me what you're no bloody good at." He felt her fingers at his nape, teasing the curling ends of his hair from the collar of his night robe.

"Subtlety, for one." No, that was not accurate. Nor even honest. "I am not familiar with what is expected when a man is in pursuit of a lady."

Her fingers stilled, and he heard her rustling around behind him. He was tempted to keep his eyes on her at all times, in case she'd taken a notion to shed her clothes and climb on the bed.

Which thought had even his cock making stupid, hopeful pronouncements.

"Are you a virgin, my lord?" She put the question casually as she resumed her seat, but she'd scooted, so she sat on her chaise with one leg on either side of him.

"You asked that merely to shock me, Hester Daniels. I will not dignify it with an answer."

"If you are"—her voice came so near his ear he could feel her breath on his neck—"then one shudders to think of how skilled you will be when you're no longer such an innocent."

He felt something—her lips, her nose—graze his ear, and then a brush was being drawn through his hair. It was the oddest sensation. He brushed his hair several times a day, but to be sitting lower than Hester while she tended him this way… Some of the tension eased out of his shoulders.

"What is the sigh about, my lord?"

"I do not excel at pursuit in the romantic sense."

The rhythm of the brush did not falter. "You're no bloody good at it?"

"Apparently not. Are you interested in becoming my marchioness, Hester?"

She hesitated, then resumed grooming him. "If you're asking whether I'm trying to trap you into marriage, my lord, you can take your bloody romantic incompetence, leave, and not come back." She wrapped her arms around his shoulders and rested her chin on his crown. "I would miss you though. Honesty compels me to admit that much."

Her words implied there were things she wouldn't admit, which was encouraging.

"That wasn't exactly my question." He laid his cheek on her forearm. "How is it you're soft everywhere? Even here." He nuzzled the crook of her elbow, which bore a concentration of lavender scent.

"I took a bath in hopes you'd come visit, Tiberius. Did you take a bath in anticipation of making a call?"

"Of course not." Except he had. And to ensure a dignified interval between the last of their evening meal and his next interlude with her.

"I've noticed something about the nights here in Scotland." The damned woman ran her tongue around the outside of his ear. This sent all manner of peculiar shivers down his spine, each of which landed with an erotic tingle in his groin.

"The nights are damp," he managed. He'd never before in his entire life labeled anything in his direct experience as a *tingle*.

"The nights are quite short, Tiberius. The sun

goes down later and comes up earlier. If you're on a particular errand, you'd best be about it."

He left off sniffing her knuckles. He'd come over here intending to seduce her into accepting a proposal of marriage. Despite her earlier rebuff, it still seemed like a sound plan—at least the seduction part did.

"You will please forgive my lack of efficiency in this regard." He turned and half rose in one movement, so he was kneeling between her spread knees and she was blinking back at him. He plucked the brush from her hand and set it aside. "Be warned, Hester. I have recalled my purpose for joining you in your boudoir."

He swooped in, lashed his arms around her, and fused his mouth to hers. She did not immediately kiss him back, but neither did she resist. In that moment, when he might have hesitated or drawn away, he eased her to her back on the chaise.

And then, ah then, she caught fire, fisting her hands in his hair and spreading her legs so he might wedge himself closer.

"You made me wait, you dratted man—" She muttered this against his teeth.

"You left me to question, infernal female—" He wasn't sure what the rest of the sentence might have been, for Hester shifted beneath him, making him abruptly aware of how his growing erection was snugged up against her sex.

Snug, but not as close as he wanted to be.

"Spath… Tiber… Tye, for pity's sake, kiss me." She dug her nails into his backside so that even through his robe, she got his attention.

"Too many clothes, Miss Daniels." He crouched

over her, vivid images of her naked on the chaise while he devoured her fogging his brain.

She went still beneath him. "Let me up. I can't remove your clothes when we're wrestling among the furniture."

He liked the sound of that, so he sat back and regarded her. Her cheeks were flushed, her breathing was deep, and her eyes held a slightly wild light. "You first, my dear. I was more than patient on the last occasion, if you'll recall."

She blinked again, the haze of passion cooling in her gaze. "Ladies before gentlemen? Are we concerning ourselves with deportment now?"

He realized two things in the next procession of instants: First, the idea of coaxing her from her clothing was not onerous in the least. He'd done it before, and he was looking forward to doing it again. The reward—her, relaxed and comfortable with her own nudity as well as his—was well worth the effort.

Second, and this took some fortitude to admit, he did not want to rush her, did not want to push her past any boundary she wasn't willing to exceed. She desired him, and that was probably as far as she knew her own mind.

And she hadn't said she *wouldn't* be his marchioness.

"Fine then, leave your clothing on. I feel no such compunction." He shrugged out of his robe and let it slide to the floor while Hester's chest rose with a substantial breath. He didn't move, but remained sitting back on his heels while her gaze slipped over his shoulders and down his torso, to the erection arrowing up from his groin, then back to his face.

"I love that you're shameless about this." She'd said it solemnly, but then her lips quirked up. "You're so proper about everything else, and in some way, you're proper about this too."

She wasn't laughing at him, exactly, but he felt a frisson of ridicule in her words. The same faint sense of puzzled censure his father turned on him in almost every communication between them.

"Shamelessness can have its rewards." He put a hand on her knee, and abruptly, she wasn't smiling. She was watching his hand as he gave her a slight squeeze through her night rail.

"I can feel the warmth of your hand even through my clothing, Tiberius. You make me a stranger to my own body."

He accepted that as a confidence, a reluctant one. He leaned forward and slipped his arms around her waist. "You are not meeting a stranger, Hester, but are encountering an aspect of your being you did not previously allow yourself to enjoy."

This kiss was decorous, because her admissions were telling and deserving of respect. Tye's usual partners knew better than to make intimate confessions in bed, knew better than to allow even a hint of deeper sentiment to pass beyond the bedroom door.

Hester didn't know better—she knew very little, in fact, and if she thought Tye was nothing more than a man driven by propriety and duty, she'd failed utterly to note the tenor of their private dealings.

He let the kiss warm up, let her be the first to slip her tongue over his lips, let her be the first to part her lips in invitation. He obliged, tasting delicately while he felt her wedge closer to him. When she ran her hand over his back, then down to clutch at his backside, he reciprocated by tracing her ribs with his fingers.

She half twisted at the waist, so he could palm one full breast. This prompted her to break off the kiss and rest her forehead on his shoulder.

"You can touch yourself like this, you know," he whispered in her ear. He closed his grip slightly on her nipple. "Bring yourself pleasure."

"I couldn't."

He did not take his hand away, but he leaned back enough to put some space between their bodies. "Undo the bows, Hester. My hands are busy."

A hint of a smile passed over her features. She started on the top bow while Tye caressed both breasts through the fabric. When she'd undone the lot, he didn't push the material aside but drew back.

"Will you let me see you, Hester?" He passed his thumbs over her nipples, the feel of them peaking beneath his touch making him want to tear the night-gown from her. He'd seen her breasts before but really hadn't done them the kind of justice they deserved.

She deserved.

"No rush." He bent his head and kissed that place where her neck joined her shoulder. She sighed against his neck, and her hand cradled the back of his head.

"I like that." Her voice was dreamy. "I do like that."

She must have liked it a very great deal, because when Tye pushed her robe and nightgown off her shoulder, she merely sighed again. Her skin was silky soft, warm, and bore the scent of lavender from her bath.

Perhaps lavender and lemon verbena both belonged

on the well-educated young man's list of aphrodisiacs, because arousal was straining hard against Tye's good intentions, to say nothing of his grand plans.

He lingered over the pulse in her throat, for his own pleasure as well as hers, switched sides, and bared the second shoulder.

Seven

To go by inches, to make no move until he was positive she desired him to make it was different... sweet, and precious in ways Tye did not want to examine too closely. He focused instead on Hester, on the rise and fall of her chest, on her fingers winnowing through his hair when he ran his nose down her sternum.

He'd neglected this before—he'd neglected a great deal having to do with her pleasure and her enjoyment of his attentions. Stupid of him to ignore such a lovely feast, to deny himself such pleasure.

In a single, slow caress, he shifted her clothing aside, baring one lovely, full breast. Hester closed her eyes and let her head fall back. Tye took it for an invitation and closed his mouth over her pink, ruched nipple.

"Oh, *Tiberius.*"

He'd never heard his name spoken in such voluptuous tones. When he drew on her gently with his mouth, she groaned and arched toward him.

She might not have the words to make intimate demands on him, but her body was eloquent with need. Hester sighed, she squirmed, she pulled his hair, and more than once, Tye felt a wool sock stroking over his bare arse. Before she could drive him to utter madness, he rose up and kissed her mouth again.

She'd caught the more languorous rhythm of his lovemaking, caught it and was offering it back to him in slow undulations of her body against his. He kissed her onto her back, and she went easily, cradling his jaw when he rested his cheek against her breastbone.

"I cannot think when you are with me like this, Tiberius. I don't ever want to think again. My wits—"

He brushed his fingers over her mouth. "Thinking isn't required of either of us right now." Thank God. Nor was propriety, nor was proper deportment. What was called for was an impressive display of shameless-ness on both of their parts.

He sat back, surveying her where she sprawled on the chaise. Her clothing was frothed around her, her hair fell about her in golden disarray, and firelight gilded her bare skin. She watched him with slumberous eyes, but when he moved her clothing aside, exposing not just her breasts but her sex as well, she did not move.

To resist what was before him, even for a few instants, was excruciating. "What I need from you, Hester, is for you to enjoy yourself." He'd never said such a thing to any woman, which in hindsight was remiss of him. He reached behind her, grabbed a pillow, and stuffed it under his knees.

Her eyes were going wide as he bent his head and brushed his thumb over her curls. "You may scream if you like. There's nobody in this wing to hear you, save myself, and I will enjoy the sound of your passion."

He enjoyed the taste of it as well. She was sweet and clean, bearing the scent of lavender even here, laced with the fragrance of a willing woman. While he nuzzled her curls, he felt her hand land in his hair. When he shifted her legs over his shoulders and drew his tongue up the damp length of her sex, that hand fell away on a sigh.

Earning her trust took time. It took long, lovely minutes while he traced each fold with his tongue and flirted a finger shallowly into her damp heat. It took the occasional stroke of his palms over her breasts, it took listening for what provoked her sighs and what—exactly—tempted her to minutely flex her spine.

He was distracted by the music of her aroused body, almost to the point where he could ignore the pulse throbbing in his cock and the soft brush of wool against his back.

He settled his mouth over the center of her pleasure and built a rhythm based on the undulations of her hips, the sound of her sighs, the feel of her body opening itself to pleasure.

She didn't scream. When her moment came, Tye sank his fingers into her heat, and she convulsed around him almost silently. Low sounds of pleasure came from her throat, and she bowed up to clutch at him while pleasure wracked her. The spasms of her release reverberated through his body, going on and on until he kept the need to spend at bay by sheer force of will.

When Hester lay back, panting and rosy, Tye brought himself off in a few quick strokes against her mons. His seed jetted onto the pale expanse of her belly, leaving him physically spent and more than a little surprised at his own behavior.

He subsided between her legs, letting himself frankly stare at the lovely, wet, pink flesh of her sex. Time enough later to be shocked at the intimacy of what they'd just done, time enough to wonder where such carnal behavior and the trust it required had come from.

He kissed her knee, nuzzled her sex once, rested his cheek on her thigh, and closed his eyes.

～～

Hester was sure etiquette existed for when a man was going to sleep between a lady's legs, his seed drying on her belly, and her vocabulary sent begging by intimacies too unimaginable to contemplate.

Tiberius would know the words for what he'd just done to her, probably know them in several languages. She traced the curve of his ear with her fingers.

"What is the Latin term?"

"It's vulgar and translates to something like 'he who licks a particular part of a woman's anatomy.' Do not move."

He rose looking disoriented. The sight of him thus—naked, his arousal fading, his hair going in all directions as a result of Hester's disarrangement of it—was disconcertingly *dear*.

He reappeared with a cloth in his hand and resumed his place kneeling between her legs. "This is not what I had planned, Hester Daniels." He swabbed briskly at her belly then more carefully at her sex. "You tempt me beyond the call of reason."

"Do I really?" *What a lovely notion.* "You ter‍
too, Tiberius."

He pitched the rag away and stood scowling dow‍
at her. "A man's sense of self-possession is important
to him, or it ought to be."

Hester hiked up on her elbows and regarded him
as he tried to be stern and proper, his hair sticking up,
not a stitch on him. With a flash of insight, she realized he wasn't afraid, nor was he anything approaching
embarrassed, but he was *uncertain*. The idea that he, of
all men, would suffer such insecurity was untenable.

She pushed up to a sitting position, which put her at
eye level with a part of his anatomy that was curiously
unassuming in its present state, and just plain curious
by any lights.

"Tiberius?" Hester caught him by one wrist and
tugged him a step closer. "My self-possession is important to me too." She leaned forward enough to rest her
cheek over his soft, damp genitals. Two could play at
the business of being shocking, though it wasn't her
aim to disconcert him.

She wanted to reassure him, in fact, and to regain
that sense of closeness with him she'd enjoyed before
he went haring off in search of a damp cloth and his
dignity. His hand gathered her hair and draped it over
her shoulder.

"Is it? Then you will accept my apology for
taking the kind of liberties a man does not appropriate with marriageable women. It was not my
intent to offend you."

She was tempted to take him in her mouth. To taste
him and learn what pleased him. But the dratted man

ranted words now, words and coherent sentences and maybe just a touch of reassurance.

Of appreciation.

"I am not offended." She kissed him low on his belly, the hair at his groin tickling her chin. "If marriageable women are denied the kind of pleasure you just gifted me with, then I pity them as a race."

"Hester?" Her name on his lips had a controlled quality.

She sighed against his skin, wondering why pleasure made her drowsy while it made him loquacious. "Hmm?"

"Nothing." He scooped her up against his chest, her nightgown and wrapper floating to the floor. "You are a remarkable woman."

"I'm a tired woman. You have worn me out, Tiberius."

He settled her onto the bed and stood back, his expression hard to read in the waning firelight.

"For pity's sake, Tye, come to bed. It's time for my vocabulary lesson."

To her relief, he put one knee on the mattress. He'd needed to be *invited* to share her bed, which was interesting.

"Would you rather go back to your own bed?" She held the covers up for him to scoot in next to her. "I hardly know how to go on in this situation. I rely on you to establish the rules."

He fluffed the pillows and got off the bed, which Hester took for a delaying tactic. When he returned, he carried her nightclothes and his robe, all of which he laid across the foot of the bed. "There are no rules, Hester, other than the ones we establish. I think one rule ought to be you don't ask me to teach you naughty language."

"I'll ask Aunt Ariadne, then." Except then Aunt would retaliate with questions of her own.

"You'll do no such thing." In an instant, he'd gone from tidily laying out their nightclothes to blanketing her with his naked frame. "If you're to be acquiring a command of indecent terms, you'll acquire it exclusively from me."

She smoothed a hand over his hair. "I'd like that. Now get under the covers. You'll catch your death strutting around in the altogether with your hair damp. Are you trying to flaunt your wares, Tiberius?"

He rolled off of her, lifted the covers over his body, and lay back against the pillows. "Yes, I am. I am flaunting my wares shamelessly. Are you tempted?"

He sounded amused despite himself—if a little exasperated—and this pleased her, to think she could make him smile even if the damned man wouldn't actually show it. "I am impressed." She rolled over to her side lest he see *her* smile. Behind her, she felt Tye shifting on the mattress, and then a voice sounded very near her ear.

"*Cunnilingus.*"

She drew his arm around her waist and snuggled her backside into the lee of his body. There was no point trying to disguise the laughter that lit her from within, no point hiding her pleasure in the answering humor she felt reverberating through him, either.

∽❧∽

How did a man clarify that he'd come to propose marriage when a woman's mouth was inches from his ill-behaved cock? Tye considered this question as he wrapped himself around his naked, laughing, prospective marchioness.

The answer was simple: *he didn't*. He hadn't, in any case. He'd been too busy resisting the temptation to sink his hand into the golden glory of Hester's unbound hair and guide her mouth a few inches lower.

"Tell me about your sisters, Tiberius. I see you are a faithful correspondent to them."

His *sisters*? Hester was naked in his arms on a commodious, soft bed, and she wanted to talk about his sisters. Very well—sisters were not a topic that far removed from marriage.

"I am blessed with three, all younger. They take after our mother in that they are very sociable."

"Unlike you." She turned her head to kiss his biceps where he'd threaded an arm under her neck.

"Unlike—?" He kissed her nape in retaliation. "If I were any more sociable at the present moment, madam, you'd be wearing my ring."

"Tiberius, did no one ever tease you?"

"Gordie." The admission was out, a truth, not a comfortable one.

"Tell me about him. All I know is he ruined Mary Fran, and then had to be brought up to scratch by the combined forces of his superior officers and the old Earl of Balfour."

"Gordie was not happy in the military." Another admission. "He said the army was changing and no longer a fit place to stash superfluous younger sons and other ne'er-do-wells. He would have done very well as my father's heir."

The words hung in the darkness, something between a shame and a regret, though the truth didn't sound half so awful aloud as Tye had always thought it would.

Hester turned out of his embrace and lay on her other side, so she was facing him. "How can you say such a thing?"

"It's simply a fact. Gordie liked to tool about the countryside, calling on the neighbors, visiting in the churchyard. He could talk politics with my father all night and knew the names of every yeoman ever to raise a chicken on Flynn property."

She pushed his hair off his brow, an oddly soothing caress. "And you don't?"

"I'm not much for visiting."

This caused her lips to quirk up in that secret, feminine smile Tye was coming to watch for. "I'd say you visit rather well."

She shifted again—she wasn't the most restful bed partner—and wrestled Tye into her embrace. He allowed it, though permitting a woman to cuddle him was a novel addition to his intimate repertoire. When he was wrapped in her arms, his cheek pillowed on her breast, his nose full of lavender and lemon verbena, she stroked his hair back off his face.

A slow, pleasurable caress that should have been soothing, though Tye's reproductive apparatus was not exactly soothed. Before she could return to the topic of his sisters—or, God help him, his parents—Tye decided to advance his artillery on the main objective.

"Do you ever consider marriage, Hester?"

She yawned, which had the effect of raising then lowering the feminine pillow beneath Tye's cheek. "Not happily."

"Don't you want children?" Even his sisters admitted to wanting children, though Joan was adamant her artistic and fashion endeavors had to come first.

"Of course I want children." Her reply held not a hint of banter. "Every woman is raised to want a family and a home of her own, and I'm no different, except my parents' union was not happy. My sister is so much more vivacious than I am, so much prettier—she's tall, you know—I accept that I might have to settle for being a doting aunt."

"Your sister could not be any more attractive than you are, Hester Daniels." He hadn't meant it to sound like a scold, but he'd seen Miss Eugenia Daniels in more than one ballroom. "There's a difference between pretty and attractive."

"That is the oddest compliment, but I think you mean it."

He didn't exactly kiss her breast, but he opened his mouth against her skin and breathed in the fragrance of her. "Pretty fades in time, and women who rely on their looks alone can all too easily become pathetic, like a man who relies exclusively on his title. You have bottom and sense."

"Now if only I were seventeen two hands and broke to the bridle, hmm?"

Bottom and sense were to Tye high praise, but it struck him as he nuzzled her breast that Hester Daniels also had a bruised, if not broken, heart.

He lifted his head and rolled to his back. "Come here, Hester. If we're to indulge in the equestrian analogies—which I do not encourage, mind you—then you can mount up."

She regarded him curiously in the dim light but obliged him, straddling his hips and curling down onto his chest.

He undertook to organize her hair. "Why should you have to settle for being a doting aunt? Why not marry?"

Why not marry me? Except winning the argument in the general case before he put a specific opportunity before her seemed the more sensible course.

She was quiet so long, Tye thought she might have fallen asleep. "I was not… I did not exercise good sense when Jasper proposed to me. I let him conduct a hasty, quiet courtship, allude to an agreement with my father, and *impose* himself upon me, all without protest on my part. Marriage is designed to make women stupid. We are supposed to be willing to do anything to gain that prize. I see this now."

For God's sake, it was exactly the argument his sisters made, frequently and at great volume. They insisted on the right to choose, said the church itself did not countenance women being forced to marry, and flounced off to the next house party completely oblivious to the marquess's draconian views on the matter.

"But you want children, Hester, and I think you would make a fine mother."

She cuddled closer and pressed her nose against his throat. "This is a very peculiar discussion to have with you, Tiberius. I did not realize you would excel at prying confidences from me."

Nor had that been his objective, but another part of him wanted to hear her confidences. "I didn't discuss Gordie with anybody until I came up here."

"And then Fee got to you, didn't she?" Hester shifted on him, letting him have more of her weight. "She no doubt had you maundering on about your late brother, and you all unsuspecting. She's gotten to me too, and this is the reason why I will eventually waver on the idea of marriage. I love that child. I would die to protect her, and if we discount last summer, I've known her only a handful of weeks. She is that dear."

"*Die* to protect her?"

"You would too." She sounded sleepy but sure of her point.

He didn't argue—a gentleman never argued with a lady—though marrying Hester hardly equated to offering his life for his niece. Instead of arguing, he stroked his hand over the warm, delicate planes of the lady's back, tracing her bones and muscles, learning her geography by touch.

When he realized he'd let the silence stretch for some minutes, he offered another point for her consideration: "Your husband would give you children, Hester." A high card, he hoped. "He'd provide for you and those children, keep you safe and comfortable all your days."

She said nothing. While her breathing evened out and she became a warm, trusting weight on his body, Tye reveled in the chance to explore her. He could reach the delectable curves of her derriere, trace the knobs and bumps of her spine, turn his nose and catch the flowery fragrance of her hair.

He fell asleep trying to find the right words to ask her—ask her in all seriousness—if she might consider marriage, were he to be the one providing her those children.

❧

Hester awoke feeling safe, warm, and *happy*. The contentment was a bone-deep bodily awareness, spectacular in its pervasiveness.

"Not only do you have sense and bottom"—a large, warm hand squeezed Hester's fundament—"but you excel at the marital art of sharing a bed. Good morning."

Tiberius Flynn, the Earl of Spathfoy, was wrapped around her in all his naked glory. In all of *their* naked glory. What did one say under such circumstances?

"Good morning, my lord."

"Miss Daniels."

She did not dare turn over to peer at him. "Are you laughing at me, Spathfoy?"

"I am cuddling with you, much to my surprise—and delight, of course."

His voice sounded convincingly serious. Hester peeked over her shoulder and found his green eyes were dancing with suppressed mischief.

"Dratted man." Wonderful man. Wonderful, warm man, holding her close and making her day start with such a sense of well-being. "The rain has stopped."

"Ah, the weather. How it gratifies me to know my lovemaking, or perhaps my mere presence in your bed, reduces you to platitudes. And here I took you for the daring sort."

"You are so naughty. Teach me another word if you don't want to discuss the weather."

That shut him up. It chased him from the bed in fact, which was a pity. Hester heard him cross the room, then heard a stream hit the bottom of the chamber pot behind the privacy screen.

She blushed. She listened, and she blushed. When Spathfoy came back to the bed, she caught a minty whiff of tooth powder.

"Will you marry me, Hester Daniels?" He spooned himself around her, making the entire mattress bounce in the process. "I've never spent the night with a woman before. I find it rather agrees with me."

"You have an untapped capacity for the ridiculous, Spathfoy." Now *she* got out of the bed, having to struggle a bit to escape his hold. She grabbed the first piece of clothing she could find—his dressing gown—and wiggled into it before leaving the bed. She didn't need to use the chamber pot, thank a merciful God, but she did avail herself of the tooth powder.

He'd appropriated her toothbrush. Hester set the thing back into the cup that held it and stared.

This was *intimacy*, to share a toothbrush, to wake together. Last night had been intimate too, but it wasn't the sexual thrill Hester would miss when Spathfoy departed.

She would miss *him*—cozy and casual in the morning, laughing with her in the bed, whispering unpronounceable naughty words into her ear, and running his hand over her backside in the most proprietary fashion as she fell asleep on his chest.

Intimacy with him was wonderful, thrilling, and

precious at once. She very much feared this combination of feelings was what vapid young ladies alluded to when they said they were smitten with a man.

In love with him.

She felt an abrupt urge to cry, ignored it, and twisted her hair into a thick braid instead.

"What are you doing back there?" Spathfoy's voice floated from the direction of the bed. "I propose marriage, and you must see to your toilette?"

"Stop teasing me, Spathfoy." She emerged from the privacy screen while tying a ribbon around the end of her braid. "You used my tooth powder."

"Come here, and I shall kiss you, then you'll appreciate my larceny. I could have done that for you."

He was regarding her braid narrowly. Hester stopped her advance before she got within range of his long arms. "Why aren't you leaping up, wishing me good day, and scampering off to your own quarters? The sun will soon be up, Spathfoy."

He looked amused, and perhaps he had cause. His dressing gown hung nearly to the floor on her, swallowing her up in its vast, comfortable folds. Then she realized he was peering at her socks, the only article of clothing to survive the night's festivities in a proper location.

"The sun will be up soon," he said, stretching out on his side, "but the servants know to leave the trays outside our doors, *Miss Daniels*. Stop grousing at me and get back in this bed." He patted the mattress as if he had every right to invite her into her own bed.

"You will not blame me, sir, if you're found here *in flagrante delicto* and we are forced to marry."

She attempted to flounce onto the bed, though his dressing gown made flouncing a rather undignified business. He had to help her get extricated from his clothing, and then she found herself wrapped again in his embrace.

"Do you wish me to go, Hester?"

How she loved feeling the way his words rumbled up from his chest. She closed her eyes, the better to feel him speak. He'd put her on her back, while he was still on his side with her tucked along his length.

"Soon. You must."

She felt his cheek against her temple, felt him hike her leg over his hip. "I'm not teasing, Hester. I have to leave within the week, and I intend to keep proposing to you until you agree to leave with me."

"Hush." She turned her face into his chest to prevent herself from saying something stupid. He *was* sincere. She heard it in his voice, felt it in his body. He was also a man bound by duty and honor to an excessive degree—witness his visit to a mere niece—and Hester was not about to take advantage of him.

She regarded him too highly for that.

"I am not ready to consider any proposals of marriage."

It was the kindest thing she could think of to say. He'd offered out of decency, and she'd declined based on the same consideration.

❧

Hester Daniels doted on her niece, but she positively melted in the presence of the small, drooling bundle that was her cousin Augusta's firstborn.

Balfour caught Tye's eye over the tea service. "We'll

leave them to it, shall we? They'll be cooing and smiling at the wee lad the livelong day while grown men go hungry and cold for want for female attention."

In truth, Tye would rather watch Hester talking nonsense to the baby in her arms. Her expression was one of such suppressed yearning, Tye could practically hear wedding bells—and naughty vocabulary whispered by firelight.

"A ramble to the burn?" Tye asked, rising. Balfour didn't look like he had any agenda other than escaping the ladies' presence, but Tye was learning not to underestimate the man.

"Sounds just the thing. Ladies, you will excuse us?"

His countess sent them along with a wave of her hand, while Hester, Fiona, and Lady Ariadne didn't even look up from where they were fussing over the baby.

Balfour led the way through the back gardens. "I look at that wee lad, and all I can think is my brother had best hie himself back from Canada soon."

"Your brother?"

"My oldest brother, by damn. We had a letter from him a year or so ago, though the man's been officially declared dead. The letter wasn't dated, you see, and my uncle was able to convince the courts it wasn't proof my brother yet breathes."

Tye had heard the gossip. The present earl was a younger son, styled as the earl with all the honors attendant thereto upon declaration of his brother's death. Gossip was apparently not up to date.

"I didn't know of this letter. I gather you would be pleased to see him?"

"Pleased? I'll kiss the sodding bugger on both cheeks and dance the Fling. The verra last thing I want is for my own wee bairn to grow up mincing and bowing his life away as the Earl of Balfour."

"And what is your uncle's interest in the earldom?" Tye didn't particularly care, but Balfour had opened the topic, and it was serving to pass the time.

"He holds the earldom's trusts, and he'll not turn loose of them until Asher is demanding he does so in the Queen's own English with a court order clutched in each fist. The day can't come soon enough for me."

"You'd relinquish the title?"

Balfour stopped walking as they gained the path to the stream. "Are you looking forward to being the next marquess? To spending half your time in the stinking confines of London so you can participate in the farce known as the Upper House of Parliament? Will you drag your family the length of the kingdom several times a year to keep up appearances in Town while trying to stay ahead of the cholera and the typhus?"

He strode off in the direction of the burn. "Bloody lot of nonsense, the title. My dear wife brought me wealth, and I share it with the earldom as she directs, but I would much rather have my brother back than all the wealth and consequence in the world. Come along, man. I want to see the great guddler in action."

Tye followed more slowly, realizing he, too, would rather have his brother back—flaws and all—than the title his father would someday leave to him.

Except that choice was not before him.

"Will you tell Fiona of her impending journey, Balfour?"

"Not today, and possibly not ever." As he ambled along, Balfour snapped off a sprig of heather and brought it to his nose. "I've been in communication with the courts, Spathfoy. Fiona was born after your brother went to his reward. She's a Scottish citizen. Your dear papa has not filed suit in any Scottish court to gain custody of her, which leaves her, I believe, in my custody, or possibly her mother and stepfather's."

"I see."

Balfour had not been idle since Tye had last seen him. He'd put two rainy days to significant use.

"What do you see?"

"You are expecting a legal action regarding guardianship of Fiona. As far as I know, none has been instituted in the English courts either."

They'd reached the stream, and Balfour was tugging at his boots. "As far as you know?" He paused, one boot in his hand, one on his foot. "Would your dear papa make you aware of such a thing?"

"I believe he would. Why are you removing your boots?"

"My niece was impressed with your ability to tickle a fish, Spathfoy. I can't have her head turned by both you and the lad."

Tye used the tree Fiona had climbed to brace himself while he pulled his own boots off. "My father hasn't any need to institute a lawsuit, Balfour."

"He hasn't?" Balfour dropped his socks on top of his boots and stood with his fists on his hips. "He's simply going to lift the child from under our noses and expect we'll accommodate his thievery?"

Tye got his second boot off, and like Balfour, draped his socks over his boot tops. Wool socks...

"My father has sent me an affidavit that ought to be sufficient to guarantee safe conduct for me and my niece from here to Northumbria."

Balfour's expression didn't change, and his tone became, if anything, softer. "Don't be keeping me in suspense, laddie. What manner of affidavit?"

Tye regarded his socks of soft gray wool. "Quinworth has sworn in writing before witnesses of good character that he's read Gordie's will, and in that will, Gordie is very clear that any children are to be raised under the authority of their paternal family. Both the will and the affidavit are witnessed, sealed, and otherwise legally valid documents. I'm sorry, Balfour."

Balfour swore colorfully and at length in Gaelic. "Write to your dear papa that I will be initiating suit in the Scottish courts to establish my custody of the girl."

"Balfour, you can't stop me from complying with my brother's wishes." Though Tye wished his brother's damned will—and his father's preferences—hadn't put him in such a contretemps.

"Then enjoy Fee while you have her, Spathfoy, because I will not rest until she's safely returned to our care."

"I will do my utmost to see that Fiona's best interests are served during her tenure with us in Northumbria. I am bending my every effort in that direction already."

"For the love of God, I wish you'd go bend your damned efforts somewhere else. Now shut your pretty English mouth before you scare the last fish out of the burn."

He stalked off toward the stream, not even turning when Tye spoke again.

"I've proposed marriage to Miss Daniels, Balfour. I think you'll agree that Fiona's adjustment to new circumstances will be made easier by her step-aunt's presence under the same roof. If Fiona's mother can entrust the child to Miss Daniels's care in Scotland, then surely the lady's supervision of the girl will be adequate in England."

And both of them knew the courts would likely see it that way, too.

Balfour turned, his expression impossible to read. "And has Hester accepted your proposal?"

"She has not—yet."

He nodded, muttered in Gaelic about the daft, horny English getting their deserts, and slipped into the frigid water so stealthily, Tye didn't hear even a splash.

❧

"He has proposed marriage, Augusta." Hester made this confession quietly, because Fiona was nearby on a blanket with the baby. Aunt Ariadne had declined to accompany them onto the terrace, making noises about her complexion that Hester suspected were intended to hide fatigue.

Beside Hester on the bench, Augusta also spoke quietly. "Is the proposal sincere, Hester? I do not mean to imply you could not earn the notice of such a man, but—"

Hester held up a hand. "I know, Augusta. My

experience with Jasper has not left me with the greatest confidence in my judgment. I thought I did not like Spathfoy, but the truth is, I did not know him. He is kind."

"*Kind?*"

Augusta's dark brows rose, and Hester could see her cousin found the notion of Spathfoy's kindness absurd.

"He teases me, often so gently I don't even know he's teasing. He does not take advantage of me, and Augusta, I sometimes feel I am taking advantage of him."

"Taking *advantage?*"

Hester nodded, though embarrassment was making her cheeks burn. "He is very skilled in some regards."

"Hester Daniels, what have you done?"

Augusta had anticipated her vows with Ian. Hester was almost sure of that. That wasn't censure she heard in her cousin's voice so much as concern. "Nothing as reprehensible as what I permitted with Jasper, I can assure you of that."

Augusta patted her hand. "I am relieved to hear it. I would urge you to continue to exercise sound judgment in this regard. Spathfoy cannot mean to tarry here much longer."

"He's leaving within the week. He wants me to go with him as his fiancée."

Augusta studied Hester for such a long time, Hester felt another blush rising. "He's told you this?"

"Yes, very plainly."

"Don't give him an answer yet, Hester. Men benefit from being made to work for their rewards— they thrive on it, in fact. Fiona, stop tickling that child or I'll make you change his linen."

Fiona desisted immediately and started singing to the baby in Gaelic.

"I know I'm lonely, Augusta, and I know my confidence is somewhat shaken when it comes to marital prospects, but Tye—Spathfoy—is becoming a friend. I can talk to him about anything—even Jasper—and we laugh together sometimes. This is…" She glanced around, again making sure they could not be overheard. "It's endearing."

Augusta was quiet for a moment while Fiona's childish soprano floated over the gardens in a high, sweet melody. "Did you laugh with Jasper?"

"Not often, but yes, occasionally."

"Did you think he might one day be your friend?"

"I hoped it, at least at first."

"You are smitten with Spathfoy, which is understandable. He's a handsome, wealthy, titled man. If you say he has hidden charms, I will not argue with you, Hester. Nevertheless, such a man can afford to court you properly, to put a ring on your finger, to escort you about all the London ballrooms, to show you off as his affianced bride. Make him give you that at least. Make him wait for your answer, make him do more than pop up here unannounced on some pretext of visiting his niece and sweep you off your feet. You haven't even met his family, haven't seen his estates."

Augusta's words were low and fervent, also very sensible.

"I don't know if I can wait for all that, Augusta. I find him very attractive."

Augusta smiled a feline, married smile. "I found Ian attractive too. I still do, but Jasper left you susceptible to any man who makes an offer, Hester. Can't you just enjoy the earl as a flirtation?"

"I thought I could—I rather hoped I could, and then he goes and turns up gallant."

"And here he comes, though how men can look gallant when they're scowling at each other like that is a mystery."

"At least they're not bringing us any dead fish to deal with. Fiona, your uncles approach."

The girl skipped off, forgetting the baby on the blanket. It was left to Hester to bundle the infant up and take him to his parents. While Spathfoy boosted Fiona into a tree, Ian and Augusta's heads were bent in conversation under a rose arbor.

All Hester caught as she moved to surrender their son to them was Augusta nearly whispering to Ian, "Husband, we *must* talk of this further."

Hester handed off the baby and wondered if Ian was the sort of husband who taught his wife Latin in bed.

❧

"Ian, that man has proposed to Hester!"

Ian settled back against the coach's squabs and regarded his countess—his upset countess—and added one more item to the growing list of things a just God was going to hold Spathfoy accountable for—though the Scottish courts likely would not.

Could not.

"Calm yourself, my heart. You'll upset the lad, and we'll be all night settling his wee feathers. Hester will never give her hand to a lying scoundrel of an Englishman."

Augusta looked up abruptly from the child in her arms. "We still haven't heard from Mary Fran and Matthew?"

"Not a word. I'm keeping the telegraph office in coin, sending wires all over the Continent. Not a single reply."

"This is not good. You are certain Spathfoy hasn't told Hester his plans for Fee?"

"I would bet my horse on it. It isn't that Spathfoy is so English, it's that he has no wife, no children of his own. He sees them as separate bits of business: you propose to this one, you collect that one for delivery to the marquess. If anything, he probably thinks having Fee at the family seat will be an inducement for Hester to marry him."

Augusta blew out a breath, her brows knitting in thought. "That is diabolical."

"That is what happens when a man has no countess to show him how to go on." He tucked an arm around her shoulders and saw that their son—drat the boy, for it meant Ian wasn't to have a turn holding him—was falling asleep in Augusta's arms. "The way the lad is tending to his slumbers now, we won't get our nap this afternoon, Wife. I would bet my horse on that as well."

"You seem to think Hester will throw Spathfoy's proposal back in his face."

"Of course she will. Hester got a bellyful of scheming, charming men with that Merriford jackanapes."

"Merriman. And you have it all wrong, Husband."

He closed his eyes. Augusta might know her own cousin, but Ian knew women. "How is that, my love?"

"Spathfoy is *cunning*, Ian. Hester might detest the man for flying false colors, for taking Fee away from those who love her just because some old man in England has rediscovered his familial conscience, but Hester will go for Fee's sake. She'll marry that useless, handsome excuse for a raiding Englishman to make sure Fee isn't all alone in Northumbria among strangers."

"She wouldn't be that daft."

"It isn't daft when you love somebody. Hester spends more time with Fiona than Mary Fran did."

Ian felt yet another cold slither of misgiving in his vitals. "Than Mary Fran *could*, you mean. Running Balfour on a shoestring took up more of my sister's energies than it should have, but Fee had three uncles about her to keep their eyes on her."

The baby let out a tiny, peaceful sigh, making Ian and his wife momentarily pause to behold their son. For no reason at all, Ian kissed his wife's cheek.

"Fiona is a child," Ian said. "All she knows is her mother was always preoccupied with household matters at Balfour, then Mary Fran became enthralled with Matthew. Of course Fee appreciates an adult spending time with her."

Even an adult such as Spathfoy?

Augusta busied herself cuddling the baby close. "And now her mama and step-papa are off on an extended honeymoon, and Hester has come to the Highlands to mend a broken heart. She and Fee are thick as thieves, Husband. This cannot end well, not for Hester, and not for Fiona."

Ian wanted to argue; he wanted to soothe and reason and offer the comfort of superior male wisdom, though he was nearly certain Augusta had the right of things. He also wanted to beat Spathfoy within an inch of the damned English border.

He settled for tucking his wife closer and drawing the blankets a little more securely around their son.

∽⊛∽

Hale Flynn, ninth Marquess of Quinworth, took his brandy to the balcony of his private sitting room. In the west, the sun was taking its damned time to sink below the surrounding green hills, but to the east, the comfort of night was making an approach.

He sank into a chair, set his brandy aside, and withdrew the letter from his pocket.

Nights were no better really, though when the sun rose, he could ride out over the vast Quinworth acreage and at least find a few hours' enjoyment at the start of his day.

He didn't need to read the letter—he'd written it himself, addressed it himself, sealed it himself. The staff knew, of course. They took the post off each day and brought him the incoming mail all sorted into business, personal, and family correspondence.

This letter had gone out as family correspondence; it came back as personal, as if by action of post, his marchioness could dissolve their marital bond—though not the decades of familiarity marriage had engendered.

Her ladyship was dissolving his sanity. Season by season, year by year, her stubbornness and independence were taking a toll on his reason and on his ability to hold his head up socially. Nobody said anything to his face, of course, but his womenfolk were not *biddable*.

Not the girls and not their mother. Taking their cue
from the marchioness, his three daughters went about
socializing all over the realm, spending the Season in
London, the summer at various house parties or by the
sea, back to London for the Little Season, and then
Yuletide with friends and cousins.

If the northern summer light didn't appeal to Joan's
confounded artistic inclinations, he'd have nobody
to share an eighty-seven-room mansion with but
Spathfoy. And Spathfoy bided at the family seat only
periodically to look in on the farms, or possibly—
lowering, odious thought—on his own father.

Quinworth's voting record in the Lords was
distinguished. His holdings prospered year after year.
He was accounted a handsome man, a man still in his
prime, and from time to time he considered forming
the kinds of liaisons available to wealthy, titled men
even long past their prime.

Then discarded the notion, unwilling to take the
final step that would prove Deirdre had won. With a
sense of growing despair, he held the letter to his nose
and inhaled.

∽∾

"Spathfoy has proposed marriage to me." Hester had
to speak slowly because her Gaelic was very much a
work in progress. She could understand almost everything Fee and Aunt Ariadne said to her, but they made
allowances for her weak vocabulary and faulty syntax.

Ariadne's face lit with pleasure. "This is marvelous!
You will be Fiona's aunt twice over. Have you told
the child?"

Hester got up to pace the small, slightly overheated drawing room where they were having their late-morning tea. "I haven't given Spathfoy my answer, and to be honest, I'm not sure what it will be. Augusta says I should make him wait, and suggests because of what happened with Jasper, I might not know my own mind."

"What happened with Jasper was unfortunate. I trust your fears in this regard have been relieved by Spathfoy's attentions?"

The question was delicately put while Aunt Ariadne fussed with the tea tray. Hester stopped her pacing and regarded Ariadne's serene countenance.

"Is there something you'd say to me, Aunt?"

"Mr. Deal checks the sconces in the occupied hall-ways twice each night, or he has one of the footmen do it to ensure the wicks aren't smoking and there's adequate oil in the lamps. He told Mrs. Deal, who told me, that he heard laughter coming from your bedroom long after the family had gone to sleep. According to him, this is proof the house is once again haunted by some previous owner of dubious political judgment."

Hester turned away as if regarding the gardens beyond the window, though she couldn't help but smile.

"Laughter in bed is a wonderful thing, young lady. A thing to be treasured, and if I had to guess, I'd say Spathfoy is overdue for some laughter wherever he can find it."

"You'll think me wicked." And still, Hester did not risk looking Aunt Ariadne in the eye.

"I'm the one who told you to get back on the horse. Aren't you going to drink your tea?"

Sly old boots. Hester obediently resumed a place on

the sofa. "I haven't, you know. Not entirely. Gotten back on the, um, horse."

"Oh, of course not." Ariadne passed Hester a cup of tea that had to be tepid by now at best. "Though in my day, we didn't buy a pair of boots without trying them on."

Hester hid her smile behind her teacup. "You are incorrigible, Aunt."

"I'm an old woman with a lot of lovely memories. If you're lucky, you'll grow up to be just like me."

"Are you telling me to accept Spathfoy's proposal?"

"I'm telling you not to let me eat all these cakes by myself. You haven't known his lordship long, but sometimes, long acquaintance isn't necessary in affairs of the heart. Has he said he loves you?"

Hester set her teacup down more quickly than she'd intended to. "Love?"

"It's all the modern rage, the love match, or at least the appearance of one. You can marry where you will, Hester, and Spathfoy can likewise. In my day a woman was bound by the preferences of her parents, at least the first time around, but so were the young men. It put the new husband and wife in some sympathy with each other, which was often an adequate basis for friendship."

"I think Spathfoy could be my friend and I his." This felt like the greater confidence, not the fact of his proposal, but why she was considering it.

"Ah. You really should have some cakes, my dear."

"You are no help whatsoever, Aunt." Hester took two chocolate cakes—Fee wasn't underfoot to appropriate all the chocolate ones before anybody else had a chance—and regarded them side by side on her plate. "I want to accept Spathfoy's proposal, but I am uncertain."

"It's hard to be completely sure, though nice if you can be. I was with my second and third husbands."

"And?"

"One turned out to be an idiot, the other was the love of my life." She took a placid sip of her tea while Hester wanted to pitch a cake at her.

"I haven't known Spathfoy long, I haven't met his family, I don't know the state of his finances, he hasn't given me a ring, and he has not declared his feelings for me."

"If you wait for a proper Englishman to declare his feelings, you will soon be an old maid. The ring can be procured easily enough, and I can assure you the man's wealthy. His mother is a genius with figures. What is the real reason you're hesitating, my dear?"

Hester considered her tea cakes, then the view out the window, then the hearth, which sported a fire despite the temperate day.

"I'm not sure."

But it had to do with love. She was fairly certain her hesitation had to do with love, and the likely lack thereof—on Spathfoy's part.

Or maybe it had to do with a lack of courage on hers.

❧

Tye had two days left before he had to leave or risk his father indulging in rash behavior. Two days and two nights to convince a shy, headstrong, passionate young lady not just to get back on the horse but to accept possession of the beast for the remainder of her earthly days—and nights.

He didn't even knock on her door this time, just pushed it open to see Hester sprawling belly-down on the hearth rug, a book open before her, her feet pointing toward the ceiling and her hair in a golden rope over her shoulder.

"I trust I am not intruding?" He strolled into the room and did not permit himself to stare at the soft, warm, wool socks on her upthrust feet.

"Spathfoy." She glanced up but did not rise. "You were very quiet at dinner. I thought perhaps you'd need to catch up on your rest tonight."

She was teasing him. She knew how to tease; he did not. It left him feeling at a disadvantage, until another thought popped into his head: perhaps she was not teasing so much as seeking reassurances.

He came down beside her, arranging himself so she was between him and the fire. "What are you reading?"

"A journal I wrote when I was Fee's age. My penmanship was atrocious—I doubt anybody else would be motivated to decipher it, which is probably a mercy."

"Were you very serious as a child?" He ran his palm down the length of her braid while she set the book aside and rested her cheek on her folded arms.

"I was a happy child as long as I could stay out of Papa's gun sights. Girl children were fortunately beneath his notice for the most part, until Genie became of marriageable age, and then he mostly tormented her and Mother."

She sounded forlorn. "Do you miss your mother?"

God knew, he missed his—particularly since coming to Scotland.

"No, I do not." She rolled to her back and heaved out a sigh. "I wish I did, but I've tried to miss her and I can't. I envy Fee having a mother and stepfather she can miss terribly."

Which topic, Tye was not about to explore any further under present circumstances. He settled his hand on her belly, let it ride up on her next breath. "Will you miss me, Hester Daniels? I leave shortly. I'd have your answer to my proposal before I ride off to the south."

"This is a time-limited proposal, then?" She captured his hand and turned her cheek into his palm, the tenderness of the gesture at variance with the pragmatism of her question.

And with her query, Tye found himself on tricky ground. In the manner of women the world over, she'd dropped him square in the middle of a conversational quagmire, where every reply was fraught with risk.

"Either you want to be my marchioness and bear my children or you do not. I am hoping you do, though I will not beg."

She regarded him by the firelight, her expression so unreadable—so unencouraging—Tye would have gotten up and left the room had she not wrapped a hand around the back of his neck. "When I left London, I did not know you, Tiberius, and now you want to give me children."

"I want to give you *legitimate* children." With Hester, he could envision having a big family. The thought had never appealed before.

"I do not intend to buy a pair of boots without trying them on, Spathfoy."

"I speak of holy matrimony, and you want to go shopping." He kissed her, because a woman could prose on about her shopping at tiresome length. And Hester would prose on while Tye watched and felt the rising and falling of her breathing, and slowly lost his mind with the pleasure of it.

"I do adore the scent of you, Tiberius." She wound her arms around his neck and scooted closer, which reassured Tye he wouldn't be stomping from the room in a rejected huff. The thought that she might, indeed, turn down his offer was... untenable. Leaving Scotland without Hester did not bear contemplation—and not because it would ease Fiona's adjustment to a new household.

"You are in the mood to tease me, Miss Daniels. Am I only to have kisses of you tonight?"

"About my new boots." She levered up and kissed him—really kissed him—her fingers trailing softly along his jaw then stealing down to slip inside his dressing gown and stroke over his bare chest. "I want to ask a favor of you, Tiberius Flynn."

Her thumb grazed his nipple, sending an electric current racing down through Tye's body. "I am disposed to grant favors to you in my present situation." He was also disposed to shift his hand so he covered the fullness of her breast through her nightclothes. Her nipple peaked against his palm, which had to be one of the most erotic sensations a man could endure.

"It's a small favor." She pushed him onto his back,

though it took him a moment to realize what she was about. He'd never made love on the floor before, but it loomed as a capital notion in those regions of his brain still capable of thought.

"You have to close your eyes." She brushed her hand down over his face. He caught a whiff of sweet flowers and tart lemon, probably from the lotion she rubbed into her skin.

"My eyes are closed." He found the bottom of her braid with his hands and slipped the ribbon off it. "What is this favor you seek?"

"In a minute."

He felt her untying the sash of his robe. This too struck him as a positive development. While she parted the folds of his robe, he unraveled her braid and enjoyed the knowledge that she was in all likelihood looking at his rampant erection. If anything, the knowledge made him harder.

"Shall you blindfold me, Hester? I'd enjoy it, I think." The night was rife with firsts—he'd never meant such an offer so sincerely: he *would* enjoy it. "I'm told it heightens the other senses, so I could better revel in the scent, feel, sound, and taste of you."

"Taste." She didn't make it a question, or maybe he didn't give her time to elaborate. Using a hank of her unbound hair, Tye tugged her closer, cradled her cheek with his free hand, and guided her down to his mouth.

"Taste," he echoed. With his eyes closed, the kiss became a lovely, voluptuous, opening ceremony for what he sincerely hoped was another step in the seduction of his future wife.

Or possibly, of her future husband.

"Keep your eyes closed, Tiberius." Fabric rustled and brushed against his ribs. "And you must not move."

At her admonition, he found himself blindfolded and bound by nothing more than the desire to please her, to be whatever she needed him to be for however long she wanted to keep him sprawled naked on her hearth rug.

"Hester?"

"Hmm?" A silky strand of hair wafted across his chest.

"Do I, or does marriage to me, perchance, in some way resemble a new pair of boots?"

More rustling. When he reached out this time, his hand encountered the smooth curve of her naked back, but the position wasn't the right one for kiss—

"More a parasol, I think."

The weight of her head settled low on his belly, and Tye's heartbeat slowed to a dull, pounding thud against his ribs. "My dear, what are you about?"

"Eyes closed. You mustn't stop me."

As if… He licked dry lips. "How do I resemble a parasol?"

He felt her fingers trace up the length of his erection, felt her breath waft across the engorged glans.

"You appear all unassuming, folded up and waiting in the corner for an outing, and then"—she *licked* him, a delicate, catlike swirl of her tongue over the most sensitive spot—"one unfurls you and reveals your beauty, and all manner of interesting uses come to mind."

He should say something, before she—

She took him into her mouth, slid her lips along his shaft, and withdrew, but not all the way. He fisted his hand in her hair and prayed for fortitude. "Hester, you *must* not."

"Must." Another caress with her tongue, and God help him, she cupped his balls at the same time. "You did, with me."

Brilliant, faultless logic. He tried to draw in a breath, but was unwilling to move even that much lest he disturb her. This intimacy was one a man usually paid for, something no decent woman ought to conceive of, and she was *glorying* in it. He drew her hair back over her shoulder. "There's a name for this."

She ran her nose up the length of his shaft, rubbed her cheek against the hair at the base. "Later, Tiberius. I'm a trifle busy at the moment."

And then her mouth was on him again, until she was drawing on him in a slow, maddening rhythm, sleeving him with her wet fingers and driving him past all self-restraint.

"No more, Hester." His voice was hoarse with banked desire, and he had to ease his grip on her hair lest he hurt her.

"I like this."

"For God's—" He pushed her away as gently as he could and used his free hand to stroke himself exactly twice before he was coming, a cyclone of pleasure and lust barreling through his body, making his jaw clench, his spine bow, and colors dance behind his closed eyes.

He suspected he'd lost consciousness. When his mind settled itself enough to process thoughts, Hester had used a handkerchief to wipe him clean. She set the cloth aside, pillowed her head on his belly, and took his cock in her hand. Her grip was just snug enough to be perfect.

He could not have borne it had she moved her hand on him or—merciful God—run her tongue over him even once more; and yet, he could not have borne it if she'd turned loose of him, either.

"You are an astonishing woman, Hester Daniels. An astonishing lady."

And she was going to make an astonishingly wonderful marchioness, too.

Eight

"Neville said you were in a taking about something." Earnest Abingdon, Lord Rutherford, let his observation hang in the air while Deirdre considered bashing him over the head with her teapot.

The Spode was so pretty, though.

"You're fishing, Earnest. Neville probably passed my every confidence to you under circumstances I do not want to contemplate."

"You are missing your children and in want of grandchildren, my dear."

She set the teapot down with an unceremonious thunk. "That is unkind, Rutherford. Has Neville said something to make you jealous?"

"We regularly do things to make each other jealous." He shot his cuffs, looking like a perfectly unruffled, lanky specimen of blond, blue-eyed English aristocracy. "It is part of the dubious charm of our circumstances. When was the last time you saw your daughters?"

"None of your business. Have a tea cake, and I hope you strangle on it. I am not old enough to have grandchildren."

She was more than old enough, which was why they took tea, not by the windows where the fresh morning light would reveal her age written plain on her face, but to the side of the room. By rights she should have a half dozen of the little dears, and be spending all her days flitting from one child's happy household to another.

"Deirdre, I like women. I like them rather a lot, and happen to be married to one I can love, after my fashion. You are nursing a broken heart, my dear. I suggest you mend it before you do something rash."

"I am doing no such thing, Rutherford, though more of this talk, and you will be nursing broken parts of your own."

"Violent passions in a woman can be so arousing." He let his lids droop, the scoundrel, as if he meant what he said. He was trying to cheer her up though, trying very hard in fact.

"What on earth makes you think I'm missing grown children who haven't needed their mama for years?"

He eyed the teacup she held a few inches above the saucer—the teacup that trembled slightly in her grasp. "When you hold your salons, my lady, you are the soul of graciousness, turning your signature smile on each guest who walks through your door. I watch while that smile fades into something very pretty but a shade less warm. You are waiting for your family to come ransom you from your pride, and you are disappointed that they do not. I'll have a word with Spathfoy, if you like."

"You'll do no such thing." She set the tea down untasted and dropped the pretense that Rutherford was wrong. "Tye is all Hale has left. I try to leave the boy in peace. The girls ride roughshod over their father, and I'm very much concerned Hale is the one plotting something rash."

"Such as?"

"Among our set, marriages are still primarily a matter of business. His lordship has the authority and the"—she searched for a word that wasn't unduly disrespectful—"the consequence to contract marriages for his daughters."

"The ballocks, you mean. He'd risk the scandal of his daughters crying off though—which might send them running to their mama."

Intriguing notion—but what of her poor daughters? The Daniels girl had cried off for reasons Deirdre suspected were all too understandable. The last Deirdre had heard, the young lady had been packed off to distant relations on some Scottish grouse moor, probably never to be seen again.

But Rutherford raised an interesting scenario. "If the girls came running to Mama, then Hale would be sending Tye around to retrieve them, and I cannot place my son in such a position."

Her only surviving son.

A silence began to spread, sad on her part. From the look in Rutherford's eyes, impatient on his. "Deirdre, I'd take you to bed if I thought it would help."

"Your idea of flattery can leave a woman feeling less than intrigued. Wouldn't Neville take exception?"

"Neville is the one who suggested we make the offer—you will note the plural. He doesn't share his toys often, and neither do I." He sipped his tea, as if they were discussing whose coach to take on an outing. But God in heaven, what did it say about her that she was considering taking them up on their questionable generosity out of sheer boredom?

She picked up her teacup and wondered what bad behavior her husband was permitting himself because he was *bored*. He was, and always would be, a handsome man to whom many a buxom diversion would come easily to hand—or to bed.

"You see?" Rutherford set his cup down. "I lay all manner of scandalous offers at your slippered feet, and you merely stare at your tea. I would be insulted if I didn't know this isn't mere coyness."

Coyness. How long had it been since Deirdre had felt *coy*—had felt anything but tired and lonely?

"I'm speechless at your generosity, Rutherford, though I fear I must decline. When did you say you had to meet Neville?"

"Apparently not soon enough for you." He rose and drew her to her feet. "Do you know why I love my wife?"

"She's the soul of tolerance, for one thing. She's also very discreet, and she looks marvelous on your arm."

He slipped Deirdre's hand into the crook of his elbow and led her toward the front of the house.

"My wife is my friend. She is the mother of my children—and they *are* my children, despite what you and all the other gossips might think—but first and foremost, she is my friend. I have her loyalty, her understanding, her moral support, and every other indicator of firm friendship, and she has mine. I think dear Hale would offer you friendship, Deirdre, if you'd give the man one more chance."

Despite the footman hovering in the hall, Deirdre turned and leaned against her guest—let the help gawk and report what they would to titillate Hale's ears. "I'm not like you, Rutherford. I can't run my life like a traveling circus, with all manner of sophisticated relationships in unexpected locations. The problem is"—she looked around and lowered her voice to a near whisper—"I do love my husband, but I sincerely doubt he loves me. He won't come ransom me from my pride, as you say, and this leaves me nothing but pride."

Rutherford, for all his business acumen, was an essentially kind man. He wrapped Deirdre in his arms, holding her closer than a mere friend, not as close as a lover might.

Deirdre could take only limited comfort from the embrace. Rutherford was not quite tall enough. He was too angular. His scent was a proprietary blend ordered from Paris, not the solid aroma of bay rum Deirdre preferred. Worse than all this, of course, was the fact that he pitied the woman he held in his arms.

Deirdre closed her eyes, swallowed back tears, and tried not to pity her as well.

❦

Fellatio.

Hester stared at the little scrap of paper that had been neatly folded under her hairbrush. The bold, back-slashing letters were in the same hand as the letters Spathfoy had addressed to his family.

She was fairly certain of the term's meaning, but on her way to breakfast, she stopped off in the library to make sure. The enormous, musty English dictionary was of no assistance, but the French dictionary defined a close cognate with sufficient clarity to confirm Hester's hunch.

Married life would be interesting, if she accepted the earl's offer, though she was unnerved to think he'd ride off come Monday morning, regardless of her acceptance or rejection of his proposal. She wasn't to be given time to consider her new boots; she was to try them on and skip away in them to married life.

Such calculation in a prospective husband gave her pause.

And yet, she was a trifle disappointed to find Spathfoy had ridden into Ballater at first light, most likely to make arrangements for his return journey to England.

Fiona looked up from a bowl of porridge liberally topped with raisins, and beamed a smile at Hester. "It isn't raining anymore!"

"Good morning to you, too, Fee. Did you leave any raisins in all of Scotland?"

"I like them, and Uncle Ian says anything that comes from the grape is good for us. Can we take a picnic to the oak tree this morning? She'll wonder where I've been."

Hester exchanged a smile with Aunt Ariadne and brushed a hand over Fee's crown. "The oak doesn't expect you to visit when it's pouring, Fiona, but yes, we can take a blanket and a snack and pay a call on your friend. Any excuse to enjoy the fine weather will suit."

She served herself eggs and bacon and two slices of toast, while Fiona chattered on about a letter she'd gotten from her parents.

"Do you have the letter, Fee?"

"I have it in my pocket. I'm going to keep it until they come home." She passed over a single piece of paper, her expression slightly anxious. "Mama says she misses me."

"And we miss them, too." Hester turned the missive over and passed it to Aunt Ariadne. "Your mother has a very pretty hand, Fiona. You must strive to emulate her."

"To what?"

A masculine voice replied, "Copy." Spathfoy stood in the doorway, looking windblown and handsome. Hester sipped her tea lest she gaze too long at his mouth. "To emulate is to copy or follow the style of. For example"—he ambled into the room—"if I wanted to emulate you and cover my porridge with raisins, I'd likely find the kitchen's supply has been raided into next week. Lady Ariadne, Miss Daniels, good morning."

He took the place to the right of Aunt Ariadne, the same place he'd taken every morning, which put him directly beside Hester and across from Fiona.

Fiona grinned at him over a spoonful of porridge. "Did Rowan jump everything between here and town?"

"He jumped every fence and ditch and even a few shadows, some sunbeams, and a brace of invisible rabbits. May I have the teapot, Miss Daniels?"

She slid it down to him, and their hands brushed as if by accident—*as if.*

Marriage to him wouldn't be boring, not sexually, but then what? When she'd presented him with an heir and a spare, and a few daughters to fire off for politically expedient purposes, then what?

Then he'd still be handsome and wealthy, and he'd probably have his papa's title as well. She'd be... consoling herself with her children's company, only to watch each child grow up and leave home, as children were wont to do.

That wasn't going to be enough. Even Jasper would have given her that much.

And friendship wasn't enough either, though it certainly added lovely potential to an otherwise fascinating bargain.

As Hester sat beside the man who might become her husband, she decided that regardless of what the future held for them, she was not going to buy her marital boots without thoroughly trying them on.

Beneath the table, she shifted her leg so her thigh was pressed up against Spathfoy's more muscular limb.

"Might I have the butter, my lord? The prospect of fresh air and sunshine seems to be reviving my appetites."

He turned to regard her, something like caution lurking in his gaze. When he slid the butter dish close to her hand, this time he did not touch her.

∽

The damned day had taken for-bloody-ever to plod past. Tye had sat under the treaty oak and tried not to stare at Hester's hands, her mouth, her ankles, her hair, her anything. Contemplation of those prizes so threatened his composure he'd climbed into the tree himself and had a protracted conversation with Fiona about her father's years at school.

Gordie had been one for playing pranks. Whereas Tye had been a proper little scholar, Gordie had made friends before the first meal in the commons. Tye had tried year after year for firsts and often gotten them; Gordie had barely attended his studies and had a grand time.

"But he did enjoy languages, for which you also seem to have an aptitude." He was resting his back against the trunk of the oak, while Fiona made a clover necklace several feet away.

"What's an aptitude?"

"An ability. It will serve you well when you take your place in society."

Hester glanced over at him, her expression difficult to decipher. When she looked at him of late, there was a measuring quality to her gaze, as if she were trying to reconcile the clothed, articulate man with the naked, incoherent heathen she'd had in her bed.

Tye himself was finding that a challenge.

Dinner passed with excruciating slowness, only Lady Ariadne's benevolent presence making a civilized meal possible. By the time they got to dessert, Tye was envisioning trifle spread on various parts of Hester's body, or—God save him—on his body, while the lady showed no sign any inconvenient thoughts were plaguing her whatsoever.

Lady Ariadne folded her serviette by her plate and sent Tye a smile that had no doubt felled princes in her youth. "That was a delightful meal, but now I must retire. Spathfoy, I wish you'd consider prolonging your stay with us. Fiona delights in your company, and I do as well."

"I wish I might stay longer, but my father's business waits for no man." He assisted her to her feet, handed her the length of carved oak she used as her cane, and watched while she made her deliberate progress out the door.

"She's slowing down." Hester made this comment from her place at the table. "She keeps up appearances for my sake and Fee's—we could hardly bide here without her to chaperone—but Ian said they were afraid she would not make it through last winter."

"You'll miss her when she's gone?"

She turned her wine glass by the stem. "Of course. I've wondered how my life might have been different if I'd had an aunt like that, somebody wise and kind to love me when I felt most unlovable."

Tye did not resume his seat. He stood a few feet away, studying the way the candlelight cast her pretty features into shadows. That she would speak of feeling unlovable no longer surprised him; it was indicative of the kind of courage she had in such abundance.

"Shall we take a turn in the garden, Hester?"

"Please." She aimed a smile at him, and maybe it was the candlelight playing tricks, but it seemed a sad smile. He assisted her to her feet and resisted the urge to lace his fingers through hers.

As they made their way through the house, it occurred to Tye that Balfour likely held hands with his countess, regardless of who was looking on, or who wasn't looking on. Tye hadn't seen his own parents hold hands since Gordie's death, or possibly even before that.

"What are you thinking, Spathfoy, to grow so silent?"

Hester twined her arm through his as they wandered among the roses, her stature not striking him as short or tall or anything, but the perfect complement to his.

"I'm recalling the day of my brother's funeral."

With someone else—with anyone else—he would have offered a polite prevarication. "It's the last time I recall my parents holding hands."

She said nothing but slipped her arm around his waist—a posture more familiar than holding hands. He settled an arm over her shoulders and sent up a prayer that this woman might be his to escort through the roses for all the rest of his days.

He had not known Hester Daniels long, he had not acquainted himself with her immediate family, he had no idea if she had a penny to her name, but he did not question the depth of his regard for her. He wanted her honesty and her courage, he wanted her trust, and he wanted her body, all for his very own.

But that list, impressive and greedy though it was, was not complete, for he wanted her heart too.

"I am going to come to you tonight, Hester, unless you tell me not to."

"If you did not come to me, Tiberius, I would surely be coming to you. Shall we sit for a bit?"

Relief swept through him, making him admit that all her considering glances and subdued smiles had caused him to doubt. The doubt did not disappear—she had not accepted his proposal overtly—but it ebbed the longer they sat side by side holding hands in the gathering darkness.

When the stars were starting to come out, Tye rose. "May I escort you to your room?"

She placed her hand in his and let him lead her into the house, up the stairs, and to her door. "Give me a few minutes, Tiberius." She kissed his cheek and disappeared into her room.

What was a few minutes? Was it five or thirty? Tye decided it was however long it took him to prepare for bed, which was not long at all. His clothes were neatly folded in the wardrobe, his body as clean as soap and water could render it, his teeth scrubbed, and—only because he'd caught sight of himself in the cheval mirror as he'd charged toward the door—his hair brushed.

His first cotillion hadn't rendered him as unsettled as he was standing outside Hester's door.

She opened the door without him even having to knock, leaving Tye for one instant to fear he was about to be rejected, so solemn was her expression.

And then she smiled. At him.

She smiled the secret, pleased female smile that had been driving men beyond reason since time began, a smile of promise and mystery, of blessings bestowed and blessings withheld. He smiled back, a man in contemplation of bestowing a few blessings himself.

"Come in." She stepped aside while Tye crossed the threshold then closed and locked the door behind him. A survey of the room revealed that she'd banked the fire, drawn the drapes, and turned down the covers on the bed.

And yet, tossing her onto her back and gratifying his lust would not do for Tye's prospective marchioness.

"Shall I braid your hair, Hester? It's lovely down, but I would enjoy being your lady's maid." He'd also enjoy undoing her braid once he got her in bed.

"I haven't had a lady's maid since I shared one with Genie during my one London Season. Here." She handed him her brush and took a seat before her vanity. "This will be a new experience."

"For myself as well." He'd brushed Dora's hair when she was small, Dora being the youngest, but that had been ages ago. "How is it your hair bears the fragrance of flowers?"

"It's the shampoo I use. That feels good."

He was making long, slow strokes down the length of it, watching light dance along each strand. She'd brushed out her hair earlier, for he'd yet to encounter a single tangle. "One braid or two?"

"One down the middle will do." She leaned forward, so her forehead was resting on her crossed arms. "We're going to be intimate tonight, aren't we?"

"Most would say we've been intimate already." He brushed her hair to the side and planted a kiss on her nape. The scent of her, the feel of her soft, silky skin made his pulse leap in low, heathen places.

"We're going to copulate." She said the word carefully, as if she might have seen it in print but not heard it spoken.

"From the Latin *copulare*, to join together." The last of his doubt drained away. If he'd held to one glimmer of reason in his dealings with her—one hint of honor—it was that only her intended ought to share such a pleasure with her. "I will enjoy very much joining together with you, Hester."

Joining his body, his life, his heart. He finished up a loose braid and scooped her into his arms, wanting the conversation and dallying and dithering to be over. She was willing; he was ready. More than ready.

And yet… for his bride, for the woman into whose keeping his heart had apparently strayed, that was not enough. He kissed her nose, laid her on the bed, and unknotted the sash to his robe.

"My goodness, Tiberius. You demonstrate an impressive enthusiasm for this intimacy." She reached between the folds of his robe and drew a finger up the hard length of his erection.

"And if I acquit myself in the manner you deserve, my lady, your enthusiasm will soon eclipse my own." He leaned down, and while she caressed his testes, he undid the ties of her robe and nightgown, though—in aid of his own sanity—he did not push the material aside.

"Come here, Tiberius." She held out her arms, as if she were inviting him to mount her directly. When he hesitated, she spread her legs. "Come to me."

"I don't want to rush—"

She captured his wrist and gave him a stout pull toward her body. "I do want to rush. I want to gallop and soar and feel the wind in my hair, Tiberius. We can hack around the park some other night."

Because, he concluded, they had many other nights—a lifetime of other nights—to test each other's paces. He tossed away his robe and covered her body with his own.

"At least permit me some kisses, Hester."

He gathered she was not inclined to argue. She got a grip on his hair that was coming to feel familiar and fused her mouth to his.

"If you ever cut your hair, Tiberius—" She'd broken off the kiss to take his earlobe into her mouth.

"If you ever cut *yours*—" The feel of her body beneath him, so very nearly joined to his, had Tye's voice sounding harsh to his own ears. He got a hand over her breast, teasing her nipple between his thumb and forefinger.

"Tiberius Lamartine Flynn." Her nails dug into his backside, sending a gratifying jolt of lust to his vitals.

"What's your middle name?" The question created a pause in the lady's attempts to wrestle her lover into submission and into her body.

"You want to know that *now*?" She hooked her ankles at the small of his back and arched her hips into him. "Now, you want to discuss names?"

"I want to know the name of the woman attempting to ravish me." He scooted his hips back. "The complete name." The name she'd say when they spoke their vows to each other.

"Wretched, awful man." She subsided beneath him, going quiet on a sigh. Her hand brushed slowly over his back, then moved down to pet his buttocks. "My complete name—and I am not trying to ravish you, but merely to effect the purpose for which you have arrived to my bed—is Hester Willamette Daniels."

"Willamette is pretty."

"It's odd." She sighed against his shoulder then closed her teeth gently over his collarbone. "I'm rushing, aren't I?"

"Trying to; I'm trying not to let you." He slipped a palm around the back of her head and cradled her face to his shoulder. "You don't need to get this over with, Hester, like your first jump after a bad fall."

"What if I don't like it?"

He was tempted to tell her she'd like it, then show her she'd like it, and hope she did like it. He kissed her cheek, hitched himself up around her, and started making a mental list of the ways Jasper Merrihell was going to regret treating Hester Willamette Daniels Flynn badly.

"I am going to impart to you now a truth, Hester. Attend me closely, please, because in about two minutes, I will be incapable of speech."

She undulated beneath him, her intimate curls brushing against him low on his belly. "I'm attending you closely, and I cannot imagine you being rendered incapable of speech. Not ever."

If she kept that up... "Becoming intimate with another this way takes time, Hester. It's like learning a language shared with only one other person. You must instruct me regarding what pleases you, and I will offer you the same insights regarding myself."

"This is the trust part, isn't it?" She punctuated her question with a glancing caress to his nipples.

"It's trust and pleasure, served together to both of us. And if you don't like what I'm doing, you tell me to desist."

"I told Jasper to desist." She said this very quietly, her face pressed to his throat. "He kept saying 'in a minute.' It was a very long minute. He did not hurt me, but he did disappoint me."

Merriman *had* hurt her, and when Tye could muster the mental focus, he'd determine a way to hold the man accountable. "If I don't desist when you ask, you simply grab my testes, and you'll have my undivided attention."

"Grab your... your command of Latin has me agog, Spathfoy."

She was talking vocabulary when what was wanted

was reassurance. Tye focused on where their bodies were close but not joined. "What about this? Does this leave you agog?"

He pressed forward, not even an inch, and she went still. "Oh, *Tiberius*." She gave a luxurious roll of her spine, as if she'd take him into her body all at once. "Yes, please. That leaves me quite, quite…"

He did it again, not enough to penetrate her sex but enough to tantalize. Her legs closed around his flanks, a snug hold embodying reassurances of its own.

The moment of joining his body to a woman's was a little interval of tedium, usually. It bridged the gap between preliminaries and escalating pleasure, and yet it required focus and patience.

With Hester sighing and moving beneath him, Tye wanted to prolong their joining in all its aspects. He moved slowly, slowly in the advance-and-retreat rhythm of coitus. He offered her kisses; he offered her an embrace that cradled her close and cherished that closeness at the same time. He shoved his own gratification as far from his awareness as he could, listening instead for the signs that her arousal was gathering steam.

"Tiberius?"

"Here."

"This is… Oh, *God*." She convulsed around him with no more warning than that, bowing up to clutch at him while he resisted the temptation to drive into her faster and harder. When her pleasure subsided, he stilled.

"Are you all right?"

"Uhn." She drew her foot up the back of his leg.

"When you plan your trousseau, you must add a number of pairs of wool socks, Hester."

"I'm not planning anything at the moment." She sounded dreamy and sated, poor dear.

"*I'm* planning something."

Against his chest, Tye felt her eyelashes flutter open. "You are the sort of fellow who's frequently planning something. Maybe you're planning your journey south."

"My journey to points south on your body, perhaps." He started moving again, slowly, but with purpose. "Shall you gallop again, Hester, and feel the wind in your hair?"

"*Again?*" She lifted her face to peer at him by the waning firelight. "Isn't it time you sprang your own horses, so to speak?"

"Soon."

For form's sake, he pleasured her once more without permitting himself to spend; and because he was a gentleman, he did not labor the point any further. Because he was human and male, he in fact *could not* labor the point any further.

"Tiberius, can we do this *all night?*"

The wonder in her tone did his heart good. "Eventually, but because you are inexperienced, to persist much longer would leave you sore."

And himself dead or committed to an asylum for men who'd suffered excesses of self-restraint.

"Sore?"

"You're going to want a soaking bath in the morning."

"I see."

"Hester?"

She nuzzled his neck, which he took for as much answer as he was going to get. He shifted so his mouth was right near her ear. "*Hold me.*"

She'd long since caught the knack of moving with him, and closed her arms and legs around him. "You'll fly with me, Tiberius? Take the last fence with me?"

He'd meant to pull out. *Coitus interruptus* was a term even the scholars failing their Latin knew before they left public school. The sweet, snug heat of her removed this useful phrase from his vocabulary, though, flung it right out of his mind, tossed it far from his heart.

He thrust steadily, hard and deep, and within moments felt her sex fisting around his cock in great, clutching spasms.

"Tiberius, *please*."

She sank her nails into his arse, bit his shoulder, and obliterated his awareness of anything save the soul-deep pleasure of joining her in a shared moment of ecstasy. He gave up his seed into the welcoming depths of her body, gave up his self-restraint, his heart, his all in the act of loving her.

❧

"Aunt Ariadne, what are these trunks doing here?"

Hester examined the brass hasps on three large valises airing out in the hallway of the family wing.

"One never knows when one might go on an extended journey." Ariadne thumped past at a stately gait. "Perhaps I'll head south soon and avoid the coming cold weather."

"Cold weather is still months off." Weeks, anyway. Hester gave the trunks one more puzzled glance, then followed the older woman to the head of the stairs. "I can't believe you braved the steps merely on a whim, Aunt. What is going on?"

Ariadne did not have to look up very far to face Hester, but rather than do that, she laid one hand on top of the other on the knob of her cane. "I do believe dear Ian has come to call again, and with more rain threatening by the moment. Go greet him, Hester, I'll be along directly."

Something was afoot, something wild horses and handsome Cossacks could not pry loose from Ariadne This puzzle added another touch of unease to a day that was already unsettled, probably because Spathfoy would be leaving in less than twenty-four hours.

While Hester would be remaining behind. She wasn't going to tell him "no," she was going to give him a "maybe"—an encouraging maybe, an almost-certainly-yes maybe, but a maybe nonetheless. She could not leave Fiona and Ariadne alone, for one thing, particularly not when the child had been through so much upheaval already.

And she needed time to sort out her feelings, to parse infatuation from deeper attachment, to test her own judgment. How she would convey these things to Tiberius had yet eluded her, but she hoped on the strength of their growing friendship that he would listen and give her the time she requested.

"Ian, welcome!" She accepted the earl's green-eyed scrutiny and his kiss to her cheek. "You've come alone?"

"Aye, my countess says His Bairnship might be coming down with a wee cold, so I'm left to wander the heather all on my lonesome. Has Fee been running you ragged, Hester Daniels? You look a touch fatigued."

"I've been up late reading old journals." Not a lie, but Ian's steady scrutiny suggested he understood it for a half-truth. He patted her hand and laid it on his arm. "We'll feed you some scones and tea, flirt with you a bit, and you'll perk up in no time. Ariadne MacGregor, are you scampering about unescorted again?"

Ian did flirt, and charm, and yet all the while, Hester had the sense he was masking an alert watchfulness, and then it occurred to her Tye was not yet in evidence. Hester had seen him cantering up the drive—yes, she'd watched out her window like the veriest schoolgirl—which meant he was likely in the stables, fussing his horse.

"If you're looking for Spathfoy," Hester said, "he's not yet back from making arrangements to ship Flying Rowan down to Aberdeen on the train. Tea, Ian?"

"Of course. Where's my little Fiona, then? Did she cadge a ride with her bonny new uncle?"

Ariadne glanced up from the tray. "The child is in the library, reading and drawing pictures. She's taken to drawing lions and is getting quite good at them."

Ian accepted his tea and stirred it slowly. "If she drew one more unicorn, I'd have to paste a horn to poor Hannibal's forehead. I'll look in on the girl before I go. You've not said anything to her?"

He aimed his question at Aunt Ariadne, which was odd. Hester had been the one to greet him, and if Fiona had learned Ian was visiting, she would have dropped her lions and stories and insinuated herself into her uncle's company in the next instant.

So what had he meant, about not saying anything to Fee?

Ariadne glanced at Hester fleetingly. "I haven't said a word."

Hester set her cup and saucer down carefully. "Is there something you two aren't telling me?"

"Yes." From Ariadne.

"No." From Ian.

They exchanged another glance, then Ian shot to his feet and went to the window. He spoke with his back to them. "Am I to understand Spathfoy has said nothing to Hester?"

Ariadne remained seated. "As far as I know, he's said nothing to Hester or Fiona."

"Said nothing about what?" Hester didn't recall rising, but she was somehow across the room, beside Ian, her gaze locked on his.

"Now, lass, there's no need to get into a dither. We'll get it sorted out soon enough."

She wondered wildly if Jasper Merriman had decided to come visit her in the Highlands. "No need to get into a dither about *what*?"

Ian shot her a single, tormented glance. "Come with me." He took her by the wrist and led her toward the door. "Ariadne, if Spathfoy shows up, kill him for me."

"Of course, Ian."

"Ian, you are not making sense. Why would you want to kill—?"

He came to an abrupt halt outside the library door. "The sodding bastard is taking Fiona with him when he leaves tomorrow, Hester. That's been his purpose for coming here, though I suspect he's a reluctant minion for old Quinworth. I've come to tell Fiona she'll be taking a journey with Spathfoy, though how I'll look that child in the eye—"

He looked away. His grip on her wrist was nearly painful.

"Spathfoy is *taking* Fiona from us?"

Ian dropped her wrist. "I canna stop him, lass. The local courts can't help, because Fee's possibly an English citizen. Mary Fran left me no documents, and Spathfoy has an affidavit from the marquess. The old man swore in writing that Gordie's will says Fee is to be raised by her paternal relatives. We will get her back, though. I vow that to you and to the child herself."

He sounded as if he was trying to convince himself, but all Hester could think, all she could take in, was that Tiberius Flynn had become her lover all the while he was planning on stealing Fiona away to be raised by strangers.

Her lover, and if he had his way, her fiancé. Doors were slamming, Ian was speaking, but Hester could not make sense of the words over the thundering of her heart.

"Balfour, I wasn't aware you'd scheduled a call."

The voice was coldly, obscenely beautiful. Hester could not face the man who spoke, the man who'd joined his body so tenderly to hers just the previous night.

"Fiona deserves at least a day to make her good-byes," Ian said. He did not offer Spathfoy his hand, and at that moment, Hester would have been glad to see Ian draw a pistol on their guest.

Their *guest*. Her would-be fiancé, Fee's long-lost uncle, Hester's suitor—his list of transgressions grew with every breath Hester took. She fisted her hands at her sides and raised her chin to meet Spathfoy's calm green-eyed gaze.

"My lord, perhaps you'd like to join us. Ian and I were just about to explain to Fiona that you'll be taking her to live in England."

"To visit," Ian said though clenched teeth. "It might be a ten-year-long visit, though I can assure you, Spathfoy, it will be the longest, most miserable ten years you or your benighted excuse for a father pass on earth. I will bankrupt you with lawsuits, spread the scandal wherever I go, trade on my acquaintance with the Sovereign, and deluge my niece with letters, ponies, and visits from her Scottish relations until that girl comes home to the people who love her—and my efforts will be as nothing compared to what Mary Fran and Matthew will do."

Hester risked a look at Spathfoy's face. His features might have been carved in marble, so austere was his expression. "You do what you must, Balfour, as do I. Miss Daniels, I regret that you've learned of this development from someone other than myself. I had intended to tell you after the meal tonight."

Was he insinuating he'd have told her when she was naked and panting in his arms?

"Ian has spared you the trouble, my lord. Perhaps we ought to concern ourselves with conveying Fiona's good fortune to her?"

She kept her voice perfectly, lethally civil.

Spathfoy looked uncomfortable. "Hester, I had hoped to be able to tell the girl you'd be joining us on our travels."

"Hopes get dashed with appalling regularity, my lord. Ian, this task is not made easier by putting it off." She took Ian's arm and let him escort her into the library, leaving Spathfoy to trail after them and close the door quietly.

"Uncle Ian!" Fiona shot away from the big estate desk and wrapped her arms around Ian's waist. "Is Aunt Augusta with you?"

"She is not, though you'll see her soon, I'm sure. What have you been drawing, Fee?" He hoisted her to his hip, as if she were a younger child, and carried her to the chair behind the desk.

"I'm working on my lions, like the lion that was Androcles's friend. I can't get the nose right, but I thought I'd go out to the stables and look at the cats, and maybe that would help."

"Any excuse to visit the stables, right?" He sat with her in his lap, leaving Hester to go to the window and try to shut out the conversation taking place. She was aware of Spathfoy standing beside her and tried to shut his presence out as well.

"Fiona, you know your uncle Tye must leave us tomorrow?" Ian's voice was conversational and pleasant, not at all the tone of a man imparting bad news.

"Yes, but he might visit again, mightn't he?"

"He's your uncle, so we'd never turn him away, but he's offered to take you with him on his journey. To take you on the train clear down to Northumbria."

Ian made it sound as if this were a grand adventure, an unparalleled opportunity, and viewed dispassionately, perhaps it was.

More likely, Spathfoy's "offer" would ruin a fragile child's last prayer of happiness. Hester wiped a tear from her cheek and tried to figure out what, exactly, Spathfoy had done wrong. She wanted to

name his sin and hold it close for as long as it took
to forget him.

"If you'll agree not to do this, I'll marry you,
Spathfoy." She kept her voice low while Fiona asked
Ian a question about how fast the trains went.

"You'd hate me if I accepted that offer, Hester. I'd
hoped you would understand. This is for the child's
own good, though if the choice were mine, I'd leave
her here."

"The choice *is* yours."

"It is not." He held out a handkerchief to her. She
ignored it and fumbled for her own.

"Tiberius, how could you?"

She hated herself for asking, mostly because there
was no explanation he could offer—not for stealing
Fiona away, not for lying about the purpose of his
visit—that would ease the ache in her heart.

"We'll talk." He squeezed her shoulder, which had
her fisting her hands at her sides again lest she tear into
him physically. Perhaps he sensed her growing ire,
because he moved away.

"I don't think I want to go right now, Uncle
Ian." Fiona fiddled with a pencil as she stared at her
drawings. "I'd rather wait until Mama and Papa come
home, and then we can all visit together. You and
Aunt Augusta and Aunt Hester can come too."

"But not your wee cousin, eh, child?" Ian had
switched to Gaelic, which meant Hester had to concen-
trate mightily to follow the sense of his words. "I do
not want to hurt Spathfoy's feelings, Fee. His old papa
wants to meet you, and that's your own papa's father."

"Is he as old as Aunt Ariadne?"

"He's quite old," Ian said, letting the inference of impending death hang in the air. "I would hate for him never to meet you, Fee, as bonny as you are."

"I'm your favorite niece." She dimpled at this long-standing joke.

"You're Connor's favorite niece too. He'll come call on you with your aunt Julia, to be sure."

"I miss Uncle Con."

"I would be very proud of you, Fiona, if you accepted this invitation. You have aunts at Quinworth, and I'm thinking there might even be a pony or two."

Hester silently commended Ian for that.

"A pony?"

"Possibly two, though Spathfoy will have to teach you to ride them. You might even find a pet rabbit. An English marquess can surely afford a pet rabbit for his favorite granddaughter."

"A *rabbit*?"

Hester glanced over to see Spathfoy was studying the rose gardens beyond the terrace. The damned man would be procuring a menagerie for Fiona at the rate Ian was making promises to the child.

"And I'll write to you, Fee. We'll all write to you, and I'm guessing your mama will go directly to Quinworth when she comes back to England."

"But that's why I don't want to go." Fiona hopped off his lap. "Mama will think I did not miss her because I went to Grandpapa's, or maybe she'll think I'm angry at her." Fiona had spoken in English and crossed the room to take Spathfoy's hand. "I don't want to hurt my mama's feelings."

Spathfoy glanced down at the girl who peered up at

him. Hester held her breath, waiting for some imperious pronouncement spoken in clipped, precise tones.

Instead he went down on his haunches and met the child's gaze. "Now here's a difficulty, Niece. I don't want to hurt your mama's feelings, either, but I have my papa to deal with. He asked me to fetch you south, and I told him I would."

"I can write my grandpapa and tell him you tried very hard. I'll come visit as soon as Mama says I can."

Spathfoy studied her much smaller hand in his. "Your uncle Ian is right, Fiona. Your grandpapa is not a young man. I think he's looking forward to meeting you very, very much."

"Do you have a pony there?"

"I'm sure we can find a pony for you."

"And you'd teach me to ride it?"

Hester could not watch while Spathfoy reeled the child in—guddled her trust—with the means Ian had handed him.

"You already know how to ride quite well, if my experience with you on Rowan is any indication, but yes, I will provide what instruction you need."

"And a rabbit?"

Spathfoy bit his lip, probably the first time Hester had seen the man hesitate over a word. "I'm not teaching you how to ride a rabbit, Niece. I've no notion how such a thing would be undertaken."

Fiona grinned hugely. "No, Uncle, may I have a rabbit for my pet when I'm at Grandpapa's?"

"Yes, you may. Now will you agree to come with me?"

"I will, but just for a visit."

"Fiona, there's more you need to know." Hester spoke with admirable calm considering her heart was breaking for the child, for herself, and for the Earl of Balfour as well.

"What else? Unicorns aren't real, and I don't want a lion for a pet because he might eat my rabbit and scare my pony."

"He would scare me as well, and likely even your uncle Tye." Hester sat on the sofa and patted the place beside her. Fiona abandoned her uncle and joined Hester on the sofa.

"Your uncle is inviting you for a visit, and Uncle Ian thinks it would be nice of you to go. I am worried, though."

"I'll write to you, Aunt Hester, and I'm only going for a visit. You'll miss me, and then I'll come back, and you can pummel me at the matching game again. Maybe I'll pummel my grandpapa while I'm visiting."

"I'm anxious," Hester said, ignoring her own urge to pummel Lord Quinworth and his handsome, silver-tongued, mendacious son. "Your grandpapa might have such a grand time when you go visit him that he won't let you come back to us when you want to."

Fiona's expression shifted to a thoughtful frown. "Uncle Tye will talk to him, and Mama will come get me." Her mouth curved into a smile. "Or I can ride my pony all the way home, like Uncle rode Flying Rowan out from Aberdeen."

"Fiona has the right of it." Spathfoy came down on the child's other side. "If she's not thriving in Northumbria, I will certainly have a very pointed discussion with my father, perhaps several pointed discussions." He was silent a moment. "Perhaps many such discussions, and I'm sure Balfour will abet me in this regard."

He looked directly at Hester when he spoke, which cast her into some confusion. He was going to deliver the child to Quinworth, then lobby for Fiona's return to Scotland? Then why take her south in the first place?

Ian rose from his seat at the desk. "Well, that's settled, then. Fiona, I'll be at the train station to see you off tomorrow, and so will your aunt Augusta. I'll have a letter for you to deliver to your uncle Con, and I want you to pass it directly into his hand. Can you do that for me?"

She bounced off the sofa. "I can do that, Uncle Ian, but I must go tell Hannibal I'm going on a journey, and the hens will want to know."

"Come along then." He extended a hand toward the child. "You'll be up half the night packing unless I miss my guess. I don't suppose you'd like to take your wee cousin with you when you leave?"

Fiona fell in with Ian's teasing and left the room in great good spirits.

Hester let the ensuing silence stretch until she couldn't bear it any longer. "Did you mean it?"

Spathfoy was on his feet, staring out the window, his back to Hester where she sat on the sofa. "That I will take my father to task if Fiona's unhappy? Yes, I meant that, though I will also make every effort to see that Fiona thrives at Quinworth."

"I do not understand why you must do this." She got up to pace, resenting the need for further conversation with him. "You are arrogant, Spathfoy, and you've been deceptive, but I don't read you as cruel or stupid. Why would you do this to a helpless child?"

"I'm arrogant? Fiona says I'm mean."

"You are not mean."

He turned to regard her. "I had hoped you would see this as an opportunity for Fiona, Hester, an opportunity she might easily adjust to if you were in the same household."

"Do not cozen me, Spathfoy. My guess is you considered having Fiona under your father's roof an inducement to sweeten the offer of marriage you made me. It matters not. I'm not marrying you, and Fiona is being taken away from her family."

"I am her family too, Hester. More so in some regards than you are."

"I love her."

She'd said as much only a handful of days ago, but he was listening to her now. Hester perceived this in the way he regarded her, steadily and maybe unhappily.

"Do you suppose I do not love her, Hester? Is that why I and my relations are such a poor choice for the child? Can a child be loved and cared for properly only in Scotland?"

She didn't know how to answer that. He looked troubled and tired standing by the window, and very much alone.

"I wasn't going to go south with you, you know."

"Ah. You were toying with me, then? Striking a blow for beleaguered women everywhere?"

She didn't quite believe the mockery in his tone.

"I was not. I wasn't going to refuse you, either. I was going to ask for some time to consider our situation when my head wasn't so muddled."

He nodded, a cautious inclination of his head that gave nothing away.

"I don't trust my judgment, Spathfoy. I laughed with you, you see, and this was... oh, why am I bothering to explain when I am so confused in my own thinking?"

"Go on, by all means. If you're rejecting a man's offer—the first such offer I've made, by the way—you can at least tell him why."

"That is not fair, Tiberius." He waited until *now* to tell her he'd never proposed to anyone else? And damn him to Hades, for she believed him. He'd lied about the purpose of his visit, but she believed him about this.

And about almost everything else, too.

He shifted away from the window and took the place beside her. "I tried to warn you, if you'll recall."

"You said not to trust you, is that what you mean?"

He scrubbed a hand over his face and nodded. "Yes, but then I got muddled too, you see. When I set out for Aberdeenshire, I thought I'd be plucking an orphaned child from very humble circumstances and gaining every advantage for her. I'd appease my father, set some other matters to rights, and be back in England within a week."

"Are you *admitting* you're perpetrating a wrong?" It would put Hester in quite a quandary if he were.

"I'm *admitting* I gave my word on a matter without properly researching it, and that as a consequence of my negligence, there are now results contrary to what I intended."

He was back to making grand, obfuscatory speeches. "That is not an apology." Which ought to relieve her, but did not.

"It is an explanation, also very likely a waste of time in present company." He closed his eyes and leaned his head back against the cushions, the image of a weary, defeated man. "I am sorry, Hester, for misrepresenting myself in the guise of a guest, and for not clearing up my purpose for being here before I became irrevocably intimate with you."

"What do you expect me to say to that, Spathfoy? That I'm sorry as well?"

"I am *sorry* I've given you cause to doubt your judgment again." He spoke very softly. "I would do anything to redress that wrong, but, Hester, has it occurred to you we might already have conceived a child?"

⁓

The list of reasons why Tye could properly label himself an imbecile—and worse—was endless.

He'd egregiously misjudged Hester's reaction to having Fiona placed in her grandfather's care.

In the alternative, he'd miscalculated Hester's reaction to not learning of this eventuality sooner and from Tye himself.

He'd also completely misunderstood Hester's hesitance in giving him an answer to his proposal. She hadn't been being coy or manipulative, she'd been... *muddled*, doubting herself.

He'd underestimated Balfour's commitment to the child, and shuddered to think what manner of legal and social havoc was going to result when Clan MacGregor took up the cause of Fiona's repatriation.

He'd badly, badly bungled matters when he'd allowed himself the ultimate intimacy with Hester last night, and for that, mere apologies would not do.

"If you are carrying my child, I hope you will reconsider my proposal, Hester."

"Our child." She shot to her feet and marched off on a circuit of the room. "How likely is it that I'm with child, Spathfoy? I know very little of these things."

"It's not impossible, not by any means. My mother would have me believe I was conceived on her wedding night." Despite the wreckage all around him and the travail lying ahead, Tye found this recollection cheering.

"Merciful Saints. I thought there were things a man did to prevent conception. Jasper assured me I couldn't get pregnant."

Tye did not dignify that with a reply.

"He was lying, wasn't he? And those things to prevent conception, we didn't do them last night, did we?"

He was not going to give her the Latin now. "*I* did not do them. I presumed unforgivably on my marital expectations with you."

"Are you trying to make me hate you, Spathfoy? Or is that grave tone to make me think you're sorry?"

She was growing increasingly agitated, for which he had only himself to blame. "I do not want you to hate me, Hester. If you're carrying our child, I want you to *marry* me. I dare not insist that you do, but I can ask if marriage to me would be so terribly objectionable."

She stopped her pacing and whirled to face him,

hands on her hips. "You've betrayed my trust, Spathfoy. I cannot marry you."

"Your judgment is not trustworthy when you're tempted to accept my suit, but it's faultless now that you're rejecting me? Do you trust that judgment enough to visit bastardy on a child who might otherwise be heir to a marquessate?"

She was once again his personal tempest, ire and indignation radiating from her posture, from her eyes, and her words. "I almost *can* hate you when you're like this, Tiberius, all cold reason and precise diction. Do not threaten me with ruin. Thanks to my previous bad judgments, I'm already ruined. I did not permit you into my bed, I *welcomed* you there. I'll bear the consequences of that folly on my own, thank you very much."

She sounded exactly like his own mother when she was in high dudgeon over some folly of his lordship's. In such a mood, a man could say nothing right, could not appeal to reason or sentiment.

Tye was halfway to the door when he realized he'd just word for word applied the very defenses he'd heard come out of his own father's mouth on so many tiresome, sad occasions. He stopped, turned around, and kept his tone civil with effort. "What are your terms, Hester Daniels?"

"I beg your pardon?"

He advanced on her, pleased to see she stood her ground—it wasn't as if he'd ever intend her bodily harm, for God's sake. "What are your terms? On what terms will you marry me if you're carrying our child?"

"I don't know what you mean."

At least she wasn't shouting, and when he leaned

over her like this, Tye could catch a whiff of her lemony fragrance and see the gold flecks in her uncertain eyes.

"I mean," he said softly, "we are two intelligent people who will want what is best for our child. We can argue over whom to blame for the child's conception—though I cannot view the matter as entirely unfortunate—but we must not allow an innocent child to suffer for our decisions. On what terms would you marry me?"

She blinked, some of the fight going out of her. "I will not live in England, not while your father is alive and making mischief like this."

"Done. I have an estate outside Edinburgh, and my mother has just finished refurbishing it. What else?"

He'd surprised her, but the renewed fire in her eyes said she was rallying. "This child will be born on Scottish soil, Tiberius, promise me that."

"I promise you that to the extent it can be brought about by mortal man. What else?"

She eyed him up and down. "If your idiot father is determined Fiona cannot live with her mother, than she'll live with us."

"I'm not sure I can arrange that. Quinworth seems to be legally in the right of the matter."

"You *can* arrange it, Tiberius." She folded her arms, looking very certain of her point. "Something is driving your father's decision to retrieve Fiona. He's ignored her existence for her entire life, and now he must have her posthaste. Figure out what his motivations are, and you will be able to wrest her from him."

Her reasoning was sound, and it spoke to the

puzzlement Tye had felt regarding his father's behavior since the first mention of this Scottish venture.

"I will not make you a promise I do not know I can keep, Hester."

"Then we do not have an agreement. You had best hope we don't have a child, either." She flounced out, every inch a woman intent on having the last word.

He let her have it, silently saluting the library door when she'd gently closed it in her wake.

They had managed to convert an argument into a bargaining session. He decided to be encouraged by that. He was also encouraged that she'd used his given name occasionally, even to express her ire toward him. Then too, she'd given him a great deal to think about regarding his father's choices in this whole, misguided matter—he was encouraged by this as well.

Though she might not be pregnant.

And he might not be able to meet her terms.

And he was going to have to find his niece two ponies and a *rabbit*.

And he was leaving in the morning.

Tye went to the sideboard and poured himself a generous portion of whisky, downed it in one swallow, then poured another.

Nine

FIONA FOUND GOING INTO BALLATER WITH THE knowledge she wasn't going to come back for quite a while exciting and a little frightening. She sat in the big coach with Aunt Hester on one side and Aunt Ree on the other, the conversation the kind of cheerful talk adults thought up to distract nervous children.

To keep children from missing their mamas and worrying that their mamas might not come fetch them home from Northumbria after all.

"I want to ride with Uncle Tye."

Over her head, Fee could feel the aunts exchanging a look that spoke silent, grown-up volumes.

"There's no harm in that," Aunt Ree said after a small silence. "You'll be sitting in the train for most of the day, and your uncle ought to understand you need fresh air as much as he does."

Aunt Hester didn't say anything. She had not said much of anything all morning, and this too gave Fee an uneasy feeling. Aunt Hester never made things up, never teased and flirted and charmed like Uncle Ian, Aunt Augusta, and even the servants did.

Aunt Hester rapped on the roof three times, and the coach lumbered to a halt. Halfway across the field to the right, Uncle Tye brought Flying Rowan down to the trot and turned for the coach.

"Don't pet the horse, Fiona," Aunt Hester said. "You'll want to keep your hands clean for when you picnic on the train with your uncle."

Aunt's voice was tight, like she was keeping more words back than she was parting with.

When Uncle rode up to the window, Aunt Ree explained the delay, and Fee was enormously pleased to find herself shortly up on Rowan, cantering toward the train station. Uncle was quiet today, too, which made Fee think maybe he was homesick or missing his family.

Rowan, though, was in wonderful form, sailing over three stone walls and a burn in fine style. When Uncle brought the horse down to the walk, Fee figured it was as good a time to ask questions as any.

"Do we have to take the train?"

"If we want to arrive in Northumbria before week's end, yes, we do. Lest you think the prospect of train travel cheers me, Rowan and I are as enamored of trains as you are."

E-nam-ored. Fee said the word to herself silently three times, and added it to her list of Words Uncle Says. Often she could tell what the word meant from how Uncle used it, and that saved her having to ask.

When they got to Ballater, Uncle got off the horse and did not let Fee get down immediately. Instead, he found a boy to walk Rowan, and when Fee thought she was going to be scooped off the horse, she was instead directed to climb onto her uncle's back.

"I won't get lost, Uncle. You can put me down."

"I need to check for wires at the telegraph office, and you would so get lost. I'd spend half my morning trying to locate you, the other half rearranging our plans when we missed our train, only to find Rowan was already in Aberdeen along with all your trunks."

He was striding along as he spoke, sounding quite bothered. Fee resigned herself to being Seen And Not Heard, which was something Uncle Con swore was written in the Bible, though nobody had shown Fee where it said that.

When they got to the telegraph office, Uncle collected his wires and stood outside on the board-walk, reading them almost as if he'd forgotten his own niece was clinging to his back.

"I'm going to swear, Fiona. You will neither emulate me nor tattle on me." He kept his voice down.

Emulate meant copy. "I like hearing you swear. You're good at it. Have we missed our train?"

"We have not, but the damned nursemaid I hired to meet us in Aberdeen has developed some mysterious blasted illness, and we will thus be cast upon each other's exclusive company for the entire perishing journey."

From the sound of his voice, that was probably a bad thing—to him.

"Can't Aunt Hester come with us?"

Because Fee was on his back, she felt him sigh, felt the way his chest heaved and his shoulders dropped. It would have been fun, except Uncle was unhappy. He maneuvered her to her feet, took her hand, and led her to a bench with a marvelous view of the train station's front porches and coach yard.

"I asked your aunt to come with us, and she declined."

"Is she mad at you?"

"How ever did you gain that impression?"

"She sat next to me at breakfast instead of you, she would not look at you, and she barely ate anything. She was like this when she first came up from London too."

Uncle looked pained, which left Fee wanting to do something to help. "I can ask her to come with us."

"Fiona…" He cast a glance at her, looking, for the first time in Fee's experience, uncertain and a little weary. Her mama had looked like that a lot before she married Papa. "It's complicated."

"Are you e-nam-ored of Aunt Hester?"

"Quite." His smile wasn't cheerful at all.

"She is e-nam-ored of you, too. You made her smile, a real smile too, not just for show so I'd leave her alone."

"I made her very upset with me when I revealed that I wanted to take you away to Northumbria. She regarded it as a betray—" He scrubbed a hand over his face and lifted his gaze as if he were talking to God. "I cannot believe I am discussing my amatory failures with a child."

Fee did not know what amatory meant, but she knew all too well what failure was.

She patted her uncle's arm, which was like patting a rock. "I get in trouble all the time. You apologize, and you behave for a while, and you try to do better next time. Everybody makes mistakes, even Aunt Hester. She told me so herself."

"Thank you for that sage advice."

"Uncle, you have to at least *try*." He was being thickheaded. Aunt Augusta said men were prone to this. Mama had not argued with her over it.

"Child, I cannot make your aunt forgive me, I cannot undo the hurt I've done, and I cannot change my father's mind once it is made up."

It occurred to Fee that he was Being Impossible, but when she was Being Impossible, it was usually because she was upset, tired, and hungry.

"Uncle, you try to fix what you did wrong not so you can have dessert and get a story before bed. You do it because you're a good person and you don't want anybody's feelings to be hurt."

He gave her a funny look. "Am I really a good person? I thought you said I was mean."

She shrugged. "That was just words, because I was in a taking."

He was quiet, gazing out over all the people and coaches bustling around the yard. "I suspect I use a lot of words, because I am in a taking too."

Grown-ups were not always very bright. Fee smiled at him encouragingly, because he was trying. Uncle Tye guddled fish and climbed trees and loved to ride his horse really fast, but he also tried to be grown-up all the time.

Which must be hard.

Fee had a cheerful thought. "Do you remember that you beat me at the matching game?"

"I was showing off, which was stupid of me."

How somebody could be stupid and win was a puzzle for another day. "You won a *favor* from me."

"Fiona Flynn, I cannot ask you to manipulate your

aunt into accompanying us to Northumbria, when the woman has made it plain she never wants to set eyes on me again."

"Then don't ask me." Fiona Flynn. She was a MacGregor of clan MacGregor, but Fiona Flynn sounded like the name of a brave Scottish girl who could befriend lions.

Uncle said nothing, which was likely more thick-headedness. When the coach pulled into the yard and the ladies got out, Fee hopped off the bench and darted directly to Aunt Hester's side. Grown-ups could be exceedingly silly, just as Fee's mama had often told her.

❧

Hester caught sight of Spathfoy sitting by himself on a bench, looking somehow alone amid all the noise and activity of the yard. She should be glad he was going. Glad he was making it easy to write him off as another deceptive, self-absorbed, useless man with no ability to govern his urges.

Except that would not wash.

She had no ability to govern *her* urges, at least where he was concerned, and that would have been a sufficiently daunting realization in itself. It was made worse by the sneaking sense Spathfoy had honestly sought to improve his niece's circumstances by taking her south, and his father—may the marquess develop a permanent bilious stomach—had somehow cornered his son into kidnapping Fee.

"Aunt!" Fiona barreled into Hester's side. The child had been a bundle of energy all morning, and the ride on her uncle's horse had only made her more excited.

"Calm down, Fiona. The train isn't leaving for half an hour at least."

And for that entire half hour, Hester wanted to hug the girl tight and tell her how much she was loved, and how badly she'd be missed by her Scottish relations—which would hardly make Fiona's departure any easier.

"Aunt, I've changed my mind."

Fiona was swinging Hester's hand as Spathfoy led his horse away to be loaded on the train. Rowan seemed to comprehend what lay before him at the same time Fiona had made her announcement, because the horse planted his front feet and showed every intention of rearing up on his hind legs.

"Fiona, you have to go. We've discussed this. It might be a long visit, but it won't be forever."

Hester watched as Spathfoy spoke sharply to a porter who'd produced a stout driving whip. The earl turned to his horse and began to scratch the beast's withers.

"Aunt!" Fiona jerked on Hester's hand in the most irritating fashion. "I'm not going, and you can't make me."

The dratted child had all but bellowed this announcement to the entire train yard. Hester had the mean thought that perhaps Spathfoy could come guddle his niece's nerves the way he was soothing his horse.

"Child, what is this racket?" Aunt Ree came bobbing through the crowd. "My ears will not recover from such an assault."

"The nursemaid Uncle hired to travel on with us

from Aberdeen has fallen ill," Fiona said. "I'm not going with just Uncle."

Aunt Ree shot Hester a frown. "Child, you adore your uncle."

Fiona's expression turned mulish, making her look very much like her uncle Ian in a stubborn mood. "Uncle is a *man*."

Through all the other emotions roiling through Hester—anger, sadness, confusion, and not a little self-castigation—she heard what her niece wasn't saying.

"He has sisters, Fee. You tell him you have to use the necessary, and he'll find a nice lady to assist you."

Fiona dropped Hester's hand and crossed her arms over her middle. "Nice ladies are strangers. I'm not going to the necessary with a stranger. And what if I get sick on the train and have to change my dress? Lots of people get sick on trains. Uncle won't even think to have a spare dress or pinny with him."

Aunt Ree looked thoughtful. "The child has a point."

"Perhaps Spathfoy will delay his departure." Even as she said it, Hester knew Spathfoy was not going to do that. His arrangements were made; the marquess was probably tapping his booted foot on the platform at Newcastle that very minute.

"Rowan is scared." Fiona made this observation very softly, and for a moment, Hester, Lady Ariadne, and Fiona all turned to watch as Spathfoy swung onto his horse bareback. The animal was dancing about, raising and lowering his head while he put one hoof on the ramp into the livestock car, then backed away.

This scenario continued until the horse was brave enough to put both front hoofs on the ramp and then stand for a moment, quivering, head down, while Spathfoy sat serenely on the beast's back. The earl might have been taking tea for all the calm in his posture.

"Uncle is telling him not to be afraid. He's a very brave horse, really. He's just young." Fiona herself sounded young, and Hester was reminded of what it had been like to come north by herself just weeks earlier. Her mother hadn't spared her even a lady's maid, meaning Hester had earned looks that varied from pitying to curious to contemptuous.

Fiona had known so much upheaval in the past year…

Rowan put all four feet on the ramp, then seemed to realize what he was committing to, and gave a little rear and spin. His rider waited a moment then aimed the horse back at the ramp.

Watching the earl's patience with his horse, Hester came to a realization: Spathfoy was not a bad man. He had erred in not announcing his purpose before becoming a guest in their home; nonetheless, his decision in that regard meant Fiona was not being carried off by a stranger, but rather by a man she had some liking and trust for.

Understanding the man's failings was not the same as forgiving them.

Fee grabbed Hester's hand again. "Rowan's going to go up the ramp soon. Uncle's wearing him down. Pretty soon he'll feel silly about making such a fuss, and he'll go right up." Fiona sounded so hopeful, as if the horse's troubles were her own. "Won't you come with us, Aunt? You don't have to stay very long, just until Uncle Con comes to visit with Aunt Julia. You'd like to see them too, wouldn't you?"

"I would." The words were out without Hester meaning to speak them aloud.

Aunt Ree thumped her cane. "Well, that's settled then, and here's Ian with Augusta to see you off."

Hester turned a frown on Aunt Ree for jumping to conclusions just as Fiona started squealing and clapping her hands, and the horse—the horse Spathfoy was so patient with—scooted up the ramp into the rail car, forcing the earl to lean right down against the animal's mane lest he suffer an injury to his head.

"I will not stay long with you, Fiona." Hester tried to sound very stern, but the idea of seeing the child safely south was creating an odd lightness where all those roiling sentiments had been. If nothing else, making the journey would allow Hester to give Quinworth a piece of her mind. "I have nothing packed, and I doubt you'll want me to linger while you're learning to ride your pony."

"Two ponies, and you can watch while Uncle teaches me!" As unhappy as she'd been a moment earlier, Fiona was in transports of delight now. "We'll picnic on the train, and we'll play cards, and Uncle can read to us. We shall have a great adventure."

Ian joined them on the platform, Augusta on his arm. "What has my niece kiting about like a spring lamb in clover?"

Aunt Ree smiled beatifically. "There's been a little change in plans. Our dear Hester has agreed to provide escort to Spathfoy and Fiona on their journey. It seems the nursemaid cannot join them in Aberdeen. We'll send a bag along for you on the very next train, Hester."

Ian's brows crashed down. "The *nursemaid* can't join them? We've a house full of nursemaid—"

"Ian." Augusta spoke softly and leaned closer to her husband. "We cannot spare your son's staff on such short notice."

Ian studied his wife's countenance for a moment. "Of course we can't, not when the lad might be coming down with a cold. Hester, does this plan truly have your consent? You need not stay in Northumbria for long."

Hester wanted to hug him, right there in the train yard, for his protectiveness. While the womenfolk were happy to consign Hester to Spathfoy's continued company, Ian alone hesitated.

"If I go with them today, it will make Fiona's transition easier and allow us a spy in the marquess's camp for a time, won't it?"

Dark brows rose. "That it will. Your Scottish heritage is showing, lass. Mind you write often, and here." He extracted a missive from his pocket. "Fee is to put that in Con's own hands. He'll be coming to call on his niece and her relations, with Julia in tow, within the week, and the letter contains as much as I know of the situation."

Fee piped up from her place at Ian's side. "I had a letter from Mama. She wrote from Paris again."

Ian glanced at his niece. "Are you sure it's from Paris? They're not supposed to be in France now."

"She's right, Ian." Hester watched as Spathfoy made a proper fuss over his brave beast, who was now in the livestock car, gazing down the ramp uncertainly. "I saw the letter myself. It was from Paris."

"Which explains why certain wires are not meriting any replies. Wife, remind me to stop by the telegraph office once we've seen Fiona and Hester off."

And with no more ado than that, Hester soon found herself in a private compartment with Fiona and Spathfoy, watching as the child waved madly out the window while the train pulled away from the station, and Spathfoy kept a dignified silence at his niece's side.

ॐ

Tye had just completed a lengthy discussion with his horse about the need to develop fortitude regarding train travel—they'd be coming back to Ballater; on that point, Tye was already quite determined—when Balfour informed him Hester was accompanying Fiona to Northumbria. Hester would make the journey with them, and stay long enough to see the child settled in.

Balfour's tone had carried a distinct sense of, "Don't be fookin' this up, too, laddie."

Tye sat back and regarded a woman he was sure would rather be anywhere than in a private compartment, knee to knee with him. He'd kept his powder dry until Fiona was asleep with her head on a pillow and her feet in her aunt's lap.

"Why did you change your mind, Hester? This journey cannot be something you contemplate willingly."

She didn't even turn her head, but answered while the scenery hurtled by beyond the window. "Fiona guddled me. Don't expect me to stay long in Northumbria."

"I do not understand."

Now she did look at him, her expression one of

bleak humor. "She tickled my sympathies, and I would likely have told her to go to blazes with her big green eyes and pleading looks, but I do not trust your father to treat her well, Spathfoy."

Tye didn't either, not now that he'd met the child. "You don't trust *me,* then, to see to her well-being?"

She averted her eyes again, which Tye felt somewhere in the middle of his chest as a desolating loss.

"Your father has not treated *you* well, Spathfoy, to send you out to do his dirty work. If Quinworth had come himself, if he'd even bothered to make Fee's acquaintance, Ian would have made sure the marquess got a fair hearing with Mary Fran and had a decent relationship with Fiona. Instead, Quinworth puts you up to high-handed legal tactics and base subterfuge. I ask again, what hold has he over you that you'd undertake such doings?"

She asked, but her tone was bored.

"I will not disrespect my father by answering that, Hester, and the subterfuge, as you call it, was mine. I fully intended to collect the child the morning after I met her, and be on my way, but then Lady Ariadne offered me hospitality, and it struck me I ought to familiarize myself with Fiona's circumstances, and then…"

The Deeside scenery was beautiful. No wonder Her Majesty had chosen the Highlands for the private castle she shared with her handsome prince.

"Then, Tiberius?"

In for a penny… "Then I met you." Met his own personal tempest ready to rage him into submission over the well-being of a child she wasn't even related to.

Silence, while they passed through Scotland's

beautiful countryside. When they reached Aberdeen, the wisdom of having Hester accompany them became apparent. Fiona needed to use the necessary, she needed to fidget, she needed to cling and whine and generally carry on like a fretful child while Tye oversaw the transfer of their trunks—and his nervous horse—for the next leg of the journey.

And fortunately, they had no more transfers to make before reaching Newcastle. This left Tye hours to regard the woman he still hoped to marry, and to consider his options.

First and foremost, he hoped she was pregnant with his—their—child. She would marry him if that were the case, he was certain of it. Even Balfour would encourage the match if a child were involved.

Second, Tye could strive mightily to convince his father to return Fiona to her family in Aberdeenshire, and forget whatever crotchet had prompted this wild start in the first place. This option had dubious chances of success. The marquess was not one to back down once he'd taken a position.

Not ever.

The third option was the one Hester had suggested: to find some means of compelling his lordship to reconsider his schemes. Tye had been reluctant to speculate regarding what leverage he could find to put the light of sweet reason in his father's eye.

Such machinations seemed disrespectful. Almost as disrespectful as presenting oneself as a guest when one intended to comport oneself as anything but.

Fiona sighed in her sleep, her second protracted nap of the day. "Shall we wake her?"

Hester brushed the child's hair back off her fore-head, the gesture tender and, to Tye, unsettling. "To what purpose?"

"So she isn't keeping you up half the night when you're obviously fatigued from looking after her the livelong day."

"I'll manage."

With two words, she might as well have kicked Tye out of the compartment, so vast was the indifference she conveyed. She put him in mind of his mother after a particularly vexing donnybrook with his father.

"Hester, I am not your enemy."

"No, you are not." She studied him for a moment in the dim light of the compartment. "You are not my friend, either."

The hope he'd been guarding for a hundred miles curled up under his heart with a weary whimper.

But it did not die. He was nowhere near ready to allow it to die.

❧

They arrived to Quinworth well after dark, though even by torchlight, Hester could see the place was imposing. The facade was a vast expanse of pale blond stone, the same shade as Alnwick Castle, but modern-ized to boast many windows, and terraces abundantly graced with flowers.

Fiona would delight in exploring the place.

"Is she still asleep?" Hester kept her voice down, lest the child slumbering in Spathfoy's arms waken.

"Out like a candle."

"I can take her."

"Get out of the coach, Hester. She's too heavy for you, and you're dead on your feet."

He sounded amused and so damnably patient, Hester had no choice but to comply. A liveried, gloved footman assisted her from the carriage and stood by while Spathfoy managed to maneuver himself and his burden out of the coach.

"Has a room been prepared for the child?" Spathfoy's voice was soft in the gloom.

The footman kept his eyes front. "In the nursery wing, my lord. There's a room for the child's nurse as well."

"Miss Daniels is not the child's nurse, but rather, my guest. Please inform Mrs. Hitchins that Lady Dora's room is to be given over to Miss Daniels's use, and have a truckle bed put there as well for the child."

The footman snapped a bow. "Pardon for my mistake, and I'll see to it at once, my lord. I'm to tell you there's refreshment awaiting you in the library, my lord."

Hester glanced at Spathfoy to see if all these obsequies were making his head spin, but he appeared quite at home.

He *was* home. She surveyed again the enormous edifice before them, and realized how humble Fiona's household in the Highlands must have seemed by comparison.

"Miss Daniels, are you coming?"

She was Miss Daniels now, not Hester. That was to be expected. She moved along at his side while footmen and porters swarmed the coach, unloading boxes and trunks and yelling at one another to have a care with that bag.

This was Tye's welcome home—three "my lords" and a tray in the library.

This was Fiona's welcome as well. Hester was not at all pleased, not for the child, and not for the son of the house who'd been sent north to retrieve the child. She followed Spathfoy through an enormous, soaring foyer, down a lighted hallway, and into a cavernous library.

"We'll need to give the servants some time to make up Dora's bed for you," he said as he laid Fiona on a leather couch, then rearranged the blanket she'd been wrapped in. "And you should eat something."

"Does it strike you as odd that the marquess is not on hand to greet his long-lost granddaughter?"

Spathfoy straightened but continued to regard the sleeping child. "His lordship is an early riser. He and Fiona will have plenty of time to greet each other tomorrow. May I fix you a plate?"

He crossed to a sideboard where Hester spied a veritable feast. "Is this how the help indicate they're pleased to see you?" Beef, chicken, and ham slices were arranged on one tray, several kinds of cheese on another; hulled strawberries were piled high in a crystal bowl; and various pastries and tea cakes with all the fixings sat on a second tray.

No chocolate cakes, though.

"Pleased to see me? I haven't a clue. This is how they indicate they wish to continue in my father's employment. As I recall, you like a deal of butter with your scones."

She let him do this, let him prepare her some sustenance, just as she'd let him manage all the details of getting them safely half the length of the kingdom.

He was good at it, in part because people seemed naturally to heed him, but also because he had the knack of anticipating which detail was about to need attention—like putting a truckle bed for Fee in Hester's room.

She accepted a plate from him, piled high with good food. "Thank you, Spathfoy, but you've served me far more than I can hope to consume."

"We'll share, then. Will you pour?"

She ought to balk. She ought to shove the plate at him, fix herself a more modest serving, and find a single chair on which to seat herself.

But it was late, they were both exhausted, and the remaining sofa looked comfortable. "I'll pour. I should also make up a little something for Fiona if she should wake in the night."

"Ring for the kitchen—one pull is the kitchen, two is the servants' hall, which will get you a footman."

He began to put away food at a prodigious rate, while Hester savored a fortifying cup of tea. She'd just realized she'd poured none for him, when he looked up. "You're not going to join me?"

"In a minute." She passed him a cup of tea, which he drained and held out to her for more.

This little late-night meal held an intimacy. Hester watched Spathfoy eat with his fingers, while the fire—a wood fire, no less—snapped and crackled softly.

"How long will you stay, Hester?"

She could divine nothing from his question, not hope, not impatience. "I don't know. Not long. A few days, maybe a span of weeks. Are you in a hurry to see me off the property?"

He paused with a rolled-up piece of ham halfway to his mouth. "You are tired, and this was not at all how you expected your day to unfold. Have I thanked you? I'm not sure how. I would have managed both Fiona and Rowan in Aberdeen. One of them would have gotten loose and come to mischief if you hadn't been on hand."

"You're very patient with your horse." He was patient under other circumstances, too, but she pushed that awareness to the back of her weary mind.

"I'm not patient so much as determined. I get it from both my father and my mother. Eat something before I demolish the entire plate." He held it out to her, an offering of ham, beef, strawberries, and two buttered scones.

And of peace. He had not allowed her to pick a fight, and she was grateful for his forbearance. "Will you check on Rowan before you turn in?"

"I probably should, but I'll see you and Fiona up to your room first. The layout of the house isn't complicated. I'll give you a tour tomorrow, and you'll catch on in a couple of days. Go ahead and eat the strawberries, Hester. They'll go to waste if you don't."

Hester. She liked it when he called her Hester rather than Miss Daniels. They were not friends, but it was as he'd said: they were not enemies either.

She ate every last strawberry on the plate.

❧

Hale Flynn understood politics. Unlike many of his peers, he understood that the role of the British monarchy was changing. Having a Sovereign with a strong familial orientation at a time when the realm was steering its way past shoals that had caused revolutions elsewhere was not necessarily a bad thing.

He understood horses and respected them for their elegance, utility, and sheer, brute strength.

He understood his place in the world, his title being a symbol of stability and tradition in a society where progress was touted on every street corner while bewilderment lurked in the heart of the common man.

He did not, however, understand his own family.

"Why the hell you put up with that idiot gelding is beyond me, Spathfoy. The blighter's going to toss you in your last ditch one of these days."

Though hopefully, not until Spathfoy had done his duty to the succession.

Quinworth's son eyed him balefully across the horse's back. "I continue to work with Flying Rowan because he's up to my weight, he tries hard, and he alerts me to ill-tempered, titled lords lurking in the saddle room when I'm trying to groom my beast for a morning ride."

"Do I employ half the stableboys in Northumbria so you can groom your own horse?"

Spathfoy went back to brushing his mount. "I've retrieved your granddaughter from her relatives in Aberdeenshire, my lord. I continue to believe your designs on the child are ill-advised, and hope you'll rethink them when you meet her."

Ill-advised was one of Spathfoy's adroit euphemisms—he had many, when he wanted to trot them out. "Is she simple?"

The brush paused on the horse's glossy quarters. "She

is not simple. She is delightful. She has a gift for languages and arithmetic, she's full of life and curiosity, and she's going to be every bit as pretty as my sisters. She's looking forward to meeting her grandpapa, because that good fellow will provide her a pony and a pet rabbit."

"Spathfoy, has your horse tossed you on your head since last I saw you?"

"If he has, perhaps it has brought me to my senses. May I assume we're riding out together?"

"You may." If nothing else, Quinworth intended to get to the bottom of his son's mutterings about ponies and rabbits.

Gordie had been the son Quinworth could understand. The boy had been lazy but likable; the man had been charming, with a venal streak, though probably nothing worse than most younger sons of titled families. The army had seemed a better solution than the church, letters, or the diplomatic service.

Quinworth tapped his riding crop against his boot, which made Spathfoy's horse flinch. "I don't suppose you ran into your mother when you were larking around Scotland?"

Spathfoy—who had two inches of height on his father—settled a saddle pad onto the horse's back. "I was not larking around Scotland. I was snatching a child from the arms of her loving family, for what purpose I do not know—except my father allowed as how, did I accomplish this bit of piracy, my sisters would be permitted to marry where they pleased, and Joan would be sent to live in Paris for at least one year. Or do I recall the purpose for my travels amiss?"

The boy had an aggravating knack for making every

pronouncement sound like a sermon. He was going to give tremendous speeches in the Lords one day, though Quinworth wouldn't be around to hear them.

"You do not recall anything amiss. So you did not see her ladyship?"

"Aberdeenshire being a good distance from Edinburgh, I did not."

He placed a saddle on the horse's back, then slid it back into place. The animal stood quietly, though it was likely plotting more mischief once the girth was fastened. Quinworth considered asking if her ladyship was still using her son's estate outside Edinburgh, but *somebody* had returned a letter he'd sent there not two weeks past, so he held his tongue.

And slapped his crop against his boot.

"For Christ's sake." Spathfoy hissed the imprecation as his gelding danced sideways. "If you're going to torment an animal, at least find one of your own to pick on."

"My apologies." He moved away, lest the gelding start kicking and stomping in the cross ties. Spathfoy spoke to the horse soothingly in Gaelic, of all the heathen languages. Quinworth had tried to learn it decades ago, when pleasing his new wife had been the sole compass of his existence.

He'd been a fool. Likely he was still a fool. He walked off, bellowing for his hunter and slapping his crop against his boot.

❧

"You must be my granddaughter."

Hester looked up from her eggs and toast to see a

tall, older gentleman with graying hair and stern blue eyes standing in the door of the breakfast parlor. The resemblance to Tye was faint, mostly in his bearing and perhaps a little around the eyes.

"Make your curtsy, Fee." Hester spoke quietly, and leavened the command with a smile. Any other relative of Fee's—any other *Scottish* relative, and even Spathfoy—would have known to brace themselves for a hug from the child.

Fiona got out of her chair and curtsied prettily before her grandfather.

"Well done, child. And who would you be?" He barked the question at Hester, making her feel about eight years old and caught snitching tea cakes from the larder.

"That's my aunt Hester. She came with us."

Hester expected his lordship to reprimand Fee for speaking out of turn, but the man instead narrowed his eyes on Hester herself.

"If you're the nurse, then you've presumed to dine at the family table for the last time, my girl. You wait outside the door for Miss Fiona to complete her meal, then escort her back upstairs for her lessons."

He jerked his chin at the two footmen standing by the sideboard, as if to indicate Hester was to be removed bodily, but at least one of them had been on hand the previous evening.

"I am Fiona's step-aunt, Lord Quinworth. My father was Baron Altsax, and I've accompanied Fiona here to ease her transition to your household. It is not my privilege to serve as her nurse."

She could not give the man the cut direct under

his own roof, so she went back to munching well-buttered toast. If this was the fare served to Tiberius with his morning meal, no wonder he'd chosen to absent himself.

"Can I sit down now?" Fiona aimed the question at her grandfather.

"May I." He sounded exactly like Tye when he offered that admonition.

"May I sit down? My porridge will get cold."

Something passed over the older man's features, surprise, possibly, or fleeting humor. "Sit."

Hester did not engage the man in conversation, though she studied him. He quizzed Fiona in French and then German, and Hester herself was surprised when the girl answered creditably well in both languages.

"When I go to Balmoral, we sometimes speak German when we play."

"*You* go to Balmoral?"

"We're neighbors." Fee studied her porridge for a moment, as if pondering whether his lordship might need an explanation of the term. "Her Majesty comes to Aberdeenshire for only a few months every year, though. Do you like raisins?" She eyed the scone sporting an abundance of raisins on his lordship's plate.

"It so happens I do. Hand on your lap, girl. I do not encourage pilfering at table, particularly not before the servants."

"He talks like Uncle Tye." This last was directed to Hester.

"I know. This is your uncle's father, which I suppose explains many of Spathfoy's unfortunate tendencies." Hester realized what she'd said as she was putting the last bite of eggs into her mouth. The marquess was staring at her, glaring at her more like, and he'd put down his scone.

"Explain yourself, woman. And be quick about it."

Fiona was looking raptly at Hester—and a little scared. Hester chose her words, though there was no disguising certain ugly truths, no matter how large and varied one's vocabulary was.

"I have low expectations of a man who will ignore his granddaughter for years, then have her snatched away without the least courtesy to her family, your lordship. Such a man has little sensibility for the feelings of others, as demonstrated by his willingness to enlist his own son in this misguided adventure, and to enforce his high-handed whims without even writing to the belted earl who has provided for the girl's every need for the entirety of her life."

She expected to be tossed from the room, never to see Fiona again.

She expected a dressing down at the least.

She expected Quinworth to raise his voice to her— her own father had done so before the servants on many an occasion.

The marquess let out a bark of laughter. "You remind me of my marchioness. This is intended as a compliment. Pass the teapot and finish your toast."

His lordship went back to interrogating Fiona, while he obliterated his breakfast. The questions ran the gamut from English history, to geography, to animal husbandry.

"I'm told you're in want of a pony."

Fiona stopped fidgeting. "I am not to have a pony just yet. I'm to be a great strappin' beauty, and I will outgrow my ponies too quickly if I start riding them now."

Her grandfather peered over at her. "This is sound reasoning, which unfortunately did not occur to me when I was nigh beggared keeping your aunties mounted practically from the cradle. Would you like to see the stables?"

"Yes, please, Grandpapa."

His lordship scowled at his empty plate. "I suppose I am your grandpapa at that. Miss Daniels, good day. Where shall I send Miss Fiona when we're done with our inspection?"

"I believe I'm in Lady Dora's room, your lordship. Though I might explore the library for a book." She should have asked for permission to use the library, but had the sense her manners would be lost on his lordship.

"Hmph." He rose and did not bow to her. "Come along, Granddaughter."

Fee bolted out of her chair, seized her grandfather's hand, and dragged him from the room.

Hester had just finished her toast and poured herself a final cup of tea when Spathfoy came in, looking windblown and bemused.

"Did I, or did I not, just see my father being led by the hand around his own stables?"

"By a small child chattering a mile a minute? You did. Tea, Tiberius?"

He paused at the sideboard, but it was too late to correct the familiar address.

"Please. Would you like anything more to eat, and was Quinworth at least civil?"

"Nothing more, thank you. To Fiona, he was quite

civil, if a little imposing. I don't like him, though. He's not only arrogant, he's…"

"My mother said he was impossible on more than one occasion. Even his cronies call him a throwback." Spathfoy took the seat beside Hester that Fiona had vacated. "Did you sleep well?"

"I slept very well. Yourself?" He was a good host, she concluded with some surprise. That had to be his mother's influence.

"Well enough. I thought to ride out with his lordship this morning—Rowan needed to settle his nerves over a few fences—though Quinworth and I were arguing before we'd reached the end of the lane."

"About?" She did not want to encourage his confidences, but the footmen had left when his lordship had departed, so she did not change the topic.

"I should have looked in on my mother when I was in Scotland. What sort of son am I, to pass right through Edinburgh and not take the time to see to her and to the estate I've turned over for her use?"

"Your father can't hop a train to check in on his wife?"

"Hopping is not within his lordship's gift. He seldom goes anywhere anymore, just rides the length and breadth of the shire in all manner of weather." He fell silent and tucked into his breakfast while Hester tried to fathom a marriage where a man did not care enough to visit his wife, but could castigate his son for the same shortcoming.

The longer she contemplated this conundrum, the more clearly she understood why Tiberius Flynn might not have been eager to plight his troth to anybody, ever.

And yet he had offered marriage to her.

❦

A week went by during which the hope Tye stubbornly nurtured for a future with Hester Daniels was severely buffeted. After the first day's outing to the stables, the marquess virtually ignored his granddaughter. The pony procured for Fiona—a rotund little slug cheekily named Albert—could not fly over fences as Rowan could, and thus his hairy company was not sufficient to distract Fiona from increasingly severe bouts of homesickness.

Connor MacGregor called with his wife Julia, and gave Tye such broodingly thoughtful looks as to make Tye wonder if Fiona ought to be put under guard, but before he took his leave, the man brought a smile to Fiona's face and promised to visit her again soon.

Which meant Fiona loudly and frequently missed dear Uncle Con and Aunt Julia in addition to Uncle Ian, her parents, Aunt Augusta, the dratted baby, and Aunt Ree.

In utter desperation, Tye bribed his sister Joan to show Fiona some painting basics while he cornered Hester in the library, which had become her haunt of choice.

"It's a pretty day, Hester Daniels. Will you ride out with me?"

She set her book aside and regarded him with an expression he was seeing on her face more and more frequently. Not a scowl, but a knitted-brow, considering, unsmiling look. "Yes, I will ride out with you. Give me time to change, and I'll meet you in the stables. Fiona will be busy with Joan for quite some time, if even half of her questions are to be addressed."

He wanted to offer her his hand, to assist her to her feet, to wing his arm at her as if she needed escort to her own quarters, but he didn't. He kept his hands to himself and settled for a whiff of lemons as she sailed past him.

At the stables, he fared little better. Hester used the lady's mounting block to climb aboard a mare Tye's sisters kept as a guest horse. As the horses ambled out of the stable yard, Hester maintained an aggravatingly serene silence.

"I've been arguing with his lordship." As conversational gambits went, Tye considered that among his worst—though commendably honest.

"I heard you. When I retire after dinner, or Joan and I are strolling the gardens while Fiona goes on a mad tear, Quinworth raises his voice at you."

"He maintains the lungs need exercise the same as the rest of the body."

This, of all things, provoked a smile. "Like you and your swearing."

"Not at all like—" He fell silent for a moment. "Viewed from a certain perspective, there is a rough parallel. His lordship is adamant that Fiona remain here at Quinworth."

"Did you really think you'd change his mind, Tiberius?"

He was in pathetic damned straits, because just hearing his name on her lips warmed his heart, even in the context of that gentle, hopeless question.

"I have changed his mind on other matters, though it's usually a Herculean labor. I am convinced you have the right of it, though. He has brought Fiona here for a purpose, to make some point, though I've yet to divine what it might be."

"Fiona does not keep to her own bedroom at night, you know."

Yes, he did know. Fiona had told him her bedroom up on the third floor was cold, lonely, and plain. She dutifully went to bed up there each night, waited until the household was quiet, then stole into Hester's rooms and spent the rest of the night on a sofa.

"I am aware of this, and dreading the day you depart for parts north."

She fiddled with her reins, then fiddled with the drape of her habit. "I should leave soon. I fear the longer I stay now, the worse it will be when I do go."

"Worse—for Fiona?"

She nodded and said nothing further. An image came to Tye's mind, of him and Fiona waving good-bye to Hester at the train station in Newcastle, of Fiona bursting into tears, and Tye not knowing how he'd comfort the child while dealing with his own upset.

Hester turned a faint smile on him. "Shall we let them stretch their legs?"

"Of course. If we trot to the edge of the trees, we'll come to the sheep meadows. The mare is a solid performer over fences if you get her to a decent spot."

"Lead on, Tiberius."

He set a reasonable pace over stone walls, stiles, hedges, and two streams, with Hester and the mare following three lengths behind. She was a natural equestrienne, one who didn't overmanage her horse, but rather let the beast have a say in how the ride went on. When they came down to the walk two miles later, Hester's cheeks were flushed, and her smile was closer to the bright benediction he'd had from her in Scotland.

"That was marvelous, Tiberius. I can see why your father enjoys riding his acres so much. Was he the one who taught you to ride?"

"He tried, but my mother had to intervene. She has more patience, which is a valuable commodity where little boys and ponies are concerned." He turned Rowan up an old cart track, unable to make small talk when he might never enjoy another ride in Hester's company. "I don't want you to leave," he informed her. "Not until you know if there are consequences from my visit north."

Her gaze went to the green hills around them, to the sheep in the next meadow, to the gray stone wall undulating up the acclivity to their right. "That will be at least another week yet, Tiberius, and I don't know if I can bear to remain here that much longer. Fiona cries, and I can offer her no comfort. Your father barely says two words to her when he comes up from the stables for breakfast, and your day is much taken up with estate matters. My heart—"

She lapsed into damnable silence.

"My heart too, Hester." He nudged Rowan back to the walk, the pleasure of the shared ride swallowed up in the pain of the parting she was determined to bring about.

❦

"Where is that ray of perpetual sunshine known as my niece?" Lady Joan paused in the door of the breakfast parlor to fire her question at Hester. In their brief acquaintance, Hester had realized a tendency to use military analogies where Lady Joan was concerned. She was strikingly tall for a woman, brisk, and bold. Her walk took her places swiftly and directly, her laugh charmed, and her penetrating green eyes were the antithesis of the term "dreamy artist."

"Fee has gone to collect some flowers for her uncle's office. I expect she's waiting for her grandpapa to come in from his ride as well."

Joan took a seat across from Hester, setting down a plate piled high with eggs, bacon, and toast. "She'll have a long wait. I swear his lordship has cast my mother aside for the company of his horse."

Hester tried not to let her surprise at such a comment show. "He cast her aside?"

"Or maybe they cast each other aside." Joan closed paint-stained fingers around the teapot handle. "I will ask Mama about this before I decamp for Paris this fall."

"Tiber—Spathfoy said you were longing to live there."

"Hah." Lady Joan sprinkled salt on her eggs. "Longing is such a polite word. I am desperate to go there, mad to live there, ready to commit rash acts and so forth. Fortunately, Tye has convinced his lordship to allow it."

"The marquess was quite set against the notion?" This was shameless prying, but Joan didn't seem to regard it as such, and Hester was willing to exploit any avenue to gain insight into the man who'd turned her—*Fiona's*—life upside down.

Joan picked up a point of buttered toast and

considered it. "I suspect Papa is contrary as a means of gaining Mama's notice, and she's indifferent as a means of maintaining his. The four of us children have learned to navigate between the two, though I must admit this is part of what makes Paris attractive."

"You want to get away from your family?" And *this* was the milieu in which Fiona was to be raised?

"I adore my siblings." Joan tore off a bite of toast with straight, white teeth. "And when I was younger, Mama and Papa were alternately squalling like cats and cooing like doves. I shudder to think what manner of husband Papa would have found for us if Tye hadn't intervened."

Hester's breakfast started a quiet, uncomfortable rebellion in her vitals. "I beg your pardon?"

"Papa was grumbling about it even yesterday: he promised if Tye brought Fiona to Quinworth, then Mary Ellen, Dora, and I might have our choice of husbands—within reason. Fiona's here, and my sisters and I are breathing a collective sigh of relief. My year in Paris was part of the bargain as well, though I suspect Tye is footing the bill rather than Papa. More tea?"

"Please." Hester pushed her cup and saucer across the table only to realize the cup was more than half-full. "Just a touch."

Joan topped up the teacup and went back to studying her toast. "When I was a girl, we were happy. I cannot pinpoint exactly what changed, but there doesn't seem to be any changing it back. Is Tye going to marry you?"

Hester took as long as she could with a sip of tea. "He has offered. I have declined."

Joan beamed a toothy smile at her. "Oh, that's

lovely. Tye adores a challenge, positively thrives on it, which is fortunate, since running the marquessate is nothing but a challenge. May I ask why you turned him down? He dotes on you and our mutual niece ceaselessly, and though he's my brother, I'm enough of an artist to pronounce him quite luscious."

"Dotes on me?" He was *luscious*.

"I cannot recall the last time he invited a guest to this house, and I cannot recall when he last went riding with a lady, even in the stultified confines of Town. He was supposed to spend two days in Aberdeenshire, you know, not two weeks, and at meals, he is forever glancing at you sidelong and pushing his food around on his plate. You've put him off his feed, I fear. I never thought I'd live to see it."

"I never intended to put anybody off their feed."

"Which is why," Joan drawled, "your eggs have gotten cold on your plate, hmm?"

Hester glanced down at the omelet congealing before her. "I served myself too large a portion. If you'll excuse me, I'm off in search of a book. His lordship's library is truly impressive."

"Books, bah. You're hiding from Tye, and I am anxious to see how this little drama plays out. If you see Fiona, tell her to bring me some flowers, and we'll paint a portrait of them. I refuse to sketch that carrot-pig masquerading as a rabbit one more time."

"I will pass your message along."

Hester rose without finishing her tea and made her way to the library, blind to the Quinworth wealth arrayed around her.

Tye had fetched Fiona here to rescue his sisters from the kind of match his parents had made into a living purgatory. This was the leverage his father had over him: three women could look forward to happy adulthoods, provided Fiona was sacrificed to a childhood away from those who loved her.

Hester pushed the library door open, lost in thought.

And Tye had said he honestly believed he'd be improving Fiona's circumstances, plucking her from penury into a life of guaranteed privilege.

Merciful Saints. That a father would put his son up to such an undertaking was an abomination against the natural order, but again, Hester had to wonder what motivated the marquess.

She did not wander the bookshelves as she had on many occasions. She instead sat at the huge old estate desk by the windows and tried to wrap her mind around the choices Tiberius had faced. Outside the windows, a lovely day was unfolding, full of sunshine and fresh breezes. Inside the library, Hester rummaged for writing implements, intent on sharing the morning's revelations with Aunt Ariadne, and Ian and Augusta MacGregor as well.

Pen and ink were not difficult to find, but the nib needed trimming, so Hester opened more drawers in search of a penknife, sand, and wax.

She found... documents. A large cache of letters addressed to Deirdre, Lady Quinworth, in a slashing hand that looked very like what she'd seen of Tiberius's writing.

Why would the lady have left her letters here if she dwelled in Scotland?

Tamping down the clamorings of conscience, Hester opened one letter:

My dearest wife,

The Holland bulbs you planted on the tenth anniversary of Dora's birth are springing up in profusions and glories, carpeting the hedges in bright colors and sweet aromas. Were you here, I would walk the paths with you. You would tell me which beds need to be divided and which might be left undisturbed for another year. Were you here, we might ride to the river and picnic there among the willows, while I read to you from the wicked French novels you used to hide under our pillows...

God in heaven. Hester folded the letter up with shaking hands. The *love* letter. She dared not read further, but glanced at the date and found to her shock it was but a few weeks ago.

And this was not a draft. The missive had been through the mails, apparently twice.

"The poor man." And the drawer was nearly full of such letters. What wrong had he done his lady to merit this treatment? No chance to explain, no chance to make reparation, no hope of forgiveness? She closed that drawer so quickly she nearly pinched her fingers, then opened another.

Still no penknife, but a single, very official-looking document. Her planned correspondence forgotten, Hester started reading.

Thirty minutes later, she was still staring at the

Last Will and Testament of Gordon Bierly Adolphus Flynn when the marquess came striding into the room, tapping his riding crop against his boot.

"Miss Daniels. Good day. Spathfoy tells me you might soon be returning to northern climes." He advanced on the desk, his expression curious. "I'd rather hoped you'd bring the boy up to scratch and do something about that moping child while you were about it. I know not who is the more cast down of late, the man or the girl."

"I wonder you'd notice such a thing, my lord, while pining for your own lady."

"I *beg* your pardon?" He gave his boots a sharp thwack with his infernal crop. That was nothing compared to what Hester would do to him.

She pushed out of the chair and came around the desk to stand directly before Quinworth. "I've read Gordie's will, your lordship. I am certain Tiberius has not been given that privilege."

"You pried into the private papers of a family who opened their home to you as a guest?" He did not yell; he kept his voice menacingly soft.

"I went looking for a penknife and found some answers, you dratted bully. How could you do this to Tiberius, to Fiona, and to her family? You lied, you manipulated, you misrepresented, you abused the trust of those around you, and the trust placed in you by a son dead and gone and unable to speak for his own wishes."

"I'm seeing those wishes carried out, Miss Daniels, and I will not be made to answer to the likes of some poor Scottish relation who thinks the hand of the Quinworth heir beneath her. Leave any time you like.

I'll manage my granddaughter *and my son* without your further interference. Good day."

He strode out of the room, boots thumping, crop thwacking, making Hester want to call him back so she could tear another strip off of him.

Many, many strips. What he'd done was an unimaginable transgression of the good faith family members owed one another, and Hester dreaded to think of the hurt Tiberius would suffer when he learned of it.

If he learned of it. Hester forced herself to spend long, long minutes pacing the library and thinking through the ramifications of what she'd read. She should not be the one to tell Tiberius what his father had done. She'd take Fiona home, and that would be the end of it. Based on what she'd learned of the marquess—and of the pertinent legalities—this sojourn in the south was over: for her, and for Fiona.

There was no need to write to Aunt Ree or Ian. Hester would have Fiona home before the letters arrived, leaving Tiberius Flynn the rest of his days to be a good son to a miserable father, a protective brother to three adult sisters, and a dutiful son to a mother who would be otherwise homeless.

The library door banged open, and Joan appeared, hectic color in her pale cheeks. "Hester, you must come! Fiona's down at the stables, and Papa is yelling at her, and there's a fox—"

"I'm coming." Fiona would not deal well with an upset, ill-humored marquess, and the marquess would not deal with an exhibition of Fiona's stubbornness and homesickness now.

But when she got to the stables, what Hester found was worse—far worse—than simple upset or stubbornness.

Ten

HESTER WAS LEAVING, AND THERE WASN'T A DAMNED thing Tye could do to prevent it. He brought Rowan down to the walk and considered kicking the marchioness out of the Edinburgh properties so Tye might take up residence in Scotland.

Or he might not kick her out. He might give his mother an opportunity to compete with his father as the primary justification—in a long list of justifications—for why an otherwise well-blessed man might take up drinking with intent to obliterate his reason.

"And you'd come with me." He ran a gloved hand down the horse's crest, feeling that today, for the first time in weeks, Rowan had been truly settled and relaxed. As if even the horse knew things weren't going to change.

Tye was composing a letter to his mother in his head when a groom came tearing down the lane hotfoot from the stable yard.

"Beg pardon, your lordship, but best come quick! I'll take the beast, for you mustn't let him add to the riot."

"Herriot, what are you going on about?" Tye kept

his voice calm as he swung down and handed off Rowan's reins.

"The marquess is taking the young miss to task, and God help us but the girl's got a fox and she's not having any of his lordship's nonsense, not none a'tall."

"A fox?"

"Please make haste, your lordship. The fox looks sickly to me."

Not good. Not good at all. Tye loped off in the direction of raised voices, and found a tableau portending multiple tragedies.

"You put the damned, rotten little blighter down this instant, young lady, because I tell you to."

The Marquess of Quinworth was standing some four yards away from Fiona, holding an enormous old horse pistol, muzzle pointed downward. Fiona held her ground, a half-grown fox kit in her arms, her chin jutting, her posture radiating defiance.

"If I put him down, you'll kill him, you awful man. You go away!"

"Good morning, Fiona." Tye forced himself to speak calmly. "Have you made a new friend?"

Her shoulders relaxed a fraction. "I found him, and I'm going to keep him. His name is Frederick."

"Like Frederick the Great?" Tye sidled closer, while dread coiled tightly in his belly. The animal was ill—its eyes were clouded, its coat matted, and in Fiona's embrace, it stirred weakly, head lolling as if the beast were drunk.

"Stand aside, Spathfoy!" The marquess bellowed this command, and even his roaring did not appear to affect the fox. "If that thing should bite you, you're doomed."

Fiona peered around Tye at the marquess. "Make Grandpapa be quiet, please. Frederick doesn't feel well, and yelling doesn't help anything."

"I quite agree with you. Quinworth"—Tye did not raise his voice—"*desist*." He got close enough to see that Fiona wasn't being defiant so much as protective. "I don't think Frederick is feeling quite the thing, Fiona."

"He's sick. We can help him get better so he can find his way home."

Tye went down on his haunches and reached out to stroke a gloved finger down the animal's ratty fur. "You think he's homesick?"

She nodded and took a shuddery breath. "He was in the petunias, falling over and crying. I think he's crying for his m-mama."

Tye fished out a handkerchief. "Compose yourself, Fiona, and let me hold him for a bit."

"Spathfoy, for God's sake!" the marquess hissed from several yards off. "The thing's rabid. I'll not bury another son of mine for some stupid—"

He fell silent while Tye gently disentangled the fox from Fiona's embrace.

"You promise you won't set him down?"

"I will not set him down without your permission. Wipe your tears."

She honked loudly into his handkerchief and sat right in the dirt of the stable yard beside Tye. "I hate it here. I miss home, and I feel sick all the time, inside."

Tye regarded the creature in his arms—there was no intelligence in the clouded eyes. Beneath the matted fur, the animal was nothing but skin and bones.

It hadn't been crying for its mother; it had been crying for death to end its pain and misery.

He glanced up to see his father looking thunderous a few yards off, and felt something shift in his chest. The way became clear between one heartbeat and the next, regardless of the consequences to him or to whatever plans the marquess was hatching.

"I don't want you to feel that way anymore, Fee. If I promise to take Frederick out to the covert near the millpond, will you find your aunt Hester and ask her to help you pack?"

"You mean I can go home? I can really go home?"

"It might take us a day or two to make the arrangements, and Albert probably would not enjoy the journey, but yes, you can go home."

Tye looked over Fiona's head to catch his father's eye. The marquess was standing very still, for once silent and not arguing.

"Fee." Hester spoke softly from behind the marquess. "I'd like nothing better in the world than to help you pack. Let your uncle Tye take the fox back to his family, and you come with me."

Fiona cast a last look at the beast lying passively in Tye's grasp. "You promise?"

She was asking if he'd keep his word about the fox, not about her journey home.

"I have given my word, Fiona. I would not break it."

She got up. "Good-bye, Frederick. Someday I'll see you again, like Androcles."

"Fee." Hester held out her hand, barely suppressed fear in her voice. And the fear was justified. Every adult watching this tableau knew that one bite, one scratch, and the girl might have been consigned to a miserable death.

Tye stroked a hand over the fox's matted pelt. "I do wonder how you'll transport that rabbit clear back to Aberdeenshire."

"I can take Harold?"

Now Tye rose with the fox in his arms. "You can if you can figure out a way to safely transport him. I'm sure your aunts will help you think of something."

When Hester and Joan had led Fiona safely toward the house, Quinworth holstered his gun. "For God's sake, some one of you lot get Spathfoy a pair of stout sacks." He stomped off, leaving Tye to keep his promise to Fiona.

The fox had the grace to expire at the moment Tye laid him among the weeds, thus allowing the stable boys to properly dispose of the remains. After muttering a self conscious prayer for the departed— Fiona might ask, after all—Tye then went to his rooms and scrubbed himself from head to foot with lye soap. Only when he'd changed and ordered his coat, shirt, and gloves to be burned, did he head down to the library in search of another beast who was ill, in pain, and creating havoc for all around him—while he very likely missed his family.

The marquess was sitting at the estate desk when Tye found him, staring at pile of folded letters and looking for the first time in Tye's experience like an old man. That was a pity and a shame, and it made not one goddamned, bloody, perishing bit of difference.

"Fiona is going home."

The marquess's chin came up, reminding Tye of... Fiona. "Says who?"

"I do. She's not safe here. That damned animal could have ended her days with a single bite, and as it is, Hester is likely still scrubbing the girl from head to toe with strong soap. Even the saliva of an animal that sick can cause death. What in the hell were you thinking?"

"What was I thinking!" Quinworth roared at his son and came around the desk. "What was I thinking? You are my son and heir, and you took that reeking, vile creature into your grasp without a thought for what it would do to your mother and sisters to watch you fall prey to madness and misery! I cannot be held accountable for the child's queer starts and obstinate demeanor. You could have been killed, Spathfoy, the title sent into escheat, and God knows how this family would have survived."

The marquess dropped his voice. "The girl stays, Spathfoy. I am Quinworth, the head of her family, and I say she stays."

Tye felt a calm descend on him, not a forced, artificial steeling of nerves necessary to weather a crisis, but a bone-deep sense of unshakable purpose. "You did not, or perhaps *could not*, act in a manner consistent with her safety. Your bellowing and obstreperousness were the opposite of what the situation called for. The girl goes home, my lord, or I will renounce your title at the first opportunity."

"Renounce—!"

"I will renounce the Quinworth title, I will provide a home for my mother and sisters, and I will dower my sisters handsomely, unless Fiona goes home to the

Highlands tomorrow, there to dwell unmolested and undisturbed by you and your damnable machinations."

"You would turn your back on a title more than three hundred years old? You'd have nothing but that paltry Scottish earldom from your mother's people, and you'd content yourself with that?"

"The girl goes home, my lord. I want your word on it."

Quinworth gave him a curious, who-the-hell-are-you glance, and Tye's calm became almost happy. Sending Fiona home was the right thing to do; he only wished he'd thought of a way to do it sooner. "Fiona is not safe in your care, Quinworth. If you can't understand a child well enough to keep her safe, then she's better off elsewhere."

"The beast was rabid, Spathfoy... I was not expecting my granddaughter to march up to the stables cradling a rabid fox in her arms. I've known her only a few days... I say she stays, and I am Quinworth."

His lordship sat heavily on the desk, but Tye was having none of these maunderings. The relevant truth popped into his head all of a piece.

"What you are, sir, is *mean*, and we none of us have to do what you say. Fiona goes home, tomorrow if I can arrange it. You can dower her or you can establish a trust for her. If Balfour allows it, you can visit her. I do not fault you for not knowing her, Quinworth, but you do not love her, and that is why she must be returned to her family by those of us who do love her."

Tye waited for a response, but his lordship's expression had become as blank as the fox's. When Tye left the library, Quinworth was still sitting on the desk, his backside half-covering some official-looking document.

∽

Hester had made Fiona take two baths and scrubbed the girl thoroughly each time. She'd washed Fiona's hands with whisky; she'd ordered the child's clothes burned and the ashes buried deep. Over and over throughout the day, she'd examined Fiona for any broken skin, even something as trivial as a hangnail, and when Fiona had finally fallen into a peaceful sleep, Hester had sat watching the girl breathe.

There was no worse death than rabies. Every child was raised with some ghoulish tale of a person who'd suffered that fate. Grown men had been known to take their own lives after being mauled by a mad dog rather than brave a death from rabies.

And Tiberius Flynn had—

Hester cut the thought off. She'd start to cry *again* if she went down that road. Cry and lose her dinner and tear her hair.

The creature staring back at Hester from the vanity mirror was pale, haunted, and miserable. She was a woman who did not deserve a lifetime as Spathfoy's wife, a woman who'd leapt to conclusions and judgments—wrong conclusions and bad judgments, yet again.

Tiberius Flynn was not coldhearted, ruthless, and self-absorbed. He had faults, *but his worst fault was that he loved too well*. His filial devotion was unswerving, his fraternal concern unrelenting, and his avuncular notions of duty and honor had very nearly earned him a lingering, terrible death.

Hester told herself she was crossing the hallway to apologize to him, to beg his understanding, and to make a final peace with him. This was not entirely a falsehood, but when Spathfoy looked up from his escritoire to regard her, she knew it was not the full truth either.

He was wearing spectacles, gold-rimmed reading spectacles that made him look more scholarly, more like a husband or a father, but no less like a lover.

"Hester." He rose and approached her, his expression guarded. "If you're having trouble sleeping, I can have the kitchen—"

She was plastered to his chest before he could finish speaking. "I'll leave tomorrow. I'll take Fee home, tomorrow, Tiberius, I promise, I just can't— You might have been killed, worse than killed, and all because I didn't keep an adequate eye on Fee, and then your father, with the gun—"

"Hush, Hester, calm yourself." His arms came around her slowly but securely, which only made the ache in her chest worse. "I've told him he'll not have the raising of her, not if he can't keep her safe. I'll take you to the train station myself, just please, don't cry."

She breathed in the clean scent of him, wallowed in the strength and warmth of his embrace. "Did you bathe, Tiberius? Did you scrub your hands? The fox was likely rabid. His lordship was right, I know he was."

"Hush. I am unharmed, and believe me, I inspected and bathed my person thoroughly, several times."

She wanted to inspect his person, and medical reasons were the least of her motivations. The need arose abruptly, barreling through all her other upsets with the raging clarity of hopeless desire.

"Tiberius, I want—" She worked the knot of his dressing gown open, leaving him standing there, his robe gaping. Her brain registered that he was not stopping her and he was not arguing with her.

Not reasoning with her. She slid her hands around his waist and leaned her forehead on his chest. "Please, Tiberius."

"The train leaves at eleven in the morning, Hester." He spoke gently, his words conveying compassion but not compromise. "I want you and the child gone from here before Quinworth can rally his defenses. It's important to me that—"

She sank to her knees and pressed her face to his thigh. "Please."

A quiet moment went by while she remained in the posture of a supplicant, then his hand stroked over her hair, a soft caress that granted her permission to take what she would of him before they parted. The frantic haste beating at her from within subsided. She took a slow, deep breath, exhaled, and put her mouth to the length of his cock.

He was not aroused, or not very aroused, which meant she participated orally in the building of his desire. By degrees, as she kissed, nuzzled, stroked, and suckled, his passion rose, until he stepped back.

"Hester, shall I take you to bed?"

"Yes. We shall take each other to bed." She paused only to remove every stitch of her nightclothes while he shrugged out of his robe. In a state of complete undress, he crossed the room to lock the door.

Hester sat on the bed and continued to drink in the sight of him as he used his tooth powder at the wash-basin. "You aren't telling me this is misguided, Tiberius."

"I don't need to tell you that, Hester. If you truly think this is misguided, you'll cross the hallway to your own room." His observation held logic, not arrogance; if anything, he was smiling slightly at the basin. "Is Fiona managing?"

"She was exhausted. She did not and does not comprehend the danger she was in."

"She'll be a mother someday." He glanced at her over his shoulder as he dragged a brush through his hair. "Or an aunt. She'll understand then. I've had wires sent to Balfour."

He would think of that. And then he was stalking over to the bed, looking not competent and practical, but gorgeous, aroused, and heartrendingly dear. "I do not guarantee that I can protect you from conception tonight, Hester Daniels."

"It doesn't signify."

Now he looked like he wanted to argue, so she rose up on her knees and kissed him where he stood by the bed. "It does not signify. I will be gone in the morning, Tiberius. I understand that. I understand much that was not clear to me until today. For tonight, please just love me."

He muttered something, which in Gaelic would have sounded very much like "I do," but words were not of any interest to Hester when his mouth finally settled on hers. No matter he was not renewing his proposals, no matter she might never see him again; he was kissing her as if she were life and breath and sun all wrapped into one, as if his soul required it of him.

As if there were no tomorrow, which for them—as far as Hester was concerned—was the sad and unavoidable truth.

❧

Hester was upset, seeking reassurances, and making a very great mistake. Tye's duty was to kiss her forehead and steer her right out into the corridor, then shut and lock his door behind her.

This was the honorable course. His brain knew it, and even admonished him to follow such a course. His body was ignoring such pleas, and his heart had clapped its hands over its figurative ears.

She would not thank him in the morning for following the honorable course; she would look at him with big, bruised eyes and silently reproach him from memory for the rest of his blighted days. And if she wasn't yet carrying his child, Tye could hope to effect such a miracle on what might otherwise be their last night together.

Duty and honor be damned, this was the woman he loved, the woman he was meant to go through life with, though she'd denied his every proposal.

Tye's self-restraint in the past was nothing compared to the discipline he applied now. He laid Hester down on the enormous four-poster where he'd tossed and turned away the past week of nights, and came down over her. When he'd feasted for a time on her kisses, he worked his way south, treasuring her breasts, her soft, feminine belly, her sex.

She denied him nothing, not her kisses, not her sighs, not the sweet, secret female parts of her body. When he tucked her legs over his shoulders, he knew a passing regret that he hadn't put a pair of his socks on her feet, the better to stroke his back with.

But only a passing regret. He deluged her with pleasure, showered her with it until he was certain she'd be sore for a week. And when at last he joined his body to hers, he vowed he'd wreak yet more pleasure upon her, so much pleasure that she would recall this night of loving for all her days.

He kept that vow, but when her body was convulsing around him, wringing the last drop of passion from their joining, Tye's self-restraint collapsed, his good intentions disappeared, and he followed Hester into a pleasure as intense and as soul deep as it was bittersweet.

❧

"This is my mother's direction in Edinburgh. You should not need it, but I don't like sending you off without even a maid."

Hester's lover from the previous night was nowhere to be found, except perhaps lurking in the green eyes of this serious, handsome man. "We'll be fine, Tiberius. I've gotten quite used to traveling about by train."

Fiona swung Hester's hand. "I'll be fine too. Will you say good-bye to Albert for me?"

"Of course, and let me stow this fellow for you." Tye held up the carpetbag housing the rabbit. "You'll have to watch that he isn't nibbling through the fabric, Niece. A rabbit loose on Her Majesty's rails will not do." He stuffed the bag on the overhead rack, and the train whistle sounded a warning blast.

"I wish you were coming with us, Uncle, and Flying Rowan too."

"I'll write to you, Fiona, and I don't want to hear about any cheating at cards either." In the cramped confines of the compartment, he went down on his haunches and hugged the child tightly. "You are my favorite niece. Never forget it."

"I'm your only niece."

And again, for the hundredth time in twenty-four hours, Hester's heart broke, this time simply from seeing Fiona share her favorite-niece joke with Tiberius, proof positive the man was secure in the child's love and affection.

"Aunt." Fiona tugged on Hester's skirts, forcing her down into what was nearly a huddle with the child and the earl. "You must tell Uncle you love him and you will miss him."

She'd spoken in Gaelic. With childish good intentions, she'd driven spikes into Hester's composure and into her heart. Hester managed an answer only haltingly, and not because she stumbled over the Gaelic.

"I will miss him badly, but it's like with the fox, Fiona. Spathfoy needs to be with his family, and they need him. They need him desperately."

"We're his family."

Hester could only nod and rise to her feet, feeling older than Aunt Ree on a wet, chilly night. Spathfoy took her hand in his without even sparing a glance at the passage beyond the open door.

"You will write to me if there's need?"

Another nod, while a lump as wide as the Highlands formed in her throat. The damned man kissed her forehead, and when he would have stepped back, Hester held on to him. "Tiberius, I am sorry."

The train whistle blasted twice, and the look he gave her was torn. "I cannot fathom what you'd be apologizing for. Please get word to me when you've arrived safely in Ballater. I want a wire, Hester, not some damnable polite letter arriving after Michaelmas."

"Uncle said a bad word."

He tweaked Fiona's braid. "I'm expressing strong feelings, probably not for the last time." Then he swung his gaze back to Hester. "My dear, I must leave you now. There are things I must resolve with my father and my sisters before I am otherwise free. You will send word?"

He was harping on this. Hester finally realized he was concerned that she was with child. "I will send word if there's need. Good-bye, Tiberius. Read your brother's will." The words had slipped out. She might send a wire, a few sentences of platitudes, but this admonition she'd give him in person.

The train whistle sounded three times, and on the platform, the conductor was bellowing the "all aboard."

"Good-bye, Uncle. I won't cheat. I love you!"

"I love you too, Fiona. Safe journey."

A swift, hard kiss to Hester's lips, and then he was gone. Hester took the backward-facing seat as the train began to move, the better to stare at Tiberius's tall, still figure growing smaller and smaller, until a bend in the tracks took him entirely from her sight.

❧

"But when are we going to get there?" Fiona's question had long since taken on the singsong quality of a child determined to pluck the last adult nerve within hearing and pluck it hard.

They'd made the transfer smoothly enough in Edinburgh, but now, not twenty miles north of the city, the train had stopped dead on the tracks.

And not moved for an hour.

"I do not know when we'll make Aberdeen, Fiona. Would you like to play another game of matches?"

"No. It's too hard to spread out all the cards in this stupid train."

"Shall we walk beside the tracks for a moment?"

"It's going to rain, and then I shall get wet and stay wet until we get home. Why isn't the train moving?"

"There's an obstruction on the tracks."

"What kind of obstruction?"

"I do not know." Just as Hester hadn't known five minutes earlier, and ten minutes, and twenty. Hester suspected it was not a trivial obstruction—a downed tree or a dead horse at least—a casual gesture by the hand of fate to make Hester doubt her determination to scurry north and lick her wounds.

"I miss Uncle."

"I miss him too."

"You should have stayed with him, Aunt. He'll miss you and miss you."

Oh, cruel child. Hester wanted to clap her hand over Fiona's mouth.

"The train is moving!" Fiona pressed her nose to the window as the locomotive gave another lurch. "We're moving backward!"

"We are indeed." Away from Aberdeen, which was maddening, to say the least. "We'll probably have to find another train to take us north, Fee. The day is likely to become quite long."

Fiona said nothing, but stood on the seat to get down the carpetbag and peer inside, as she'd done frequently throughout their journey.

"It doesn't smell very good in there. Harold is unhappy."

"Then Harold will be relieved to reach home, as will we."

"But home's that way." Fiona jerked her thumb to the north.

Swear words paraded through Hester's weary brain—nasty, percussive, satisfying Anglo-Saxon monosyllables that would have sounded like music on Tiberius's tongue.

"I am damned sick of this day, Niece."

Fiona's brows arched with surprise. "That was very good, Aunt. May I try?"

They turned the air of the compartment blue on the twenty-mile trip back down to Edinburgh, and shared not a few laughs, but when Hester was told there was no way to reach Aberdeen by nightfall, she wanted to cry.

"We could hire a carriage," Fiona offered helpfully as they stood outside the busy station in Edinburgh.

"It would still take us days, Fee. We need to find decent accommodations for young ladies temporarily stranded far from home."

"And a rabbit." Fee tucked her hand into Hester's. "Don't forget Harold."

Hester did not wrinkle her nose. "I would never forget dear Harold."

"Uncle has a house here on Princes Street, and a very nice house in the country too. My grandmamma lives here."

Hester was reminded of Tiberius tucking a folded piece of paper into her reticule when he'd parted from them on the train. "Princes Street, Fiona?"

A short ride by hack took them to the New Town address Tye had given them, and much to Hester's relief—and probably Harold's as well—the lady was home.

And she was breathtakingly beautiful.

Tall, stately, with classic features that would not yield much to age, Lady Quinworth also sported flaming hair going golden at her temples.

"Miss Daniels, I'm afraid you have me at something of a loss, but any friend of Tiberius is a friend of mine." Her smile would warm a Highland winter and only grew more attractive as she turned it on Fiona. "And I am dying to meet this young lady, who I can only hope has also befriended Spathfoy."

"He's not my friend, he's my uncle."

The marchioness blinked. "Spathfoy is your uncle?"

Hester felt again the sensation of the train pulling out of the station at Newcastle, gathering momentum, and hurtling her at increasing speed in the wrong direction. "I can explain, my lady."

"I'm sure you can." Lady Quinworth turned to a waiting footman. "Take the ladies' things up to the first guest room, Thomas. We'll want tea with all the trimmings in the family parlor."

"What about Harold?" Fiona held up the malodorous carpetbag. "He's ever so tired of traveling too." She grinned at the marchioness. "Bloody, damned tired."

"Fiona!"

But the marchioness only smiled. This smile was different, warmer, with a hint of mischief. This smile reminded Hester painfully of Tiberius in a playful mood, and on the lady, it looked dazzling.

"The child no doubt gets her unfortunate vocabulary from her uncle. Come along, ladies, and bring Harold."

~

Deirdre considered two possibilities. The first was that Tiberius had developed a liaison with a lady fallen on hard times, and the little girl was his love child, which was a fine thing for a mother to be finding out from somebody besides the son responsible.

Except Tiberius would have married the mother; without question he would have.

Which meant this was Gordie's child. Fiona was old enough, and she had the look of Gordie in her merry eyes and slightly obstinate chin. When the child had been sent off with the housekeeper to enjoy a scented bath, Deirdre considered her remaining guest.

"Now that we are without little ears to mind us, Miss Daniels, I'd like to know how you came to be at Quinworth, and what exactly Spathfoy's involvement is in that child's life."

Miss Daniels—who bore no noticeable resemblance to the child in her care—used the genteel prevarications. She sipped her tea, nibbled a sandwich, then set her tea down. "I believe Fiona is your granddaughter, my lady."

"Are you her mother?"

"I am not. My brother Matthew is married to Fiona's mother, Mary Frances MacGregor Daniels, or I suppose she's Lady Altsax now, though they don't use the title."

"You're *that* Miss Daniels?"

She showed no sign of being discommoded by the question, except for a slight tipping up of her chin. "I am the Miss Daniels who cried off her engagement to Jasper Merriman."

"Have some more tea." Deirdre decided the immediate liking she'd felt for the girl had been grounded in solid maternal instinct. "I received the most peculiar epistle from Spathfoy not a week past. I am to ruin young Mr. Merriman socially, to hint he has a dread disease that renders him unacceptable as a marriage prospect for any decent young lady."

Miss Daniels's smile was radiant. "That is diabolically clever. You must thank Tiberius for me when you see him next."

Tiberius? "You won't be seeing him yourself?"

The smile died. It did not fade, it died. "I do not think so. I rejected his proposal too, you see."

"We will discuss that in due course. First, tell me how Fiona came to be in her uncle's care."

This necessitated a darting glance at the fat white rabbit reclining like a drunken burgher against the fireplace fender. "Quinworth demanded that Tye bring Fiona to him, though I did not learn this from Tiberius. Lady Joan explained it to me. She said

Tye—*Spathfoy* agreed to retrieve Fiona in exchange for Quinworth's willingness to allow her to live in Paris for a year, and to allow all three of your daughters to marry where they chose."

"Quinworth devised this bargain?"

"He did, and somehow Tye got him to undevise it where Fee is concerned."

Tye. She'd slipped more than once, using the earl's name and even his nickname.

"This is interesting, Miss Daniels." Deirdre took a leisurely sip of her tea, which had lost much of its heat. "I'd heard rumors Gordie had left us an afterthought, and I pleaded with my husband to follow up, but he was adamant it would be a waste of time."

Waste of time, indeed. The wrath she'd directed at Hale previously was going to be nothing, *nothing*, compared to the peal she'd ring over his head now.

"I wish you would not be too hard on his lordship, Lady Quinworth. If he has been high-handed in his dealings regarding Fiona, I believe his course was set in part because of the way you have dealt with him."

Deirdre's teacup nigh crashed to its saucer. "Explain yourself, Miss Daniels."

Little Miss Daniels got up and went to the window, turning her back to her hostess. It was a slim back, but straight. Strong. "He keeps all the letters you send back to him—Quinworth does. He has them in a drawer, and they look as if he's read them time and again."

Inside her body where she thought she'd long stopped feeling anything of note, Deirdre experienced small tremors of emotion. "What has this to do with me, Miss Daniels?"

"They are love letters, my lady. I read perhaps two sentences of his most recent epistle, and I know a love letter when I'm reading one, though I've never received any myself."

"Love letters? Listing all the things I've left behind me in a vain attempt to gain that man's notice? Those are taunts, Miss Daniels. When you've been married to an arrogant, domineering Englishman for thirty years, you'll know the difference."

She tried to pick up her teacup, but her grip was too unsteady, and her speech had acquired more than a hint of a burr.

"He's taken to stealing children in an effort to entice you to return to his side."

"*He has not.*"

Miss Daniels turned to face her hostess. "The Earl of Balfour has sent regular reports to Quinworth regarding Fiona's well-being, my lady. It's been years, and Quinworth has never acknowledged the child until now. Fiona is legitimate under Scottish law, and she is a wonderful child. Quinworth sent his son to bring her south, and I am convinced this is all in aid of luring you back to the family seat."

"He never admitted to me we had a grandchild." Deirdre's voice, the melodious, cultured voice she'd been complimented on since she'd put up her hair, came out broken and empty. "That man… I told him there had been a child, and he ignored me and railed at me and told me not to hang onto dreams that could never be. We fought and fought until I could not fight anymore."

"Your husband compromised his relationship with his only remaining son to get his hands on Fiona." Miss Daniels had moved again to resume her seat across from Deirdre. "He lied, he sacrificed control of his daughters' futures, he moved heaven and earth to gain custody of Fiona, and I am certain in my bones it was the only way he could bring himself once again to your notice."

"He *has* my notice. He has always had my notice. I am tempted to order my traveling coach and take my notice to Quinworth in person this very moment, but I will not pass up the opportunity to spend even a moment with my granddaughter."

Miss Daniels said nothing. She fixed Deirdre a fresh cup of tea, as if that would help with the mess Deirdre's marriage had become. As if anything would help.

When Deirdre began to cry, Miss Daniels took the place beside her, tucked a serviette into Deirdre's hand, and put her arm around Deirdre's shoulder.

All of which only made the marchioness cry harder.

⁂

"She's not coming." Quinworth spoke quietly, though there was nobody to hear him who'd repeat his words. "The child left more than two weeks ago—the child who might have finally lured your mother home—and still, there is no word from Edinburgh. Not a scathing letter, not a request for a formal separation, nothing."

He swatted at the grass with his riding crop. "Each day, my boy, I envy you your repose a little more. Your mother would say I'm being petulant and dramatic."

Quinworth eyed the headstone to which he addressed himself. "I'm being pathetic, but when you are all the family left to me, at least I can indulge myself privately in this regard." The alternatives did not bear thinking about. Her ladyship was probably halfway to Vienna by now, and if fetching her home from Edinburgh had been a daunting prospect, the Continent was a patent impossibility.

"Your brother has gone off to the north again, though whether he'll sort matters out with the little blond, or take up the latest family tradition of solitudinous brooding remains to be seen. You used to be able to jolly him out of his seriousness at least occasionally, but then, you did not lie to him about a material matter."

The child had been good for Spathfoy, though. About that much, Quinworth was certain. The child and the little blond.

"Fiona has your chin, your eyes. You would love her—anybody would love her." Which wasn't something he'd bargained for, not at all.

"Hale."

Quinworth blinked, wondering if he was finally to be granted the mercy of losing his reason. He was even hearing his wife's voice on the slight summer breeze, a voice that had been silent except in his memory for two years.

Quinworth did not put any stock in summer breezes.

"I miss your mother," he went on. "I miss her until I am ready to crawl on my knees to beg her forgiveness, but she won't... she will not acknowledge my letters. She will not see me; she will not hear me; she will not speak to me. To her, I am as dead as you are, perhaps even more so. I fear her sentence in this regard to be irrevocable."

The wrought iron gate creaked, a distinctive, rusty protest that was no part of Quinworth's imagination. A curious shiver skipped down his spine and settled low in his belly.

"Hale, why are you sitting here all alone on the grass?"

Angels might have such a pretty, gentle voice. He closed his eyes and felt a hand pass softly over the back of his head. The scent of roses came to him.

"Hale, please say something."

His marchioness, his beautiful, passionate lady sounded sad and frightened. When he opened his eyes, she folded down from her majestic height to sit right there beside him on the grass.

"Dee Dee." He did not dare touch her, though with his eyes he devoured her. She would always be lovely, but two years had made her dignity and self-possession a luminous complement to her beauty. "You came."

Her gaze was solemn as she took a visual inventory of him. "Tiberius told me to have done with things, one way or another. He said he gave you the same speech."

Quinworth could not stop looking at her for fear if he blinked she'd disappear. "Spathfoy had many choice sentiments to impart to me, in which the words happiness, compassion, forgiveness, and honesty figured prominently. The boy—the *man*—was not wrong."

She rustled around to organize her skirts, sending another little whiff of roses into the air. "He lectured me about love and everybody erring occasionally, often with the best of intentions. The Lords will have a fine orator in him one day."

And then silence, which had so often presaged verbal gunfire between them. "Dee Dee, have you come to ask for terms?"

He forced himself to put the question calmly, and she stopped fussing her skirts to stare at him. She'd more than hinted over the years that a formal separation would be appreciated.

"Yes, Hale." Her voice was not so gentle now. "Yes, I have come to treat with you regarding our future. Why did you keep that child a secret?"

This was… good. This was a chance to explain, a chance to preserve the hope that whatever the legal posture of their marriage became, they might be civil with each other, cordial even.

Provided he was honest now.

"When Gordie died, you went to pieces, Dee Dee. You grew quiet—you, who roar and laugh and bellow your way through life. I could not bear it."

"*I* went to pieces? Did I limit my sustenance to hard liquor and my company to the hounds and hunters? Spathfoy says your drinking has moderated, but your horses still see more of you than your own daughters do. You became a stranger to me, Hale." She looked away, giving him a fine view of her profile. "You no longer came to my bed, and when I came to yours, you were a stranger still."

He heard in her voice not accusation—which might have permitted him a few words in his defense—but *hurt*.

"Dee Dee, sometimes a man can't—"

"For God's sake, Hale, we're not children. Sometimes I couldn't either. I hope you recall that much of our marriage."

"It's different for a lady, my dear." And he stopped himself from pursuing this digression further, even in his own defense. "To answer your question, I did not learn of the child until the present earl took over the management of the estate, which was almost a year after…"

She swung her gaze back to him, concern in her eyes—and chagrin. "After our son died. I had to practice saying it, had to learn how to make the words audible while thinking of something else, of anything else."

Before Quinworth's eyes, she hunched in on herself. "I call him 'our son.' I do not speak his name in the same sentence as I mention his death."

To see her so afflicted was… unbearable, and yet in a curious way, a relief too. He used one finger to tip her chin up, then dropped his hand and spoke very slowly. "I did not learn of the child's existence until almost a year after… Gordie… died."

While he watched, her gorgeous green eyes filled. She blinked furiously then dashed her knuckles against her cheeks. "Go on."

"Dora was battling cholera, and you were a wraith, my dear. I feared to lose you and her both, more than I'd lost you already. Balfour sent only a short letter, saying the child thrived, and condoling me on the loss of my son. I burned the letter, and forgive me, Wife, I almost hoped the child would die. Why should some scheming Scottish girl get to keep a part of Gordie, when I was left with nothing but guilt, regret, and a family unable to put itself to rights?"

She did not fly into a rage; she did not start on one of her scathing lectures in the low, relentless tones of a woman intent on delivering thirty-nine verbal lashes.

Quinworth's wife spoke softly. "You were a good father, Hale. You knew when to set limits and when to wink. You have only to look at Spathfoy to see how Gordie would have turned out, given time."

"Dee Dee, how can you say this? I arranged for Gordie to have his colors, knowing full well military life was not going to bring out his best traits. The drinking and wenching and travel…"

She cocked her head as his words trailed off. "Why did you do it, Hale? I've often wondered."

And now he could not look her in the eye. "I've wondered myself, and often wished I hadn't, but I've had years to consider it, and all I can come up with is: I did not know what else to do for him. In his brother's shadow, he was bored and becoming…"

"Troubled." She finished the thought for him, and to his consternation, reached out to lace her fingers through his. "Gordie might have stood for a pocket borough in a few years, but not right out of university. I thought a few years of service might give him the maturity Tye seemed born with."

"*You* thought?"

"I encouraged him to ask you to arrange his commission. I never foresaw him getting into trouble in Scotland and taking a transfer to Canada in disgrace."

"And I did not want you to know." He studied their joined hands. "He compromised the girl, Dee Dee. I learned this when the child was a little older, and I could not see how to tell you of our granddaughter

without also admitting Gordie had behaved dishonor-
ably toward the mother."

"So you told me nothing at all."

She wasn't wrong. He could let matters stand and
be grateful they'd been able to clear the air this much.

But he'd missed his wife, missed his best friend, the
mother of his children, the woman who'd seen him
drunk, ranting, and insensate with what he now realized was loss and guilt. "I cannot undo the harm I've
done, Dee Dee, but I have never stopped loving you.
That is all I've wanted to tell you for more years than I
can count. I am sorry for the decisions I've made, sorry
I could not be the husband you needed and deserved.
The fault for what has become of our marriage lies
with me, and I sincerely regret—" His voice caught.
Her grip on his hand had become painful, but he
managed a few more words. "I regret the situation
we find ourselves in and would do anything to make
reparation to you for it."

He raised her hand and pressed his lips to her
knuckles.

He'd been honest. At last he'd been honest with
his wife, and while there was no joy in it, there was
peace. For long moments, Quinworth sat with his
marchioness, side by side in the grass. A robin landed
on Gordie's headstone, then flitted away as if nothing
within view could be of interest.

"I was so angry." Her ladyship spoke quietly,
worlds of sadness in her words, but she did not retrieve
her hand from his. "I was angry with Gordie for dying,
angry with myself for living. Angry with you for not
being able to understand what I did not understand

myself. You always used to talk to me, Hale. I love
that about you. I loved just to hear your voice."

She had used the past tense—she loved just to hear
his voice—but she'd also used the present: I love that
about you.

Quinworth remained still and quiet, her hand held
in his.

"I've realized something, Husband. I've realized
the anger was a way to stay connected with Gordie,
and to pretend I wasn't the mother who sent him off
to wheedle his colors from you. I pretended I wasn't
the *useless twit* wishing him into some regiment so he
wouldn't be causing a scandal when his sisters made their
bows. I became very good at pretending." She frowned
at the headstone. "But not good enough. All the anger
in the world does not make the grief go away."

"No," Quinworth said, kissing her knuckles again.
"It does not. Drinking, shouting, and galloping hell-
bent across the countryside don't either."

Her ladyship withdrew her hand. "Tiberius says you
are a man in love and must be forgiven much, and he
recognizes the symptoms because they've befallen him."

"Spathfoy has a certain pragmatic wisdom about
him. He'll make a fine marquess."

She smiled at him faintly, a wifely curving of the lips
that had something to do with forbearance. "He makes a
fine son, and I have made a very sorry wife. This is what
I want to say to you, Hale Flynn: When you needed me
most, when you were, for the first time in our marriage,
not indulgent, doting, and unrelentingly kind to me, I
failed you. When our son…" She stopped and bowed
her head, speaking very softly. "When Gordie…"

Her shoulders jerked, and Quinworth's throat closed up to see her so tormented.

"Dee Dee, please don't." He shifted to tuck an arm around her shoulders, willing her to silence. She took a steadying breath, and he felt her gathering her great reserves of courage.

"When… Gordie… died, I failed you." She pitched into him, lashing her arms around him and sobbing quietly against his shoulder. "Forgive me, Hale, for I failed you terribly."

While the summer breeze wafted the scent of roses around him, Hale Flynn held his dear wife in his arms and wept. He wept for their departed son, for the years wasted, for the hurt his spouse had suffered and suffered still, but mostly he wept in gratitude for the simple comfort of having her restored to his embrace.

∽∾

Ian MacGregor kept his voice down, because His Wee Bairnship had for once taken his nap at a time convenient to his parents' plans—some of those plans, in any case.

"All they need is a nudge, Ian." Augusta smoothed a hand over the child's sleeping form, which had Ian nigh twitching with the need to stop her. Anything, anything at all, was sufficient provocation for the baby to waken and start bellowing, and God knew how Ian was supposed to handle matters without his countess to direct him.

"Spathfoy is cooling his heels in the library with a dram of the laird's cache, Wife. Come away with me."

Ian escorted his wife into the corridor and closed the nursery door very, very softly. "Is Hester lingering over her tea?"

"She's tarrying in the garden, last I checked. I thought I'd steal a peek at the baby before I wish her on her way."

"You thought you'd dodge out on me." Ian took her by the hand and led her to the steps. "There's a sound and lengthy scold in it for you if you desert the cause at this point, woman."

"A *lengthy* scold?" She stopped and bestowed a wicked smile on him. "Marriage to you is growing on me, Ian."

He could not help glancing at her flat middle, where he suspected another aspect of her fondness for marriage was having repercussions. "We'll see how matters unfold with our guests. Spathfoy will not appreciate our meddling."

"Yes, he will. So will Hester."

She kissed him, which was no reassurance, none whatsoever. Ian parted company with her on the first floor and went to do business with an errant earl whose wanderings had once again taken him into the Scottish Highlands.

"Spathfoy, I do beg your pardon. The lad will fret, and then the wife will fret, and then a man needs a tot lest he fret as well."

Ian's guest shot him a curious look. "You take quite an interest in what transpires in your nursery, Balfour."

"A wise man usually does." Ian topped off Spathfoy's drink, poured one for himself, and faced Spathfoy. "Hester tells me your brother's will did indeed state that Fiona is to be in the care of her paternal family, but Gordie specified that you, and not Quinworth, were to be her guardian. I asked you to come here so we might settle the business like gentlemen—unless you'd rather take it up in the courts?"

Spathfoy had apparently given up declaiming the eternal verities in Her Majesty's English in favor of awkward silences.

When Ian made no effort to leap into the conversational breach, Spathfoy eventually deigned to speak. "And how does Miss Daniels fare?"

As the closest thing Hester had to a head of her family, Ian allowed Spathfoy's question was the right one to ask. Fee's situation was not urgent. Ian had concluded that much when, two weeks after the child had returned home, no lawsuits had been filed, and no demands for settlement or surrender of the child had been received.

"Hester is coping."

Spathfoy peered at the best damned whisky Ian would ever be privileged to serve, but took not a taste. "What the bloody hell does that mean?"

"Hester's in the garden, Spathfoy. I was supposed to use all manner of subterfuge to lure you there, as I'm sure my countess has employed with Hester, but it's clear to me I'll get nowhere negotiating with you until you've been put out of your misery."

Spathfoy set his drink aside. "It's that obvious?"

"For God's sake, man. You're pathetic. You can barely hold a conversation, you're moony-eyed in the broad light of day, and you've not been keeping in good pasture, from the looks of you. You're an affront to single manhood, a disgrace to the gender, and worse

than all of that, you're wasting some of the best pota-
tion ever brewed in Scotland."

"Suppose I am." He tossed the drink back in a
single swallow. "Fiona stays here, unless she wants to
come terrorize the bachelors of Edinburgh when she's
older. Assuming my parents have found their common
sense, my mother will be happy to sponsor her."

"As will my countess."

"We understand each other."

"We do." Ian stuck out a hand and clapped
Spathfoy on the shoulder. "Now quit prevaricating,
laddie. Faint heart never won fair maid, and my son is
likely to wake up at any minute."

"You'll be watching, I take it?"

"Somebody might have to drag you off the field if
you bugger this up as badly as the English bugger up
most of what counts in life."

Spathfoy smiled the smile of a hopelessly smitten
man. "Half English, but also half Scottish."

"Then we've a wee glimmer of hope." Ian spun
him by the shoulders and shoved him toward the door.

కావ

A rose garden past its peak was a sad place to spend
a summer afternoon, but Hester hadn't wanted to
accompany Augusta up to the nursery, and the stables
had to at least throw a saddle on a horse before a lady
could safely ride home.

Tea had been awful, full of knowing silences on
Augusta's part, and sidelong glances that alternated
between sympathetic and speculative, while Hester
stared at the carpet or out the window and tried to

make conversation. If Aunt Ree hadn't forced her to accept Augusta's invitation—her summons—Hester would still be sitting by the burn, losing games of matches to Fee.

In a few short weeks, Hester had learned the difference between a bad judgment—such as allowing Jasper Merriman liberties—and a terrible judgment, such as flinging Tiberius Flynn's proposal back in his face. She hadn't made him a proper apology, and that rankled almost as much as the relentless pain of his absence from her life.

"I wasn't sure you'd still be here."

The pleasurable shock of hearing Tiberius Flynn's voice was quickly doused in the reality of seeing him standing on the garden path, looking mouthwateringly handsome and well turned out in his riding attire.

"Tiberius." She wanted to rise, to go to him, but dared not. She wanted to speak but couldn't find the words.

"May I sit?"

She twitched her skirts aside in answer. "You're here." A stupid thing to say—an imbecilic thing to say.

"Your cousin and her earl have connived for it to be so. I cannot regret their scheming. Hester, are you well?"

What was he asking? She did not meet his gaze but hunched forward, the better to hide her blush. "I am in good health. You?" He looked thinner in the face to her.

"I am…" He trailed off, and Hester could feel him taking in her features one by one. Tired eyes, hair not quite as neatly braided as it should have been, fingernails a trifle ragged. "I am going to be honest, Hester

Daniels, for the rest of my life, with you, with all of those who matter, I am going to honest."

She said nothing. This sounded like the introduction to a painful admission, though—painful for her. For the pleasure of hearing him speak, she'd bear it. Somehow, she would bear it.

"I am unhappy... no, I am miserable. Abjectly, profoundly, unendingly miserable. I have transgressed before a woman who deserved honesty and more from me, and now my life stretches out, decades of meaningless time... I am making a hash of this."

He scrubbed a hand over his face, and Hester dared a glance at him.

"Whatever it is, Tiberius, I promise I will listen."

His expression was solemn, grave even. He had never looked more dear to her, or more distant. "Do you carry our child, Hester?"

"That is of no moment." Oh, how she wanted to shoot off the bench and hide in the stables. How she wanted to throw herself into his arms. "If you are here to propose marriage again, I will not have you trapped. I know what it is to be trapped, to feel as if duty and honor leave one no reasonable options."

He sighed—perhaps a sigh of relief, maybe of frustration.

"What of love, Hester? *Amo, amas, amat*? You recall the word."

"Please, Tiberius, no Latin now." But her heart had picked up the rhythm of his conjugation: I love, you love, he loves, we love, you love, they love... A steady, anxious tattoo that wanted desperately to hear what he'd say.

He moved, and the loss of even his proximity threatened to choke her. "Don't—" She reached out a hand to stay him, when he slid to his knees before her.

"My great, impressive vocabulary fails me, Hester Daniels. My wits fail me; my reason fails me. I only know that I have met the love of my life, a woman who can help me to face life's hurts and wrongs with courage, a woman in whose love and trust I can repose my entire heart, if she—if you—will have me."

"This is not—" She was supposed to tell him this was not necessary, this dramatic offer, but she saw that for the man she loved, when he was looking for a way to redeem what he believed to be his compromised honor, this was necessary.

And when she had promised to listen, he'd given her back her own words.

"Tiberius, I understand that you had no choice, that the people you love were in terrible, terrible difficulties."

"I am in terrible difficulties." He looked like he'd say more, but then bowed his head. "I love you, Hester Daniels. When I think of you, I want children for us to love too. Swarms of them, all with red hair, to sing to the trees and scare the fish and cheat at cards with their uncles."

He fell silent while the images he spun took root in Hester's mind and in her heart. She wanted him to go on, to give her more lovely words, more dreams built with his sonorous tones, but he folded forward, sliding his arms around her waist.

"Please, Hester." A simple word. A beautiful, honest, heartfelt word rendered profound by the hoarse plea in his voice.

A single word that banished her misgivings, her self-doubt, her fear.

"Please. *Please* will you marry me, will you be the mother of my children? I've already told Quinworth he can keep his damned title, and I think he and my mother have finally set each other to rights. We'll bide here in Scotland. Just... please, marry me."

She grasped his hands, feeling as if every good, blessed thing in creation had been given to her with his words. "Yes, Tiberius. Yes, I will marry you. We'll bide in Scotland, and we'll have swarms of children, and they'll have red hair, and we'll love them all, each and every one of them, and we'll love each other, for I do love you, so very much."

He said nothing, not one word, but when she kissed him to solemnize her promises, she felt his body and his heart and every fiber of his being resonating with agreement.

And as it turned out, Hester was right: they married; they bided in Scotland; they had swarms of red-haired children—the first showing up something less than nine months after the wedding. That one was joined shortly by others who sang to trees, scared every fish in the burn, and cheated at cards when playing with their uncles and with their many, many, *many* cousins.

ONE GLIMPSE OF LADY MARY FRANCES MACGREGOR, and Matthew Daniels forgot all about the breathtaking Highland scenery and his misbegotten purpose for this visit to Aberdeenshire.

"For the duration of your stay, our house is your house," Lady Mary Frances said. She strode along the corridor of her brother's country home with purpose, not with the mincing, corseted gait of a London lady, and she had music in her voice. Her walk held music as well, in the rhythm and sway of her hips, in the rustle of her petticoats and the crisp tattoo of her boots on the polished wood floors.

Though what music had to do with anything, Matthew was at a loss to fathom. "The Spanish have a similar saying, my lady: *mi casa es su casa*."

"My house is your house." She either guessed or made the translation easily. "You've been to Spain, then?"

"In Her Majesty's Army, one can travel a great deal."

A shadow creased her brow, quickly banished and replaced by a smile. "And now you've traveled to our doorstep. This is your room, Mr. Daniels, though we've others if you'd prefer a different view."

She preceded him into the room, leaving Matthew vaguely disconcerted. A proper young woman would not be alone with a gentleman in his private quarters, and Mary Frances MacGregor, being the daughter of an earl, was a lady even in the sense of having a courtesy title—though Matthew had never before met a *lady* with hair that lustrous shade of dark red, or a figure so perfectly designed to thwart a man's gentlemanly self-restraint.

"The view is quite acceptable."

The view was magnificent, including, as it did, the backside of Lady Mary Frances as she bent to struggle with a window sash. She was a substantial woman, both tall and well formed, and Matthew suspected her arms would be trim with muscle, not the smooth, pale appendages a gentleman might see at a London garden party.

"Allow me." He went to her side and jiggled the sash on its runners, hoisting the thing easily to allow in some fresh air.

"The maids will close it by tea time," Lady Mary Frances said. "The nights can be brisk, even in high summer. Will you be needing a bath before the evening meal?"

She put the question casually—just a hostess inquiring after the welfare of a guest—but her gaze slid over him, a quick, assessing flick of green eyes bearing a hint of speculation. He might not fit in an old-fashioned bathing tub, was what the gaze said, nothing more.

Nonetheless, he dearly wanted to get clean after long days of traveling. "If it wouldn't be too much trouble?"

"No trouble at all. The bathing chamber is just down the hall to the left, the cistern is full, and the boilers have been going since noon."

She peered into the empty wardrobe, passing close enough to Matthew that he caught a whiff of something female... Flowers. Not roses, which were probably the only flower he knew by scent, but... fresher than roses, less cloying.

"If you need anything to make your visit more enjoyable, Mr. Daniels, you have only to ask, and we'll see to it. Highland hospitality isn't just the stuff of legends."

"My thanks."

She frowned at the high four-poster and again walked past him, though this time she picked up the tartan draped across the foot of the bed. The daughter of an earl ought not to be fussing the blankets, but Matthew liked the sight of her, snapping out the red, white, and blue woolen blanket and giving it a good shake. Her attitude said that nothing, not dust, not visiting English, not a houseful of her oversized brothers, would daunt this woman.

Without thinking, Matthew picked up the two corners of the blanket that had drifted to the blue-and-red tartan rug.

"Will you be having other guests this summer?" He put the question to her as they stepped toward each other.

"Likely not." She grasped the corners he'd picked up, their fingers brushing.

Matthew did not step back. Mary Frances MacGregor—*Lady* Mary Frances MacGregor—had *freckles* over the bridge of her nose. They were faint, even delicate, and they made her look younger. She could have powdered them into oblivion, but she hadn't.

"Mr. Daniels?" She gave the blanket a tug.

Matthew moved back a single step. "You typically have only one set of guests each summer?" Whatever her scent, it wasn't just floral. There was something spicy in it, fresh like cedar, but not quite cedar.

"No, we usually have as many as the brief summers here permit, particularly once Her Majesty and His Highness are ensconced next door. But if your sister becomes engaged to my brother, there will be other matters to see to, won't there?"

This question, alluding to much and saying little, was accompanied by an expression that involved the corners of the lady's lips turning up, and yet it wasn't a smile.

"I suppose there will." Things like settling a portion of the considerable Daniels's wealth into the impoverished Balfour coffers. Things like preparing for the wedding of a lowly English baron's daughter to a Scottish earl.

"We'll gather in the parlor for drinks before the evening meal, Mr. Daniels. The parlor is directly beneath us, one floor down. Any footman can direct you."

She was insulting him. It took Matthew a moment to decipher this, and in the next moment, he realized the insult was not intentional. Some of the MacGregor's "guests," wealthy English wanting to boast of a visit to the Queen's own piece of the Highlands, probably spent much of their stay too inebriated to navigate even the corridors of the earl's country house.

"I'll find my way, though at some point, I would also like to be shown where the rest of my family is housed."

"Of course." Another non-smile. She glanced around the room the way Matthew had seen generals look over the troops prior to a parade review, her lips flattening, her gaze seeking any detail out of order. "Until dinner, Mr. Daniels."

She bobbed a curtsy and whirled away before Matthew could even offer her a proper bow.

❧

"Miss MacGregor?"

Mary Fran's insides clenched at the sound of Baron Altsax's voice. She pasted a smile on her face and tried to push aside the need to check on the dining room, the kitchen, and the ladies' guest rooms—and the need to locate Fiona.

The child tended to hide when a new batch of guests came to stay.

"Baron, what may I do for you?"

"I had a few questions, Miss MacGregor, if you wouldn't mind?" He gestured to his bedroom, his smile suggesting he knew damned good and well the insult he did an earl's daughter by referring to her as "Miss" anything. A double insult, in fact.

Mary Fran did not follow the leering old buffoon into his room. Altsax's son, the soft-spoken Mr. Daniels, would reconnoiter before he started bothering the help—though big, blond, good-looking young men seldom needed to bother the help—not so the skinny, pot-gutted old men. "I'm a bit behind-hand, my lord. Was it something I could send a maid to tend to?"

The baron gestured toward the drinking pitcher on the escritoire, while Mary Fran lingered at the threshold. "This water is not chilled, I've yet to see a tea service, and prolonged travel by train can leave a man in need of something to wash the dust from his throat."

He arched one supercilious eyebrow, as if it took some subtle instinct to divine when an Englishman was whining for his whisky.

"The maids will be along shortly with the tea service, my lord. You'll find a decanter with some of our best libation on the nightstand, and I can send up some chilled water." Because they at least had ice to spare in the Highlands.

"See that you do."

Mary Fran tossed him a hint of a curtsy and left before he could make up more excuses to lure her into his room.

The paying guests were a source of much-needed coin, but the summers were too short, and the expenses of running Balfour too great for paying guests alone to reverse the MacGregor family fortunes. The benefit of this situation was that no coin was on hand to dower Mary Fran, should some fool—brother, guest, or distant relation—take a notion she was again in want of a husband.

"Mary Fran, for God's sake slow down." She'd been so lost in thought she hadn't realized her brother Ian had approached her from the top of the stairs. "Where are you churning off to in such high dudgeon? Con and Gil sent me to fetch you to the family parlor for a wee dram."

Ian's gaze was weary and concerned, the same as Con or Gil's would have been, though Ian, as the oldest, was the weariest and the most concerned—also the one willing to marry Altsax's featherbrained daughter just so Fiona might someday have a decent dowry.

"I have to check on the kitchens, Ian, and make sure that dimwitted Hetta McKinley didn't forget the butter dishes again, and Eustace Miller has been lurking on the maids' stairway so he can make calf's eyes at—"

"Come, you." Ian tucked her hand over his arm. "You deserve a few minutes with family more than the maids need to be protected from Eustace Miller's calf eyes. Let the maids have some fun, and let yourself take five minutes to catch your breath. Go change into your finery and meet us in the family parlor. I'll need your feminine perspective if I'm to coax Altsax's daughter up the church aisle."

Ian had typical MacGregor height and green eyes to go with dark hair and a handsome smile—none of which was worth a single groat. In Asher's continued absence, Ian was also the laird, and well on his way to being officially recognized as the earl. While neither honor generated coin, the earldom allowed him the prospect of marrying an heiress with a title-hungry papa.

Mary Fran did not bustle off to change her dress for any of those reasons, or even because she needed to stay abreast of whatever her three brothers were thinking regarding Ian's scheme to marry wealth.

She heeded her brother's direction because she wanted that wee dram—wanted it far too much.

∼⊷

Matthew enjoyed a leisurely soak in a marble bathing chamber that boasted every modern convenience, then dressed and prepared to find his way down to the formal parlor. As he moved through the house, he noted the signs of good care: a faint odor of beeswax and lemon oil rising from the gleaming woodwork, sparkling clean windows, fresh flowers in each corridor, an absence of fingerprints on the walls and mirrors.

Lady Mary Frances, or her minions, took the care of Balfour House seriously. A swift drum of heels from around the next corner had Matthew stopping and cocking an ear. A man did not lose the habit of stealth simply because he was no longer billeted to a brewing war zone.

The hint of acrid cigar smoke warned Matthew that his father was in the vicinity.

"Miss MacGregor, perhaps you'd allow me to provide you an escort down to the parlor?" Altsax spoke in the unctuous tones of a man condescending to an inferior, though Lady Mary Frances was arguably the baron's social superior.

Matthew eased far enough down the corridor to see that the lady was attired in a dinner gown of green-and-white plaid that did marvelous things for her eyes—and riveted the baron's attention on her décolletage.

"That's gracious of you, Baron." Her smile was beautiful, though it did not reach her eyes. "I hope Mr. Daniels will escort your womenfolk?"

The baron winged his arm. "I'm sure Matthew or your own brothers will see to that duty."

As the lady tucked her fingers around the baron's elbow, Matthew's gut began to churn. Altsax was never polite to anybody, much less to pretty young women, unless he was maneuvering toward his own ends.

"So why aren't you married, Miss MacGregor?" Altsax stroked his fingers over her hand. "You're comely enough, well born, and intended for better than spinsterhood as your brothers' household drudge."

The observation was Altsax's version of flattery, no doubt. Matthew felt a familiar urge to scream, or find a fast horse and gallop straight back to the Crimea.

"Marriage seems to be the topic of the day, my lord." While Matthew watched in a conveniently positioned mirror, Lady Mary Frances smiled back at her escort, revealing a number of strong white teeth. "You are blessed with two comely daughters, Baron. It's a pity your baroness could not accompany them on this journey."

As if Altsax would have allowed *that*. Matthew's mother knew better than to come along when her husband had decreed it otherwise, and quite honestly, Matthew envied his mother her freedom from Altsax's company.

"My wife and I have been married for thirty-some years, my dear. I hardly need to keep her underfoot at all times. Marriage is, after all, still a business undertaking among the better classes. I'm sure you'd agree."

Altsax walked with her toward the sweeping main staircase, a monument to carved oak that suggested at some bygone point in the MacGregor family history, coin had been abundant.

Matthew had an instant's premonition of the baron's intent, a gut-clenching moment of knowing what was about to take place. The baron took his opportunity at the turn in the hallway where carpet gave way to gleaming bare floor. He made a show of catching his toe on the carpet and jostling his companion sideways with enough force that she fetched up against the wall.

This allowed Altsax to mash into her bodily, and his hand—like one of the big, hairy spiders common to the tropics—to land squarely on the lady's generous, fashionably exposed bosom.

"I beg your pardon, Miss MacGregor." Altsax made an effort to right himself which of course involved clumsily, almost roughly, groping the lady. Matthew was about to reveal himself to his disgrace of a father, when the baron flew across the hallway as if propelled out of a cannon.

"Baron, do forgive me!" Lady Mary Frances was standing upright and looking creditably dismayed. "I did not mean to step on your foot, I sincerely did not. Are you all right, my lord?"

Her strategy left Altsax trying to look dignified and innocent of his crimes while not putting much weight on one foot. "The fault is mine, Miss MacGregor. I beg your pardon most sincerely. Shall we join your family downstairs?"

"Of course."

As they moved toward the stairs, Matthew noted that this time, Altsax did not offer the lady his arm.

First skirmish to Lady Mary Frances, though as Matthew waited for a silent moment at the top of the stairs, it occurred to him that rising to the lady's defense might have been enjoyable.

Tricky, given that he'd be defending her from his own father, but enjoyable.

❧

"A word with you, if you please, Lady Mary Frances."

Mary Fran tore off a bite of scone and regarded Mr. Matthew Daniels where he stood next to her place at the breakfast table. The baron had taken a tray out to the terrace, there to read his newspaper as he let a perfectly lovely breakfast grow cold at his elbow, while Ian and Miss Augusta Merrick, the younger of the two chaperones, had disappeared to the library.

And now Mary Fran's favorite meal of the day—sometimes her only decent meal of the day—was going to be disturbed by this serious gentleman waiting to assist her to her feet. No doubt Mr. Daniels's shaving water had been too hot, or not hot enough. Perhaps he objected to the scent of heather on his linen, or he'd found a footman using the maids' staircase.

Mary Fran folded a napkin around the last of her scone and put it in her pocket, then placed her hand in Daniels's and let him assist her to her feet. Thank God her brothers weren't on hand to see such a farce.

"In private." The gentleman kept his eyes front as he appended that requirement, as if admitting such a thing made him queasy.

"Shall we walk in the garden, Mr. Daniels? Pace off some of our breakfast?"

"That will serve." He tucked her hand around his arm, which had Mary Fran about grinding her teeth. They skirted the terrace and minced along until they were a good distance from the house, and still Mr. Daniels said nothing.

"Is there a point to this outing, Mr. Daniels? I don't mean to be rude, but I've a household to run, and though you are our guest, my strolling about here among the flowers isn't going to get the beds made up."

He stopped walking and gazed down at her with a surprised expression. "You do that yourself?"

"I know how. I expect you do as well."

Something flashed through his eyes, humor, possibly. He was one of few men outside her family Mary Fran had to look up to. She'd been an inch taller than Gordie, and she had treasured that inch every day of her so-called marriage.

"I do know how to make up a cot," he said. "Public school imbues a man with all manner of esoteric skills. The military does as well. Shall we sit?"

He was determined on this privacy business, because he was gesturing to a bench that backed up against the tallest hedge in the garden. They'd be hidden from view on that bench.

Even if she were amenable, Mary Fran doubted Mr. Daniels was going to take liberties. Good Lord, if he was this serious about his dallying, then heaven help the ladies he sought to charm. Though as she took a seat, it struck her with a certainty that Matthew

Daniels needn't bother charming anybody. For all his English reserve in proper company, he'd plunder and pillage, devil take the hindmost, when he decided on an objective.

Former cavalry could be like that.

"You are smiling, my lady."

And he was watching her mouth where he stood over her. Mary Fran let her smile blossom into a grin as she arranged her skirts. "I'm truant, sitting out here in the garden. I suppose it's fair play, given that my brothers—save for Ian—are off gallivanting about with your sisters and your aunt." And Lord knew what Ian was up to with the spinster cousin—probably prying secrets from the poor lady.

"About my womenfolk." He took the place beside her without her permission, though she would not have objected. "I have sisters."

He had two. The lovely Eugenia Daniels, whom Aunt Eulalie had spotted as a possible wealthy bride for Ian, and the younger, altogether likable Hester Daniels. Mary Fran held her peace, because Mr. Daniels was mentally pacing up to something, and he struck her as man who would not be hurried—she was familiar with the type.

"I have sisters whose happiness means a great deal to me," he went on, leaning forward to prop his elbows on his thighs. "You have brothers."

"My blessing and my curse," she said, wondering *when* he'd get to his point.

"My sisters are dear to me." He flicked a brooding glance at her over his shoulder. "As I'm sure you are dear to your brothers."

"Their hot meals and clean sheets are dear to them."

He sat up abruptly. "They would cheerfully die for you or kill for you. Not for the hot meals or the clean sheets, but for you."

She regarded him for a quizzical moment, trying to fathom his intentions. Insight struck as she studied the square line of his jaw and the way sunlight found the red highlights in his blond hair. "They won't kill your father while he's a guest in our home. Rest easy on that point."

"I cannot rest easy, as you say." He hunched forward again, the fabric of his morning coat pulling taut across broad shoulders. "My father's regard for women generally lacks a certain…"

"He's a randy old jackass," Mary Fran said. "I don't hold it against him."

Whatever comment the situation called for, it wasn't that. No earl's daughter, not even a Scottish earl's daughter running a glorified guesthouse ought to be so plainspoken.

"I'm sorry," she said, gaze on her lap. "I don't mean to be disrespectful. Your da's a guest in my home, and I'm responsible…"

"Hush." His finger came to rest on her lips, and when she looked up at him, he was smiling at her. He dropped his finger, but the smile lingered, crinkling the corners of his eyes and putting a light in his gaze that was almost… gentle.

God in heaven. The man was abruptly, stunningly attractive. Mary Fran felt a heat spreading out from that spot on her mouth where his bare finger had touched her.

"My father *is* a randy old jackass, I was searching for those very words. He can offend without meaning to, and sometimes, I fear, when he does mean to."

"He's not the first titled man to show uncouth behavior toward women." She linked her fingers in her lap lest she touch her lip as he had.

"No, but he's my father. If he should come to a premature end, all the burdens of his title will fall upon me, and that, rather than filial devotion, makes me hope your brothers will not have to challenge him to pistols at dawn."

The daft man was genuinely worried. "My brothers are Scottish, but they don't lack sense. If Ian took to dueling with his guests, God Almighty could live next door, and the most baseborn coal nabob wouldn't give a farthing to spend a day with us. Her Majesty has just about frowned dueling out of existence."

Plain speaking wasn't always inappropriate, and Mary Fran sensed Matthew Daniels could tolerate a few home truths.

"I fear, my lady, you underestimate your brothers' devotion to you, and"—he held up a staying hand when she would have interrupted—"you underestimate the depths of my father's more crass inclinations."

Mary Fran studied him, studied the serious planes of his face, and noted a little scar along the left side of his jaw. "I can handle your father, Mr. Daniels. I won't go running to my brothers in a fit of the weeps because he tries to take liberties."

"Tries to take liberties again, don't you mean?"

He had blue eyes—blue, blue eyes that regarded her with wry sternness.

"He's too slow, Mr. Daniels. He can but try, and I shall thwart him."

He peered at her, his lips thinning as he came to some conclusion. "Your brother had the opportunity to take my father very much to task the other evening for a verbal slight to you. Balfour instead suggested I see my sire to bed. I'd suspect the reputation of the Scots' temper to be overrated, except I've seen Highland regiments in action."

"Our tempers are simply as passionate as the rest of our emotions."

As soon as the words were out of her mouth, she realized she'd spoken *too* plainly. Ungenteelly, though that was probably not a proper word.

"I agree," he said, rising and extending his hand to her. "Having fought alongside many a Scot, I can say their honor, their humor, their valor, and their tempers were all formidable. Still, I am asking you to apply to me rather than your family should my father's bad manners become troublesome. I assure you, I'll deal with him appropriately."

She wouldn't be *applying* to anybody. If the baron overstepped again, he'd face consequences Mary Fran herself was perfectly capable of meting out. God had given each woman two knees for just such a purpose.

"I can agree to bring concerns regarding your father's conduct to you, Mr. Daniels, before I mention them to my brothers." She placed her hand in his and let him draw her to her feet.

And there they stood for a long, curious moment. His blue eyes bored into her as if he were trying to divine her thoughts.

"My name is Matthew," he said, still holding her hand. "I would be obliged if, when we are not in company, you would do me the honor of using it."

He was so grave about this invitation, Mary Fran had to conclude he was sincere. He would be *honored* if she addressed him familiarly—there was no accounting for the English and their silly manners. She nodded, put her hand on his arm, and let him escort her back to the house in silence.

She did not invite him to address her as Mary Frances.

Maybe being born with red hair, slanting green eyes, a mouth that personified sin incarnate, and a body to match made a woman sad—for Mary Frances MacGregor was a sad woman.

Matthew drew this conclusion by watching her at meals, watching the way she presided over the table with smiles aplenty and little real joy. He drew further evidence of her sadness from the way her brothers treated her, verbally tiptoeing around her the way Matthew had learned to tiptoe around his wife when she was tired, fretful, or in anticipation of her courses.

And she worried about her brothers. The anxiety was there in her eyes, in the way she watched them eat and kept their drinks topped up. To Matthew, it was obvious the MacGregor clan was not happy about having to trade their title for English coin, but the Scots as a race could not often afford the luxury of sentiment.

Because she was sad, and because he genuinely enjoyed dancing, when the middle brother, Gilgallon

MacGregor, challenged Aunt Julia to a waltz—those were his words, he *challenged* her to a waltz after dinner—and Julia had laughingly accepted, Matthew joined the party adjourning to the ballroom.

"Who will play for us if I'm to show Gilgallon what a dance floor is for?" Julia asked the assemblage.

Before Genie could offer, and thus ensure she wouldn't be dancing with Balfour, Matthew strode over to the big, square piano. "I will provide the music for the first set, on the condition that Lady Mary Frances will turn the pages for me."

Genie shot him a disgruntled look, but stood up with the youngest brother, Connor MacGregor, while Balfour led a blushing Hester onto the floor.

"What shall we play for them?" Matthew asked. "Three couples doesn't quite make a set."

"I believe my idiot brother demanded a waltz," Lady Mary Frances muttered as she sorted through a number of music books stacked on the piano's closed lid. "Take your pick."

She shoved a volume of Chopin at him, which wasn't quite ballroom material.

"I take it you don't approve of dancing?" Matthew flipped through until he found the Waltz in C-sharp Minor and opened the cover shielding the keys.

"Dancing's well enough," the lady said. Her tone was anything but approving.

"Maestro, we're growing moss over here!" Julia called, but she was smiling up at her partner in the manner of a younger, more carefree woman, and for that alone, Matthew would dust off his pianistic skills.

He launched into the little waltz, a lilting, sentimental

confection full of wistful die-away ascending scales and
a turning, sighing secondary melody.

"You play well, Mr. Daniels."

Lady Mary Frances nearly whispered this compliment, and Matthew could feel her gaze on his hands.
"That's Matthew, if you please. I've always enjoyed
music, but there wasn't much call for it in the military."

Out on the dance floor, by the soft evening light
coming through the tall windows, three couples
turned down the room in graceful synchrony. Beside
Matthew, Lady Mary Frances was humming softly
and swaying minutely to the triple meter. He finished
off the exposition with another one of those tinkling
ascending scales, which allowed him to lean far
enough to the right that his shoulder pressed against
the lady's.

"Page, my lady."

She flipped the page, and Matthew began the
contrasting section, a more stately interlude requiring
little concentration, which was fortunate. Lady Mary
Frances had applied a different scent for the evening.
That fresh, cedary base note was still present, but
the overtones were more complicated. Complicated
enough that Matthew could envision sniffing her neck
to better parse her perfume.

"What scent are you wearing, my lady? It's particularly appealing."

"Just something I put together on an idle day."

Matthew glanced over at her to find she was
watching the dancers, her expression wistful. "You
haven't had an idle day since you put your hair up, and
likely not many before then."

"A rainy day, then. We have plenty of those. Your sisters are accomplished dancers."

"As are your brothers." For big men, they moved with a lithe grace made more apparent for their kilts. "You should take a turn, my lady."

"No, I should not. I've things to see to, Mr. Daniels, but it is nice to watch my brothers enjoying themselves on the dance floor."

"Page."

She turned the page for him, and Matthew had to focus on the recapitulation of the first, delicate, sighing melody. The final ascending scale trickled nearly to the top of the keyboard, which meant Matthew was leaning into Lady Mary Frances at the conclusion of the piece.

And she was allowing it.

"Oh, well done, my boy, well done." Altsax clapped in loud, slow movements. "I'd forgotten your fondness for music. Perhaps you'd oblige us with another waltz, that I might have the pleasure of dancing with Lady Mary Frances?"

"When did he slither into the room?" Lady Mary Frances muttered, resignation in her tone.

Matthew rose from the piano bench. "I'm afraid that won't serve, your lordship. My compensation for providing music for the ladies is a waltz with my page turner. Perhaps Hester will oblige at the keyboard?"

Gilgallon turned a dazzling smile on Matthew's younger sister. "And I'll turn the pages for her."

"My lady, may I have this dance?" Matthew extended his hand to Lady Mary Frances, who smiled up at him in a display of teeth and thinly banked forbearance.

"The honor would be mine, Mr. Daniels."

He led her to the dance floor, arranged himself and his partner into waltz position, and felt a sigh of recognition as Hester turned her attention to Chopin's Nocturne in E Minor. The piece was often over-looked, full of passion and sentiment, and it suited the woman in Matthew's arms.

"I hate this piece." Lady Mary Frances moved off with him, speaking through clenched teeth.

"You dance to it well enough." Which fulsome compliment had her scowling in addition to clenching her teeth.

"It's too—"

"Don't think of the music then. Tell me what it was like growing up in the Highlands."

She tilted her head as Matthew drew her through the first turn. "It was cold and hungry, like this music. Never enough to eat, never enough peat to burn, and always there was *longing*…"

Her expression confirmed that she hadn't meant to say that, which pleased Matthew inordinately. That he could dance Mary Frances MacGregor out of a little of her self-containment was a victory of sorts. "What else?"

"What else, what?"

"What else was it like, growing up in these mountains?"

He pulled her a trifle closer on the second turn, close enough that he could hear her whisper. "It was lonely, like this blasted tunc."

"Your brothers weren't good company?"

"They are my *older brothers*, Mr. Daniels. They were no company at all."

She danced beautifully, effortlessly, a part of the music she professed to hate.

"And yet here I am, my lady, an older brother along on this curious venture for the express purpose of providing my sisters and their chaperones company."

She huffed out a sigh. "I appreciate that you're preserving me from your father's attentions, Mr. Daniels, but I assure you such gallantry is not necessary."

"Matthew, and perhaps I'm not being gallant, perhaps I'm being selfish."

He turned her under his arm, surprised to find he'd spoken the truth. A man leaving the military in disgrace was not expected to show his face at London's fashionable gatherings, and had he done so, few ladies would have stood up with him.

"What was it like growing up in the South?"

Her question was a welcome distraction. "I didn't. I went to boarding school in Northumbria. I was cold and hungry for most of it."

Her gaze sharpened. "Why the North?"

Another turn, another opportunity to pull her a bit closer and enjoy the way her height matched with his own. "The North is cheaper, and Altsax isn't what anybody would call a doting father. I made some friends and spent holidays with them to the extent I could."

Though those same friends would probably be careful not to recognize him now.

"So you weren't lonely."

He distracted her with a daring little spin, one she accommodated easily, and from there, conversation lapsed while Matthew tried to enjoy waltzing with a gorgeous, fragrant woman in his arms.

Her last comment bothered him though. In boarding school, he'd been lonely. The schoolmates who'd taken pity on him for a holiday here or there had not been the sort of companions to provide solace to a boy exiled from his home and family. The military had been a slight improvement, for a time, and then no improvement at all.

As Matthew bowed over the lady's hand to the final strains of the nocturne, he admitted to himself that he'd been lonely for most of his boyhood as well as most of his military career.

And he was lonely still.

Acknowledgments

Not every publishing house would allow an author to shift focus just a couple of years into the happy task of building up a backlist. I delight in my Regency stories, but I have to say, these Scottish Victorians are proving a wonderful undertaking too. Thanks to my editor, Deb Werksman, and my publisher, Dominique Raccah, for allowing me to branch out, particularly in a direction that justifies the occasional tot of whisky in pursuit of literary accuracy.

I'd also like to acknowledge the other authors writing for the Sourcebooks Casablanca line. If you look at your keeper shelf, they are no doubt well represented. In addition to being enormously talented, these folks are also the nicest bunch of people you'd ever want to talk over your book with. They regularly do favors for me and my books above and beyond the call of duty, and make being a published author a lot less bewildering and challenging than it might be otherwise.

About the Author

New York Times and *USA Today* bestselling author Grace Burrowes hit the bestseller lists with her debut, *The Heir*, followed by *The Soldier*, *Lady Maggie's Secret Scandal*, and *Lady Eve's Indiscretion*.

The Heir was a *Publishers Weekly* Best Book of 2010, *The Soldier* was a *Publishers Weekly* Best Spring Romance of 2011, *Lady Sophie's Christmas Wish* won Best Historical Romance of the Year in 2011 from *RT* Reviewers' Choice Awards, and *The Bridegroom Wore Plaid*, the first in her trilogy of Scotland-set Victorian romances, was a *Publishers Weekly* Best Book of 2012. Her historical romances have received extensive praise, including starred reviews from *Publishers Weekly* and *Booklist*.

Grace is a practicing family law attorney and lives in rural Maryland. She loves to hear from her readers and can be reached through her website at graceburrowes.com.